SWEET OBLI

**Sweet Obli**
**A War of the Wo**

by Samuel P

For Jess.

# I.

Anyone with a modicum of common sense, if told that this world was being watched keenly and closely by intelligences greater than ours, would have believed it.

By the Third Millennium's early years it was natural for people's thoughts to dawdle on space's unnervingly boundless gulf. It was all we had left to explore – and so we talked of asteroid mining and Martian settlement and colonisation of the cosmos until we basked under every star. None of this had yet materialised but, eventually, maybe it would. Naturally, in that place of wonderment, all kinds of threats, too, were imagined. These fantasies manifested in literature and cinema with man's triumph over invaders – sometimes militarily, sometimes philosophically, but always morally – inevitable. Man, you see, would always win in the end – we couldn't imagine an alternative. We're too cool to lose.

Yet, with a complacency as infinite as the space we contemplated, we were serene that nothing would *actually* come from that dark and endless sky. It was, simply, too big. Space might have played host to an endless array of civilisations but we would never know for all were beyond our reach and we beyond theirs. It is curious to recall some of the mental habits of those lost and comfortable days – when we thought the Earth untouchable. Yet across that void, minds that are to our minds as ours are to the snails I used to squash on the way home from school, intellects vast and cool and unsympathetic regarded this delicate little world with envious eyes – and slowly and surely drew their plans against us.

The Solar System, I hope the reader knows, has a whole bunch of planets. The Blight must have touched all of them, for it is thought that their spread across the stars was no calculated move but an act akin to a dandelion dispersing its seeds in all directions, the wind dictating their fate. All but the tiniest sliver of their civilisation must have perished in this desperate effort to find a new home for, beyond our own world, we know of no hospitality to be found. They couldn't live on Pluto, which people still derange themselves into thinking a planet – presumably they also think Woking a thriving metropolis. The Sun is so distant that in the Plutonian sky it becomes indistinguishable from the rest of the stars, and so the dwarf world is deathly frozen. No life can sustain itself there. They couldn't live on Neptune or Uranus, perpetually cold worlds, composed of unbreathable gases in which all life is impossible. Those Blight adventurers who approached might have been briefly excited by Saturn, a fantastical world with its many moons and magical rings, but this feeling would have faded once they descended into its poisonous, crushing atmosphere. The next world was giant Jupiter, where the atmospheric pressure is terrible – thousands of pounds to the square inch. They couldn't go there. Nor could they survive Mars, nearest planet to our own, which we had been slowly excavating for years and found no evidence even of water – the most critical ingredient for life – and whose atmosphere, if ever there was one genial to life, has long been stripped away by the solar winds. Venus, Earth's sister planet, is an ugly twin – she is boiling beyond imagination with an atmosphere of sulphuric acid. Good luck to those who try planting a flag in her soil. Mercury, nearest planet to the sun, was a tall order, too; it has no air, and the equatorial temperature is that of molten lead. All of these options, to be frank, sucked. But there was one more. For of all the worlds that the Blight could consider, only our own warm little Earth was healthy with vegetation, inviting with water, and possessed a bright and fertile atmosphere. It didn't occur to mankind – her often-absentee stewards – that a swift fate might be hanging over us.

Why, we ponder in scientific journals and spooky documentaries with traumatised interviewees against black backgrounds, did the Blight come? Two theories prevail. The first, a more sympathetic proposition, holds that their world is a dying, decaying waste – that their scattergun spread onto every planet (their *assumed* spread – we're still trying to find evidence of landings on our neighbours) was a desperate bid to find and cling to a new home, somewhere out in the sky. Over the aeons, maybe they landed upon many thousands of worlds and found none to be accommodating, all perishing in the effort. The evacuation of their homeworld perhaps amounted to nothing more than flinging themselves into the open maw of extinction. In a way, there's a poetic tragedy to the Blight's story – to journey across the universe, in hope of a new home, only to perish. We British, who lionise Captain Scott and the Light Brigade, should find something admirable in their glorious failure – though I doubt that will be forthcoming after all they have done. Rich Carpenter, a dear friend whose surname reflects his occupation but whose forename does not reflect his success at it, put it succinctly to me one evening at the Red Lion – "people are stupid, the Blight are stupid, everything is stupid."

The alternate interpretation, well worn by those uncomfortable with applying any sympathetic notes to the Blight's swansong, is that there is no discernable difference between our conquerors and great buzzing herds of locusts. That they are nothing more than 'viruses with keyboards,' as the well-regarded Dr Forrester of Merton College recently suggested on a daytime talk show, sat alongside a reality show host and a pet nutritionist. The three were given equal airtime, answering viewer questions about what's in for autumn and chihuahua deworming, but Dr Forrester's words stuck with me – especially when he talked about how our invaders must see man. To them, we are nothing; not in a cruel way, but an objective one. They don't even consider us, he said, because they aren't capable of consideration. We may be insects to them but, from a psychological perspective, *they* are the insects, incapable of all thought and emotion beyond motorised instinct. I've seen many disregard this possibility out of their narcissistic need for the extermination to have 'meant something' – as if meaning can be applied by ants towards a boot. There is in the human soul a need for her fate to be entwined with some lasting reason and, were this second theory true, we'd find no meaning in our suffering. I disregard all this talk of the Blight being mindless, though, for different reasons – because I saw things during those dark days. Things no others saw.

And is my friend so wrong about people? We, the creatures who claim this Earth as our own, who must be to the Blight at least as lowly and alien as those ants I'm going to mention a lot are to us, readily admit that life is a ceaseless struggle for existence – it would seem that this is the belief of minds beyond the stars, too. And if these minds did in fact know what cruelty they wrought, before we judge them too harshly we must remember the destruction our own species has wrought, not only upon animals, like those hundreds going extinct each year, but upon our own. How many people, undeniably fellow humans, have been brutally wiped from existence for the crime of occupying a parcel of land which some other person fancies? How many empires have emerged from seas of gooey blood, cutting thousand down with every step, all to secure reliable supplies of sugar cane or apricots? Glance at a globe and you won't see a single nation placed there peacefully. Here in Britain there isn't even, really, such a thing as an indigenous person. We are colonisers of our own islands – the first ancient peoples who inhabited these lands were butchered, and their conquerors followed, until many bloody generations of supplanted races and aborted bloodlines later we find what we pretend is the fixed point of modern society. Who are we to complain when the Blight treat us as we have already treated ourselves?

When they came, hoping for the best in their dandelion distribution, it was from a deep and forbidding and so far unknown corner of the beyond – many theorise that they originate from Betelgeuse, the tenth most brilliant of stars, for in recent years its luminosity has dimmed and brightened to imply that supernova approaches. Any orbiting planets are, surely, being cooked in the cataclysm. Others have calculated that Ross 128, one of Virgo's red dwarfs, might be home. Yet it is just as possible that they came from even further, beyond any constellation to which we have assigned a name, with Betelgeuse and Ross 128 and all their luminous siblings just road signs on a much longer journey. What a relief it must have been to see Earth in their windscreens. But they may have arrived longer ago than we think.

Eight summers ago, a great light was seen passing between the Earth and the Moon. Anyone across Eurasia who looked skyward that night witnessed it. I didn't, being busy setting alight the local playing park's climbing equipment and then passing out on a friend's bedroom floor, but the agencies who make observing the skies their business were sent haywire. We are now inclined to think that this light may have been an early comer, skimming the Earth and failing to connect, or perhaps a scout, or something else entirely, but the prevailing attitude at the time was that a particularly majestic superbolide had passed by. It was, all in authority said, entirely benign and entirely natural and entirely fascinating – though plenty of people were furious that it hadn't been detected, and calls for a global outer space surveillance system were elevated for a few days.

Much was thought to have been learned to astrophysics's benefit by that February 13 event, little of it within my then-juvenile mind's comprehension, particularly the gravitational effect of two bodies upon an object's momentum when it passes between them. Anomalous behaviour, such as the way the object seemed to briefly slow as it reached its closest point to the Earth before speeding up again, was taken as priceless example of a slingshot effect by the cooperating gravities. Plenty more was assumed by the army of conspiracists who stood ready to leap upon natural phenomena as anything but. How well I recall the video I stumbled across online which alleged connections between St Valentine's Comet and a coming conquering of the Earth with unnerving accuracy. They would have been bang on the money had they not insisted that the invaders acted in concert with various ancestrally Jewish merchant banks and shapeshifting neo-liberal politicians. Slowly, then all at once, the topic of the fireball faded from the public zeitgeist and was left to the astrophysicists to ponder.

Yet there were soon to be other strange celestial events, primarily a greater volume of meteoric showers across the Solar System's outer planets, but it is an eternal mystery which if any had a relationship with the coming of the Blight. Perhaps it was all just a big coincidence. One event in particular, though, stays with me. A mere six months after the passage of St Valentine's Comet there came an almighty explosion which shattered the asteroid 4062 Schiaparelli as it drifted harmlessly between Mars and Jupiter – contemporary science presumed this the result of a simple and routine, but unexpectedly violent, collision between it and a fellow barren rock. Another rare and exciting and harmless moment in space's endless ballet. Now we all wonder, spurred on by a viral tweet postulating the theory, if a Blight capsule mistook 4062 Schiaparelli for something worth exploring and met a predictably grisly fate. If so, I wonder, how many more of the Blight made such mistakes? How many missed their targets altogether and were condemned to drift endlessly in the darkness – or made it safely to some bleak world where they rapidly found they could neither breathe nor, having landed, escape? It must have happened somewhere, perhaps in thousands or millions of somewheres. How many, too, could have reached the Earth were it not for Jupiter, our mighty shield, whose gravity sucks away far larger celestial threats daily, or the cosmic Hadrian's Wall which the asteroid belt may have accidentally formed, as the example of 4062 Schiaparelli attests? What an appalling irony, that asteroids – another commonly cited threat to human existence – may have saved us all from a fleet which ought to have conquered every inch of Earth.

The storm burst upon us a few years ago now. A glorious Indian summer taking hold of Cornwall, where I lived against my wishes but in line with my moribund academic qualifications, NASA set the astronomical community palpitating with the amazing news of a celestial object settling in one of the five Lagrangian points. These are the unique spots of space in which the Earth and Sun's gravitational forces become so balanced as to make them perfect for anything seeking an unimpeachably steady orbit. The visitor, known first as 1I/2008 U1 and then as Oumuamua, was no stranger – first glimpsed years earlier from an observatory in the Hawaiian mountains, it was the first object of interstellar origin ever detected passing through our Solar System. Now the massive artefact had settled in the most impossible of places, held against its will, we thought, by the Sun and Earth's competing gravities, like a salmon forever trapped in a river whose current perfectly matches its exertions, apparently doomed to drift in the same little oval forever. The Advanced Composition Explorer, studying energetic particles carried on the solar winds, went silent after colliding with the great body. It was feared that more damage could be inflicted were man's other gadgets, many of which were sprinkled in this scientifically convenient region of space, permitted to get too close. Terror overcame space authorities – but there were no more disasters. At least not out there.

Oumuamua's settlement had occurred towards midnight of the twelfth, shunting away headlines of Ethiopian water warfare, Satanic rituals at a Middlesbrough comprehensive school (alleged), and a minor royal pregnancy. Every terrestrial and space-based telescope which could turn towards our new neighbour did so – all registered a fuzzy mass of darkest grey, rugged and topographically indistinguishable from any asteroid which it may have batted its way through to get there. Most unusual was its shape, highly elongated, like a tightly rolled cigar, and its brightness – Oumuamua was of a luminosity quite unusual for a meteor. Despite widespread public agitations at the uncomfortable reality of an uninvited guest sat on our cosmic doormat, it was taken as unquestionable by those with the authority to speak on the topic that Oumuamua was – yet again – mere natural phenomena. Her settling where she did, it was argued, was perhaps mathematically inevitable – if inconceivable – once she came within a certain distance of a Lagrangian point; like a bit of driftwood circling a whirlpool. It was pointed out with great regularity to the nervous masses that no radio signals of any form emanated from the visitor – it was just another lifeless rock among billions. Beautiful – but harmless.

Unhealthily pale even in good times, the NASA chief herself, flanked by serious looking individuals in charcoal or taupe suits and occasionally colourful pantsuits, leaned over the White House lectern and – almost drowned out by snapping camera shutters – firmly assured all who would listen that faint Oumuamua was utterly benign. No alien incursion nor impact event was underway – the chances of anything coming to Earth were a million to one, she said, and so its arrival ought to be celebrated as a little moon which had found a new home against all imaginable odds. The uneasily increasing number of celestial events were no more than a coincidence, and one which should be enjoyed while it lasted. Misinformation, she made clear, was only muddying the waters of truth.

"Screeching about it won't help," she said, and then had to apologise for having said, while our own government didn't acknowledge the event at all besides a departmental press release and a joke at Prime Minister's Questions at the Opposition's expense; the barbed exchanges on no-fault benefit debt and East Grinstead rail services, unnoticed by all except political obsessives and mad Christians in wheelchairs, went on.

Despite her apology, Dr Ferrier's phrase about screeching proved singularly appropriate, it was felt, and the quote was splashed across the papers the next day, from broadsheet to tabloid, all giddy with excitement about Earth's new Moon and eager to belittle those who worried. So the human race went in ignorance of one of the gravest dangers that ever threatened it. Those anxious there might be more to events than what we saw were roundly ridiculed – the greatest fear among many was not 'aliens' at all but that gravity may, in time, drag Oumuamua closer until she struck the Earth, or that her presence might alter the tides or Earth's rotation. It tended to be those without an education in gravity who suddenly developed such strong opinions about it. The prolific commentator and verified tweeter Marcus Prospere (real name Daniel Hartley-Green), taking a moment of time away from blasting gender non-conformity and celebrity activism, distinguished himself with a long thread attacking the scientific authorities for their "egomaniacal intransigence in the face of doubt. Here we have world-changing news – we suddenly have a new moon for goodness sake – and all who feel natural anxiety and dare question the official narrative are written off as a nest of loonies!! What if it IS a giant egg???"

As for me, I couldn't care less – at the time I was uninterested in even the most world-shattering news. My long litany of poor life choices hadn't left me the most put together individual the Earth could assemble from its dust. I was one depressed creature, languid in both mind and body – at the time, a staircase would put me out of breath and the very phrase 'difficult literature' would have made me want to kill you and then myself. I was a long way away from how I am now, attempting to replicate semi-sophisticated prose because in dealing with my trauma I'm on a classics kick and, I am sure, doing a great job at it. Few things were as unlikely to catch my attention in those days than talk of a new rock in space. That was until I met Angus Plain, a fast-talking, lanky, and very excitable amateur astronomer with curly red hair like spaghetti bolognese, whom I bumped into in the gravelly car park at the foot of Rosewall Hill.

Here, the outskirts of St Ives become a great sweep of empty fields and protected moorland for people to walk terriers and fornicate in Corsas. All I wanted was to play *Splatoon 2* and smoke one or four poorly wrapped psychoactives to suppress my period cramps. Angus had come bearing a heavy telescope and – delirious at Oumuamua's arrival – in the excess of his feelings invited me from my Golf and up the hill to take a turn on it. Bemused by this funny little fellow, I followed – soon tasked with carrying the telescope myself, puffing and panting and cursing my ever-abandoned fitness plan, while he fiddled with optical equipment lugged in an overstocked backpack – and we climbed the craggy National Trust hillside beneath the stardust.

In spite of all that has happened since, I still remember

that vigil very distinctly: the hill's black silence, struggling to navigate the telescope around a wooden stile, the distant scrabbling of what Angus assured me would at worst be a foraging badger, my intense fear of the badger, purple heather and overbearing ferns which itched at my exposed ankles, placing the telescope down and the ticking as he focused its lenses, cold sea breeze reaching up the hill, continuing to fear the badger, the overpowering glow of my phone's torch to guide our – mostly his – efforts on the lens. It's as if it's all still right in front of me.

Angus moved about, triple-checking that we hadn't missed the summit's best ground for the telescope's tripod, invisible in the dark but audible with his stammer and gentle Highland cadence, wondering aloud if cloud cover would come, explaining that he had never forgiven clouds since they spoiled the 1999 eclipse, until he returned and trained the scope toward a cluster of stars.

"There you are!" he cried triumphantly, after a period of silent scanning. "Incredible... exemplary..."

"What is?" I asked, looking up at the stars and seeing nothing particularly unique. They seemed to be where we'd left them.

"Oumuamua," he answered, and finally I knew how to pronounce it – I was, vaguely, aware of the thing, having seen a notification or two pop up on my phone but had assumed it was a new superhero film. "It's one of the most amazing astronomical events ever observed. They'll be writing *libraries* about this!" I found his enthusiasm delightful as he explained why it mattered.

"Which one is it?" Angus pulled away and pointed with his freckled finger.

"Up there. It's super dim, but you can still see it. Right?"

"Right...?" I said, unsure, following his finger. Stars tend to all look the same from a distance.

"Fancy a proper gander?" he asked, gesturing to the telescope, and I did, so I looked, one eye pressed painfully against the lens and the other tightly closed.

Looking through the telescope, it was hard to know which star wasn't a star. They all looked alike – until, suddenly, one didn't. Looking closely, I realised that one was different. Luminescent, like the Moon merely a reflection of the unseen Sun, a rough and blurry oblong swam in the light it emanated. Grey beneath this light, a dull sheen was visible, and once you noticed the exotic effect it was impossible for Oumuamua to blend back in with the stars. So small and still, it seemed such a small thing, pock-marked with what must have been the grooves of a thousand smaller asteroid encounters, and the phrase 'cigar-shaped' which was doing the rounds materialised in my head of its own volition. So this was what had set the world alight. But it was so little, so grey and cold, and it seemed even to quiver, but that was just the telescope trembling on uneven ground. I withdrew from the lens to rest my eye and, as Angus gobbled up the chance to gaze again, I looked down on St Ives and all its hundreds of people, aglow with white and gold from waking windows, the floodlights of the rugby club and triangular steeple of the Congregational chapel standing highest, ring-fenced by a growing and overpriced and seasonally occupied prefabricated suburbia. Beyond it all was the black Celtic Sea, impossible to make out but for the occasional automated ping of light from distant Godrevy Lighthouse across St Ives Bay and the lights along the neighbouring Godrevy headland. Being on the bay's opposite end, these lights gave an impression of the sea's boundary but not entirely of its location. I pointed this out to Angus and he suggested, without taking his eye from the telescope, that it was often easier to establish where something was not than where it was, which was a perspective I didn't quite understand. I returned to the lens when offered and, as I watched, the rock seemed to grow larger and smaller and to advance and recede.

"Should we be worried about that?" I asked.

"About what?"

"The thing's moving."

"Moving?" He took over and sighed at my innocence.

"What?"

"It's just autokinesis," he laughed, and I didn't know what that meant, but the 'just' carried the implication that all was well, so I believed all was. Besides, the thing was almost a million miles away – almost a million miles of void completely blank but for gamma rays and darting tachyons and swimming dust and countless other busy things. Space, you see, isn't empty. Few appreciate its immense fullness.

Near Oumuamua on the lens' rim, I remember, were three faint points of light; three infinitely remote stars. Angus – proud of his encyclopedic astronomic memory which I found vaguely frightening in a vaguely horny way – told me they were "the Cassiopeia family." All around them: empty space's unfathomable darkness. I'd always known how deep the blackness looks when lit by stars, when the night sky seems more made of light than dark, and that darkness which survives is so contrasted that it even absorbs itself. But, with my eye to the telescope, I saw that even those black patches were alive with the noise of stars. I should reply to my mother's texts more often, I thought, as I stared into what I now saw was not darkness but endless light and for the first time appreciated my true smallness and surprised myself by being glad to realise it. And as I did, flying swiftly and steadily towards us across that incredible distance, invisible to me and Angus and the rest of the world, as cold as the mind which piloted it, drawing many thousands of miles nearer every minute, came the Thing they were sending us, the Thing that was to bring so much struggle and calamity and death, the Thing which silent Oumuamua was watching and guiding and wishing well. I never dreamed of what was coming – even as I must have been looking it in the eye.

Midnight struck and Angus took my place. I reflected both on what an odd little acquaintance we had formed and how little astronomers actually did with their time; to me it seemed mostly to constitute ceaselessly staring at what was not just inanimate but lies. Some of those stars were dead, now, and we'd never know which ones.

The night was warm and I was thirsty, and I went clumsily stretching my legs and feeling my way in darkness through which my dying phone's torch bored a hole. I went back to the car where I retrieved a gradually warming bottle of vodka and orange squash from the boot. With it I returned to the summit, short of breath, thighs chafing in jeans unsuited for all this hiking.

"Don't you get bored?" I asked Angus, face glued to the lens, then voicing my thoughts on how a person could go mad stargazing.

"What makes you think that?" Angus asked. I shrugged and took a burning sip – home was so close, and town so unpoliced, that I could dare risk drinking. I was a worse person then – but, in other ways, after all that has happened, a far better one. Or maybe we are always what we become – even before it happens. It only takes a nudge to expose it.

"It just makes me think of that phrase," I answered; "about looking into the abyss for too long and it looking into you."

Angus replied: "Nietzsche is so overused. And misunderstood. Besides, that'd work if it was an abyss – it's not. Every spot is a star."

"I know that *now*. I just always thought of the universe as cold and uncaring, you know?"

"The universe isn't uncaring," Angus exclaimed, "for we are part of the universe – and we care."

"That's pretty cute," I replied.

"It wasn't meant to be." With some struggle, as I had no light to do it by now my phone had died, I lit another joint and shared it with Angus. Reluctant though he was, and coughing plenty as he did, he proved amiable, though more keen to share vodka shots in the bottle's upturned cap. Little did we suspect the beastly missile rocketing toward us. Angus kept up at the telescope until the clock struck one and the air grew frigid, and then even he became tired of the exercise – we drifted, tipsy, back down the hill towards the car park.

Angus was loaded with speculation about Oumuamua and, buoyed by drink and skunk, scoffed at the vulgar idea of it being piloted. His idea was the same as that of all the very serious and excitable scientists – you can be both – that our visitor had, despite mathematical impossibility, drifted into one the Lagrangian points by chance and, its momentum cut short, frozen to an effective stop. Was that not exciting enough? Why did aliens have to get involved to make science interesting? He pointed out how unlikely it was that extraterrestrial beings, having somehow located our speck of dust in the first place, would ever have the patience to travel the infinite streams of space separating us. It takes more than four years to reach us just from our nearest star at the fastest possible speed – almost three million from our nearest galaxy. All that in the name of something as needless as conquering a speck of dust.

Thousands of observers studied Oumuamua that night in Cornwall alone, millions more on every inch of the turning world, and the night after, and again the night after; and so for ten nights, until the crowds dwindled as Oumuamua failed to do anything to maintain their interest. Why interest seemed to cease by the tenth day is fairly simple – human beings grow bored easily and, outside the scientific realm, the fascination with Oumuamua came to fade as it became clearer that it was just a rock not doing anything more than simply being a "bloody big rock," as my friend Anne referred to it with a dismissive wave of the hand while we watched *Strictly Come Dancing*.

The daily papers, happy to milk the disturbance while it

remained one, realised the public's boredom and new stories both real and imagined shunted their way onto the front pages, like the Essex family swept away in an Indonesian typhoon or pony meat found in supermarket mince. Those of a scientific disposition still bleated that Oumuamua remained fascinating. Talk of an official expedition, perhaps a joint enterprise between the Americans and Chinese, said the more geopolitically optimistic, simmered. Maybe in a few decades, mumbled the White House, or a bit later, once their public-private plans for Martian settlements and a telescope beyond the Moon were done and dusted; things with a little more economical promise.

Remarks flew that, if humanity wanted to keep putting satellites in the sky at our current pace, Oumuamua would have to be gotten out of the way eventually. The invaluable Lagrangian points couldn't be forfeited for a bloody big rock and, so, progress and conservation fought their own little flame war over something likely irrelevant for decades. The latter pointed out that the Lagrangian points were huge and Oumuamua no obstacle, and the former pointed out that they really wanted to blow it up. An eccentric tech-tycoon or two, suffering from severe cases of personality, put forward their own lightly detailed expedition proposals – heavily subsidised by the state, rather than their own net worth, of course. One fortnightly satirical magazine, I remember, made a happy use of Oumuamua in their front cover's political cartoon – a strange and slightly forced pun on its name, if I recall, drawing on its similarity with the embattled Minister for Europe's surname – and in doing so provided later generations a haunting image of complacency. All the while, unsuspected, those missiles drew earthward, rushing now at a pace of many miles a second, hour by hour and day by day, nearer and nearer, closer and closer. It seems almost wonderful, in a strange way, that we could go about our petty concerns as we did. I remember the day before the denouement how jubilant my friend – and occasionally more than friend – Amber Robbins was at securing half a million followers on her food-themed Instagram. For my own part, I was occupied in my part-time apprenticeship, pursuing motorcycle mechanics as a route out of this godforsaken county, and busy upon a series of posts discussing the probable developments of moral ideas as civilisation progressed. In other words, tweeting in all lower-case to my two-and-a-half thousand followers nonsense that I wrote without really thinking about it. When I next saw Angus, as he left Pizza Express while I walked to work, neither of us shared any words and his telescope was nowhere to be seen – though I guess he wouldn't have it with him at *all* times. Normality rarely dawdles in returning.

One night, with the first missile then scarcely a few hundred thousand miles away, I met with a Tinder date as was routine. He was stocky, like a pitbull, but sickly – it only took a few minutes for him to bring up his severe kidney damage – and, it being starlight, he made it worse by guiding me through the Signs of the Zodiac and telling me it "explained a lot" when I said I was a Gemini, before explaining that Oumuamua, towards which so many telescopes were aimed and which you could literally see even without one, wasn't actually real. Conspiracies, you see, were underway to drum up support for Big Tech's intrasolar political machinations, the end goal being "making it so you *are* your money," and the Oumuamua "fairy tale" was designed to accelerate that. This he explained in great and certain detail while I half-listened.

Coming to his holiday flat on that warm night – the kidney damage and spiritualism and deranged conspiracism not having spooked me enough to say no – a party of thirty-something excursionists piled from Wetherspoons, singing Kesha, one in a wedding gown and sash and carrying a half-inflated sex doll under her arm. We continued down the narrow cobbled street between cottages refurbished into holiday lets with holidaymakers drinking from bottles on the balconies. There were lights in the upper windows of guesthouses and, as a metal shutter was pulled clanging over the Sandpiper Gallery's doors, fat herring gulls bickered atop a wheelie bin. We stepped onto the wharf and lights blinked out in the St Ives Grill seafood restaurant, adolescent staff glaring at leftover diners still not getting the message, while a line of young Chinese tourists queued for chips besides a gathering of leather-jacketed motorcyclists outside the booming arcade. Waves, gentle and reflective, lapped at the stone wharf. From the distant branch line came the clank of a shunting train's outdated engine, pulling away to Lelant, then to terminate at St Erth, softened almost into melody by the distance. Those seagulls still awake cried from above. The sky over the bay, towards the horizon, beyond Godrevy's island lighthouse, was still tinged a deep, thoughtful blue. On the gradient's edge, where blue became black and black became blue, I saw Cassiopeia and recognised Oumuamua again, balancing on the very boundary. I stared for a moment before my impatient date pulled me along, past a police car parked in a disabled bay, football fans crowding the Miners Inn for white-shirted England versus honey-shirted Moldova. A howl of anguish rang out from them. Teenagers sat at the Methodist church's wooden door, comforting one with watery vomit on his knees, a blonde toddler wailed at his dropped raspberry ice cream, and a girl in a tiara bickered with a taxi driver. My date, whose name I forget, jeered at a bearded tramp lying etherised by cider on the curb – for that I didn't go home with him after all, though I was still insulted by how easily he accepted it.

It all seemed so safe and tranquil.

Then came the falling star.

# II.

The star burst the dawn open, rushing north-eastward over Pendeen, a line of flame high in the atmosphere startling all across the peninsula. Thousands saw it and took it as a shooting star in the early blue. One photograph, taken by an early rising dairy farmer in Zennor and circulated online, showed it to leave a greenish streak which glowed as it cut the sky. Flying from Penzance to the Scillies, a helicopter pilot stated that the height of its first appearance was about ninety or one hundred miles. A budget airline pilot, shepherding half-cut and now quite exhilarated passengers from Cork to Majorca, tentatively reported that it fell to earth at a sharp angle about forty miles east of him. The report was dispatched by Shannon air traffic control to the Irish Aviation Authority who passed it to their British colleagues. From there the chain of command, as the stagnating Robbins Inquiry has since learned, became fuzzy and unclear – the Chichester civil servant at the Civil Aviation Authority who got the email, being new and unwilling to bother his line manager, simply forwarded it to the Meteorological Office's social media team, who duly informed the public at large, or at least their followers, in characteristically dry language. Only as the retweets began cascading did the relevant authorities, such as the military and a dormant government action group without even an office to meet, belatedly become aware.

At that hour, I was at home and watching *Riverdale* again, my sleep schedule entirely broken and my black cat, Disco, asleep on the desk beside my laptop, his tail brushing the keyboard and fur kept warm by the fan. Although my bird-shit flecked windows, against which the desk was pressed, faced across the bay towards Godrevy and the blind was up (the mechanism had long been broken, of course, because what good is a set of blinds which don't immediately break?), I saw nothing of the falling star. Yet this strangest of all things which ever came to Earth – as far as we know, that is, given I've heard there's still questions about the Pyramids – fell while I was sat right there. Had I only looked up from my laptop as it passed, I would have seen it. Some of those who did say it travelled with a hissing sound – this noise was reported as far away as Bristol's Leigh Woods where it disturbed *Countryfile*'s filming. I had headphones on, and I liked the sound *up*, so I remained ignorant. It's a little bit hilarious that, being directly (I've checked – I was) below the thing's path, I still found a way to miss it. It seems the rest of the Westcountry all the way to Sidmouth and the Quantock Hills saw the fall, and the collective assumption which spread across social media was that a meteorite had come crashing. What else could they have thought it was?

Having alarmed much of the South West in its journey from the heavens, the falling star impacted with a colossal smash into the heathland on the clifftops of Clodgy Point, the northern boundary of St Ives, barely missing the snarling ocean. The resultant thunder shook the town awake, rattled windows, provoked car alarms to screech, and startled gulls which took flight en-masse. Having seen its fall everyone who was near now had some desire to look for it – except me, who thought the impact a passing lorry, and so I went on unaware of what had touched down practically outside my door. That was probably for the best.

Closest of all was poor Angus, who – illegally camping on the heathland for its perfect absence of light pollution – had been briefly deafened by the impact as it struck just beyond the nearest hill. Wide awake, scrambling from his tent with ears ringing he set out over the cliffs to investigate, dust falling like rain around him. One hillside trek later, he found the site and, convinced at once that a meteor lay upon the South West Coast Path, was too delighted to stop himself from getting closer. An enormous hole had been excavated by the projectile's impact, mud and Cornubian granite flung violently in every direction over the heath and stonecrops, and it seemed to shimmer in the early sun. Delicate clifftop protrusions had been shaken and crumbled into the sea. Thus was the Blight's first effect on the Earth; a slight redrawing of Ordnance Survey maps would be in order. The heather was ablaze eastward and thin blue smoke rose against the dawn – a beacon for the curious to follow.

The Thing lay almost entirely buried in its crater, the mud scorched to glass which explained the shimmer, amid ferns shivered to fragments by the descent. Smoke from the burning heather drifted away from Angus and shrouded the hillsides. The uncovered part of the object had a diameter more than three times longer than a bus, from above appeared like an oval with a tapering point and a bulbous top, and was covered on all inches by a thick, scaly, and brutally unnatural blood-coloured incrustation. Tentatively, Angus approached the mass, surprised at its size and more so at its shape; it had apparently survived both atmospheric entry and impact without a scratch. With each footstep, glass crinkling under his feet, he wondered at his good luck in being close enough to be first on the scene yet far enough not to be squashed. Upon reaching the crater's edge, though, and gazing down its glass walls and seeing the paranormal crust, he realised his mistake in thinking this a meteor.
"Oh, lord..." he mumbled at the sight, the crater's petrified lip cracking beneath his feet, instantly certain of the Thing's alien

nature as steam hissed from its body. He was then overcome by a nervous cackling. How he wished to get closer – the bowl was, however, a furnace, as agonising heat emanated from the object. Angus dared an additional forward step, edging into the Pit's bowels, only to roast himself. Instinct propelled him back. Frustration boiled within Angus, even hotter than the object that he couldn't reach, nor place a hand on, for he then heard a stirring noise within. He was sure this was the wandering of a pilot. Having consumed every sci-fi novel available once, twice, then thrice, then a few more times, Angus had always assumed that the natural reaction to first contact would be the mental anguish of culture shock – childlike joy, though tempered by an overwhelmed numbness, was therefore a surprising thing to meet instead.

"Hello?!" he shouted stupidly, balanced at the Pit's edge, staring down at its strange resident, astonished at every unusual feature and dimly perceiving his own place in events. "Anyone in there?" There came no reply – only the hiss of steam.

"So this is how it happens," he then said quietly, realising his esteemed position as discoverer, then worrying about the effect on his ego, as with each passing second he saw more evidence of design in both the visitor's arrival and appearance. The early morning was brisk in a way he loved, and the sun, rising over the blue-silver horizon, was already warm. Those few clouds which had come out dawdled, wispy almost to the point of non-existence, on the sky's edges, sparring with each other like swords. Seagulls, still insulted by the disturbance, shrieked through the sky all over the catchment area. Waves were to be heard throwing themselves onto the clifftops and a salty breeze carried in off the water. Despite the many available distractions, Angus, all alone, had eyes and ears only for the cindered bulk and the faint movements within.

Suddenly, he noticed that the grey and ashy crust was falling off. Like noxious snow, it dropped in flakes and rained onto the crater's glass bowl. A large piece fell with a shatter that yanked his heart into his mouth. As the crust fell away, so emerged the sheen of black metal. Angus thought himself sophisticated enough to realise what all this meant and, with the heat becoming if not healthy then at least tolerable, he at last clambered down into the pit, unable to resist, desperate for any answer he could wring out. He fancied that the Thing was rapidly cooling and, in so doing, shedding a protective film intended to shield from the heat and violence of impact. Perhaps this second skin, made of materials he couldn't imagine, absorbed all heat and kinetic energy while leaving what it covered unharmed. What things could be learned just from that technology alone!

Slowly, Angus picked his way around the whole circumference of the crater several times in succession, angling to see every inch of the black Thing that he could before the stupid masses bumbled along and crowded him out. Steam jetted from the newborn glass beneath his walking boots, scorching a loose lace, and with each step he heard the tinkling of rounded, bead-like shards grinding against each other. Angus' internal biological circuits, of course, were screaming for him to run away at full sprint. He perceived the almighty threat he put himself under – even if he were to slip he risked requiring a skin graft or two, made abundantly clear as each new step left a melted rubber footprint on the glass – but he found himself much too overawed by the alien geometries to care.

In one place on the object's bulbous top, where the red crust was still peeling away to form a porthole of black skin beneath, Angus had seen and stared and wondered at the metal, so dark it seemed almost inexplicable. Then, in his scrambling around the circumference and briefly taking his eyes from the Thing to watch his footing, he realised that same shaped hole in the crust now faced the other direction. He scarcely understood what this meant, until he heard a muffled grating sound and saw the black mark was gone again. Then, in a blinding flash,

the truth burst upon him. This top was a lid – and something within was unscrewing it!
"Oh, *shit*!" cried Angus, leaping back and falling against the crater's glass wall. Vanishing into the smoothed shards, his hands seared with the heat, but in the moment he barely noticed the pain. His phone buzzed in his pocket and he mindlessly threw it at the Thing as a chimpanzee might a stone. "No!" he yelled as he did. "Stop that!" His phone bounced off the Thing and smashed.
"Damn it," Angus rambled, heart attack nearing, as he gathered up his phone's plastic cadaver, brain starting to catch up with his body, "I didn't even come to Cornwall for the stargazing! I just had to do that poxy funeral and wanted some time for myself! This is bollocks!" He silenced himself as, with a quick mental leap, he linked the thing to Oumuamua – he looked up, expecting to see it, but the blue sky drowned out its luminescence just as it did to the stars. There then came a dread that more were tumbling earthward – and who knew how many? Overcome by this feeling, his heart a vandal in his chest, Angus tried to climb from the pit only to slip and fall onto the object's scalding hull. At the first touch his hands hissed and, with a pitiful scream, he pulled them away to stare at skin now bubbling a caustic red.

Dazed, Angus turned, scrambled up and out of the pit, and then set off running madly down the coast path through the smoke and past his tent, past a herd of stern alpacas, past an overflowing dog muck bin, and in St Ives' direction. All the while his eyes were either fixed to his fingers, burned to whitening crisps, or the skies from which he anticipated a shower of falling stars. He imagined they must now be landing every which way, on every continent, an overwhelming invasion; the very type he had scoffed at. Fantastic pictures invaded his mind of identical craft burying themselves in Norwegian glaciers and Californian ranches and Kalahari savannah and Indian slums – all unscrewing. The time then must have been somewhere about seven o'clock.

Beach Road, which the coastal path eventually emptied onto after winding along the cliffs between rocks and itchy ferns, was silent as the grave. Tall terraces lined it, looking out over golden Porthmeor Beach, all still asleep. Angus first met a delivery driver who stopped for him at a zebra crossing. He tried to make the driver understand the situation, but his tale and appearance were so wild – his roar of "my hands are fucked!" didn't help – that the driver, after recording him for TikTok, simply drove on. After cooling those fucked hands in the Porthmeor sea, where the salt introduced him to a new conception of pain, he was equally unsuccessful with the beachside cafe's kitchen porter wheeling out a trolley of £20 inflatables. The fellow saw the smoke rising from Clodgy just as well as anyone else, but Angus' insistence of an extraterrestrial invasion met a mind too small to accept it – it wasn't really, the guy had a mathematics masters' from Royal Holloway and had dealt with enough insane tourists to think this just another in a long list, but that was how Angus felt in the moment.

Sobered by all this unexpected and maddening stonewalling, Angus made a much greater effort to make himself understood when he saw the next man – Joe 'Call Me Henderson' Henderson, a local publican and RNLI volunteer, who was walking three uncooperative springer spaniels across the beach. Already people, awoken by the commotion which the Thing had brought, were coming onto the road and the beach and looking toward the smoke which wafted over the hills. Some, being holidaymakers unfamiliar with the area, were already searching for paths to Clodgy Point.

"Hey!" Angus called, hurrying across unhelpful sand towards Henderson. "Mate!"

"You alright?" Henderson asked, tensing as this strange man running at him, looking his ragged form up and down. Once

Angus reached him, he realised he was no threat, while Angus realised he had no idea how to word what he wanted to say.

"You see that meteor?" Terrible start.

"That was that was?" Henderson asked, intrigued and looking towards Clodgy, where the smoke from the burning heather was growing thicker. "That's mental, that."

"It's on Clodgy right now!" Henderson looked back at Angus.

"Mental, that," He said again, nodding to himself.

"But it's *not* a meteor!" Angus cried impatiently, seeing a few heads turn his way, but being far beyond self-consciousness now. Henderson knelt down to scoop up his dog's mess with a plastic bag. "I swear to God – it's alien! There's something inside! I heard it!"

"What you on about?" Angus closed his eyes in agitation and tried to slow down.

He explained: "I was right where it came down. It basically landed on top of me and I swear on my life it's metal and it's making noises and it's *not* a bloody meteor! You've seen the news, haven't you? About Oumuamua? This is it! The invasion!"

"Happened to your hands, lad?" Henderson asked suddenly. Angus looked down – at the sight of the burns, his hands so wrinkled they looked like they'd been underwater for a thousand years, he felt a terrible sickness.

"I don't..." His head went cloudy, bile pooling in his throat, and he stumbled. Henderson shot forward to catch him before he fainted.

"Steady, mate, steady," he said reassuringly, bag of dog muck swinging from his wrist, its warmth pressing against Angus' side, lowering him onto the sand. "Just hold them out for me, yeah?" Angus did so, two spaniels licking his face with sandy tongues as he sat, the smell of burning Clodgy reaching the beach now, while Henderson unzipped his bag and from a tangle of fishing wire produced a roll of clingfilm. He tightly wrapped it around the seared hands and, after fighting the capsules out of their packets, dropped ibuprofen into Angus' mouth.

"Thanks," Angus said, breathless, swallowing the white tablets dry and the putrid bile with them.

"Don't mention it. You're lucky I'm first aid trained, you know, but you should get yourself to a proper doctor. That's some proper nasty burns you've got, you know."

"No time!" insisted Angus, forcing himself to his feet, panicked by the sight of more people excitedly making their way toward the coastal path and the distant smoke.

"Chill! Chill!" Henderson shouted. "What you saying about meteors? What's up there?"

"We can't let people near!" Angus squawked, hurrying back in the direction he'd come from. Henderson followed; the dogs couldn't have been more excited by this change of pace. "You've gotta call the police and tell them not to let anyone near! And then call the RAF and make them bomb it! They *have* to kill it! Before it's too late!"

Bemused but concerned for his safety, Henderson followed Angus up the coastal path, shunting past several enterprising explorers, and, having half-believed Angus was living entirely in his own fantasy land, found what had caused the ruckus. Beside the torched heather there lay what to him appeared like a gigantic and mostly-buried arthropod – at the first sight, the three dogs began barking.

"Christ on a crust!" Henderson exclaimed, precarious on the crater's glass rim, pulled forward by the straining spaniels – he nearly slipped as it crumbled beneath his feet, but, with cling-filmed hands, Angus caught him by the elbow and with some effort dragged him and his three troublesome sons back. "Cheers."

"Don't mention it – I still owe you one." He held up his hands. Wrapped in layers of reflective clingfilm, they looked like futuristic oven mitts.

"Yeah, yeah; mine's a Strongbow. Crumbles! Enough!" He yanked one of the spaniels back. "You say you heard something inside?"

"Yes, definitely," said Angus. "Definitely." But now the sounds had ceased – the great majority of the incrustation had now fallen away to reveal a cold, black, metal shell. Steam still rose from the crater walls and, with a thin sizzle, air could be heard either entering or escaping the Thing. More people were arriving and lining the rim. "There's something in there. Or some*one*. I'm sure of it."

"Well..." replied Henderson, crouching to pick up a rough fragment of granite jettisoned by the impact. With the skill of a cricket bowler he threw it at the Thing and, with a metallic smack, it bounced off in three pieces. Everyone around, apart from the dogs, fell silent. "Oi! Anyone in?"

"Relax," Angus hissed through gritted teeth. "I'd rather not piss this thing off." But Henderson threw another stone and the growing group listened; Henderson even journeyed down into the crater and, with a scaly and burnt stick from some shattered shrub, rapped on the black wall. Meeting with no response, Angus sighed and looked to the sky, embarrassed to find himself disappointed by the invasion's glacial pace. This wasn't what the American films had promised.

"Sure you heard right?" Henderson asked – other people were jumping into the crater now, making circuits about the Thing, and Angus realised he might not be getting discovery credit after all.

"If I didn't, I burned my hands for nothing," he complained in return, starting to feel more secure now he wasn't alone, even if his new companions included oblivious parents with very small children. Somebody was on the phone to the fire brigade. "Maybe it's a probe or something, I don't know, unmanned. It's not like *we* send people to other planets before we send remote controlled cars."

"Well, maybe it's not alien at all, you know?" suggested Henderson. "I mean, come on, you know, Occam's razor and all that. More likely to be a drone or something stupid, you know? One of ours. Something experimental – Culdrose ain't far from here. Bit much to just say aliens – they wouldn't land in Cornwall, would they? New York's over that way." He pointed over the sea in the direction of Ireland. Angus' certainty, though, was unwavering.

Of course, it was beyond the power of the two to do anything but be swiftly overwhelmed. Gawping holidaymakers, shaken awake by the impact and sent into a tumult by news of a meteor by the beach, were now pouring down the coastal path and ignoring all shouted warnings not to get too close, trampling wildflowers as they came. Henderson, furious at the sight of a police car making two separate rounds past Beach Road without realising it needed to turn, went off back into town to get help and remove his increasingly psychotic dogs from the situation. Disordered and excitable, the crowd was a river to wade against in the narrow cliffside lane, until he was in the harbour running down little cobbled streets in the bright sunlight. Shopkeepers were only just pulling up shutters and people opening bedroom windows; many had heard the explosion and thought it merely grumbling of thunder.

Henderson went into the Lifeboat House where he could plug into Wi-Fi – 4G having dreadful coverage in these tight streets – and tried to find the "meteor emergency number." It turned out that no such thing existed but, with the lifeboat gleaming beside him, he found the UK Meteor Society's website – only to realise with mounting agitation that its citizen scientists hadn't included a phone number in their 'contact us' page and their bulletin board had been last updated four years ago. Then, considering that as an RNLI team leader he possessed a duty to public safety, Henderson summoned the rest of his volunteers to guard the crash site from the excessively curious onlookers. The object hadn't seemed dangerous to him, sure, but the Thing was still deathly hot and a crowd could easily push someone against it. In the back of his mind, all the time, haunted Angus' horrified face and his certainty that there was a special kind of danger about this intruder. He didn't want to be the man who ignored the warnings when they came true.

Henderson, unfortunately, was bolting a long-redundant barn door – within the hour everyone knew. Even those who slept through the explosion were waking up to phone calls or the sound of growing crowds or the acrid smell of burning which by now permeated through much of St Ives. News travelled quickly that a meteor – or, maybe, not a meteor – had come down on Clodgy Point. That was the form the story, now beyond anyone's control in the online waterfall, took. Some parents roused their children early, or were roused by their children early, for who could imagine a better day out than seeing a real life meteor? Amid it all there was still at least one child, a few paces from the crater, sat on the grass and poking at a tablet instead.

As for me, I heard the news first when, half an hour into trying to sleep before my shift started, my WhatsApp group chat constituting most of my surf shop colleagues, except Colin ever since *that night*, exploded. One of them, Isobel, who usually just told us we should be voting Green, was there on the cliffs – she sent photo after photo of the Thing snug in its glass pit. After my initial fury at being woken subsided I was, naturally, startled and, naturally, pulled on jeans and joined the herd. It was fifteen minutes from my house to Clodgy Point, via the country lane which wound past the Rugby Club and along the clifftops, and not for a second did I question the wisdom of going.

# III.

Several dozen people formed the chattering crowd surrounding the glittering hole in which the Thing lay. I was taken aback by the colossal bulk's appearance, embedded in the ground, with its remarkable blackness, and the burned heather between the crater and sea (the fire having largely burned itself out), but saved my greatest astonishment for the glass from which the pit was formed. It sparkled like crystals in the rising yellow sun and, once the meteor was safely removed and shipped to the Royal Cornwall Museum before its inevitable and controversial rehousing in the Natural History Museum, would make a hell of a photo trap for influencers and travel blogs. There'd probably be signs up soon, imploring visitors not to take any of the glass, which they would anyway.

Henderson and Angus weren't there – perceiving that there was little more to achieve now that a pair of Community Support Officers were on the scene and giving up on talking people away from the crater's edge, Henderson had driven Angus to the cottage hospital for his hands while his lifeboat volunteers stood about, unsure of what to do, becoming little more than additional spectators. There were four or five young boys amusing themselves—until a stout PCSO stopped them—by throwing stones at the black mass. Chastened by the firm speaking to, and the Thing rapidly becoming uninteresting as it kept sitting there doing nothing, they began playing on one of the groups' phones instead. Their parents, all hungover young professionals, took turns photographing each other with the fallen star behind them. Four young Japanese tourists shyly kept to themselves on one side of the crater, all taking pictures and painstakingly editing each one in turn. Two middle-aged joggers passed by and stopped to stare. The air stank of smoke – an old woman complained about this to me at length and, by her tone, it seemed she thought it was somehow my fault. Tourists can be like that.

Families were aplenty – some children were on the shoulders of fathers or siblings to get a better view of the Thing. Many scooped up a handful of cooling glass to take home or tripped on the upturned rocks which now littered the cliffside. Clucking filled the air – everyone possessed their own theories as to the Thing's origin and nature. Most just gawped and took endless collections of photographs, in search of angles as yet undiscovered, jostling for a glimpse. This was the group to which I belonged. The word "aliens" didn't, as far as I remember, come up – though I'm sure it was being thought. The consensus seemed to be that a meteor had indeed come down and that this was very exciting, at least for the time being. Looking back, I'm surprised that so few of us reached the same instant conclusion as Angus – maybe we were just more naive than we cared to admit.

Growing bored or not wanting to waste the day looking at a lump of metal, some went away, declaring that they had a table booked or needed to get going if they didn't want to miss their bus to St Just or Lands End, sometimes dragging a child away with the assurance that it would still be there when they got back. Others went to admiring the view of the increasingly choppy sea and St Ives Island (actually a peninsula, but that's not important right now) on Porthmeor's opposite side instead. But, more people coming than going, the crowd only grew until the coastal path couldn't accommodate them and they spread out onto the unburned heathland. It was coming to feel like a festival was organically springing up here on Clodgy Point. Eager and curious, I clambered into the Pit itself, joining plenty of scrabbling others.

"You be careful down there," one of the PCSOs warned me, a plump woman failing to keep people back and resorting to these bland pronouncements. The black occupant was now cool enough to touch but warm enough to make this unwise for an extended period, and I held my hand against it for a few moments. It was exceptional in its smoothness and the man next to me, doing the same thing, seemed to feel just as I did.

"Curiouser and curiouser," he said, and I glanced at him, and he glanced back, and I saw deep indigo bags under his eyes. "Isn't it beautiful?"

"I guess so," I agreed. "I've never seen a meteor before." He grinned and, just then, I thought I heard faint movements grumble beneath my feet.

To those without great scientific credentials the Thing was really no more exciting in its design than a Volvo or a tree blown across the road. It required a certain amount of scientific education, which I lacked, to perceive that it was more than just a big pebble, that its black bulk was no common element, that it was of an unnatural hue unfamiliar to this world, and that any rock thrown at it wasn't bouncing off but being repelled. All these things I read in an article by someone much smarter than me, with my failed criminology degree and my failed English Literature degree and my failed Etsy business selling preserved moths, and I kicked myself for not having realised them at the time. Given all that would come to pass, and all the horror that we would be bathed in, warnings which the Thing whispered then are now remembered as screams.

Yet, despite my ignorance, it suddenly became clear in my mind that the Thing had come from Oumuamua. This was a connection much of the rest of the world was slowly making, too. But it wasn't entirely correct – Oumuamua had pointed the way and no more. Nonetheless, even with the light bulb of "oh, so aliens are real? Sick!" I felt the same as Henderson and judged it improbable that it could be anything other than some unmanned probe; I imagined a great technocratic civilisation shooting out tens of thousands, maybe millions, across the galaxy to every heavenly body, for no purpose other than to scan the atmosphere, with this one in the process of reporting back that Earth didn't have enough nitrogen to be worth their time. "Worthless," I imagined it saying. "Fail planet. Don't bother."

Rumours swirled of movement within, but I thought this merely an example of people's nature to interpret the unexplainable into something familiar. There couldn't be a funny little fellow hanging out inside; that'd be insane. My mind, still trying to adjust to the shift from meteor to alien capsule, sprinted through alternate possibilities of what it might contain – probably just motors and gears but we'd soon find out, I was sure, when it was eventually stripped and reverse-engineered and its presumably far-advanced circuitry adopted for the next generation of smartphones and self-driving cars. Yet, the Thing was a just little too large for me to feel completely assured of its harmlessness – after a while in the Pit, I felt I was looking too deeply into its dark foreboding metal, and came to sense that if I continued I might sink into it. I climbed from the Pit, feeling an intensifying impatience to see it opened. About ten, as nothing seemed happening besides the crowd's growing and shrinking and growing again, the arrival of some local journalists, and the orbiting of a black-yellow police helicopter, I walked, full of thoughts, to work, regretting my aborted nap. But though I sort of tried, I found it difficult to focus on my job, which largely constituted telling of patrons that we didn't permit pushchair access owing to fire hazard guidelines – and receiving much abuse for this, as was traditional, as if I had any authority at all. At least I wasn't

Helena who, on her first day, had misinterpreted the rule as applying to wheelchairs as well, and been passionate in defending this incorrect policy to the customer. She didn't work at Surf Shack anymore. All the while I leaned over the counter, I would sneak chances to check news updates, and as I did I felt the object's presence through the walls, as if even from this distance it were somehow regarding me and sinking into me as I had feared I might into it.

In the afternoon, the appearance of the town through my shop window, or at least the strip of narrow cobbled Fore Street visible through the cardboard window displays, had changed profoundly. There was a greater traffic of people, gripped by excitement, trooping up the street and a greater hum of sirens in the distance. Customers could only talk about the meteor, unless they were complaining about our offers, or agitating about our cashless policy because "but it's legal tender" even though that's not what 'legal tender' means, or shouting at me for not letting their toddler use the staff toilet. At times, vehicles – often emergency vehicles, once a transit van with a plastic Stormtrooper in the window – passed and parted the crowds against the walls. One woman complained about this to me – "can't you do something about the street?" she asked. Would you believe me if I told you this wasn't even the first time I'd been asked?

Hurrying police officers, usually travelling in pairs, like badgers, were an increasingly regular sight as the day trudged on – one came in and bought some sport sunglasses. There was a sense in the shop of the town swirling into crisis just outside our four walls. The authorities, we learned from an upset out-of-towner who wanted to fetch her daughter to see the meteor but now wouldn't be allowed back into St Ives, were locking down the roads for everyone except residents and those with booked accommodation, in an effort to halt a flood of sightseers. The gravity was becoming apparent. Snatched

glances at my phone when Sue, the area manager, wasn't looking showed that the star which had fallen upon St Ives now had the attention of all the world. How surreal it was to see my little town dominating the front pages of the Guardian, CNN, the Times of India, Botswana Today, and so forth; the New Guinean tsunami and an online streamer accidentally blowing off the top of his head with a revolver vanished from the newsfeed. Instead, the unreal words UFO CRASHES IN CORNWALL sat splashed across the BBC's banner headline. The object's mechanical nature was becoming undeniable. An ITV camera crew passed down the road hauling equipment – despite our momentary excitement not stopping to interview or otherwise speak to us till monkeys in the Surf Shack. The rumble of helicopters was a constant above our heads. Work, the tension mounting, closed early – Sue pleaded with head office in Camborne that the feeling of unease in a town threatened by aliens was overpowering. She finally convinced them by pointing out that our last paying customer had been two hours ago and then laughed heartily when she put down the cord phone – there were several customers in the shop and I was in the middle of a transaction.
"Thank God Nikki doesn't check the records," she sighed. Overexcited, I took the opportunity to return to Clodgy Point under three helicopters' watchful eyes and, assuming I could get back to the crater, see what had transpired in my absence.

As it turned out, it was a lot. From Beach Road, the Thing was invisible behind a hill, accessible only via the coastal path, and so the road swarmed with people.

Many had come, in spite of the day's heat, and the crowd was considerable – any effort to put up a police cordon had patently failed and now the crowd completely overwhelmed the heathland along the Clodgy Point cliffs. Beach Road and the adjoining streets were swamped by emergency vehicles – police cars and vans, fire engines, several ambulances, a Land

Rover with HM Coast Guard decal. Navigating it all out again would be a logistical nightmare. One motorist, leaning from his BMW, was in passionate argument with a paramedic whose ambulance blocked his second home's driveway. Glaringly hot, not a cloud in the sky nor a breath of wind, the sea now hauntingly still and half of Porthmeor dark from a shadow cast by the Tate Gallery, I sensed that tempers could quickly snap. I pushed my way through, itching to get as close as I could again, thinking of those sweet Instagram likes, while Devon and Cornwall Police officers urged us back and few obeyed. They hadn't the numbers to enforce anything like a proper cordon and anyone who wanted to could flow right past. So I pressed on with many others down the coast path again and back to the Thing. How I wanted to see it again. To touch it again. It felt like I was being called in – like a sailor to a siren.

The burning heather may have extinguished but the ground towards the sea was blackened as far as one could see. Vertical streamers of smoke seemed to come from every inch. Of course, people still stood about in it. Helicopters circled menacingly above, like vultures, and an enterprising ice cream van had come the long way, now perched halfway up a nearby hill, to overcharge on Cornettos just beyond the stone hedge. Many, clearly, thought this all a big jolly. Some onlookers had climbed rock formations to see over the heads and to the Pit. I passed a profusely sweating police officer, bald with glasses, who, into a bulky walkie-talkie, engaged in animated conversation with whoever sat on the line's opposite end.
"No," he was saying quickly, "we can't get anything done with this crowd in the way. We need help getting people off the cliffs and after that we need some actual direction on what you want us to do with this bloody thing… no, we can't get a digger down here." All I could think about was getting to the Thing again. I might not get another chance, I thought.

The Pit itself, which I couldn't yet reach as here at least a police cordon had been successful, was occupied by about half a dozen officers – chief among them the bronze commander of the operation, the tall, fair-haired Detective Inspector William Stent stood atop the black rock itself, evidently now much cooler given he wasn't melting, he gave instructions in a high-pitched voice.

"Ladies and gentlemen, please, for your *own safety*, stay behind the line!" His face was crimson and streaming with perspiration and he seemed perpetually irritated as he shouted everyone back.

"Safety?!" someone shouted back. "You're standing on a UFO, ya gimp!" Laughter broke out.

Over the multitude of backs of heads I could just about see DI Stent, a small black scribble of a figure against the green hill, before, much closer, I recognised the back of Angus' head – he was being questioned by another officer who scribbled down his account of the initial encounter with mild interest. I slapped him on the shoulder and he flinched before turning and, recognising me, his eyes brightened and he hugged me tightly which I found somewhat uncomfortable.

"Can you believe this?" he asked with tremendous excitement as he pulled away, still gripping my shoulders.

"Not really," I admitted, and Angus let go and looked back toward those officials on the crater's rim.

"He shouldn't be standing on it," he growled.

"It's a bit dumb," I agreed, as someone shoved past me and I tried not to start drama I'd surely regret. That was the old me – besides, too many police around. "You'd think he'd be careful."

"None of this is going how it should be. Who *stands* on the ship?! I told them – they ought to evacuate the whole town! They're not listening. Everyone's in danger. Everyone." He looked around in wonder at all these people who didn't seem to notice the dagger hanging over them.

"So what you doing here, then?" I asked.

"I'm the discoverer," he replied proudly, and at once I saw how his vainness would trump most else – I wondered if he found a fondness for astronomy only because he hoped to get a comet named after himself. "And what's more, I-"

"What happened to your hands?" He looked down – they were both heavily bandaged, so much so that he couldn't hope to adjust a telescopic lens for days.

"Burned them."

"How'd you burn them?"

"Just burned them."

"That's fair. So what's the deal with that thing? Was hoping to get a proper look." Self-consciously, I chose not to tell him I had already been here once and hungered for more – I didn't think that would reflect well on me. Aloofness is sexier.

"They can hear something inside – something stirring."

"I heard something about that; it's just the engine or whatever, right?"

"Maybe. I sure hope so. I heard it too, right at the start; it's coming and going, like a really slow heartbeat."

"I'm rooting for an engine. There's nothing scary about an engine."

"Clearly you've never seen the old Thomas the Tank Engine illustrations." I laughed.

"Well, I'd rather that than it turning out to have a heartbeat." Angus nodded. "This is mad."

"And gonna get madder," Angus replied, putting on a spooky voice. "But you might as well go home; you won't get near and we won't find out what's in there for days *and* you might die any second.

"You *always* might die any second," I replied, crossing my arms. "Why won't we find out for days?"

"Well, the case must be *so* strong to fall to Earth like that without breaking. It'll take forever to cut our way inside.

"Or for it to cut its way out," I added brightly and darkly – I love doing both.

"Hopefully. But there's not gonna be anything in there – it's just a probe or drone or something. Which is amazing, obviously, it's the most amazing moment in human history – it's just hard to feel that way when your hands are like this and there's someone prancing about on the alien vessel."

"And they're selling ice cream."

"And they're selling ice cream," Angus agreed.

"They're definitely okay, right?" I asked. He glanced at Stent, still balancing atop the Thing.

"I don't know – he looks a bit mental."

"I mean your hands."

"Oh, they'll be fine. Told me I'd have to go to a burns centre in Plymouth and here I am instead. Wouldn't miss this for anything. Can't be in Outpatients at a time like this."

"That sounds like a... bad idea."

"Who's fussed? I've got far too much adrenaline to worry. Anyway, whatever those noises are, I'm not bothered. Even in the worst case scenario – least I got to see."

"Could be a bomb."

"It's not a bomb." Someone in front of us whipped their head round.

"It's a bomb?!" he cried.

"I said it *could* be a bomb," I replied, and he looked back to the Pit, a worried look on his face. I looked back to Angus and raised my eyebrows. "It could be a bomb."

"It's not a bomb. Hey – treat you to a poke?" I stared at him. *Here*?

"A what?" Angus blinked.

"A cornet. You bloody dirty-minded English."

"Sure," I laughed. "Only if it has a flake."

"Do I *look* like a barbarian?"

# IV.

My back was to the Pit as I dawdled in choosing between strawberry or mint chocolate chip – Angus was outraged that I'd even consider the latter – and, in a way, enjoying not being so consumed by its presence. That was until the sound of screams from its direction washed over me. Swinging around, being on a hillside I could see the crowd of a hundred people, perhaps, suddenly scattering in all directions away from the glittering crater. Strange imaginings passed through my mind.

"Something's going down!" Angus cried, his strawberry ice cream pinned between two ridiculous-looking wrapped hands, hurrying back down the hill and dropping it as he went. I followed, forgetting the ice cream and stumbling as I went, until Angus stopped somebody coming past. I nearly slipped and rolled down the rest of the hill as I halted.

"I don't have the shoes for this!" I protested.

"What's happening?" Angus asked the pale-faced man with urgency.

"It's feckin' opening!" he wailed back. "There's something trying to get out! No more of this for me!" Angus' eyes widened as much as I ever saw someone's eyes go and, dropping his expensive ice cream to be brutally trampled into the grass, he pushed his way through the crowd to get as close as he might achieve.

"That doesn't strike me as the right way!" I shouted after him, unheard in the commotion, and then realised I was going to be there too – the pull was too much to bear. "For God's sake!" I gave chase. DI Stent, who had been thrown from the meteor, was now on the crater's edge and, waving grazed hands, bellowing, he and his officers desperately linking their arms to form a chain.

"Get back! Everyone get back!" A little blonde boy in a Minecraft shirt came running past me.

"Nope, nope, nope," he repeated to himself; "I'm not having that, I'm not, I'm going home."

Not being so wise, I dove into the crowd with Angus, trying to stay close to him, afraid of falling under all these feet and ending up like his ice cream. There were, I should think, a hundred and a bit people elbowing and jostling one another, one tracksuited girl flinging a Sports Direct bag about as she screeched that the crowd was suffocating her.

"Get him out of there, for God's sake!" I then heard someone yell over the din.

"Stay back!" shouted DI Stent, his officers – far outnumbered – trying and failing to keep the squawking crowd from surging back towards the Pit, having regained some courage after its initial flight. I elbowed my way through the excitement hearing a peculiar humming sound from the Pit but not seeing see a thing. With all these bodies in the way, whatever was causing the commotion was invisible to me. "Fucking stay back!"

"You can't shout at my child!"

"This is ridiculous!" Angus wailed as the crowd encircled the Thing, we were a mere pace or two from the edge and still I had to jump up and down to catch a fleeting glimpse of the black bulk. "You don't even know what's inside! It's dangerous!"

"Then *why* are we getting closer?!" I yelled.

"Because I wanna see a spaceman!" he shouted back like it was the most obvious thing to say in the world. A face appeared over the lip of the crater, then vanished again; a young officer, who had lost his helmet, had been pushed into the hole by the crowd and, having broken something in the fall, was failing to scramble out. Two of his colleagues were reaching down to help, others holding them so they didn't themselves fall, but still they couldn't reach. I grabbed the shoulders of two people in front of me and hauled myself up, trying to view the whole scene, and, at last, I saw what was happening.

The Thing's bulbous upper portion was breaking open in a strange, fluid kind of way, like a pair of eyelids slowly separating, still connected by strands of syrupy gunk. Only darkness could be seen inside. Just as I got to the front to join the effort to haul the officer out of the hole, the instinct to help having taken over, somebody blundered against my back. One foot slipped down the side of the crater. Shrieking in an uncomplimentary way, my legs split as it went, the other foot staying on firm ground, until DI Stent grabbed me by the wrist and heaved me back up.

"Everyone get back!" he insisted, ignoring me and my repeated thanks, as he hauled me back onto non-petrified ground. I was then nearly knocked down again as, suddenly and with a ringing concussion, the object gave out a metallic bark.

The crowd ducked as one and fell silent – even the guarding officers had turned to watch the Thing, now just extra bodies in the crowd, and even those helping the trapped man stared silently too. Droning helicopters were all I could hear. An elbow jammed into my ribs, its owner swearing passionately as he scrabbled to nope his way out of the crowd – despite everything I knew about common sense, I didn't follow, nor even try getting my elbow to him in return, instead staring with the rest at the opening capsule. Pungent stinks of vomit and iron swept out from inside. Squinting, a fierce glare of the Sun bouncing from the metal, I gagged as it washed over me.

I think everyone expected to see *something* emerge—in imagining what, all manner of freak shows swept my mind. A big-headed man made of sludge, perhaps, or an army of

Harlequin babies, or just a funny little fellow. Something mental, anyway, whose emergence would prove I should have stayed at the ice cream van, or never come at all, or just died in the womb and spared myself any involvement in this doomed world. Whatever was in there, it was stirring, and it smelled. Then something cumbersome, a big pinkish rounded bulk, the size of a bear, came rising slowly and painfully out of the meteor's top with the most revolting of squelches. Bulging up, catching the light, the being glistened like wet leather – it put me in mind of a giant heaving brain, slimy and brown-pink, slowly forcing itself upwards. There was nothing human about it; nor anything animal. It was beyond alien – a creature so defiant in its reprehensible morphology that its very existence seemed an insult. When it had squelched high enough, two luminous discs – eyes of a deep and unkind black – became visible and at this awful sight a sudden burning chill rushed over me. The crowd found its voice again. They retreated with screams. My ear hurt from a woman screeching beside me. Half-turning as I ran, unable to tear my eyes from the beast, I saw those haunting eyes fixed upon what could have been me but more likely were all of us at once, and joined the rout from the pit's edge.

Everyone was running, many of them backwards, putting space between us and the hideous It. I saw astonishment and indefinable horror on their faces and I imagine I looked the same. None had expected *this*. I looked back, saw the officer struggling still on the Pit's edge, then tripped and fell under the crowd. I lay there, expecting shoes to come a'trampling, and I was lucky only one landed on my ankle. Somehow, it didn't snap; even if it had, the smell was so intrusive and so all-encompassing that I think it would have distracted me entirely from the pain.

The crowd disappeared around me like a withdrawing wave and, suddenly, I found myself alone on the prickly grass.

Pushing myself up, I saw the people on the other side of the Pit running off, DI Stent among them, a clearing between crowd and crater forming on all sides. Now slowing, the crowd watched from what they must have thought a safe distance, some hiding behind rocks or bumps in the terrain, many of them filming the scene, myself and a handful of others scattered about the newly formed clearing. Ungovernable terror gripped me at the sight of the still-heaving Thing with its unnatural body, like a living blood clot. Petrified, I couldn't move, only lie there and stare as a sloppy, writhing tentacle came wriggling from the capsule – and then another.

Wet goo dribbled from the formless mass which was this Thing's ugly body and down the metal cylinder – it appeared to be trying to heave its way out altogether, like a living fatberg clogging a pipe, grim gases burping out with it. More intestinal tentacles slithered into the pit or swayed in the air. Convulsively heaving, pulsating, the monstrosity came to seem satisfied with its resting place and ceased trying to push its way out – maybe it had realised it was fighting a losing battle against our gravity. Now able to study it, though my eyes watered from fear and the smell, I saw that beyond its own eyes there was nothing which could be called a face. There was no mouth nor nose; it was little more than a motorised blob of matter with an unspeakable nastiness in the way its tentacles clumsily deliberated. I was overcome with disgust and dread.
"Help!" My attention snapped to the policeman who, still trapped in the pit, now had a thick oozing tentacle gripping his calf and dragging him deeper down the petrified bowl. Several onlookers, Stent and Henderson among them, dropped their caution and surged forward to the pit where, beneath the monster, they reached for his hands. Being nearby, I joined them, less out of the natural impulse to help than the self-conscious realisation that I was too close not to. At the vocal encouragement of those unwilling to get so near, we engaged in a tug-of-war with the Thing looming over us.

"Oh, Jesus! Oh, Jesus!" the officer wailed, clinging painfully to my hand, wedding ring digging into my fingers, unable to take his eyes from the maggoty monster which had him. Even with a dozen people holding both arms I felt him being pried from our grip. It was then I saw Henderson seize a rock and – leaping with exceptional courage into the Pit – hammer at the tentacle itself.

"Get! Back! In! Your! Box!" he yelled with each strike. After a few more blows, drawing purple bruises in the slimy red flesh, slowly and obligingly it released the man. To my shame, the moment it did, I was the only one to let go of him. I stumbled backwards fast. The rest of the group helped him and each other out of the Pit and all hurried away, the officer limping badly, except for a Chinese man who had been among the rescuers, and who was now barking some appeal at the creature.

"We're friends!" he pleaded, hands held out. "We welcome you!" Slowly, without reply, the monster slipped back into its metal nest to vanished again. It rattled off a peculiar thick cry as, slowly, its tentacles followed; I felt a powerful hate at their slow retreat, as if this leisurely withdrawal reflected how little it cared for us and any threat it thought we posed. A muscular need festered in me to show it whose house this was.

The beast having disappeared from view I became suddenly aware of the adrenaline flooding my system. Powerful sickness took over my stomach as I examined my hands and nearly laughed at how hard they shook. I turned and, stumbling slowly and without consistent direction for even now I couldn't avert my face from where the Thing had been, made for the stone hedge, perhaps a hundred yards away. Surf crashed against the cliffs below. Again the white stones, assembled in an ancient and unwritten era, I stopped, leaning against them, dryly retching several unpleasant times. Nothing came up. Taking a few deep breaths, staring into the sparse vegetation, my mind tried to make sense of what I had seen and failed. It took on the feeling of a dream. After a time I stood and sat upon the wall, waiting for further developments with no eagerness for them to happen, staring at the object, which seemed in the moment to have turned a darker shade of midnight since last I looked. Its top had closed again while I wasn't looking. Henderson, with great energy, was wiping the Thing's slime from his hands against the rough bracken.

"You ever seen anything like that before?" someone asked another as, in a daze, they walked by me.

"Once, in Weston-super-Mare." They laughed nervously.

"Ladies and gentlemen," DI Stent was shouting, as his handheld radio shouted louder about military reinforcements, "please learn your lesson and stay *well* back! I'm not asking you; I'm telling you!" Those with the guts to remain had learned their lesson and stayed far from the crater's edge, for a bit, before, inevitably, many returned to the lip. Transfixed terror reverberated through the crowd. Misty steam ebbed from grooves in the object's exotic metal. The ice cream van stood on the hillside still, comical against the scene, and in its service window a fat seagull fed greedily on wafer cones.

# V.

After glimpsing the grunting Blight in its steaming capsule, a kind of morbid fascination paralysed my instincts. I stood knee-deep in fluffy heather, staring at the black machine that hid it, unwilling to step closer and unwilling to step further away. Fear and curiosity fought a running battle inside me.

Despite a passionate longing, I dared not go back near the Pit; resisting the urge to snatch a harmless peek was torturous. Therefore, I had been walking in great circles, seeking some point of vantage and finding it at another of the stone hedges which, being positioned further upon a hill, permitted me to overlook the Pit with some presumed safety. Nothing more happened for a time besides the police helicopter passing back and forth overhead. Then, suddenly, the machine gave me good reason not to draw closer. A leash of thin black whips, like the arms of an octopus – or a grotesque otherworldly being whose existence was a crime against God, which seemed the more appropriate simile right now – flashed from the hull and across the sky. The crowd jumped back again. For a moment I imagined these whips intended to ensnare all those foolish enough to have gotten closer; some sort of self-defence mechanism. Instead, this strange display ended after a few moments, the coils slowly withdrawing back into the hull just as the pilot, or passenger, or whatever it was, had done. That sense that I should not be here grew inside me – but, oh, look, I still wasn't leaving.

By now, the police had successfully driven everyone far from the Thing, and most of the spectators had gathered in two groups – one crowded on the heather either side of the coast path, the other was a string of people behind the assumed safety of the grey rocks nearest the Thing. All, evidently, shared my mental conflict – to stay or to go. There were few along my hedge until I began moving down the wall for a better view. One man, dressed in the thin fabric of an Aston Villa shirt which didn't bode well for articulate conversation, turned and engaged me as if we were long-time neighbours.

"I just got off the phone with my brother – he says there's more coming down in London, Paris, um, fuckin' somewhere in Surrey – but also Bristol, Liverpool, Manchester..." He tried to catch his breath. "I think these things are gonna be everywhere. The whole world, maybe. I don't think we'll be able to move for them soon." This was not, as I would soon learn, even remotely true – ours was the only one. His brother spent too much time on Twitter.

"We're being invaded by the ugliest things I've ever seen," I mumbled, half-listening to him, my mind still too much of a whirr for talk – or to panic over the news he'd just given me. "Christ, they're *so* ugly!" I repeated this several times over.

"Not much of an invasion if they're just sitting there, though!" he said hopefully. He suddenly had a Lion Bar in his hand. I don't know where he got it. "You saw the bastard couldn't move, eh? Think they bit off more than they could chew with our gravity, eh?"

"You think so?" I asked, hopeful – his eyes lit up at the possibility that he could have landed upon something himself.

"Look at it," he said. "It's useless. Just a bit of junk. I don't fancy being all cocky but I'm not impressed so far – one copper with a busted leg ain't really world-conquering. You ever heard of the Dieppe Raid?"

"No."

"Been reading about World War Two. It's, like, my thing. Six thousand Allied troops landed in Dieppe in France to hold the port. Planned it like shit so it completely failed. Half of them killed. A whole invasion stopped just like that cause they planned it so bad. This reminds me of that. They're here, so, what now, ey? One Hellfire missile and it's done. It's all very Dieppe, you know?"

"Yeah," I answered. "Very Dieppe. And after that, of course, the Allies gave up and stopped fighting and never invaded France again and Germany won. Right?" He didn't acknowledge my wit – instead he held his hand not busy with a Lion Bar in front of his face and examined it, with an interest I hadn't yet seen him afford the crashed alien spacecraft right before him.

"What is it?" I asked. "Got burned?"

"No," he replied softly. "I'm not shaking. Not at all. Are you?"

"No."

"I was expecting a bit of... I don't know... shock. Just found out aliens are real. Just fought one – in a way. But I'm *very* unbothered. Maybe I'm a psycho. Maybe after all the shit these last few years I'm not even surprised aliens're next! This'll be out of the news cycle in a week, I bet. Even if they did conquer us. Everything happens too much."

"You were in that melee too?" I asked.

"That what?"

"Melee."

"What?"

"Fight."

"Oh, yeah, I was," he said proudly. "Look at us – making first contact by throwing hands. That's the human way, innit? Definitely the Brummie way." He laughed and I pretended to join in – customer service had trained me well.

"So now what?" I asked.

"Fuck knows – people with degrees will figure it out."

"That rules me out, then."

"Same." He looked to the sky – I followed, expecting to see falling stars streaking across it with tremendous, silent speed,

but there was nothing. "They'd better be quick. You got family nearby?"
"Does a cat count?" He laughed.
"You should evac 'em if you do. God knows what'll happen."
"I take it that's what you're doing?"
"Don't have family round here. I mean... I've got a niece but the alien can fuckin' have her."
"Right. How's the guy who fell in?" He made no answer to that – just started texting. We became silent, and stood watching for a time side by side, deriving, I reckon, a certain comfort in one another's company. Then, seeing someone else vacate it, I shifted my position further up the hill for a yard or more of elevation. When I looked back, the man was walking away down the coast path towards St Ives, limping as he went. Slipping my hands from my pockets, I examined them – they *were* shaking. I stared with the same intense fascination to which he had given his own.

Slipping from its moorings, the Sun was drifting towards the horizon before anything further happened. Directly ahead of me, down the hill, lay the Pit, and beyond that the cliffs and the roaring sea. The crowd far away on the right, on the path to St Ives, seemed to grow, journalists and police and media people in greater abundance, and its murmuring grew correspondingly.
Buffeted by a growing wind off the bay, which insisted on flicking my hair into my mouth, the chain of people with me along the rocks dissipated and the crowd on the path, closer to the Pit, grew. I guess folks were becoming confident enough to get near once again. A slow, intermittent movement upon the crater began by some of the authorities, clad in high-visibility jackets like fluorescent insect shells, still unable to persuade the gawkers, like me, to leave. I, at least, wouldn't get in the way – even as I found myself alone behind the rocks, and gradually working my way down the hill, the Pit now just a couple dozen feet away as I joined some of the others, I refused to obey the

burning want to venture over. I had no desire to be within the reach of those tentacles – even if I could outrun their sluggishness. Then, over my rock, I saw a group boldly venture into the upturned and fossilised mud and back towards the crater itself. The foremost, bald and in smart-formal dress with obnoxious brown aviators, was holding a white bedsheet and waving it with some unease at the apparently inactive capsule. There had been a hasty consultation and since the Blight were, though repulsive, clearly intelligent creatures, it had been resolved to try again at showing them that we were intelligent, too.

A hand on the flagbearer's shoulder, Stent joined the apprehensive advance, which moved perpendicular to me, so giving me a perfect view of their every timid step toward the fallen star. The intent, since denounced as needlessly provocative and meant only to lure the creature into showing itself again, was rather more charitable. It was strongly felt, in the moment, that the Thing was frightened and ought to be somehow calmed down. The sense that it might be aggressive was dwindling – the capsule had no visible weaponry and, though the Thing was grotesque, it was also, obviously, utterly helpless. There was a genuine, and woefully naive, desire to help it.

This little group dragged inward, so to speak, the crowd as it advanced. Figures followed at discreet distances like nervous deer. Angus and Henderson were among them. Near to me, someone was murmuring the lyrics to Don't Leave Me This Way to himself. Suddenly, when the group came to within a few paces of the crater's edge, there came bursting from the capsule, in three intense puffs, luminous greenish smoke. They drove up, one after the other, straight into the air to be carried on the wind. Some of the crowd scattered while others, including Stent, took it for some unconnected exhaust fume. After an anxious pause and nervy glances at each other they continued their advance. How I wanted to scream at them all to turn and run. But I didn't – for, intuitively, I knew what was coming and I didn't want the Thing to know I, too, was there. Sometimes, when I close my eyes, I can still see them and I still won't scream. Hissing, faint and electronic, became audible from the Pit. One of the group lost his nerve, turned, and ran. Stent was calling something I couldn't hear to the machine – I don't think anyone could hear over that hiss. If they could, well, that wouldn't make a different. Slowly, the hissing passed into a cold hum, into a long, loud, droning noise, and then this passed from noise into something else, something which made the same sound yet seemed different; like a voice doing an impression of what it had replaced. Suddenly, quick as that had come, fell silence. And then the delegation turned into fire.

Writhing and dancing, I saw them stagger and fall, little black toys in the flames. Screams and heat filled the air. Those behind them fell backwards or scattered in every direction. They were chased – all, as far as I saw, were caught by the invisible beam which swept from side to side and painted the clifftops with death. Fire erupted where before there had been people, huge billowing balls of it, swallowing everyone. Staring, not moving, flames bursting in front of me, I was a spectator. People pushed past me, sprinting and bounding from the cliffs to escape the Thing's reach, falling under each other. No weapon could be seen firing this beam – the comet willed fire upon whatever it thought needed it. My eyes stung from the flames' brightness and, rooted to the spot, unable to move, fingers digging into the rock, I saw a woman stumble towards me, naked but newly dressed in fire. Her eyes melted and poured from the sockets like milk. As the unseen shaft of heat came nearer, fire erupting along the grass in a straight-line towards me, I ducked behind the granite rocks and the improbable salvation it suggested. Every piece of vegetation on the clifftops had become a thunderous mass of fire. Back against the rocks, pained eyes slammed shut and certain of my demise in this whirlpool, I waited for death. When I opened my eyes, the inferno's roar bellowing in my ears, I saw the reach of this inevitable sword of heat – the hillsides beyond erupted and a cottage, barely a speck hidden at the pinnacle of the incline, was consumed. Its white plaster and slate roof fell away as the firestorm took it. At once, I realised I sat in a lonely little island within the fire, with nothing to hear but the fire and the screams and the distant chime of an ice cream van. Oxygen eaten away by the fiery vortex, I found myself unable to breathe. Above, the orbiting police helicopter was sliced in half and, with a strange grace, its two parts separated and fell into the sea.

Perceiving some chance of survival if I ran but none if I remained, I looked about wildly for some pathway to safety through the flames, tears yanked from my head by the flames and streaming down my face. Death's approach could be seen by the flashing bushes, approaching me with great speed and bursting onto the rocks like waves, and I stirred and ran for the nearest clearing I could find in the whirling black smoke. I pushed past one, two, three figures all in a floundering confusion or already alight themselves, heard the squeal of a child that was suddenly stilled, saw a woman laying across the floor with steam gushing from a skinless scalp, felt a red-hot hand try and fail to grip my ankle. I felt played with – like the fire was appearing everywhere I wasn't and that it was happening on purpose. Still I ran until through the smoke I saw the coast path and registered its gridlock of people. My imagination materialised the burning finger drawing right down it.

"Nope!" I yelled hoarsely as I turned from the path. "I changed my mind! I don't wanna die!" I instead threw myself into the deep, as-of-yet unburned heather.

Crawling, licked by heat, I fell into a sodden ditch and, as I covered my head with my arms as if it afforded protection, prayed it'd be adequate. Blinded, fire roared all around, and I knew that if I felt myself alight there was nothing I could do. In my own pit, whenever I peeked up I saw nothing but fire in every direction, heard distant screams still, slowly falling silent. I coughed relentlessly on the smoke, the sky invisible for it, until, dumbfounded, I lay motionless and dazzled in my crypt. What I knew to be the world was suddenly unfamiliar – there was a sense of it having vanished from around me and something else taking it place.

Clodgy Point choked in the smoke's blackness – nobody outside could see inside and vice versa. Laying in my hole, time passing at an unknown speed, soon I heard nothing but the crackle of fire – no voices or, as I feared, cries, joined it. Shrouds of toxic smoke thinned enough above me that I could see the sky was still a pale, bright, almost greenish blue and, as the ringing in my ears faded, I heard the sea just beyond the cliff's delicate edges. The hillsides which looked down on the Pit, where I had been just moments before, were consumed in tangy orange flame. Slowly, warily, I pulled myself up the ditch and peered over the edge, out over the killing field. The ground all the way to the Blight appliance, a vague black shape through the fire, glowed molten. The crowd had been swept from existence – I saw blackened charcoal in the shape of human beings scattered about the glowing ground, powderised by the heat, and I wondered which one was Angus. I couldn't find the coast path I'd rejected – it and the surrounding vegetation had been rendered to ash and dust. The beast torched everything it saw – had it landed in a more elevated position it may well have scorched everything all the way to Bodmin.

It came to me that I was helpless and alone and probably going to die soon – what way out was there which wasn't in full view of the Thing? Sinking back into the ditch, face and body feeling as though they *were* aflame from both stress and the firestorm, I absurdly giggled at my own ridiculous circumstances. Then,

I thought of my cat, Disco, and realised I couldn't die here – he needed his medicine. He had a bad body.

With my sightline close to the ground, I kept peering, and thought I saw an avenue of ferns which had been pulverised to ash but were no longer aflame. Forming a path in my mind, its terminus I had no idea, I slowly climbed from the ditch, laying as low as I could, looking towards the capsule as smoke obscured it again and hoping it couldn't see me, either. Ash stuck to my hands and seeped into the wrinkles, turning them black, like ancient stones. With an effort, I stayed on all-fours and began a rather pathetic crawl low through the wreckage, flames trying to touch me from either side, praying I was beyond the Thing's reach, spluttering on fumes which in a moment of great queasiness I realised probably used to be people. Corpses scattered all around in twisted poses – I crawled over one which fell apart beneath me, a hard and burned outer layer crumbling into boiled orange goo, and bit my tongue to keep whimpers from escaping as I kept going.

I'd never known you could feel fear like this – it was not just of the Blight and the fire, but of the stillness and the feeling of sudden reduction all about me. It was as if I could sense the vanquishing of all these people's energy all at once. Now I lay in a vacuum. Remembering stories of Lot's wife in my old Church of England school, I did not dare look back at the Thing in my crawling through the dead undergrowth, teeth gritted so tightly I thought I might sand them down. At one point I saw a figure appear from the smoke and realised it was a man, flash-fried where he stood, shielding something small in his arms, reduced now to a coal statue.

As I crawled further, the ash faded, the plants either side no longer wallowing in it but blackened and steaming. Dragging myself along the hot ground, leaving grooves in the dead flora, I came across a lifeless man who lay in my path. His face was burned away, all the sinews and muscles exposed and seared white, his lips gone so his teeth grinned at me, and I stopped to look at him. His phone, the screen cracked, lay next to him, vibrating with missed calls. After a few moments his eyes opened. He looked at me. Regarded me. He looked almost wistful.

"Well, don't *stop*," I thought he passively said, somehow enunciating while lacking lips, and I obeyed, crawling further, the ground getting hotter until I couldn't go any further. Unless I wished to burn my hands, feet, and everything else which touched this cooked land, I'd have to get up and run. But I dawdled, terrified, certain that the moment I did the Thing would turn me to coal, too.

"Yeah, this is a good idea," I whispered, slapping myself across the face. "This is an awesome idea." I slapped myself again.

After what must have been minutes of quietly begging myself to do it, then not to do it, and still ignorant to whether I were in full view of the Pit and wondering what damage was being inflicted on my psyche minute by minute, I climbed to my feet. Hoping that smoke still hid me, and that this would even make a difference, I sprinted along the clifftops as my thighs begged me to stop – unless they wanted a much worse fate, I thought, they'd better start cooperating.

Running, I felt a hopeless terror that I was being messed with. That this mysterious death could see me and, when I was on the very edge of safety, would leap after and upon me.

# VI.

Blundering through the smouldering heather, under a sky shifting orange I left eighty-or-so people, charred and distorted into hideous shapes, one of a stream of bloody and burned survivors – for around twenty of us had escaped the Death Ray's clutches – stumbling in any direction away from the Pit. A couple, who had jumped from the cliffs and found the sea, were swimming to shore. A couple more, who had jumped from the cliffs and missed the sea, were not. Others, having been on the opposite side of the Pit to that which led to civilisation, escaped along clifftops and, when night fell, found themselves marooned between open ocean and the Thing or even clinging to sheer cliff faces.
From Beach Road and all those parts of St Ives which could see only the hillsides which guarded Clodgy Point from view, all anyone saw at first were flashes of bright light; many imagined an RAF bombing run was underway, or that the Thing had self-destructed. Then, with a wave of heat, fiery curtains burst over the hills and rose in great pillars of fire, sweeping section by section, in doing so betraying just how calculated and deliberate it was. That had the effect of making people quite aware of the situation.

Survivors trickled in from the coast path, many bringing grisly wounds and fantastic stories with them, and panic swept away the crowd's initial shock. Embers, like fireflies, drifted

on the sea wind over and around them. Any scintilla of doubt as to what had transpired was removed when, suddenly, through the confusion, a woman came galloping with her hands clasped over a blackened head, screaming until she was dragged to the beach and thrown into the water. She was only the first – a platoon of burned, barely human figures, melted wax faces and fingers, came trooping the path, like ghouls from mist. Children didn't cry but watched, surprised, as if their dreams had been given form. It was not quite like what the military-funded superhero films had promised them about alien invasions; where every shot misses every civilian. This was altogether more real.
"They're coming!" someone else, sprinting by with tattered clothes and bloodied face and missing teeth (unconnected), screamed incoherently, like in a film, and then everyone was turning and pushing at those behind, the Thing's mechanical shriek which must have started up again but which I had been deafened out of hearing becoming clear, the flames flashing bigger and brighter. Many bolted – others didn't. Instead, they ran and dived into the flames to help those left behind. It was one of these people into whose arms I collapsed.

News of the massacre travelled fast along the information superhighway. The iconic image that night was the bright orange glow from Clodgy Point, two sunsets on opposite horizons, St Ives bathing in the flames. Emergency authorities near enough to witness the carnage but not be overcome by it now declared a major incident and the hastily convened command centre ordered the entire population of West Cornwall be somehow evacuated. This idea they quickly gave up on; for now. The government, undergoing its own blind panic, beset on all sides by scientific and military pressure, endorsed the order, then withdrew the endorsement as the fear of overreaction grew. After all, the Thing was stuck there. What more harm could it do? Questions arose about who was making these decisions.

By the time Clodgy Point was obliterated, the crowds beyond its immediate periphery into the wider area, just out of sight and so out of the Death Ray's hateful reach, had already grown into what must have numbered over two thousand. Many had poured in from adjoining towns, gridlocking the A30, for a chance to see the Thing before it was carted away. Any effort by an underfunded rural police service to turn them back was bound to fail. With little means or numbers to keep so many out, being more specialised in pub fights and domestic abuse calls than vast crowd control operations, Devon and Cornwall Police were helpless. Many, therefore, poured through, and plenty did as I did.

"Fools, they cut their own throats!" a paramedic yelled to a news camera. Most, though, did as they were told – there was, even before the killing started, a regular chorus of boos greeting those who passed through the police lines onto Clodgy Point. Having been told not to go, and gone anyway, sympathy for the incinerated was not entirely universal. An editorial waxed lyrical on the lessons we should all learn about human curiosity.

Some, it was unkindly suggested, even deserved it – so too did the onlookers who'd shown up after the attack to gawk, not heeding warnings to stay back, sneaking past barricades on the roads and dodging over fields to get a glimpse of the Thing, but not ventured onto Clodgy. One can imagine these people, thinking it all a lark, suddenly coming face to face with survivors gathered about Beach Road and the adjoining areas, many irreparably scarred by burns or in varying states of hysteria, emergency vehicles screaming past, makeshift triage centres roping in retiree doctors and members of the public, corpses in lines along the pavement under bedsheets and rugs from adjoining houses. What lesson they were expected to learn from this wasn't made entirely clear. Police officers went door to door across the town, advising all who could to take flight, but many ignored them. Traumatised St Ives was infected by fright and horror – and this had frozen it rigid. Many just couldn't comprehend what had descended upon them as the smell of burning, of plant matter and cooked meat, wafted through the tight streets.

Before his untimely death DI Stent, anticipating some possibility of a collision, had insisted on help from whatever military resources could be brought to bear. St Ives was, as far as places go, quite remote from any armed units of significant firepower. They were all in Aldershot or Warminster or training Estonians to one day shoot down Russian fighter-bombers. It could take twenty-four hours at least to deploy to Cornwall, if they were deployed at all, which they probably wouldn't be, because what were they meant to do? And why was this country bumpkin cop demanding air cover? How ridiculous, Stent said with furious frustration at the time, that twenty-four hours was all the Royal Marines needed to jump into Pakistan or Somalia but they couldn't cut that down for Cornwall! The best that could be provided at this short-notice was a Merlin helicopter from RNAS Culdrose outside Helston. It proved fairly useless in preventing or even reacting to the massacre, being equipped for training crews in the search and rescue of surfers caught in rip tides, and so could only report with detached objectivity on the orgasm of fire. Their live report of the slaughter, a tape of which was distributed by the Ministry of Defence and broadcast by the BBC (audio only) that night, matches my own – the three puffs of green smoke, the deep humming note which they heard even beneath powerful rotors, and titanic flashes of flame blinding their thermal imaging. After the carnage, room was found in the defence budget to scramble two RAF Typhoons from Lincolnshire, and they orbited the town until they ran out of fuel and left again.

# VII.

I remember little of my escape except how much it sucked. Exhausted by what my online therapist insists I call "the violence of my emotion," I fell straight into someone's arms as they came the other way. It wasn't very feminist of me. Gently, frenzied shouting all around, hot air blowing over us, my limp form was lowered onto a bench with a memorial plaque for 'Paul Alex Tindall, Beloved Husband & County Bowler, 1947-2009' beside the fenced-off bowling green. Voices, close to my ear, asked after me but, staring into the ether, I gave no response, slowly laying across the bench, the heat and smells and pain still consuming me. People flourished all around and sirens screamed beyond the bushy hawthorns and explosively bloomed hydrangeas. Though I overlooked the green, still and pleasant and devoid of threat, I could still only see the flames – and all those people swallowed, like flies by spiders, inside it.

I must have lain on the bench for some time until I sat up, strangely perplexed, for a moment unsure of how I came to be there. Blinking myself from the stupor, people still running about around me, helping the injured to Beach Road, I looked down at myself. My jeans were dirty and singed, the deliberate fabric tears stretched out far beyond acceptability, and I picked healthy leaves caught in the sinews over my knee. Feeling an insect bite on my wrist, I looked and saw a white burn no larger than a thumbnail. Beyond that cork of pain I seemed untouched by the butchery. A tide of ironic laughter washed over me again until, realising how badly mauled some others were, I forced myself to quieten down.

Eyes stinging still, I sat up in wonder. My terror had fallen from me like a prom dress. Just moments before, there had only been two things occupying me – my sense of feebleness and the inevitable coming of death. Now, with both things apparently out of my immediate future, the presence of St John's Ambulance proving quite the confidence boost, my point of view abruptly altered. Now I was in my skin again. There was no clear transition from distress to calm – it was almost as if both existed inside me but had found a way to cooperate like uneasy bedfellows. I felt like myself – but how was I to be sure? Perhaps I had simply accepted my lot and drifted in that feeling, uncaring towards my eventual fate, whatever the Thing may choose it to be. I'd seen what nobody should see – the flames, the massacre, the immense *being* which had tried to crawl onto my Earth and which would have taken me if it could reach. Anguish at being entirely at the Thing's mercy coursed through me.

Yet grasping for these memories felt like trying to reconstruct a fading dream, as if my mind rejected the pictures it was being shown. I asked myself, even with crazed people all around me and wounded victims streaming by, some lacking sizeable chunks of their bodies, whether any of it really happened. How easily I could simply look west, where thick smoke and an intense glow emanated beyond the hillside, but I suppose though I asked I didn't want an answer. Not even with all the proof the world wanted to give me.

Unsteadily, against the advice of the paramedic trying to push a water bottle into my hands, I rose and walked down overcrowded Beach Road – I ignored, or didn't perceive, all efforts by authority figures to stop me. People, so badly hurt as to be barely worth the word, were hurried by on stretchers or carried by wrists and ankles. There weren't enough ambulances for them all – a GP was on his knees staring down at a man whose chest cavity was gaping open, like a shark's mouth, laying on the pavement.

"What do I do with this?" he asked someone. A, ashen-faced child, stood next to him, watched in silence. To my left, the sea pounded powerfully up the beach, and gulls circled. My blank and awestruck mind had nothing to offer anyone – not even myself. Though my body felt drained I managed to navigate the tiny gaps between the clustered emergency vehicles and climbed the hill past the sprawling old cemetery and towards home. Cars and fresh onlookers raced by in the other direction, some staring at me as I went by, none inquiring as to my state. Maybe they did ask and I didn't listen. I must have looked wasted by how I staggered. Maybe I was, in a weird way, for I wasn't injured – I knew my body felt pain but couldn't feel it myself. Me and myself, in that walk, felt like two separate forms, two shadows on the ground intermingling and dispersing with each step. It's a feeling which still occasionally overtakes me, even now, but was as strong as it ever could be on that long walk home as the chaos was left behind and the streets fell quiet in the still evening. I coughed almost constantly, my throat tortured by the hot fumes, and my legs ached but whatever piloted me instead of my brain insisted I keep going. A little boy ran by, in the beach's direction, and I thought to warn him not to, but I didn't. Still I see him sometimes, still I want to warn him, and still I don't.

Now the nightmare seemed to drift into the ether as, with each step, the town became quiet and almost normal again, besides the distant sirens and that haunting glow from over the rooftop edges. From the gate of a house's tiny front garden, a French Bulldog with a big stupid tongue yipped in a friendly manner at me, and I stopped to reach through the metal and stroke its scruffy head. He seemed grateful. An old red bus, empty, a long caterpillar of lighted windows, rumbled by in the rugby club's direction. Schoolkids chased each other in a plastic playpark across the street. Why was this town behaving as if all was well?

At the gravel entrance to a dimly populated caravan park, a group of people talked frantically, a sight which relieved me for it said I wasn't going crazy. I paused at the bus stop, besides a donation box full of canned goods and old books, and looked around, realising that, even with the sirens and the burning smell, St Ives seemed so placid. So untouched. After a mere few turns, the town had made itself feel normal. Everything was so real, so familiar, and what was behind me was so absurd. I thought again about the Thing, tried to remember its body and its eyes and those awful tentacles, and again it was like scrabbling at the sides of a vanishing dream.

"You been at Clodgy?" someone outside the caravan park shouted at me from across the street. It was a thin woman, wrapped in a fluffy pink dressing gown, bony arms tightly crossed over her chest. She and her companions, stood around the entrance sign for KERNOW HOLIDAY VILLAGES and smoking like the Clodgy heather, were watching me closely.

"You what?" I said blankly.

"You been at Clodgy?" she repeated, slower and tersely.

"No," I said, having no appetite for conversation, but I must have delivered my reply unconvincingly. I was never much of an actor; my E in GCSE Drama is demonstrative.

"Yeah you 'ave," a man, older and with rounded glasses, laughed. "You just came up from that way."

"Well, I didn't," I said angrily. "Alright?" He held up his hands in mock-surrender.

"So there aren't any men from Mars?" he teased and it was quite enough – I kept walking, turning onto Laurel Street, as they chortled together and returned to their conversation. I caught snippets of it – they were trying to pin the blame on a child called "Ugly Noah" for an outbreak of nits.

"You'll find out for yourself," I muttered beneath my unsteady breath as a pair of police cars screeched by. "Soon." It was a mere few more corners before I arrived home.

I startled Disco in the hallway, smacking his hindquarters with the door as it opened, and he grumbled in protest as I stumbled into the kitchen, Scuttling under my feet, trying to trip me with each step, mewling, I ignored him. Yanking the fridge door open and frustratingly trembling fingers negotiating open a San Miguel can, I went back to the lounge to crumple onto the loveseat, where I tried to catch my breath – but it kept slipping through my fingers. For a time I just poked at the burn on my hand, making it hurt, proving it was really there. I should have been dead. Why wasn't I? Did it let me go?

I was most of the way through the can before I could sufficiently collect myself and realise Disco was sat on the floral Ikea rug staring at me with big, green eyes, pawing at my ankle. I looked away. His food bowl, laying empty in the utility room atop the tumble dryer, would have to wait until I was done staring at the wall.
"At least they're slow," I said aloud, distant sirens the dusk chorus, trying to talk myself down from the ledge my fears had placed me on now. Digesting all which had happened and might now happen was a very uncomfortable experience. I then looked down at Disco and started directing my words to him. "That's something. Maybe they can kill you if you get close but they can't move – and if they do, they'll get shot in a fuckin' heartbeat. But…" I took another long sip, too long, and choked, having to splutter out my next words: "…Jesus Christ, they're so disgusting. Oh, God, I hate them so much." Disco jumped up and put his paw on mine, which I took to be a sign of comfort – or of wanting food. Unable to neglect him any longer, I rose, he followed, and after lifting him with a squeak onto the tumble dryer I emptied a packet of wet food into his purple bowl. Slimy when it slipped out, for a moment I stared until Disco's black furry head obscured it, reminded of the

Thing, if you can be reminded of what you're already thinking of.

"Poor Angus," I mumbled, not imagining a worse way to perish than ravaged by fire. I hoped it was quick but fire doesn't have a reputation for ending you mercifully. Disco ate *so* loudly. I stood for some time watching, feeling great envy at his lack of concern, not even noticing the food's pungent smell. I'd smelt worse.

Withdrawing to the bathroom, washing the dirt from my hands, trying to scrub it out from under my nails, splashing my face with cold water, I stared at myself in the mirror. My face was deadly white. "I wonder what his last name was."

"*They'll come here,*" said a voice and I went to the kitchen for another can. Disco fixed me with his big eyes and mewled obliviously.

"They can barely move," I told him, thinking all I needed for reassurance were the right set of words, pressing the cold aluminium for a time against my hand's dinky little burn, until I stripped and, naked and clutching the can, stood for a long time in the steaming hot shower drinking and prognosticating and feeling frozen no matter how high I turned the temperature. The bathroom, the fan long since broken, became impenetrably foggy but I refused to open a window in case a tentacle slithered in. More than once I left and, without a towel and dripping everywhere, fetched another can and returned with it to the shower. To hell with gas bills. "They can barely move."

I thought about the man in the Aston Villa shirt, whom I hoped survived, and his excited certainty that gravity made the creature incapable of crawling out of its capsule. I hoped he was right. Maybe on its home planet it could slither about at two hundred miles per hour. Were it not for our planetary core's dense metals, it would now be chasing people up and down the land, probably eating them, which would have been unpleasant, at least until someone painted a tunnel onto a wall. Maybe it was better, for the sake of avoiding farce, that it hadn't gotten out.

Wherever that ugly Thing had come from, however intelligent it was, it had clearly made a terrible mistake – this, I was glad to find, was also the scientific community's common opinion. St Ives' initial panicked evacuation order was even being criticised in some quarters for its blow to local business. Those who had died, ignoring all orders not to approach, were just Darwinism at work. One moderately famous biologist postulated online that the helpless Thing had acted out of spasmodic self-defence, being swarmed by so many strange beings, and this view gained traction. Given the choice between sympathising with a few dozen dead fellow humans or a giant slug, a surprising number of people chose the latter. Retweets came my way when I highlighted what a tragedy it was that first contact with an intelligent race had to start with such misunderstanding, even if it was disgusting and hateful and needed to be destroyed at once. Vengefulness, I was surprised to find, didn't really exist in me even after all I'd seen. Everyone, I think, overlooked the possibility that there might be more to the Blight than met the eye – that they hadn't gone through all this effort just to deliver what one tabloid called "a big ugly useless silly snail."

Plying myself with alcohol, the online whirlpool demanding I drop my needless fear, wry jokes and memes at the lonely Thing's expense taking over the newsfeed as bodies smouldered still on Clodgy Point, my terror fell away and I grew as courageous and secure in my comfy suburbia as a renter ever can – especially as, outside, I heard no panicked crowds and the night fell as quiet as normal, besides the chorus of distant sirens. But I didn't hear that – I had headphones on. I don't spend my evenings with ear against window, listening to the traffic, going "I think that one was a van."

"What a moron," I said of the Thing, finger trapped in a Budweiser bottle, to Disco – by now curled upon my lap while I watched *Friends,* a kind of comfort food while I tried to shake off my shaking. "It must be petrified – I bet they never expected to find living things on Earth. Definitely not living things that can fight back. All it'll take is one bomb..." I childishly mimicked the bombastic noise of an explosion, not quite realising I spoke more in hope than belief, "that's all it'll take to kill the bitch."

The day's intense emotional whiplash had, no doubt about it, left me grasping to stay sensible, and it was a funny thing, I suppose, to just walk home after all of that. I could have done with some significant psychiatric treatment, maybe. Despite its alcoholic blurriness, I remember that evening vividly, even now. My perfect cat's sweet black face peering at me from around the sofa, the notifications blowing up my tablet, beer cans warming in my hand, even a resilient itch in my armpit. All of it stays with me – but though I remember such tiny details, the carnage of the attack has only recently returned, and I can only guess at some of it. I suppose my mind doesn't want to reel it all back in.

At one point I found myself on Facetime, anxiety tempered with a fat joint, sat on the backdoor steps and ignoring the cold night air, telling my sister how rashly that crowd and I had behaved and denouncing the stupidity of both ourselves and the Blight for ruining what could have been a peaceful coming together of civilisations. But, as I told her almost as much as I told myself and not nearly as much as I told Disco, the Thing was marooned and helpless and ignorant and without a paddle. We, however, were not. It was more than enough to make you feel secure. I imagine that, a few centuries prior, a dodo must have glared onto a beach, at pitiful, hungry, lost-looking sailors, and said "oh, we'll peck them to death tomorrow, for sure."

# VIII.

Of all the strange and horrendous things which happened that Friday, probably the one that grates the most today is not the unnecessary pile of simmering corpses but how our social order decided to react to them. For sure, as the condolences and offers of assistance flooding in from foreign governments attest, all the world's emotions were affected by the newcomer – but, as I've said, a self-assured confidence reigned supreme nonetheless. Some were surprised that the most important moment in human history, the answering of whether we were alone in the universe, didn't make the expected sensation – it felt like an inconvenience, said one, not an epoch-defining moment. "The alien was just too pathetic to really respect." There was, after all, no vast fleet of starships slicing through the ionosphere, nor essentially humanoid beings preaching peace or surrender on hijacked airwaves. Capital cities weren't blowing up and presidents weren't revealing their faces to be masks. It was simply this one wretched, rather pitiful creature which, after tumbling onto a seaside resort best known for misidentified sharks and a Georgian nursery rhyme, had thrown a fiery tantrum and made the whole business of first contact kind of complicated.

Now this Thing lay there, tetchily silent and sticking into our Earth's skin like a poison dart, with nobody quite sure what to do about it. Certainly, it was an appalling danger if approached – but, our good luck not yet turning, it had landed in so sheltered a spot that there was nothing left for it to harm. Property damage, which is always a concern, amounted to one cottage, one helicopter, and one ice cream van. Everything, and everyone, which could burn had already burned.

Necessity and public image demanding it, the Typhoons returned, greater in number and orbiting the town at all hours through the night, kept aloft by a Voyager refuelling tanker from 101 Squadron, training their laser designators on the motionless crater. There emerged some early kerfuffel when it was alleged that the government hoped to withdraw the Typhoons. They were also needed to patrol the national (and, as they couldn't do it themselves, Irish) airspace for more falling stars. Instead, Number 10 hoped to rely on a company of The Rifles from Truro; they would ring the crater with weapons trained on the capsule just in case the creature "tried it on." Public outcry followed at putting "our boys" in unnecessary harms way as well as outrage in some quarters at such a militaristic response. Many words were shouted in the Cabinet Office as ministers jostled for precious limelight, leading first to the alteration of these plans and then to the denial that they ever existed.

6th Battalion, augmented by sister detachments from Barnstaple and Poole, were commanded instead to keep their distance from Clodgy and leave the Thing be, for now, at least until two reinforcing squadrons of the King's Royal Hussars arrived from Tidworth. Their Ajax armoured fighting vehicles, transported by flatbed truck, were an eerie sight on the Hayle Bypass and it was altogether unclear what use they would have in dealing with a mostly buried target on a clifftop inaccessible to any vehicle larger than an E-scooter. The plan, if it came to it, was very simple, the Ministry of Defence told a privately antsy Prime Minister – were the Thing to act up, a few guided air-to-ground missiles would be more than enough. Infantry patrolling the streets and tanks on the perimeter were for the locals' reassurance, the authorities' reinforcing, and the cameras' pleasure. Someone, naturally, asked how much this was all going to cost.

Amid all the confidence there was, of course, plenty of horror, too, at the massacre which had so sharpened attentions – eighty-four were eventually counted incinerated by the Visitor; a title which many objected to. Many hours later, those bodies still rested across cindered Clodgy Point, impossible to recover without risk. Civil servants tried to figure out how best to explain to livid relatives that many, being reduced to ash, were unrecoverable no matter what. They drifted on the wind, now. Somehow, journalists got hold of my number, surviving witnesses very much in vogue, and I had to spend part of the evening angrily denying interview requests. Demands for swift, brutal revenge were easy to find in St Ives, along with a deepening hatred of those who espoused cautious restraint. At a hastily assembled emergency Downing Street press conference, scientists offered earnest hope that it would all shape up as a simple misunderstanding which man and alien would get past. The value of peaceful contact was too great to pass up. They were preaching to a fidgety kingdom, characterised by a twitchiness, hungover with yesterday's emotional turmoil, and a snapping of nerves as to what would come next.

Beyond St Ives, where dead townspeople and visitors both foreign and out-of-towner were mourned and the local Diocese promised a splendidly respectful memorial service, the world was not so traumatised and passionately debated the consequences of the Visitor's slaughter. The threat even to Beach Road, just round Clodgy's corner, seemed non-existent, so why would Fleet Street or Wall Street be worried? What were its political implications, they asked? Would this impact the expected Cabinet reshuffle, next year's local elections, or the priorities of the coming G7 summit in Munich? How would the tourist trade fare? Would your investment property's value recover? Shares in defence and space firms and foreign travel companies went up – shares in domestic travel companies and restaurateurs went down. Ghouls, of which the population has a healthy supply, aired half-baked views on radio phone-ins and podcasts otherwise dedicated to superhero films and Premier League fixtures. Social media, the non-world we all nonetheless choose to inhabit, sizzled with pent-up opinion which tended to reflect what one's opinions already were. A public poll, posted by one regional broadcaster, was swiftly retracted and replaced with an apology for those "who may have been offended" at its tongue-in-cheek solutions to the crisis. Others pointed out all the disproportionate attention given to the dead on Clodgy Point – predominantly upper middle class, probably, as they could afford a holiday, while everyone else scraped by eating birdseeds and brake fluid. Compare that grief to what was afforded to the homeless veterans, the downtrodden refugees, the hungry children of Bolton! Nobody, as of yet, blamed immigrants for the mess – though, given the nature of the Internet to devolve into the politics of the bowel movement, some drew parallels between the government's apparent tolerance for the Blight and "the Muslamics swarming in."

As of yet, concern whether more stars might fall didn't hasten the global airspace lockdown some craved. Wait until at least one more comes, said officials, ignoring that once more came it would be too late. Only South West England's airspace was tightly restricted, with exceptions for any airport of economic importance, which turned out to be most of them. Even the Minehead airfield, where a very important balloon festival needed to get started, was business as usual. Cross-Atlantic flights still passed close enough to glimpse, if one squinted, the blackened landing site. It was just one lonely alien – there was no need to disrupt the planet over it.

Retailers, amid renewed fascination at the boundless void, reported an explosion in sales of amateur astronomy equipment – many, trying to stargaze from a bedroom window in Enfield or a Wigan park, mostly came to appreciate light pollution's pestilence, as well as how deeply boring it all got once the excitement of recognising Orion's Belt had worn away.

Concern was far more focused towards other, more nebulous, threats – particularly what foreign pathogens the Visitor must have brought with it. Xenologists, already delighted by the tentacles, were finally justifying their education. Alien microbes had surely spread to the populace given direct physical contact had been made – I refer to that whole icky business with the tentacle. Yet, it was uncomfortably noticed, that risk may have been quite a lot less than thought – for everyone who could have been infected, and the landscape which could have hosted any microbes, had afterwards been very thoroughly torched. There was no better solution to the problem – if there ever was a problem. I'd gotten pretty close myself and didn't seem to be coughing up my own heart just yet – perhaps our DNA was too foreign to interact, like jamming incorrect batteries into a television remote and expecting a current, or maybe we were just very lucky.

Non-militaristic solutions to the Thing were being proposed, too – some suggested a team of helicopters drop a flame resistant blanket or 'dome' over the capsule, permitting a safe approach, or that it be provoked to unleash the Death Ray on a drone. That way its weapon could, from a distance, be identified, targeted, and disabled. De-fanged, perhaps it could be examined properly, even reasoned with. Or maybe it just needed a healthy dose of knockout gas. Then, of course, there was Oumuamua, undoubtedly the source of the capsule – yet its direction of travel had been nowhere near this supposed mothership. It couldn't *possibly* be a big coincidence, couldn't it? A debate for another time. Ought it not, now we knew it was probably-maybe-perhaps hostile, be blasted from the sky? Whether to investigate or detonate, any such mission was years away but the White House promised they'd "work closely with our international partners to find a solution to the Oumuamua issue." Only later would we figure out that Oumuamua was entirely unmanned and nothing more than a guide, a cartographer, lighting the Thing's way. They must have sent millions to every planet in the sky – and this lucky one found something blue and green and swimming with life.

Torrents of scientific authorities poured into St Ives that night, called in from across the world to figure out a solution, settling into the fancy Belyars Castle estate-turned-hotel where years earlier I sat on the grounds and cried my way through prom. It was clear that some intelligent response was being formulated. Press packs swarmed every car rolling up the castle's stone driveway, experts from government and military and academia shook hands and trooped inside, and we were told to "be calm and trust the process." After all, they were already forming working groups.

While the world crackled with nervous energy, the place actually afflicted was inert. Blind shock was omnipresent in St Ives – any other mood, I suppose, would have been bizarre. And so, even with the Thing buried so close, so close that all the way to the Cripplesease dairy farms the town slept in the smell of burning flesh, people carried on. They had no direction to walk but the ones already laid down were the Blight never here. So, like good little citizens, they mostly kept going to work – I found the local Spar open as usual the following day, though rather more sparse of shelf, and an email warning Harbour Guest House staff not to skip work went viral. If they couldn't bear staying tightly locked in their homes as was advised but not ordered, people murmured down to the harbour to join the gathering throngs. Soldiers, usually unarmed, were appearing on the streets and knocking on doors for awkward wellness checks. Appeals for those still missing crowded social media or pinned to telegraph poles. Makeshift field hospitals which had sprung up just beyond Clodgy Point, where the wounded were treated in emptied restaurants and guesthouses, were emptying of patients – but ready to receive new ones. Air Ambulances and Army helicopters had gone back and forth from beaches and school playing fields to lift the grievously injured to the Royal Cornwall Hospital or the rapidly overcrowding Plymouth burns unit or an approaching Royal Navy hospital ship. Angus had refused to go to Plymouth. He really shouldn't have. All the while, as ever, the waves rolled up and down the beaches.

Battered into shock, having lost so many and unable to process the absurd circumstances in which it happened, my little town drifted into a kind of denialistic slumber. Even soldiers arriving in defence of the townspeople often met an angry reception. The desire for revenge wasn't universal – it was felt by some that the situation, which had already sucked away so many lives, was being needlessly inflamed.

"Just leave it alone!" one mourning mother wailed at a visiting minister, dry blood like irradiated skin on her brow, and she could find plenty who agreed. Elsewhere the pubs – the Wetherspoons and the Five Weasels, locally famous for its HIV outbreak sourced to an unchaste bouncer, being the most frequented – were busy even with some seats empty of their regulars. Juvenile booing greeted those officials who entered to meekly suggest everyone return home – some rejected that this was happening to them at all. All the while, with trains and roads shutting down, Army barricades at every junction, the lockdown tightened. Nobody was getting in. Bus services stopped at Hayle. Residents with a bit more sense packed bags and, without ceremony, took to the dual-carriageway and fled for relatives or Premier Inns upcountry – as anyone who lived anywhere else would be – but, stunningly, they were a minority. Those not shattered by grief's black fist, like me, were of the opinion that it couldn't get any worse, so why flee? A terrible thing had happened – but what was there left to fear when the Thing, hidden round that corner at the edge of the world, was now so harmless? Out of sight, out of mind.

Curious crowds, therefore, lingered restlessly all throughout the traumatised town, thousands more pouring in from the rest of the country and impatiently gathering at every roadblock. Police grew equally restless with their troublesome curiosity. By the morning they were newly equipped with truncheons and polycarbonate shields, many sets provided by neighbouring forces with more experience of urban trouble, some still with labels identifying them as Metropolitan Police property. A police sergeant went viral briefing his officers.
"We *will* hold the line!" he roared. "It is the last line to hold!"
Gradually they pushed onlookers further and further away from any place in which St Ives – a town now known to authorities as the Red Zone – might even be visible. And yet it was the Red Zone which proved to be the only place they proved unwilling to shove people around. I suppose they felt we'd been through enough.

Adventurous souls, it was found, had deduced alternate ways to Clodgy Point by tramping the western coast path – until this too was shut down with guards and barbed wire, several had made the trek, and some never returned. So it was that the only spot of St Ives which was silent and desolate was that part which provoked frenzy everywhere else. Nothing more was heard from the Pit and, as remote controlled drones performed their own close-up investigations, no activity was seen either. That was until late on the first night, when the capsule began emitting puffs of green-white smoke which whirled into the starlit sky. This new behaviour aroused enormous trepidation; enough so that medical-grade respirators were distributed and a stand-by order given for pummelling Clodgy Point with explosive ordnance. Yet there appeared no change in the populace's health – the gases' composition, now thought to be nothing but exhaust fumes which hinted at our visitor's wastefulness and inefficiency, was written off as entirely benign.

About eleven on the second day, the first soldiers of The Rifles crawled through springy sward grass onto Clodgy Point to form an overwatch. Dressed in flame retardant overalls, they lay along the overlooking hillside at the boundary where the grass turned black and burned. Strictly instructed not to make themselves any more visible than utterly necessary, they were stripped of weaponry to remove all risk of a provocation, tasked with setting up a ring of cameras providing constant surveillance the Thing before scurrying away again. Their fellows from a separate company, here permitted service rifles, formed a nervous cordon on Beach Road. Several ranking officers were taken for a closer inspection of the Pit and one, Major Eden, was reported as missing for a time – he eventually turned up at the Bombay Spice takeaway, regarding the whole affair as a supreme overreaction, while a colonel flanked by scientists answered local questions at a hastily assembled Guildhall meeting. Farmers' market stalls were still being put away while he spoke and took the occasional heckle.

The local people came away satisfied that the military appreciated the situation's gravity – the military, meanwhile, were not satisfied as to the government's appreciation. Much of their needed equipment was either not to be found or "in transit," and it swiftly became clear that those soldiers sent – while of the utmost professionalism (apart from the private who got caught in a hotel room with three college-age waitresses) and eventually of great effect in calming a frightened town – were unprepared for anything more than a solitary, stationary target with no ability to counter them. Thankfully, that's what they faced – nonetheless it was rapidly clear, as the King's Royal Hussars unloaded their heavy equipment in fields and the emptied comprehensive school car park only to find themselves missing key spare parts and almost every road too thin to even permit such vehicles' entry into St Ives, that Her Majesty's Armed Forces were in no sense built to repel a hostile incursion. Inquests loomed.

At least, everyone kept saying, over and over again, there was only one. Then, late on Saturday night, a star was seen coming down from heaven. It had a greenish colour, and caused a silent brightness like summer lightning as it crashed into the sea to the north-east, just past Godrevy Lighthouse, on St Ives Bay's opposite end. This was the second capsule.

# IX.

I had, on Friday night, eventually, put down the cans and crumbled to sleep – in a fitful, uncomfortable way, sprawled across the sofa, with Disco curled up on my chest and his tail in my mouth. Murderously hungover all of the following day and drinking again the following afternoon into the evening while watching Graham Norton highlights and Fleabag and avoiding the news, this was also how I slept on Saturday night – weekends are there to be wasted. Alcohol having kept my sleep light, I woke early on Sunday morning. It was not yet quite eight which is very early for a girl like me. With a curdling headache I made bacon sandwiches and carried them into the garden and its irritating birdsong. The Indian summer showed no sign of pitching up, the Sun thriving over St Ives and the air newly crisp and fresh, lilac butterflies chasing each other around the palm tree. The stink of burning, a day and a half later, had finally faded. There, in the pale overgrown grass, beside the moulding shed I never used because the landlord would go mental if I did, I stood listening. Suspense hung over Sunday like drapes. But, though aircraft rumbled overhead, dark shapes in the sky, and sirens cawed unseen, I heard nothing which I would associate with the Thing on Clodgy Point.

"Sorry, Angus," I sighed, feeling awful guilt; I wasn't certain my memory of his face was accurate. I wandered back inside to feed Disco some ham. Disco liked ham.

The postman came early, which I respected given the tricky circumstances, and upon hearing the final notice bills fall from my letterbox and Disco pounce on them, I hurried around the side gate, tugged it open, and shouted after him.

"Oi!" I called, surprising him. He'd shaved poorly – long hairs poked out in irregular intervals from his stubble, like little proboscises – and his face was splotched with tart rashes. "Any news?"

"About what?" I stared at him.

"Really?"

"Oh, the alien?"

"What else could I possibly be…" I sighed, my headache making me impatient. "Yes, *that*."

"Well, there's another one now," he said uncaringly, slinging his red bag over his shoulder, sending a chill tap-dancing along my spine. "Landed off Godrevy."

"Shit," I said, mouth rapidly drying, which may have been the hangover.

"It's no big deal," he said. A dog walker passed by behind him, her gold-coated Shiba Inu trying to eat every flower it found, and glanced at us. "They reckon there'll be plenty coming eventually but it's amateur-hour with the lot of them. Fat lot of harm it can do in the sea, anyway, right?"

"Maybe," I said, shivering nonetheless at the thought that now two lived in my little sliver of the world. Getting out might be a good idea.

"Anyway," he said, "Army's got the first one surrounded and it's just sat there, so that's good."

"I guess it must be," I answered – a familiar, reassuring bus rumbled by, empty of people, making my headache worse.

"They're promising not to kill it," he added sourly, "if they can help it."

"Can they help it?" He shrugged.

"They're the Army – they're not here to fuck it. Is that your cat?" I looked down – Disco was stood between my feet, watching him warily.

"Yeah."

"I'd love to pull on his whiskers. See how angry he gets." And then he left for the next house, where my neighbour was already loudly trimming his hedges – the best time to do that was, of course, eight in the morning on a Sunday – and I momentarily wished he had been among the eighty-four before going back inside to ignore the bills and make marmite toast. The bacon, its rashers paper-thin, hadn't been enough.

*Good Morning Britain* was on, and I watched for a time, perched on the sofa's armrest while Disco tried to climb up to investigate my toast. A Scottish astrophysicist with an impressive moustache was of the opinion that, while the Godrevy landing proved more Blight stars would surely fall to Earth, if they were at all like the first then it would prove a rather abortive invasion. They were absurdly vulnerable to our own military might, after all, and many nations – including our own – were belatedly waking up to the threat and assembling countermeasures.

"They may not even make it to the ground in the first place, now," he said. Bodmin Moor, a cutaway demonstrated, was hosting Sky Sabre missile batteries with a range suitable for clearing the skies all the way to Monmouth while the Americans were dribbling with glee at the prospect of a morally uncomplicated fight against helpless aliens – their military had recorded the highest one-day recruitment drive since the Twin Towers went crumbling down. Even Russia wanted a piece of the action – they were asking if they could send military attaches to St Ives, just to watch the expected show, while we just smiled and nodded and didn't really answer.

But just how many did the Visitors plan to send? What if thousands ended up laying claim to Cornwall, landing in every field and front garden? How many would it take before their mere presence overwhelmed us? Talk abounded that the government sought to ban anyone entering Cornwall altogether unless on "official business." Even second home owners might not be exempt – at this, the town found its much desired silver lining, while the owners cried foul.

"It's a rotten shame they're behaving like this," the physicist was saying thoughtfully. "They may have technical know-how, flinging themselves across space and landing with such accuracy, which is genuinely astounding, but you can't shake the feeling that simple common sense is lacking. There's a lot we could be learning from each other."

"But probably them more than us!" chortled the host, gaily.

"Possibly – but we have to stay vigilant. We've still got no idea what they're capable of and shouldn't act like we know. The only thing more dangerous than ignorance is arrogance." The host, perhaps egged on by a producer in his ear to remain somewhat uplifting, moved the story onto viewer texts concerned about falling debris when the Blight capsules were inevitably blown from the sky. Would their home insurance cover that?

After breakfast, which I mostly chucked having forgotten I hate marmite, masochistic temptation took me and against every ounce of common sense I walked down the main road towards the harbour where the real action was. I hadn't gone on the Saturday, being medically incapable of lifting my head above my pillow, but was passingly aware that after Friday afternoon's extraordinary trauma I should really have stayed at home. Leaving St Ives, let alone Cornwall, didn't occur to me for a second.

The old harbour had swelled with serious-looking military and governmental officials along with what must have been most of the world's press. Army and police vehicles lined the streets. I recognised a famous BBC correspondent, hair tied back, talking to a tripod-mounted camera and made sure to stick my tongue out as I walked by behind her. The route into the harbour was blocked by armed barricades so, instead, I went uphill, past the catholic church and to the bus depot which overlooked the harbour, surprised not to be stopped at any point.

Once there, across the bay I could, just about, see a grey Merlin helicopter hovering low above the second capsule's impact point off Godrevy. It was lowering a bulbous dipping sonar beneath petulant waves. Trucks, all darkest green, were coming and unloading and going from the depot with no buses to be seen. Outside the neighbouring hairdressers, shuttered with photos of beautiful people who had *never* gotten a haircut here in the windows, I came across a group of young soldiers – Royal Engineers in olive berets, baggy fatigues camouflaged like moorland, off-duty and perched on a wall drinking iced coffees. They warned me, in a tone as if reciting a script, not to bother trying to reach Porthmeor or any adjoining streets. I sensed they had been telling it to a lot of people. Looking skywards, I saw one of the Typhoons, a silver sentinel streaking between elephant clouds. They launched and landed from Newquay, an airport recently closed and hurriedly reopened to accommodate them, or a dozen other airports in the South West struggling to accommodate both military traffic and overbooked package holidays to Tenerife and the Algarve.

The engineers seeming down to earth and relatively chill, I talked with them as the lorries kept rumbling by, asking what they knew – they were, at first, aware of their orders and so dismissive of civilian fraternisation. That was until I told them I'd seen the Thing for myself. Realising I came bearing a first-hand account, they plied me with questions, and this opened up a discussion. Not one out of their teenage years, I found them to be surprisingly thoughtful, as they debated the possibility of a fight.

"It'll go one of two ways," said one, acne bedevilling his cheeks but handsome for his sparky attitude. "Either we blow them away in a heartbeat – or they blow us away. Either way, *we-*" He pointed at himself and each engineer in turn with a smirk, "-are useless."

"What do you mean useless?" I asked, looking from one to the next. "That's not what you want to hear your own Army call itself."

"He means there's no need for infantry," another, ginger-haired and sniffing away a cold, answered. "It's, like, the *most* basic military tactics in the world. You've got one big, stationary, *metal* target and you've got the RAF circling it like fuckin' birds of prey – you're *never* gonna throw foot soldiers at that when you can drop a Brimstone or two and be done with it."

"Too bloody right," agreed the first. "It's not the Somme, you know? Fixing bayonets and rushing a fortified position – we don't do that anymore. It's so unfair – must have been travelling through space for millions of years and had to arrive *now*. Could have been in twenty more years; then this whole thing'd be done with drones and we'd be at barracks playing FIFA like normal."

"Or two hundred years *earlier*, and then we'd all be buggered, maybe," I offered.

"We're here for PR, innit?" said the third, abruptly – tall, loud, roughly Hackney-accented. "Looking busy. Being all burly and impressive. So if that thing turns out it can take us, and we're all lying dead, that's a ministerial resignation waiting to happen."

"And isn't that the *real* tragedy?" laughed the ginger soldier, and the rest laughed too.

"You get proper close to the thing?" asked the Londoner. I told them what I could of its physicality, of its black eyes, and how I'd grappled to rescue that officer from the tentacles.

"Shit a brick!" exclaimed the ginger. "That's heroic! Where's your medal?"

"It's nothing," I said. "Lots of us were doing it – I haven't thought about it. I haven't thought about any of it, really, I just went home and got pissed."

"Yeah, that's how I deal with my PTSD, too," laughed one of them.

"You wait a week or two and they'll be naming you for a George Cross, after that display," the ginger laughed to me, nudging my shoulder. "Fuck me. Wrestling with an outer space octopus."

"So… tentacles, ey?" asked Grey – belatedly, I'd realised that each had a name tag on their uniform's breast. Hackney was Grey, Ginger was Scott, Acne was Howell. "That's original. I mean, we've all seen the footage, and that thing's nasty, but I didn't know there were tentacles to worry about. Gets worse and worse with each passing second."

"Won't be getting too close to that shit," shivered Howell. "Don't want any alien fingers up my ying-yang."

"I strongly doubt that's the shape the invasion will take," I replied dryly, which made them laugh – I enjoyed that.

"Japanese would be jealous," sniggered Scott, and we laughed again.

"Christ," exclaimed Howell, "I'm sick of waiting. Can't we just get it over with so we can go home and let all these lovely people get back to their boring lives and mourn their dead and that? We're just extending the misery right now – *and* we're gonna miss the Merseyside derby. I should be four pints deep at the King's Head right now and heading for six before my Toffees even start warming up. Scouse solidarity."

"You're from Guildford," said Grey. "And you can't just go murdering an alien visitor."

"Killing monsters ain't murder," retorted Scott.

"Probably just scared shitless and lashed out, I read."

"Yeah, where?"

"The news."

"Twitter?"

"Yeah."

"Of course."

"Well, I'm still right – and no matter how peaceful it turns out to be, it's gonna be a job getting folk to forgive it. You know; for everything it's done. People don't ignore eighty-whatever dead – unless they drowned in the Channel, obviously." Scott spoke up.

"Just bomb it and get it over with. I mean, look at that shit!" He pointed across the bay, where the Merlin hovered still, and where the second capsule lurked just beneath the ocean's lapping surface. "How many more you reckon'll come? Fuck knows what they'll do. Everyone's chatting shit 'bout how stupid they are, how they came here without a plan, don't know what they're doing – what if they do? And we're just waiting to find out. Useless." On they bickered with great energy.

After a while, being something of a bystander and feeling insecure in front of young lads confident in their life choices, I left to push deeper into the tight and cobbled harbour where I could get my fill of gawping.

But I won't weary the reader with a description of that infinitely long morning and the afternoon which managed to feel longer than that. I failed to get any glimpse of Clodgy Point or anything near, for all the harbour and everything near Clodgy was as Red Zone as could be, and soldiers or police curtly sent me back at each attempt down a different route. Every street and alley was blocked off – Operation Horsell, as it was termed, saw hotels, restaurants, shops, and houses within the Red Zone emptied, residents moved to commandeered holiday parks, and so the promised memorial service at St Ia's Church would have to wait. I was told another was happening at Knill's Monument, a granite obelisk on nearby Cock Hill, with the Lord Mayor presiding. I've never been going around mourners so I stayed away.

Even the bare, tiny St Nicholas Chapel atop the Island, which peered just around Clodgy and glimpsed the blurry black shape of the Thing, was in the military's hands, now. Offering excellent views of Clodgy to the west and Godrevy to the north-east, where the presumed drowned second cylinder rested, a command post had been established and the Union Flag waved defiantly over the Coast Watch station/second-hand bookshop.

The engineers turned out to be the only uniforms cool enough to divulge anything resembling opinions or knowledge – everyone else, from private to officer, didn't answer any of my inquiries. One yelled at me to "get the fuck back!" which couldn't have been in the plan for winning hearts and minds. Yet, watching scientists in official Range Rovers pass through the roadblocks towards Clodgy, relatives of the dead shouting demands for their recovery and bombing runs across the barricades, I found myself feeling increasingly secure in the military's presence. Perhaps it wasn't so much confidence in the protector as contempt for the aggressor – our invaders had two ships, and, as nobody could stop pointing out, one had crashed into the sea while the other was stranded on a cliff. Scott might have had his opinions but they were hard to take seriously. What was there left to fear?

I got home about two, exhausted already for, as I have said, I was still hungover and the day was hot. I was sweating buckets into my Ben Sherman shirt. Hoping to restore some sense of myself, I took a cold shower, Disco pawing at the door the entire time, and by half four I was locked on social media – the day was already a write-off and had been from the start as far as work was concerned. Until the situation was resolved, my shop – slap bang in the middle of Red Zone – was closed for the unforeseeable future. Even if commuting staff were permitted past the roadblocks, there wouldn't have been much point in opening. Soldiers were unlikely to buy surfing equipment at this delicate time. I got what I hoped – but knew was unlikely to be – a more detailed and accurate picture of the crisis from Twitter.

The picture was an unmoving one. Still the Blight refused to show an inch of themselves – their only activity was the almost continuous streamer of near-neon green smoke emanating from their capsule. This provided much anxiety and speculation – even as the Scientific Advisory Group for Emergencies, sequestered at Belyars Castle, insisted that the longer it went on the less dangerous it seemed to be. Maybe they'd given up – maybe they were already dead. And if not, it was noted, if air could come out of that shell then air – such as the enormously destructive air pressure changes wrought by a bunker-busting bomb – could go in. For the first time, also, I learned from Facebook that Clay Barry, with whom I had tolerated a brief fling in Sixth Form (he cried during a handjob), was among those lying as barely human forms on Clodgy Point. I hadn't seen him.

"We believe the second object missed its target and the occupant drowned in the sea," Sir Richard Pierson, Chief Scientific Advisor, was saying with confidence, flanked by Major Eden, doused in the light of snapping cameras. "Army divers have been scouring it all day and they've found nothing – no movement, no activity at all, certainly not any attempt to shoot at them. As for the Clodgy object, we've been making fresh attempts to make contact throughout the day. We've had no success." This had first been attempted with a set of musical notes, played from a loudspeaker in a pattern emulating the prime numbers, before a second attempt in which a drone projected pictograms onto the ground in front of the Pit. The Blight took as much notice of such olive branches as we would a sheep's bleating. Well, as *some* would a sheep's bleating – I'd have given it a little "baa" back.

Seeing all the firepower being brought to bear, with more always available from a world eager for a spot of guilt-free carnage, I began sensing a surprising twang of sympathy for those two little metal pods, a far cry from my bloodthirsty initial reaction. It hardly felt a fair fight. Swift and embarrassing rout loomed and I started to find myself sucked in by the growing number of voices preaching restraint; even pity. Maybe there was a strange humility to the Thing, I told myself, in its sluggish movements, its helpless groaning, its whole misguided venture. Worry took me that it would be exterminated because that was the most convenient thing to do – and so much which could be learned if we exercised patience would be stomped into the ground by the murder machine.

About six o'clock that warm evening, as I sat under the tree which sat under an amber sky in which swam fighter jets, surrounded by overgrown grass and eating cardboard pizza and vigorously stroking Disco to calm my bubbling nerves, I was trying to focus on a podcast. Their intense discussion about which American president they'd sleep with was keeping me well-distracted from the dream around me. Then, over their voices, I heard a sole, distant detonation from Clodgy's direction. It slowly rolled and rumbled thunderously over the rooftops, scattering terrified seabirds as it swept over us, before fading into the distance. I pulled out a headphone.
"Well," I said to Disco, black fur stood to attention, my anxiety dissipating like dust at the realisation that it was all over, "that's that then." But then, on the explosion's heels, came the yonder crackle of gunfire. I stood, slowly, Disco falling from my lap and mewling in outrage, and listened. The sounds reminded me of crinkling sweets packets as they carried over from the cliffs. It almost sounded peaceful, reassuring – like a distant fireworks display – yet I knew that something was wrong.

Then, all at once, there came a violent, volcanic crash which shook the ground. Disco bounded inside. I heard windows shatter and looked wildly about, expecting to see billowing smoke, but instead, just over the top of my shed roof, I saw the puffy beech trees on the hill towards Belyars Castle burst into smoky red flames. Then, a splat behind me; I slowly turned. A seagull – burnt crisp black and steaming – had fallen, dead and charcoaled, into the grass. More fell, pitter-pattering, one bouncing off the roof and rolling down into the garden, taking a slate tile as it went, another a few inches from concussing me. I became aware of the sudden absence of screeching which a few moments prior filled the sky.

Running inside, I pounded upstairs to my bedroom window and reached it in time to see the St Ia Church tower slide down into ruin. Then came new, repeated, thuds. Fistfuls of dirt and rock were battering like hailstones across the whole span of the town – the bathroom skylight smashed, car alarms cried outside, a chimney cap burst. Expensive terraces towards Carbis Bay, in a line affording premier harbour views on the westward hillside's furthest reach, suddenly erupted in orange flames. I could feel the heat from here, the fires filling my eyes and freshening memories, stonework crumbling like a collapsed meringue. I stared until a rock took down the drainpipe above my window.

Colossal plumes of muddy smoke, I then realised, were rising from Clodgy Point's direction. Certain that we would never deploy such powerful ordnance in the first instance, I was at once sure the Thing had either self-destructed or deployed some weapon obliterating much of the neighbouring geology. Stunned, it became clear to me that with this geographical reshaping half the town must now be within the Death Ray's sight. The hill which had hidden it was gone – now the deadly beam could scythe through the air, cutting down any unfortunate birds, and strike those parts of the town at the highest altitudes, such as the church tower or the terraced hillside with the burning beech trees.

At that realisation, horrified that I might now be within the Death Ray's sight, I ran back downstairs, three steps at a time, balls of petrified dirt still pelting the house, cursing myself for staying this long. Through the window halfway down the stairs, I saw someone run by, shielding his bloodied head with his arms. The neighbour's estate car in the opposite driveway was missing a windscreen.

"Disco! Disco!" I yelled through the house – I found him in the lounge cowering beneath the dining table, and as I heard another window upstairs shatter I realised he might be safer there. Instead, I crawled beneath the table to join him, we both listening to the storm, begging it to stop until, after what felt like minutes but could have been seconds, it eased.

Without ceremony, I scuttled from under the table, grabbed Disco despite his insistence on staying, and scooped him into my arms before running out into the road. Fine, dirty dust lay low over the town now, blown in from the site of the destruction, and I tried to take small breaths so I wouldn't set myself on a date with lung cancer in fifteen years. Others were coming out of their own houses, astonished, looking about wildly, drumbeat of explosions and gunfire audible from Clodgy Point.

"What's happening?!" someone yelled at me from halfway down the street.

"I've got some notion!" I yelled back, unhelpfully. Disco sank his raptor claws deeper into my shoulder. One of the Typhoons screamed overhead, a blurry silver triangle, lower than I had ever seen a plane fly, and vanished over the rooftops towards the plume which used to be Clodgy. Disco meowed at it as it went.

"Heads up!" I didn't know where the shout came from but I obeyed – looking heavenward I saw a rock, as big as a coach, falling from the sky, curving at an angle which told me it had been blasted from the Clodgy bedrock. Motionless, I just watched it fall, smashing through the roof of a house two streets over. Its windows blew out, walls caved in, and a great mist of dust quickly obscured the ruins. Cloud of dirt growing thicker in the air, itching my eyes, I opened my Corsa's back door, the car battered by the falling debris, and threw Disco onto a seat.

"You'll be safe here," I told his furious face, as if he were a person, which he kind of was, before slamming the door.

In search of answers, I ran down the street onto the main road, kicking aside piles of dirt with heather and blackthorn roots still dangling out. A bevy of police cars screamed by, people were running to and fro with little idea of where they were going, and to the north-west, the smoke rose thicker and thicker from Clodgy, so huge I thought I saw lightning dance about inside. The din of battle wasn't stopping.

"We're kicking the shit out of 'em!" a man shouted, gleefully.

Then something came flying from the smoke, a tiny object growing bigger and bigger, turning from black to white as it approached. At last I realised it was a Land Rover Discovery, cartwheeling through the air, and I ducked as it tumbled overhead, took out a string of power lines, snapping a wooden telegraph pole as it did so, and smashed straight through the Costcutters roof. I stared at the sight, the roof caving in, the glass bursting outwards, the burglar alarm screaming, the automatic doors opening and closing and opening and closing, a woman with a bloodied face staggering out...

Two soldiers were running from house to house, pounding on doors, demanding people evacuate regardless of their legal right to do so. I saw residents stumble from their houses into cars with bags and pets underarm – many had clearly packed and been ready to go for a while. A Typhoon – perhaps the same one, perhaps another – roared overhead, higher than last time, little more than a triangle against the orange sky, and from a soldier's radio I heard panicked voices through static as she ran by.

"*Target active! Target active!*" one cried.

"*Drop everything you've got on the green smoke! Now!*" screamed another. Then...

*"Evacuation order alpha, I repeat, evacuation order alpha! Everyone fall back! Fall back!"* The sun, shining through the smoke wrapping around the town, seemed blood red, and threw that same red light upon everything.

Panic gripping the streets, people pouring from houses and cars fighting for space with the fumes of battle drifting our way, I hurried back to the house, nearly getting hit by a speeding van for my trouble. Wiping dirt from the windscreen before climbing in, Disco mewled a confused mewl at me as I started the engine. With some protest and me yelling "come on, you piece of shit!" in reply, it spluttered to life – the radio turned on, still tuned to Radio 1 which, having not yet caught up with things down here, was playing some Ed Sheeran thing. Taking care not to collide with any of the growing crowd storming from Clodgy's direction, I pulled from the drive and tried to figure out a plan before I was pushed down a route which might be impossible to return from. I elected to make my way down the B3311 towards Penzance where the Thing could certainly not reach us. I would put together a plan with more than one step once I arrived – in all likelihood, I realised, I would end up at my dad's flat in Carlisle. I gritted my teeth – I'd rather take my chances with the alien.

Passing the Iron Horse pub on Blackwood Road, I saw a soldier urgently directing people out. Some stubborn patrons still gripped pints as they filed through the double-doors; I slowed and, pulling onto the curb, rolled down my window so hard I nearly broke my arm. The noise of war flooded in from Clodgy way.
"Fuck's going on?!" I roared at to the soldier over the pitter-patter of distant explosions. He turned, stared, said something about how we were all fucked, and ran on to the next building. Before I could set off again, I saw in my rear-view mirror something else falling from the sky – craning to look over my shoulder, I witnessed a Chinook helicopter, its fuselage

vomiting flames, coming down hard and vainly trying to settle. It vanished behind rooftops and satellite dishes and in its place rose a ball of tar-black smoke. Gritting my teeth I pulled away, part of the slow-moving stampede of traffic, until the two cars in front of me collided and I broke all Highway Code conventions and mounted the pavement to overtake them. Almost everyone ahead was pulling onto leftward roads, towards Carbis Bay, hoping to cut across onto the St Ives Road into Hayle and then, via the bypass, the A30. This left me suddenly alone as I crossed a military barricade, the soldiers hurriedly dismantling it, fetching cones and moving jeeps, to let through escaping traffic. In another moment, we were clear of the smoke and noise and joining the unnervingly empty country road past Rosewall Hill – where Angus had first stumbled into my life – towards Penzance.

In front was a quiet evening landscape, sky towards the horizon shifting from morning amber to blue, a patchwork of empty fields either side of the road, and the Hellesveor Inn with its children's play area and Happy Hour sign and rapidly packing up ITV news crew. Before the next turn I looked to the mirror to glimpse the town I was leaving, maybe forever, but all I saw was a barn and some bushes and a Weight Watchers advert. Beyond, chaos reigned; past the hills, thick streamers of black smoke were driving up into the still air, throwing dark shadows onto the browning fields southward. The smoke was already overcoming the harbour, encircling the Island in a whirlpool, and crawling around the hills among which St Ives nestled. Faint now, but very distinct through the warm, quiet air, I heard another crack of defiant gunfire. A helicopter of some military model sliced through the sky, driving for St Ives. By now the radio had changed, too.
"*This is the BBC from London*," said a monotonous female voice, as I wondered what had become of their correspondent I had seen on my earlier visit into town. "*Please remain tuned for news updates.*" Jessie Ware's new single followed.

# X.

Penzance is almost twelve miles from my house; it can feel much further, depending on whether an alien invasion is happening or how badly the McDonald's queue at Long Rock blocks traffic. If you've been stupid enough to take the long route – as I had, into a world of fallow fields and cattle grids – then it really is much further.
Manure thick in the air and a brilliantly blue sea stretching to an inviting horizon, I sped through a green and pleasant land wholly unprepared for its new situation – council contractors were still cutting back a wildflower verge as I passed. A strange serenity existed out here, just a short bound from chaos, and it unsettled me. Moments earlier I had been in the depths of what military analysts might call a rapidly deteriorating situation. Now, with every glance to my rear-view mirror, even the sky above St Ives had vanished from view, replaced by knolls and hills and paddocks. Tranquillity restored itself. Yet, when I pulled into a muddy track leading to a shuttered farm gate so I could vomit out my stress while some ponies regarded me from across a fence, I still heard distant booms and felt the ground quaking.

Disco was curiously silent throughout the drive, unusual given his penchant for near-hysterical screaming by way of greeting, though he still found time to bat unhelpfully at the handbrake. Maybe, I thought, he sensed evil's presence in some weird spiritualistic kind of way. Cats have powers like that. Then, as we passed a field with Warrior fighting vehicles still trapped on their flatbeds, soldiers breathlessly rushing to unload them, it occurred to me with a flash that in my panic I'd left *everything* behind in that hell. Everything, of course, included Disco's medicine. He had, since the day I found him squeaking behind Froggie's Fish and Chips, been burdened by an intemperate heart. After his last clot-related episode he had regular tablets (which he was *not* a fan of) to prevent the devastation of arterial thromboembolism – which you knew was dangerous just by how long it was. There may not be units of time measurement yet invented which quantify how little it took for me to resolve that I'd return to St Ives and fetch those tablets; it came before the thought that my purse and phone might be worth retrieving, too. Some may regard me as risking myself unnecessarily but, I say, consider this – Disco is a very excellent cat.

The road being empty even at the height of summer, for the military had been expelling tourists from the area over the last twenty-four hours, I had little sense of how awake West Cornwall had been shaken by events. Nor did I know how St Ives behind me was doing – the radio was still trying to reach their correspondents and so busied themselves by uselessly speculating with someone from the Royal United Services Institute. Indeed, I saw so few cars on the road – and those I did seemed to drive with no more abandonment than normal – that were it not for foreboding black warplanes in the sky, which always went in only one direction and never seemed to return, I would have mistaken it for yet another day of peace. Misadventure, however, I knew couldn't be far away.

I turned left at hauntingly silent Treen and traversed winding roads to Gulval, a little parish of granite and the last stop before the A30 and Penzance. Here, the chaos crystallised. Hedges like a madman's frizzled hair rose over both sides of the narrow road, rendering me unclear on what awaited us, but when they fell away I found that the whole population must have come out onto the street. Cars were being packed up and I thought I saw several people atop the church tower, trying to glimpse towards St Ives, in whose direction some men in a white van were heading. Others were running beside their window pleading with them to stay. I had to drive slowly, daintily, as pedestrians kept forgetting themselves and wandered in front of me. Not even my horn roused Disco from his worrying malaise. One woman sat on the curb, phone to her ear, crying profusely. Eventually, I broke out into the outer edge of Penzance, the new builds and retail park of Eastern Green, where things were even worse.

Long queues snaked from a Texaco forecourt and, as I passed, I saw fists traded along with the unleaded and the Fruit Pastilles. A tall man in a high-visibility vest struggled to direct the queuers.

"*You're doing a swell job, Ian*!" came a shout from the tannoy. The eastbound A30 was already blocked like a sewer pipe with traffic as people made haste in fleeing. I supposed they must have feared more capsules falling near us and didn't blame them. There wasn't a single sign of the military, which induced my nerves again, and in their absence authority was doled out by another high-visibility hero; a Tesco worker with glasses and curly black hair who directed traffic clogging up the roundabout outside the superstore. It was a fool's gambit; vehicles were already laying empty and forsaken, others bumped into each other carelessly, with frightened people – the word 'refugees' popped into my head and sat there uncomfortably – streaming through the corridors between them and down the dual-carriageway, weighed down with bags, emergency lights intermittently visible along the many rooftops. Everywhere I crept my Corsa, looking for somewhere to park so I might take a moment to figure out my plan for going all the way back again, I heard the same rushed, frightened voices – they talked of St Ives' destruction, of the Army's crumbling, and exodus before more stars fell.

"They'll come 'ere soon, hurry!" a woman barked at her two small children, dragging them by the hands down the pavement. Many were stood looking to the sky in search of the next capsules to dole out slaughter. One man on the roundabout's centre, feet buried in the arranged daffodils declaring "Welcome to Penzance," wasn't just looking at the sky but roaring blue murder at it and the RAF's conspicuous absence. From my window I, for some reason, shouted to him that I'd seen several jets.

"Yeah," he replied, "American ones! It's *our* bloody sky!" I left him to his strange repudiation of help which didn't have the Union Jack splashed across his saviour's wings.

Anxious for Disco's health and needing to get back as soon as possible, I ended up leaving him in the care of an elderly woman living out of a dirty Trevarrack caravan park. Disco had to stay somewhere. I might go back to St Ives but he most certainly would not. The woman, who seemed a bit lost, demanded payment in the form of a pint of skimmed milk, and when I returned with it from the petrol station she poured a handful of pennies into my hand. I stared at them for a moment, unsure of how to reply, then blurted a thanks. I'd leave them at her doorstep once I left. She seemed a bit mad – but not nasty, and that was good enough for me. Mad people, after all, are great with cats – and Disco, perking up, seemed to like her vibe.

Telling me her name was Evelyn and then remembering it actually might be Daphne, she was totally unconcerned by the Blight, declaring it "all a lot of fuss over nowt," and I found myself in some agreement – for, though the invaders could deal out devastation, they still couldn't move. If you ran away they couldn't follow. Anything they saw they could burn – so as long as they couldn't see you, you were safe. It was reassurance I badly needed – there was no version of events I foresaw in which I didn't return so, perhaps against a lot of my common sense, I needed to believe it would all be okay. I grew feverishly excited. War fever swam in everyone's blood. Some in Penzance were eager to make their way to St Ives themselves as spectators or combatants even with no knowledge of how to go about the latter nor the safety of the former. Ridiculously, I even found myself afraid that I might return to St Ives only to find it being cleaned up, the dust settled and guns silent, and the Blight dead in their silly pods. I hoped to witness the end myself – not in a documentary. Fear of missing out is quite something.

It wasn't until eleven that night, with the roads clearing and the sky reddening, that I could return, having tried and failed to nap in my car in a lay-by until then. The radio told of heavy casualties, of terrible damage inflicted upon St Ives, and the Army undergoing what they called a "strategic withdrawal" one too many times in their press conference for it to sound confident. A "ring of steel" would be thrown around either side of St Ives Bay, promised the Prime Minister to a packed and sombre Commons, from Zennor in the west, across the Hayle Estuary, and to Camborne eastwards. The threat would be contained and the two menacing objects on Clodgy's cliffs and under Godrevy's lapping surf would be destroyed. Where all that steel would come from was unclear – the defence of the realm was proving tricky enough as it was. Mobilising the necessary forces would take time – maybe weeks – and reports of missing parts and creaking logistics were already triggering a storm of anger. That anger often came from those same people who, when given the chance to vote on spending cuts, had happily waved them through. Now one lollipop lady was alleging that she was all that manned the defence of Camborne.

"We probably could have thrown up all these defences, once," a retired general told Sky News, "but that was a few budgets ago."

Details on the course of the fighting were spreading far and wide – this was what, by then, I'd come to learn.

The Thing had, without warning or apparent provocation, suddenly unleashed a barrage of sonic energy in all directions. In a heartbeat this excavated and threw skywards the hillsides overlooking Clodgy Point as if they were burst sores. This was what rained down on my house – I'd been lucky; closer to the site, colossal mounds of earth and rock had buried whole streets, families, and Army detachments. The front-line not merely breached but smashed and, as I'd thought, the Thing now enjoying a view of great tracts of St Ives, the Death Ray was brought to bear upon everything in its sight. Ground forces readied for battle until, to their horror, black smoke of an extraordinary quantity and an extraordinary blackness came gushing from the Pit and rolling over the town. This revealed itself as a prolific nerve agent. It choked the life out of everything it touched. All of St Ives and the surrounding outlands drowned in this smoke with only those few with respirators they could get on quickly enough surviving its poisonous grasp. At the stories I thought of my town, of everything I knew, gurgling on liquefied lungs, and for the first time felt the seething hatred for the Blight which had quickly taken others but dawdled before seizing me. The deliberativeness of their atrocity now clear, I felt foolish for ever affording them pity.

Our defenders' plasticity revealed, the Army crumbled to men now only called "survivors" lucky enough to reach high ground. Killer smoke flowed freely through streets and over rooftops. Waves of bombing runs were launched by the RAF and, as had been strangely condemned by the man on the roundabout, Super Hornets from an American aircraft carrier in the Channel. They must have pelted the Pit and its maybe-dead-maybe-not sister off Godrevy with thousands of pounds of ordnance and done no good – the Thing was unharmed, its black skin a peculiar element immune to kinetic and thermal energy, and through the carnage it just kept firing back. Two Super Hornets went down, slapped from the air by the Death Ray like they were paper planes and it a Maths teacher finally losing his patience. No British aircraft were lost – a sign of our superiority, some puffed, or, I thought, a sign of the Americans' eagerness, and ability, to deal all the biggest punches.

The ring of steel nowhere close to assemblage and all our forces retreating from the smoke's reach, in the unexpectedly black night I crept back unmolested back towards St Ives, taking the same empty and unguarded roads. All the while I knew how stupid I was being by coming back – but every second thought was met by the mental image of innocent Disco and I kept going.

There was nobody to be seen. I saw things too normal to feel real in this odd new world. A badger snuffled obliviously in the undergrowth; the clouds drove fast, dimming the stars; even the air's quietness, with not a single drumbeat of war on the distant wind, was perturbing. The roads were pitch-black, severed cables in St Ives having snuffed out windows and lampposts even this far away, and as I came past the Otter Inn I saw what must have been the proprietor stood with arms crossed and watching me silently. I turned one more corner and picked up speed along the empty moorland at Penderleath and saw along the northern horizon in my destination's direction a glow of deepest blood-red. This crept up the sky as if it were infected. A gathering thunderstorm, building its power over the northern sea, mingled with masses of black and red smoke funnelling from unseen St Ives. Constantly, remembering the gas and how if it returned it could take my breath too, I thought to turn back – yet I didn't, for I thought of little Disco, and his medicine, and so, though the bare moorland made me feel terminally vulnerable in my little car, I pressed onward.

The B3311 into Penbeagle, where open country turned to semi-detached suburbs, was deserted but for cars strewn about the place like toys. With a shine of my headlights I saw the dark shape of a body crumpled on the pavement. A victim of the gas, no doubt; I clicked off the lights both to hide myself and that foul sight. I'd seen enough death these past days. Doing so, I quickly realised, wasn't necessarily wise as I narrowly escaped an accident at the corner of the Higher Stennack when a golden retriever bolted across the road and into the thickets. At that, I sat for a time with fingers clinging painfully to the steering wheel, trying to encourage myself along until, finally, I opened the door and abandoned the Corsa – if nothing else, my house wasn't far, and I was terribly nervous that my engine would attract trouble no matter how softly it purred. All I knew of the Blight was that they sat in the Pit – and yet, somehow, I sensed danger all around.

Tucking my Corsa into a driveway available to rent for £500 a week opposite a pottery workshop, spitting at the sign offering the deal as I passed, I stepped gingerly down the main road and deeper into silent St Ives. The red glare was hidden now behind the nearest houses, its edges peering over the roofs, but I was too distracted by the content of the road to pay it much mind. Traffic must have built-up in the town's final moments, as all who first dawdled tried to flee, and the smoke had consumed them all. Body after body sat in seats, or was frozen half-out of their doors, some still ensnared by seatbelts. Others lay scattered about the tarmac and I had to walk past, or step over, all of them. Birds were feasting on some already. I didn't know if the silent houses either side were houses of the dead or if, perhaps, some survived simply by going upstairs. Indeed, I didn't even know even if their second storeys were high enough to afford protection – I'd never learned the height of the black cloud and whether, if it rolled it again, I could even hope to save myself.

Mounting fear of the smoke's return gnawing at me, I chose to detour a longer route home which would take me via the hopeful safety of uphill. Maybe I could find some obviously non-existent way to get home while sticking to higher ground. So it was that I ascended Penbeagle towards the industrial estate. Seeing nobody, or at least nobody alive, I still didn't feel safe and so climbed higher, trees about me shivering with the first intimation of the storm, and then the hill levelled and I came upon the industrial estate with its cuboid warehouses dealing in mackerel distribution and the manufacture of electronic cigarettes. It, too, was empty. Looking about, desperate to see wide-eyed survivors I could convene with, I saw nobody. Cold loneliness pricked at me. Having reached as high an altitude as St Ives allowed me, with any route home downhill, I turned and pressed into winding residential streets which would lead me to my house and, if it came, the smoke. There was no choice. Ahead the town dipped, valley-like, before ascending again and plateauing as it approached the coast. Red glare crept over the rooftops and, now, I could see dark houses in Clodgy's direction smouldering or still ablaze. Past them the vacant farms and National Trust heathland burned too. Rugby Club floodlights, marking the peak of Catherine Road, were thin black sticks against the burning heath's glow, which I realised must stretch to the coast. Odd – that land was neither within range nor sight of Clodgy.

As I beheld this, there then came a lurid green glare which lit the road all around me – I sprinted for shelter beneath an oak tree, terrified of being spotted, though I didn't know what by – and then spread over the whole town. Looking up through the tree's canopy, I saw the clouds pierced by a thread of green fire, falling fast and vanishing behind the rooftops to my left. It was the third falling star – many saw it fall at the old engine house in Cripplesease, due south of myself. Now it lay as an obstacle between me and any return to Penzance. As it disappeared I saw, over the sea towards Clodgy and blindingly violet, the first lightning of the gathering storm dancing across the sky. Thunder burst like a sonic boom overhead. Seagulls, previously unseen by me and having a torrid few days, bolted en-masse, filling the air with cries.

Penbeagle's throng of terraces are built on an incline leading down to the Stennack, the main road bisecting St Ives, and I clattered down it, eager to get home and get out again. Once the lightning had appeared over what once was Clodgy, it went on in an unnaturally rapid succession of white flashes, brightening and dimming the clouds, over and over, like someone kept tugging at heaven's light switch. The thunderclaps, treading one on the heels of another, didn't sound right either – they came with a strange crackling accompaniment and there was an unnerving mechanical whir to their rumblings. It was like I could hear them powering up before they sounded. Still driving down the slope, thin rain gusting into my face, I found my attention held by this confusing flickering of light beyond the Rugby Club. Something, I realised, was moving shrouded in the darkness there on the hill – and with each flash of light I saw uncanny shapes which I couldn't piece together into a single whole. A floodlight strained then toppled onto the pitch with a great crash. At that I realised I was focusing my vision too low. Whatever lurked there was far taller than I had dared realise and, then, with another burst of lightning, it formed clear and sharp and bright into the whole I was looking for.

A monstrous tripod, of glittering bone-like black metal just like the Clodgy capsule, surely a hundred feet tall, strode upon the rugby field – in its canter, a leg clipped and smashed the white grandstand in half. It didn't seem to notice. This walking engine, many steel tentacles curling from a cuttlefish head held atop those three thin legs, vanished and reappeared with each flash of lightning – I realised that its head was the capsule buried in the Pit. It had grown legs.

The Thing strolled at its leisure, stopping to take stock of its surroundings, and in the flashes of visibility I saw it examine another floodlight with some strange care. A tentacle coiled around the structure only to tug it down with the ease of uprooting a flower. And I, I realised, was galloping down the hill to meet it! I slowed and slipped in the wet tarmac, just about steadying myself, moving to shelter behind another tree's thick mossy trunk. I peered out at this dreadful thing which looked this way and that like a heron fishing in a brook. Rain, heavier now, lashed at my face and I clung to the tree with my heart in my throat, a hot lump of ice, fearing I would faint. My house was between the pair of us – I had to get there. Just had to. But what could this monster do to me if it saw me? Then, all of a sudden, the tripod was coming towards me, over the houses, so tall that it covered a dozen feet with a single bound. Had it spotted me? I felt utterly trapped as it stomped its way nearer. Palm and beech trees parted like reeds, the Thing picking its way through the town, each step shaking the ground with greater force. I too shook, either from the Thing's steps, from the cold, or from sheer, bleak fear. My hands gripped the tree tighter, breaking off a chunk of bark, and I found I couldn't move. The dense black shadow now climbed my hill, its titanic size making it seem like a knoll, and, by instinct, I crouched, still clinging to the tree – further down the hill there stood a line of trees and, through a gap between them, I saw a police car vanish beneath a metal foot. In another moment the colossal mechanism – having either not seen me or just not cared for something so puny – went striding by two streets across from me, smashing through houses as it went, and passed uphill into Penbeagle and toward the open country of campsites and ancient mineshafts. Oh, how I prayed for the banter of it slipping into one!

In an instant it was gone, but beyond the trees and newly broken rooftops I heard a frightful mechanical howl, like a warped animal hoot, drowning the thunder. As it faded, though it remained and remains deeply embedded in my mind, I was left with the rain.

For some minutes I remained crouched there in that lashing rain – bullets from the ether – and darkness watching for the monster to reappear over the rooftops. Hail was coming, mixing with the rain to form slush in the gutter, and a mist made even the rooftops past which the tripod had vanished grow unclear. Now and then came the lightning, rendering sharp their edges, but I saw nothing more of the Thing.

Soaked through and shivering, cold raindrops running off my fringe and chin, it took some time before my blank astonishment let me go and I could struggle on. In stickily wet clothes, I picked the rest of the way down the incline towards the Stennack. What a moron I'd been not to imagine the stupid thing might sprout legs. Of course it would! Idiot! My one comfort was that, as long as it was over there, so it was no longer here, and I could make it home – there was only the one tripod and it wouldn't be hard to miss.

"Just..." I mumbled to myself, "...just stay frosty or whatever it is they say in *Predator*." Under cover of trees which lined this part of the Stennack I succeeded, still soaked and still shivering, like all those PE lessons which taught me never to try physical exercise, in picking my way through the darkness and around obstacles which only came into view when I was a few steps from colliding with them. Only in the brief spasms of lightning could I see my way. I stopped for a time, in some strange silent admiration, at the sight of the tripod's crushing footsteps which had squashed the police car, torn caverns in the road to expose broken pipes, and pierced holes in nearby buildings. Navigating between and around scattered cars, the bodies within formless in the dark, hailstones fell in a growing torrent as I hopped over the thinner edge of one hole in the road. Muddy water collected in the bottom, hailstones splashing into it, and I thought I saw a body face-down in the muck but didn't look long enough to be sure.

My motive for getting home remained and it was all I needed to thrust me forward through the gloom. Picking between cars, I found even the pavement was crowded by them; this included an improbably overturned cement mixer whose cab and drum I scrabbled between, before tripping over a dead soldier and thumping my knee on an Audi which had smashed into a garden wall. Then I came across the Five Weasels, now a blackened shell barely recognisable but for its half-readable sign, and in the darkness a man blundered into me and threw me to the floor. We both cried out in terror and, with raised hands and a breathless apology, he rushed on – I didn't dare shout anything after him for fear of alerting the Thing, wherever it was. For a moment I lay there on the asphalt, pounded by hail, watching the man's vanishing silhouette and reflecting on this very strange day – it was a hard task to get back to my feet, grinding my hands against the cold ground to push myself up, and upon reaching Catherine Road with arms tightly crossed at last I made my way up the hill. Wind and rain bit at my face the whole time.

On the yellow lines outside the house before mine I stumbled on something big and soft, and, by a flash of lightning, saw between my feet a pair of army-issue boots. Knowing what I would see at the next flash, at least in a general kind of way, I stood over him waiting for it. This wouldn't be the first corpse I'd seen today – but somehow, perhaps because it was so close to my house, I knew it was one worth looking at. When the lightning came, I saw that a man in baggy military fatigues lay crumpled against the stone wall my neighbour had been building. It looked, from the shape his body had made, as if he might have tried to climb over it to reach the house, but been

overtaken by the black smoke and fallen off again. I objected to the wall's planning application, I recalled, and so wondered if I would have played a hand in saving him had it not been built. A handheld radio lay in the gutter beside him, inches from falling down a drain down which rainwater rushed. From it a female voice, barely audible in a blizzard of static, crackled.
"*Flash... NBC-3 chemical... bravo... NBC one seven... three seven... four five... Delta... ninety degree grid... India... Kilo... ninety seconds... second target active...*"
With both hands, slowly, I rolled his heavy body over – the chance remained that he was alive and, in the dark, I patted about in search of his neck. When I found it, I felt no pulse.
"*...be advised... chemical contamination detected... observed within radius of one point nine miles... personnel within two miles of red zone must execute evacuation order...*" The lightning flashed again and his face leaped upon me. I sprang to my feet.

It was Howell, the Royal Engineer with the acne-ridden face, only much of that face had been stripped away. Across one half only raw, bloody flesh and bone were left where skin once was. His eyes, staring up into the rain, unblinking as it hit them, were glassy and empty and grey. Another flash lit the scene and I looked up from Howell to see that bodies were strewn about the place, but different from those choked by the gas – they were in pieces, tattered dolls, limbs and various segments missing or half-wrenched away – and the whole street, and the cars, too, was thickly scarlet with blood. It was then that I noticed that it was not rainwater gushing down the drain.
"*Hostile forces active... all personnel within AO avoid contact... civilian evacuation priority one...*" Something particularly awful had happened here.

Gingerly, I stepped over Howell and onto my empty driveway, then came running back to guiltily close his eyes and – with some struggle – search his uniform for a weapon which he didn't have and I wouldn't know how to use.

"Sorry," I mumbled awkwardly to his empty face. Distantly, I heard another metallic hoot, and at that I hurried for the door – the hillsides were no longer aflame, though from Clodgy there still murmured a red glare. So far as I could see by the flashes, my house had enjoyed a lucky escape of sorts – many others were weathered or stomped on, and piles of wreckage half-blocked the road further down. Rocks, of course, lay everywhere, having rained down from Clodgy's obliteration. Also further down the street were voices and what sounded like footsteps, but I hadn't the courage to shout or go to them – though the need for human company felt particularly deep at this moment.

It took my shivering hand several attempts to unlock the front door but once I succeeded I let myself in, closed and locked the door again, staggered into the pitch dark living room, and, overcome with shallow breaths and stubbing my toe on the coffee table, collapsed onto the sofa. Entombed in the dark, my imagination was full of striding metal monsters, and of Howell's ghostly face, and blood streaming down the street. I realised, too late, that I had tread bloody footsteps onto the carpet. I kicked off my shoes, opened the window, and threw them out into the camellia bush. Shivering violently, I went to the bathroom tearing at my wet clothes, seeking anything which might lend warmth, and found with resignation that the shower didn't respond to its buttons. Instead, I changed into pyjamas still warm from the dryer, wrapped myself in a fluffy dressing gown with towel around my hair, located my phone, purse, and Disco's medicine, and hid myself in the cupboard beneath the stairs with a wood-handled bread knife in hand. Now I was ready to fight the aliens, I thought with biting, livid sarcasm.

# XI.

After a time, having broken from my solitude beneath the stairs to fetch rosé slowly warming in a dead fridge, my emotional firestorm, like most wildfires, was burning itself out. I was exhausted. Cheap wine splashing in an empty stomach, I was moved to go upstairs. I don't quite know why, as the last thing I wanted was sleep when Disco – and the tripod – was waiting for me.
The staircase was dark and at each creak I froze like a child fearing waking her parents. Reaching the doorway, I stood with my hands against the frames to keep myself on my feet. Compared with the rest of the house's impenetrable darkness, the bedroom was alarmingly bright, reds and yellows gushing in through the windows, and I realised that in the hurry of our departure one had been left wide open. A lost crane fly jerked about in the ceiling corner, inches from the open window, unable to find it despite how close it was.

Noiselessly, I hoped, I closed the door behind me so the rest of the house wouldn't be illuminated. I crept towards the window and deeper into the red light. As I did, the view opened up until it reached over the chimneys towards St Ives Bay and, across that dark expanse, I could see Godrevy. To the right were the wrecked houses and blackened woodland in Carbis Bay's direction, which I had seen explode what felt like such a short time ago. The thunderstorm was passing right overhead now yet I paid no attention to anything but Godrevy for, lit by the vivid red glare, I saw things were a little stickier than I realised.

Godrevy was on fire – the bay and the clouds above the headland splashed bright red with the reflection of flames, their minute tongues swaying and writhing with the gusts of the storm, the lighthouse standing lonesome and untouched beside the furnace. With this emanating light I saw the tripod again, on the hill and glaring down over St Ives it, and I ducked beneath the windowsill to hide. Across the bay another black shape, grotesque and strange, moved carefully through the inferno. With a bit of squinting I recognised it as a second tripod, surely from the capsule which had fallen off the coast and crawled ashore, and I wondered both if the two intended to link up and how long it would take for that third meteor to activate. The second machine stepped in and out of the haze shrouding Godrevy, as if it didn't notice the flames at all, and then the nearer one let out another hideous howl. I dived to my bedroom floor and lay there, hands pinned to my ears, silently begging it to go away. Minutes must have passed before I dared peer over the windowsill again – when I did, it was gone from the hillside. Now it could have been anywhere. How could a thing that big sneak off?

From my vantage point I could see that on the Stennack a black shape, unfamiliar to me, lay across the road beside shattered Costcutters, just visible past the neighbour's horse chestnut. Then I perceived this was what remained of one of the Super Hornets; the American fighter-bomber's carcass lay flat on the ground, like a halibut, having left a long trail of debris behind itself before resting at the corner shop's charity clothes skip. Both wings had severed, one partially lying in a cottage's flowerbeds, and the cockpit's glass casing was missing – though this provoked hope that the pilot had survived, I could only really feel gloom at the sight of something so powerful so effortlessly humbled.

Through the window, with burning Godrevy providing enough light to spy on those streets visible from my window, I looked for some sign of life, something which would tell me this wasn't a town of the dead. I was sure I saw a number of black figures hurrying one after the other past the Costcutters and up the hill to Carbis Bay, maybe in silent pursuit of the nearer tripod, whose footsteps I thought I could hear in that direction. Having no reason to doubt it, given how mad the world had gone, I half-reasoned that they could be alien infantry combing for survivors. As I look back, I suppose they could have been stay-behind soldiers maintaining surveillance on the Thing, or hoping to attach plastic explosives to an ankle, or perhaps just a few survivors who couldn't shake their curiosity. Regardless, I saw no more of them, and even if I had my attention was so attuned to staring at Godrevy and looking out for the tripod that I couldn't focus on anything else for long. So strong was my interest that I dragged my moulted antique chair – which I had always intended to have fixed and never did – to the window, sat down, and stared at the orange headland as if it were a performance.

Obviously, the sluggish creature I'd seen and, in a way, wrestled with, piloted the tripod – another surely drove the Godrevy one, marching on its perpendicular bearing. I wondered how it must work, whether the tentacles operated different levers or if the Thing's very brain was plugged into the controls, whether it hurt to be crammed in there, and why they chose three legs instead of four or seven or twenty-nine. Thoughts ran away from me to form all kinds of strange ideas – that wine hadn't so much squatted in my belly as moved in.

The sky was clearing as the thunderstorm passed on, stars daring to show their faces, and over the smoke of the burning dream in waking life I saw Venus' pinpoint.

"Couldn't you of gone there?" I muttered. I watched it for a moment, wondering if the Things ever looked skyward and felt wonder at constellations they had never known, and as I thought it I realised that not once had I seen them look up. Remembering Angus I thought of how, were he to land upon an alien world, that would probably be the first thing he'd do. My hatred for the creatures grew as I sensed a lack of appreciation for their place in the universe. Annihilate man, if you must, but don't be animals about it. From out in the bay, wind – warm, carrying the heat of flames – gathered and drifted through the window.

I must have gained a certain hyper-awareness of my surroundings – the presence of clanking cosmic war machines may carry that effect – because my ears, being vigilant little bits of cartilage, pricked at a noise from the street on the house's front. Rousing myself from the lethargy that comes with velvet chairs and wine and apocalyptic scenery, I rose and hurried to the porthole above the stairs – on the street I saw a dim silhouette which, a few paces from Howell's body, sat against the concrete wall of the opposite house. He held his knees to his chest. Grappling with the window catch, I pushed it open and poked my head out into the fresh, surprisingly warm night.

"Hey!" I hissed, eager for human contact. Alert eyes, bright enough for me to spot in this darkness, darted in my direction – the stranger slowly pulled himself up the wall to his feet and, softly, stepped towards my front garden.

"Where are you?" he whispered back, scanning the lawn and driveway, stood like he was ready to bolt in the other direction.

"Up here!" I waved and, taking a step back, with a painful squint he saw me in the gloom. "Where you going?"

"Christ knows," he said, in a voice I recognised but couldn't place.

"You trying to hide?"

"Well, I'm not here to fuck spiders." Rolling my eyes, hoping he couldn't see in the red-tinged dark, I nonetheless was glad of the company.

"Get inside," I said in a commanding voice which I was rather proud of, and, not waiting to be told twice, he came to the front door, his baggy clothes rubbing together frustratingly loudly.

"Could you be any louder?"

"I'm not doing it on purpose!" he hissed back, trying the door. "It's locked."

"Shit, damn it, sorry," I said quickly, and I hurried down the stairs, unlocked the door, let him in, and locked it again, testing the handle several times to ensure it was so. I don't know what I thought a locked door would do against one of those machines. It being darker inside than it was outside, where the stars and glow of distant Godrevy provided some semblance of light, I couldn't see the man's face – he was nothing but a burly and somewhat formless humanoid who rested himself against the wall and drew in deep, pained breaths.

"Fucking hell..." he mumbled slowly, as I willed my eyes to adjust and identify this stranger. Or was he a stranger? I was *really* sure that I knew that voice – and I had no idea what to say to him.

"Can I get you a drink?"

"Oh, I would literally stab an infant for one," he answered gratefully, which made me chuckle, and I led him by his arm into the living room. He followed me, mechanical as the tripod, inside.

"Tread carefully," I said. "Don't remember what I left lying round here." Immediately, his foot collided with the DVD player, and we froze at the noise. Silence reigned for a few moments – no alien tentacles came bursting through the windows.

"Oops," he said, finally.

"Just..." I breathed. "Just mind it." I found my bottle of Zinfandel on the coffee table.

"Wine?" I asked, pushing it into his hand, which pushed back.

"Is it red?"

"Uh, I think so." Think so? I knew it was. What a stupid answer.

"No, thank you, I'm allergic."
"To wine?"
"To histamines."
"Fair, fair. Whisky?"
"Is it apple?"
"Sense the situation, mate."
"Sorry."
"It's normal whiskey. For normal people."
"In that case, oh, God, yes, please." I felt my way to the kitchen, which was a little better lit as it faced glowing Godrevy. The stranger didn't follow me – I heard him crash down onto the sofa – and so his identity stayed a mystery for now.
"I've got this weird Japanese whiskey and some Scotch stuff," I called from the kitchen, opening a cupboard where the bottles sat waiting for me. "Any preference?"
"Whichever's harder," came the reply.
"I think that's Scotch." Pouring out more of the brown liquid than any responsible bartender would, I downed half of his glass. "Grim." I walked back, slow as I could, feeling my way again. I'd lived here long enough to remember where things were, I thought, but apparently not.
"Here you are," I said, passing him the half-full glass, trying to find his hand in the dark.
"Thanks." He took it but didn't seem to be entirely here. He was sighing the same thing, over and over: "Poor James."
"James?"
"He's on the road outside," he said, quietly. "I thought he made it." He drank the entire glass in one, just as I had, which made me smile. I thought it best to wait until he poured a refill himself than offer him another. I feared dangerous emotions might lurk behind a gate for which whiskey had the key. "I'd pour one out for him but, you know, it's your house."
I replied: "Trash it, if you want. Might as well. Think I'm gonna move out – I don't like these new neighbours." He nodded slowly, looking down into the empty glass, gripping it so tightly I worried it'd shatter in his hands and we'd have a whole

new thing to worry about.

"Really, really thought he'd made it."

"You mean Howell, don't you?" I asked and, in the obscurity, I saw him look up at me with surprise – and at once I realised where I knew him from. He was another of the engineers whom I had bantered with at the bus depot. As my eyes adjusted I saw his bright red hair begin standing out in the dark. "Scott, right?"

"No way?" he asked. "Small world. Well, not really, same town, but hey-ho. And call me Harry. I'm no soldier – this uniform's just a fuckin' costume, now. Might as well be. Against those things."

"You sound like you were in the thick of it." He made a despairing gesture.

"If I was in the thick of it, I wouldn't be here. Everyone who *was* in the thick of it, like you say, well, they got torn to bits – just torn to bits." He repeated this several times. "You saw those other folks outside, I assume?"

"Yeah. I didn't go looking too closely."

"Keep it that way." He sighed.

"Want another drink?"

"Please." I fetched the bottle and he took it from my hands – after pouring himself another, to the brim, and downing it in what might have been record time, he dropped his head into his hands and, in a perfect passion of emotion, loudly pounded his fist on the table.

"Damn it!" Harry wailed with each pound, on the edge of sobbing. "Damn it! Damn it! Damn it!" I kept my distance until the third or fourth punch, before I stepped forward and laid a hand on his shoulder, trying to think of something nice to say and coming up short. I worried 'they' could hear his tantrum – no, not tantrum, that's dismissive, let's call it an outburst – but felt it'd be polite to let him have his moment. Even if it wasn't good for my new table.

It was a long time before Harry could steady his nerves enough

to answer my questions. His engineering unit had been called upon to fashion a route for articulated vehicles, which I took to mean a pontoon bridge or something like that, so they could access Clodgy and retrieve the Thing's wreckage.
"Wreckage?" I asked.
"Well, obviously there'd be wreckage, we were gonna kill it in two seconds flat, right? *Right*?" He laughed and drank again before carrying on with his story. Nerves had overcome him throughout the day, he said, whispering in his ear that things weren't as cosy as they seemed. His friends teased him for it.

Harry took a long time to explain how he actually survived, focusing instead on the minutiae of what happened to those who didn't make it, and how before the fighting even started he had become become sure that everything would go wrong.
"It was like an itch in my brain," he said. "Just telling me to run." It was then that he revealed his shame – being certain of impending doom, he deserted his unit before the fighting even began and left them to their fate.
"Oh," was all I could offer in response. I then added: "But it sounds like you made the right choice."
"Still let everyone down," Harry said. "But I got lucky. Once the gas came, I just so happened to be on high ground. Wasn't high enough – but I climbed a tree and just managed it. Most everyone else didn't. I heard it all over the radio – voices crying out – then choking and silenced. Casualties must be in the hundreds and we didn't leave a scratch in return. All the scientists in the castle got away after saying there's nothing to worry about, obviously, but not us. They sent all those men to their deaths for nothing!"
"Who did?" I asked.
"The government," he growled. "Just a show to them, innit, just panicking and trying to look good and throwing us in the fire. We used to be able to defend the country, you know, when my granddad went to the Falklands, when we had National Service, back when the word 'service' actually

*meant* something!" For a deserter, he seemed very concerned about duty. "But now? They just left us there! Where was the artillery? The air support? The Typhoons were just flying in *circles*! Fucking clowns! At least the Yanks tried; I saw their jets come in, just get swept out of existence, but at least they tried! At least they tried." Later, he told me, as night fell on the ruins, he saw the capsule again. It rose, he said, suspended in mid-air, levitating, before out of nowhere legs burst from its body.

"That's insane," I said, dumbfounded by the mental image.

"You're telling me!" Harry exclaimed. "I swear to God, it was just this big rock, flying, then these legs grow out of it like... well, I don't know what it's like. Like nothing I've ever seen. I'll tell you what – if it was CGI, you'd say it looked like shit. That's how weird it was."

"That's an oddly good way of putting it," I replied. "I think."

"It seems to prefer walking over flying," he observed. "Maybe it doesn't have the energy to stay aloft, I don't fuckin' know, but the one in the sea must've done the same thing."

From his distant view, Harry told me, he saw the feeble resistance that second machine met as it rose from the water off Godrevy – flashes of gunfire from sparsely deployed infantry, the pitter-patter of a pea-shooter rocket against its black shell, and then fire rose everywhere across the headland. Satisfied, it drifted over the land, sprouted its legs, and began its business. It seemed extraordinary that so terrible a thing could walk unhindered upon England and yet here it happened, and here it continued to happen, as they stomped about without challenge. I told Harry what I'd heard on the radio, about the "ring of steel," and he choked with laughter.

"They think they can just contain it! Incredible. Ain't nothing bringing one of them down. It's like they're made of adamantium or something – nothing's getting through their armour. I saw the Hornets get a whole bunch of direct hits and each time nothing happened – swear I saw a Hellfire bounce right off! Defies description, I swear, it's not even alien – it's

like they're something out of a dream." He continued with his story, telling how the St Ives tripod wandered about the town, strangely aimless as it went about.
"Like it was looking for something but didn't know what," he said, thoughtfully. "Same with the other one. It's big enough to have made it to London by now, if it ran, but it's not. Why?"

The one in St Ives, meanwhile, was keeping busy. It would punch great holes in any structure it deemed offensive with foot or tentacle, having tugged up the branch line and thrown fishing boats across the bay, while power lines were fried and Bussow Reservoir's stone dam smashed, flooding the surrounding fields. The Titan seemed thorough, exploring, moving back and forth across St Ives, with no urgency to its actions, like it had all the time in the world. Occasionally, it would find survivors.
"I always closed my eyes when it did," Harry said. "Wish I could close my ears."
"Is that what happened to the people outside?"
"Gas doesn't rip your limbs off." Harry hid in a garden shed for a long time, furtively peeping out between power naps next to the sander, checking if the tripod was near or far, subsisting on a jumbo pack of Monster Munch. For hours the monster walked leisurely to and fro across the town, its headlike hood turning about like the head of a cowled human being, a few times passing within sight of Harry. He told me it put him in mind of a primitive man skulking through a stream hunting for fish to spear.

As evening sequestered there was, so far as Harry could see, not a living person left in St Ives, or at least not any who dared make themselves known. The tripod slowly expanded its area of patrol, deeper into the country, satisfied that the town was cleared. Moorland further south was spared fiery death in favour of another liberal dousing of black gas. Wispy tentacles of the stuff penetrated far into the surrounding villages. At that news I realised that, had I attempted my entry merely ten minutes earlier, I might have driven straight into that cloud. Instead, it had only just dissipated by my arrival. How far was my luck planning on carrying me? Harry left the best for last: he was sure, he insisted, that more than one machine had come out of the Pit on Clodgy Point.

"I can't prove it," he said, "but I *really* think I wasn't always seeing the same one."

"Why do you think that?" I asked. "I only ever saw one. Well, two, one here, and one over on Godrevy."

"Yeah, yeah," he replied quickly, "I thought so, too. But there's something about it. It's like... every time I see it, I think it's a different one. You know? I've heard rumblings from the crater down on the cliffs. I think there's more crawling out – maybe their ship's way bigger than we realised. Maybe they'll keep coming. Exciting times, right?"

Harry's face lit up, though, when he told me he had a plan – he seemed very proud of the fact. He intended, as a first step, to gather supplies from the houses then begin, "very cautiously, more cautious than I've ever been before, so cautious it'll blow your mind," making his way uphill to the imagined safety of the moors. Out there, it wasn't hard to come across a disused tin mine, the shafts not used since the Victorians but very much still hiding beneath the undergrowth for unleashed dogs to fall into every now and then. Strange conceptions existed in Harry's head that one would make a handy shelter now the Blight were done with their gassing.

"This was my plan from the start," he said proudly, explaining he'd already been to the moors once to scout and been called mad by the refugees streaming over the fields who couldn't understand why he'd stand still for even a second. "That's why they died and I didn't – I took the time to actually think."

"They died?" He explained: while exploring one promising shaft, and trying to convince his fellow refugees to entertain climbing down it, the metal giant appeared upon the moorland. A steady stream of frantic escapees from St Ives, many burned and scalded, were broken up by its presence – but not Harry, who found a way to get himself a few feet down into the hole. From the shaft's safety, which he peered out of like a meerkat, he watched the machine pursue and catch people with its steely tentacles and deposit them into a hole in its body. The purpose of this couldn't, he said to my agreement, have been pleasant.

Harry concluded at the sight that hiking dark moorland, invisible mineshafts all around, hunted by giant machines which could never be evaded in open country, was a nonsensical risk. Reluctantly, having nowhere else to go, he returned to St Ives. There he hoped to squat in a house and gather supplies, darting from building to building and ransacking under the invaders' noses, until they left or at least thought the depopulation complete. The owners of whatever house he chose – unlikely to still be breathing upon this Earth – wouldn't object. Then he could properly survey the mines and realise his strange vision.

I asked if there were others – oh yes, said Harry, there were plenty of people left in St Ives. All were hiding in the upper floors of their dark houses just like myself, not daring to make a sound, like rabbits huddled in warrens. The black smoke couldn't climb hills – but, as a few cocky survivors learned, the wind could help it up. Others stumbled their way across open country, got lost, and probably either died of exposure or got snatched up by the tripod. Or *a* tripod – the mystery remained as to how many stalked these lands. Those who still had Internet access talked of a naval flotilla taking shape off the south coast, evacuating everyone who could reach it. Many were risking it all and abandoning shelter in St Ives to press hopefully in that direction. Harry had been consumed by more simple needs – thirst – until he found me and my whiskey.

That was the story I got from Harry, bit by bit. He grew

calmer telling me and trying to make me see the things he'd seen, and to understand there must be dozens of machines prowling the countryside, though I thought he'd just lost it a tiny bit. Maybe he was just crashing. He hadn't eaten anything but Monster Munch since mid-morning, so I thought to warm up some gnocchi before remembering the lack of electricity. Searching the cupboards for something else, our hands would occasionally touch, which did nothing for me, and I found myself feeling increasing unease about this combat trained and clearly distressed man in my house. At least they didn't give him a gun. Nonetheless, he seemed willing to remain a perfect gentleman – for now. As for the cupboards and general food situation, we could only settle for Coco-Pops in lukewarm oat milk – Harry ate them gratefully.

When we had our fill of whiskey and childrens' cereal, we stumbled upstairs – I embarrassed myself by joking that Harry ought not expect any especially pleasant treats and he replied with "I'm as gay as the day is long, don't worry yourself" – and fell asleep, fully dressed, sharing the bed in a strangely platonic way that I never imagined doing with a soldier.

When I woke from unpleasant dreams I can't recall, a mere few hours later, I pulled the blinds apart with two fingers and looked again out of the open window. A dawn sky was painted deepest blue, the blue you find in the ocean just before it turns black, the Sun not yet having burst from below the horizon. Godrevy's fires had dwindled now – the headland was charred and smoking. Countless ruins of shattered and gutted houses and blasted and blackened trees hidden by night now stood gaunt and terrible in dawn's pitiless light. Yet here and there some object had had the luck to escape – a plastic Let Agreed sign here, a Cornwall Council street-sweeper there, untouched amid the wreckage. Birds were even singing. And shining with the growing light over the bay, upon Godrevy's black headland, I saw three metal giants stood together in the desolation, as if in consultation with each other. Smoke rose from every field around them – streamed up, whirled, broke, and vanished.

"Jesus," Harry whispered, making me jump, having also woken.

"Jesus indeed," I said, shuddering, my heart in my mouth from the surprise. Harry rested his elbows on the windowsill, morning breath creeping over me like the black gas, holding his own bit of blind open with both hands. Dark blue light gushed in.

"Three of them," he muttered. "I knew it. The proof's right there."

"I guess so," I said. "One's bad enough. I saw another meteor earlier when I was walking in. There could be way more."

"Yeah, I saw that too," he replied. "Who knows how many are coming? We're gonna be swamped. And where's the frigging RAF?! Do the Army Air Corps have to do *everything*?"

"Army Air Corps? You guys have planes, too?"

"A few. Mostly helicopters." He smiled at my lack of military knowledge.

"Well, maybe they're regrouping, the RAF," I suggested. "Somewhere. I don't know. I'm not a strategist. I'm not Rommel."

"Nobody's Rommel."

"Or maybe we slept through the whole invasion and we're the last ones from here to Torquay."

"Doesn't bear thinking about," Harry sighed. The smoke turned bloodshot at day's first touch.

"Doesn't matter either way," I said, rolling off the bed and pulling on my shoes. "I've gotta get back to Penzance."

"Right," he laughed. "Your cat." I'd told him my mission just before falling asleep – he'd laughed then, too.

"Exactly," I said with the utmost seriousness. "And I won't be having any piss-taking; I'll tell you that right now."

"No piss-taking taking place," he replied with some sarcasm. Over the bay, an electronic hooting from the tripods – we tensed up and looked in its direction. All three machines which, just a moment earlier, had stood on the headland, had vanished. The stage was empty.

"What the fuck?" I exclaimed.

"What happened?" Harry cried, trying to keep his voice down and failing to keep his voice down. We both crawled back over the bed to the blinds and peered. "Do you see 'em?"

"I don't see jack," I replied. "Great – last thing I need is for them to get all light-footed. Could be standing right over us. Maybe they can jump, too."

"Oh, *fuck* that," hissed Harry, outraged. "That's how God made spiders true evil. Giving them jumping powers. Don't need *them* doing it, too."

"Spiders aren't so bad."

"Don't say that," Harry said. "When you're around me, you don't say that."

"Sorry."

# XII.

Dawn brightening and Godrevy smouldering, we withdrew from the window and, quietly as we could, went downstairs to root around for breakfast – I warned Harry of the creaking steps, of which there were many, and he did his best to avoid them. He failed – but he did his best. Over a breakfast of fruit – Harry teased me for cutting my apples into slices – we remarked simultaneously that the house, the town, even the county, was no place to stay.
"Now I've slept on it, I think I've realised that whole thing with the mines was pretty stupid," he said. He proposed making our way eastward where, after donning civilian clothes to avoid court martial on the way, he'd find his partner in West Wellow outside Southampton, assuming such a place still existed. Soldiering was a life he'd tired of a long while before the aliens came and now seemed like a decent time to pack it in. With each distant metal hoot of a tripod beyond our four walls, I couldn't blame him.

My plan, of course, was to immediately return to Penzance for Disco; so obvious was the Blight's outrageous strength, and their eventual spread across the Earth possibly infinite, that I'd decided to take him aboard a boat where we'd live a new life on the waves until the struggle was over. All I needed was a fishing rod, a replacement fishing rod, a manual for using a fishing rod, and a spare manual for using a fishing rod. Disco,

I was certain, would make an ideal ship's cat – I just needed to find him a tricorn. Between me and Penzance, however, lay the newest capsule; the one I saw fall in the night. By this morning, metal giants had undoubtedly crawled out of the ground there, too. Were I alone, I'd probably have taken my chances and driven back across the barren moors, no matter what waited for me. Harry talked me out of this.

"Don't go getting yourself killed for nothing," he warned. "Come with me – you can break off when you need to, maybe at the St Erth Roundabout or something, but don't go straight into the jaws of death like that. Need to go *around* them – you're not doing your cat any favours by dying." From the emotion with which I had told him about Disco and how he needed his medicine, Harry had come to appreciate how important this was to me. I never heard him doubt my goal again – and, annoyed, I realised he was right.

"I got it! I got it!" he suddenly cried, staring at his phone.

"Got what?" I asked.

"4G!" He beamed. "It's working!"

"Oh, shit, how'd you fix it?"

"I didn't – it's just working. Hang on. There's gotta be news..." I watched him scroll with his thumb, eyes lighting up. "Okay, things aren't *so* bad, after all."

"No?"

"No – they haven't even got as far as Hayle."

"Oh." I was surprised; and trying to get a connection myself, which wasn't happening. "So I guess the world isn't conquered just yet."

"Nope – earthly men still man the barricades." He smiled.

"And unearthly men lurk everywhere else."

"That they do," Harry agreed.

"Find out about that third meteor," I said, urgently. "Anything come crawling out?"

"Hang on..." he said. "Aaaand my Internet's gone again. Cool."

"Alright, well, let's assume they *did* come crawling out," I said.

"Yeah?"

"Yeah. So maybe you're onto something," I conceded. "Going around instead of straight back." Delighted, Harry agreed, and it was settled.

The plan was simple: under cover of Steeple Woods, across Carbis Bay's outer edges, we'd walk our way to Hayle. Harry suggested, or wildly guessed, that judging by the landings they'd managed so far the Blight were going to fall *very* methodically. The invasion would plod along, acre by acre, he thought, so slowly we'd barely notice its advance. We had to get out of Cornwall, at the very least, before they landed in every hamlet – but, even if I had to drag myself by my tongue, I was going to Penzance first. Then Hayle and the Army's safe, muscular, tattooed… excuse me, arms.

Chivalry being dead, Harry didn't offer to accompany me – he wanted out. We'd part at St Erth, as he said, then I'd go alone back to Penzance, keeping to the country roads parallel to the A30 – I imagined that the dual-carriageway would either be impossibly crowded by refugees, jealously guarded by the Army, or torn to shreds by the Blight. I really hoped that Disco's caretaker hadn't upped sticks – all this effort and peril just to find an empty field where her caravan had been. I imagined myself stapling "have you seen this cat?" posters onto a wall otherwise covered in human faces and didn't like the impression I'd leave.

We ought to have left immediately but my companion had been in the services and I'd been to university – we knew better than that. We first ransacked the house for whatever supplies, particularly alcohol, we could find, filling two backpacks, knowing the whiskey would be useful either for ourselves or for haggling our way out of any scrapes which society's collapse might make more common. I made a joke, which didn't quite land, about using it to bribe my way out of sexual assaults. All it earned me was a blank, nervous stare from Harry. As we left through the front door, though, I suddenly ran back inside – I emerged a few moments later, sheepishly holding Disco's medicine and stuffing it into my backpack, having nearly forgotten the one thing I'd actually come here for.

Creeping onto the empty street into the fresh and bright morning, studiously ignoring Howell's body sodden from the overnight hail, we pushed through the next two front doors in search of anything else which might prove useful. Non-perishables were a good idea, and we hoovered them up, the same fate befalling batteries, the contents of my neighbour's first aid kits, and several months worth of rent squirrelled in a kitchen drawer. You would have done it, too. Going from door to door, I averted my eyes from the dismembered corpses down the road – but I could still smell them. That grisly stink of wet meat and sewage. Eventually, well-stocked in Kopparberg and canned tuna – which I would save for Disco – as quickly as we could we took the route with which I'd come into town; down the street, onto the Upper Stennack, and up again southwards into Penbeagle. There was no sign of the tripods – besides the general carnage, of course.
"Didn't you drive here?" Harry asked, as we made our way towards Steeple Woods.
"That I did."
"Do you wanna check on your car, at least?"
"To be honest," I replied, "I'd forgotten all about it. I'll just leave it there and claim it on my insurance later. Why not, right?" Harry sniggered.
"There goes your no-claims bonus." I laughed, trying to keep it down, knowing a machine could be eavesdropping from any direction.
"The insurance people probably already know this'll be costing them a pretty penny," I said. "Who's gonna check if I'm lying?"

The houses seemed as deserted as before. I heard nothing but the wind, though more than one front door must have been left ajar and blown open, for several batted against inner walls, and a dog barked angrily from some nearby street. Little heaps of bodies piled outside some of the houses, overcome by gas as they clawed to get in, and I tried not to look, especially at the ones who had gotten bloodied hands through windows but were still too late.

"It must hurt a lot," I said. "If you're that desperate to get away. Do you think they knew they were dying?"

"Don't look at them," said Harry. One man lay halfway into a lounge window, gutted by shards, and all about lay little balls of tangled feathers; corpses of rooks and songbirds. That I can describe all this to you may tell you how well I did at not looking.

Here and there were things deserted in the stampede – plastic bags pinned to the ground by clothes or trapped on a wing mirror, an overturned pink pram, heavy rucksacks and backpacks, even a mattress which had fallen from a Fiesta which now stood static, engine still running, halfway onto the pavement, all of its doors open. A baby seat was empty inside. At the corner, turning up towards ChipsAway where I got that nasty fever, a Jeep Wrangler, overloaded bags and duvets pressed against the back windows, lay on its side in a puddle of its own sprinkled glass. The driver was crumpled inside against the windscreen; just another piece of spilled luggage. His head was smashed open in a way that reminded me of an ostrich egg – yet, from the hardened black-red slime bubbling and oozing from his mouth, I knew it was the gas which got him, too.

None of the houses around here had suffered very greatly – the tripods must have felt the gas was enough. Were it not for the human tragedy all around it could have been any quiet morning. Chimney tops had been shaved by the Death Ray and the taller trees suddenly ended in a horizontal line, their upper portions sliced away as if with medical precision, but besides this there was no structural damage to be seen. Desolation, therefore, reigned. Save ourselves and the obliviously chirping wrens, nobody else was out. Either the survivors Harry told me about had escaped or they had been found. Yet, more than once, from the upper floors of some houses I thought I saw curtains pulled back, momentarily, but each time I averted my eyes. I wonder now if this was for fear of unnerving the residents – perhaps it was a simpler need not to be bogged down by distractions.

Pebbledash lower-middle-class suburbia gave way to the aluminium business park and then silent million pound houses tucked behind tall fences and beneath tall trees. At last we broke onto a muddy path into Steeple Woods, my back already aching from my overburdened backpack, a gathering chill in the air. Newly sheltered by the green canopy I came to feel vaguely secure even while aware that the Titans were never so far away. There were no howls or footsteps to be heard but I was coming to realise that their absence might not mean they were gone. The woods nearer to the town were dessicated ruins, caked in grey and white ash, serving as a helpful reminder of which direction not to walk in. We picked our way through segments of the woods almost entirely felled, so freshly cut that the foliage was still green, while I made unhelpful remarks about how grateful to the Blight local developers would be and Harry unhelpfully encouraged me by laughing, but there were very sharp edges to it. Nerves punctuated our every step.

Hayle was a mere two hours walk away but, rapidly, we came to realise that we'd be taking quite a bit longer. While waiting for Harry, who had gone behind a tree to answer nature's call, and listening to him quietly curse the complexity of his belt, I felt the ground tremble. At once I sank to a crouch, holding the nearest ash trunk for stability, looking around through the trees on all sides with wide eyes. I dared not call out to Harry to warn him – besides, he ought to know on his own. Another tremble. Stronger. Closer. I closed my eyes, begging the next one to feel further away, but it didn't – I fell onto my rear when it came.

"Just fuck off," I whispered, sitting there in the undergrowth, with the helplessness of trying to ward off aircraft turbulence, "just fuck off, fuck *right* off." It didn't – then came a crash, the snap of a cracking trunk, and perhaps a hundred yards directly ahead of me a dark shape moved swiftly between the trees. It was the sweeping leg of a tripod cutting through the woods – slowly I backed behind my tree, staring as it went, hoping the canopy made me as invisible as it made the machine. Three legs passed harmlessly by and were gone – I stayed frozen still, watching where it had been, waiting for another, until I dared rise to stand. I felt a touch on my shoulder. I span round and threw a punch – it struck Harry in the jaw.

"Fuck!" we yelled together, both falling backwards onto the hard muddy ground. Harry glared at me, rubbing his mouth.

"I blame myself," he said.

"Yeah, I blame you too!" I hissed. "You see that shit?!"

"Yeah – I was trying to piss through it!" he said. He seemed on the verge of giggles. "That's *not* how I intend to die!"

"I was hoping they'd stay put," I said, looking around again, half-expecting the next to pass by and revealing the start of a whole cavalcade. "Maybe they're drifting out now. What if they're going to Hayle? We're in trouble then."

"Maybe," Harry said gravely. "But find us another choice, you know? Come on." He patted my shoulder, lightly this time, and we rose and hurried through the tangled and redecorated woods.

"Sorry about the punch, by the way," I said, as I clambered over a fallen tree.

"It's cool," he answered. "You've got good form."

"First time I've punched someone who wasn't in, or near, a nightclub." Harry laughed, trying to keep it quiet, and I bit my tongue to stop myself from joining in.

"I've never laughed as much as I have been during the end of

the world," he sighed at last.
I replied in a matter-of-fact way: "I read that laughing evolved as a shared response to the passing of danger, you know."
"Oh yeah?"
"Yeah – makes a lot of sense right now."

This would not be the last time a tripod came near – before we were even out of the woods there came another, marching in the opposite direction, and we darted over the felled trees it left in its wake as we made for the St Ives Road. At the woodland's edge, trees suddenly vanishing to become neat brown and green farmland, we froze solid again – some fields away there loitered two more machines, while a third wandered westward, picking its way across the pastures. With its head bowed as it walked, it had an almost timid quality.
"Great," muttered Harry, sitting against a tree. "This is just what we need."
"Nice view, though," I offered, crouching to tug a jumper from my bag, unfold it, and lay it down so I could sit on it. Enough mud was on my arse already.
"What do they remind you of?" Harry asked, regarding the machines, as he reached into my bag for a packet of Nik Naks. This was becoming one strange picnic. One tripod was beginning to drift away now – there was an aimlessness to their movements, almost a drowsiness, which didn't make them appear very ruthless.
"Insects, maybe," I replied. "A praying mantis or something. They're kind of amazing."
"Amazing?"
"You can't pretend it's not a bit fascinating; all of this."
"It'll be fascinating once I'm not around them. You don't find a snow leopard cute when it's got its jaws round your throat."
"I guess you don't, no," I conceded.

Distantly, over the hills, I saw the dark shape of another meandering machine. The Things were often enough a sight that it became disorienting and I couldn't guess at how many were out and about. One was rough enough. Harry and I returned to the woods, for the sake of keeping hidden, and I kept watch while he napped. Eventually, we hoped, the machines had to leave. Then we'd continue – but, for now, they blocked our route. Within the hour, Harry was woken by a metal hoot, and he scrambled over to me.

"What I miss?" he asked.

"Nothing," I said. "They're just standing there." But, at the hoot, the machines seemed to stir – we watched from the treeline as, slowly, they wandered back towards St Ives. Once satisfied they had actually left, the landscape now relatively normal apart from all the deep footprints carved into the farmland, we hurried out of the woods, across an open field at what approached a full sprint, and onto the empty St Ives Road.

From there, keeping low and watching every horizon, it was a straight shot to the pretty village of Lelant. Its tidiness was somewhat ruined by the corpse in the road, a tabby cat chewing its way into an eye socket, which seemed to twitch every few moments.

"You hear that?" Harry asked, as I stared at the cat.

"What?"

"Listen." I did – in the distant sky, the far-off rumble of a jet engine.

"England lives, then," I said dryly.

"Yeah, for now," said Harry. "Not here, though." He was right – in Lelant, as in St Ives, we appeared the only people left. The empty roads were as spooky as ever. We stopped for lunch at the granite Celtic cross beside the road upon which was inscribed the names of "the men of Lelant who gave their all in the Great War 1914-1918 and the World War 1939-1945." Everything through which we had walked so far must have either been choked to death or busily evacuated at the end of a gun. The dead body round the corner, certainly, implied the gas had come at least this far, but the Blight machines, which we hadn't seen since, must have been content with St Ives. For now – as Harry would say.

"It's like they're waiting for something," I said, to no reply. There was no longer even a breath of wind this morning. Harry and I shared some more whiskey and reflected on how swiftly such a great swathe of country had emptied. Shrubs, poking from a cottage garden, were freshly trimmed, only half their mass having been parsed back before the pruning's sudden interruption. Tools still sat about the scaffolding which scaled the Trevithick Inn like stainless steel weeds. Distantly, there came a hoot.

"That sounded close," I said.

"If you can hear it, it's too close," Harry replied.

"That's pretty agreeable. We should get going." We hopped off the memorial and onto the road, trusting in the birds to stop singing if a tripod came too near, to hurry further through Lelant towards St Erth. Harry and I only spoke when vital; and then only in whispers.

After a time we passed Gentle Pines Nursing Home, empty, and down the winding road stepped out of the shade and onto the St Erth Roundabout – the alternate paths to Hayle or to Penzance via St Erth were at last upon us. The roundabout's emptiness was disorienting, as I expected a car to come speeding round at any moment – I was less used to standing in the road than I was to seeing cadavers at this point.

"Well, I guess this is it," I said to Harry.

"I guess it is," he replied. "Sure you won't come with me?"

"Penzance or bust," I replied, shrugging, and he nodded.

"Well," he said, holding out his hand, "it's been fun."

"Hasn't it?" I said, smiling, and I fist-bumped his open palm. He looked to the ground, smiling, as I turned and began walking. It took only a few paces before the palm trees in the roundabout's centre were out of the way and I now saw that my route to Penzance was blocked by an Army barricade.

"Ah, shit," I said, stopping in my tracks.
"What is it?" I heard Harry ask, alarmed, and his boots were loud as he hurried to my side. I heard his voice in my ear: "Oh."

A Scimitar light tank of the Queen's Royal Hussars held the roadblock, turret poorly disguised under plastic vegetation, and red-white chequered fencing had been placed over the lanes. One soldier was busying himself by directing sunlight from his iPhone screen onto the ground, to the terror of a column of ants. Several others, all holding heavy rifles, stood around, a pair crouched beneath street signs, and at the sight of us these two reflexively raised their weapons towards us.
"Don't come closer!" one shouted.
"Oh, grow up!" I shouted back, hands up, staring at him with disbelief. "Do I look a hundred feet tall to you? Come on!"
"How many of you?"
"Count us!" They lowered their weapons, glaring, and another – his name tag read 'Dickens' which I found childishly humorous – hurried towards us from the roadblock, holding his round helmet to his head as he did. We moved to meet him – I kept my eyes on the nervous pair under the signs, but they kept their weapons, if not their eyes, lowered.
"Good to see someone else made it!" Dickens exclaimed, his accent flowery and Welsh, as I realised I'd always somehow assumed you couldn't be in the Army if you wore glasses. "Sorry about my lads – everyone's a bit overexcited right now. Either of you hurt?"
"No, sir," I said, annoyed at myself for my submissive lexicon, while Harry kept quiet and tried to edge away – I suppose he feared outing himself as a deserter, but it just made him look like he was concealing drugs.
"Don't call me sir, love – I'm from West Wales."
"Okay, Dickens, then."
"Lieutenant's fine," Harry mumbled next to me, shifting on his feet.
"Anything without an attitude's fine," Lieutenant Dickens, sir,

said coldly.

"Sorry," I said, "just really, *really* eager to get to Penzance."

"Okay, well, that's not happening," he said firmly.

"But-"

"Not a chance, love." The men behind him stared curiously. A jet rumbled by, unseen behind clouds, but close. "We're under a mandatory evacuation order for everyone west of the Tamar. No ifs, no buts."

"The Tamar?" I asked, stunned. "That's all of Cornwall!"

"Or thereabouts," muttered Harry.

"We're lucky it's not the whole country," Dickens answered. "These things are unbelievable. They *own* pretty much everything west of us. I take it you've seen 'em for yourself – you can understand the worry, surely."

"But I really need to get to Penzance," I pleaded. "I've got family there." I could hardly have told him I needed to fetch my cat – he had a gun and, frankly, it'd probably be completely fair if he shot me in reply.

"No, you don't," he replied. "Whole town's emptied – I guarantee your family's on the A30 right now and a whole lot safer than they would be in Penzance. Trust me."

"You don't know that," I stammered; fear, then a blinding panic, flooded through me at where Disco might end up when in the care of strangers. I might never see her again whether she lived or not!

"I'm not arguing with you, love; I've got a gun. I don't need to," he answered with finality. "Get yourselves down to Hayle, fast as you can; the last buses will be out of there soon and you do *not* want to miss them. We're not far from Hammerdown."

Harry suddenly exclaimed: "Hammerdown?!"

"That's the one."

"You're joking."

"I ain't." Dumbfounded, I looked from one to the other.

"Jesus..." Harry looked at me. "Thank fuck we left when we did!"

Cautiously, I asked: "What the fuck's Hammerdown?"

"Later this afternoon," Dickens replied, glancing at his watch, "not sure when exactly, but I've been hearing thirteen hundred, we're dropping every missile we own on the aliens all at once. A dozen countries are joining in. I hear the Yanks even have some stealth bombers lined up for the party. You don't think those contrails are flights to Malaga, do you? It'll be a hell of a display but if the enemy's in Hayle at thirteen hundred, then they're bombing Hayle; so I'd want to be gone when it kicks off."

"But…" I imagined St Ives, Hayle, the whole beautiful area, turned to one great field of craters and rubble, a Somme in the Westcountry, and confused little Disco limping through it with his ears ringing. "Why're you doing that?"

"Because they're winning." Over the hills, back towards home, a warbling hoot – everyone looked in its direction. Dickens looked back at me, unrepentant sternness across his face, like a teacher you know you'll never reason with. "There's more all up along the north-east coast, all the way to the lighthouse. It's like a termite infestation. We're bombing them, too. Any minute now, I reckon, and they'll move on Hayle – classic pincer movement. So I'll repeat – get out of here, get evacuated, and stop your bickering."

"But I…" I put my face in my hands. Black despair overcame me.

"Need directions?" I looked through my fingers, like cell bars, at his awful smirk. One of his teeth was stained yellow.

"I know the way," I said with resignation. "We'll get there."

"Course you know the way – there's signs." A couple other soldiers sniggered. "But you'll have to take the road past the estuary and go through Hayle itself – bypass is blocked."

"By what?"

"Plane crash. Recon flight strayed a bit too close and got himself cut in half. Took out the overpass. It's decidedly unhealthy that way."

"That's mad!"

"Well, there *is* a war on. You can hike the fields if you want and get bogged down in the mud, but it'd be faster to just go via town. That's what everyone else is doing."

"Alright," I sighed, "well, thanks, I guess. For your service and all that."

"Please don't say that to me again," Dickens laughed. I turned back the other way down the roundabout, circling towards the road which ran along the River Hayle and towards the town, as suggested.

"Don't walk, run," I heard Dickens call behind me. "It's nearly two miles and those things can cover it a lot faster than you!"

"Yes, yes, fine," I said glumly, not picking up my pace, and Harry hurried after me down the carriageway's edge. Abandoned cars lay here and there. Walking, I noticed more soldiers clustered in the trees, invisible until they weren't in their green camouflage.

"Nice shoes, mate," called one, his voice oozing sarcasm, and Harry looked down to realise he hadn't disposed of his Army-issue boots. Despite the horror upon his face, no drama came of it beyond a few sets of narrowed eyes.

The carriageway skirted the Hayle Estuary, tall white seabirds paddling in muddy water, and on the other side was the quiet Lelant woodland through which cut the local branch line. On the road's other side stood a petrol station where a car, burned to a crisp, stood halfway in a ditch. A dead body, of indeterminate gender, lay besides it and, feet away, a curly-haired man calmly jet-washed his BMW at a bare petrol station. I stared at him for a moment. Beyond, through a gap in the trees, I saw what had once been a concrete bridge constituting the Hayle Bypass's beginning. Its span was severed, taken out by the aforementioned plane crash, whose remains lay smouldering in some unseen field. At the bridge's edge, held up by a grey girder, stood a battle tank with turret turned to aim over the estuary.

"That's good," I said, pointing it out. "They'll get one fair shot, at least."

"Sorry about your cat," Harry said, suddenly.
"You don't need to pretend you give a shit," I replied.
"It matters to you – so it matters."
"Other people're probably losing their whole extended family right now," I said, shrugging. "I can't complain." Harry just grimaced and we continued down the carriageway. The view across the water was calm and peaceful in the morning sunshine. Nonetheless the empty road, which should have been crammed with day-trippers by now, made our newfound apocalypse more plain than any alien machinery or simmering stiffs.

Hayle's urban confines growing around us, trees turning into warehouses and office parks and a historic brewery's visitor centre, we found it equally silent until we came across the stretch of empty Wickes and Tesco car parks. Distributed across it, positioned at neatly equal distances, stood six more Challenger 2 tanks.
"Bows and arrows against the lightning," Harry muttered bitterly. Men and women in the same uniforms he had discarded busied themselves around the tanks, loading them, readying equipment, barking orders. For the first time I became aware of commotion further down the streets and deeper into town. "I think they know, too."
"Know what?"
"Come on," Harry said, shooting me a dirty look which I thought unearned. "They know their shells can't do nothing – they've wasted enough on them already to know it. They're here to delay the enemy, not beat them. A lot of posthumous medals waiting to happen." Silenced by this comment, I walked with hands in pockets past the car parks and a number of men in camouflaged fatigues, to a checkpoint through which we passed without challenge, and then into the heart of Hayle. Groups of people, all hurrying in the same uncertain direction as us, were turning into crowds, which we were being absorbed into. Soldiers, some with unmistakeably French or

American accents, helped families with their luggage – one carried a cage containing a perpetually hissing cat, which further depressed me.

Onto the main road, the scene now dominated by the great brownstone Hayle Viaduct, we walked along the river's quayside finding the town crammed with people. It was a carnival of confusion and fear. It seemed as though everyone who had escaped the Blight had been funnelled here, then kept here, as the transportation to get them out became available much too slowly. Bureaucratic derangement reigned; the authorities had refused to let them make their own way. Now, at the last minute, the evacuation order had come, and many felt, no, *knew* it was too late. Exhausted and desperate faces were everywhere and it took me a while to appreciate that, far from being a spectator, I was now just another one of those faces, anonymous in the horror.

From snatched conversation I learned that the A30 eastbound to Camborne, the primary evacuation route, was now cut off. The Godrevy machines had torched a swathe to non-existence. What escape could be mustered would now have to navigate requisitioned buses and coaches through tight country roads instead. This they would somehow do all the way to the A394 with tripods lurking all around. In this tightening siege, there was a sense of short distances made impassably great – and the quickest glance at a map would tell you that, with the tripods of St Ives to the west and the tripods of Godrevy to the north, it would be Hayle where they intended to link up. Everyone had predicted this – and the decision makers had ignored them. I began wondering if I'd gotten myself into a bit of a pickle.

At the realisation that the moment for safe and orderly withdrawal had passed Hayle had fallen into its current tumult. Countless refugees had camped here, many cramming into homes opened up by endlessly generous owners, and now they learned that the tacticians' failure to see Hayle was no sanctuary might cost them everything. Fearing that the narrow roads still available could be hopelessly clogged, private vehicles were banned, and people, shepherded along by the panicking authorities, were limited to one bag each as they were hurried to waiting buses of which there were too few. A retail park off the Hayle Bypass had become a makeshift depot to which all were being pointed. We hadn't long – the tripods, it was rumoured again and again, were on the move.

"I guess we should follow the crowd!" I shouted to Harry over the bustle.

"I guess we should!" he agreed so, swept up, we joined the parade.

Somebody was screaming at a blameless young private that "you facking idiots" had "killed the lot of us" by leaving the evacuation too late – though the fault, as so often, lay with unseen men in clean suits, not visible men in dirty uniforms. In the middle of the road, lined with wailing emergency vehicles, a fresh-faced police officer with a powerful megaphone stood on his car's bonnet and barked instructions over the sea of heads.

"Please, no pushing!" he pleaded, constantly adjusting his cap, people streaming past like water around a rock, "everyone please just stay calm and show kindness to each other and we'll all be alright." His pleas were drowned out not just by the crowd but by the low grumble of jet engines above the town, as well as an obnoxious woman who hysterically wailed three inches from my ear about how death is coming, death is coming, death is coming. Clearly there was no difficulty to be had in making these scores of people realise their situation's gravity. Grown men shook in anguish in their certainty that the Things, which only a few had actually seen themselves, were approaching, and a young child tearfully watched a soldier explain to her flushed parents how to attach her respirator – supply being so limited, these priceless tools were reserved for the under-fourteens. Over my shoulder I heard

squawked accusations of a mask snatched from a toddler's hand. Somebody else, a freckled teenage girl in a cherry beanie, held a digital camera aloft and filmed for YouTube.
"Excuse me," she asked, turning the camera on me, her next interviewee, "what do you think of all this? Crazy, right?" I ignored her and, her narration shifting seamlessly to the criticality of her viewers subscribing "for more content like this," pressed on through the crowd, trying to stay close to Harry. Down an adjoining street and through a garden greenhouse I saw a shrivelled old fellow stood at his terrace's patio, warped by the glass, clad in cyan pyjamas and leaning over a walking frame, in no state to travel and no clear desire to – from his orchid garden he watched the frenzy with vapid acceptance. Unhelpfully, in a misguided wartime spirit, the polyphant stone St Elwyn's Church was incessantly ringing its bells above the excitement until the Army persuaded the vicar to desist – it being pointed out that the enemy might take an interest in the noise.

Despite all this madness, nobody in Hayle could tell me if the tripods actually *were* coming at all. The military seemed more confused than you'd ever want the people in charge of defending you to be. According to the Internet, a nest of conjecture I couldn't trust but which was all I had, the resources still weren't in place to properly track the tripods and relay their whereabouts to us common folk. Command and control had already fallen apart, if it was ever together – probably not, if they couldn't even track a handful of gigantic metal beasts dawdling in open country. Hayle was a madhouse and I needed out – but to where? Some awful, grisly fate awaited this town, obviously, but I hadn't a clue where to be instead now that Penzance was off the table. I had no West Wellow to call my own. Were I to climb aboard one of those buses, I was sure, I'd be surrendering my fate to the incompetents running this clown show – I'd prefer not to. Some vague, ghostly phantasm of a plan existed in my head, like a cloud too thin to be called fog, to go to Penzance anyway, by any route I could find. Free spirit, and all that. But Disco wouldn't be there. I don't know the difference between improbable and impossible but finding him was certainly one of them. And then there was Hammerdown, inching ever closer, to contend with.

"Maybe you were onto something!" I shouted to Harry.

"About what?"

"Hiding in a hole!" He laughed.

Harry and I eventually came to be seated, with legs dangling from the Copperhouse Pool quayside, eating dry steak and ale pasties. A chain bakery was freely handing them out to all who asked. Fishing boats were coming and going from the quay, picking up evacuees, braving the gauntlet of the St Ives Bay in full view of every Blight machine at once – and Harry hoped to hitch a ride. He'd already signed a waiver which I warned him didn't look legally enforceable, being written in Comic Sans. Yet I, too, lacking any better idea, had joined the slow-moving queue despite not being sure I'd actually have the guts to get aboard when my turn came. Once I stepped onto that boat, I was out of Cornwall – but, to the reader's undoubted frustration, I wasn't sure I was ready to abandon hope of finding Disco. This was very silly and I knew it, so I didn't mention it to Harry, instead mostly talking to suppress his insistence that we should jump the queue. We, I told him, are English – besides, the local fishermen coordinating this exodus were unlikely to tolerate it.

Each time a boat arrived, a soldier with a clipboard came over to warn the fishermen that they ought to abandon the folly of seaborne evacuation – it was dangerous and, more importantly, not officially sanctioned – but he didn't have the heart to actually stop them. Don't do this, he urged those of us queuing; go to the staging area outside Hayle. A seat aboard a bus was guaranteed – so he said. I got a glance at his clipboard as, having received universally negative replies, he turned away – the pages were entirely blank.

Given their two rotten choices, many were happy to leave in old boats under the tripods' noses rather than be wedged in a Gwinear Downs country lane where they could gurgle on nerve gas in a poorly upholstered seat. The crowd, thusly (ooh, get me), swelled along the quay.
Boats, some from as far as South Wales and Ireland, chugged in and out, weighed down by bodies, overcrowded to the point that water splashed over their decks, bringing with them stories of machines on the headland and drawing closer. Amid this knowledge I found myself eerily calm, even numb, realising with each ticking second that I was indeed getting on one of these boats and my life in Cornwall, as I knew it, was over.

Huge vessels, we were told, had gathered over the northern horizon to pick up all who could reach them – the world's eyes, trained on Cornwall, were now training on Hayle. Salvation was a fingertip away. Despite the dreadful stress whipping through the rapidly growing queue I was relieved to see no great misbehaviour – and even witnessed places swapped for children or the elderly. When push came to shove, people did neither. Goodness prevailed though the world burned.

Harry and I parted at last once his turn came, the *Snake Eyes* having room for him but not me, and I felt a bit silly waving goodbye as the boat pulled from the quay so stared at the watch I'd pilfered from my neighbour's house. Ah, yes, I forgot to mention I did that, didn't I? I must have been a bit embarrassed. Oh, well, it's relevant now.

Since the stroke of midday I'd been nervously glancing at this watch every few moments awaiting the so-called Hammerdown. It was a word passed about my fellow refugees – what time it took for me to recognise myself by that name, as if people like me can never be rendered into one – and all were excited by the prospect that, at last, the assault might be halted and we could go home. From Hertfordshire, Strategic Command spared no details in explaining Hammerdown or, as it was formally known, Operation Undercliffe.

"I don't choose their names," sighed the operation commander, General Sir Ed Humphreys – he batted away questions regarding whether it was wise to make the operation public, saying the Blight probably didn't read The Times, while repeating promises that this day-old conflict was nearing its conclusion. He said: "It's just an infection. Today we intend to sterilise it."

Several hundred aircraft from half a dozen NATO nations, General Humphreys said with a certain feverishness, would gather "beyond visual range," putting them far outside the Death Ray's deadly reach, and launch warheads upon the occupied region between Hayle and St Ives. Property damage would be minimal, Strategic Command promised – all machines were, contrary to rumours, being tracked with laser designators singling them out for direct targeting. Each and every tripod would be pounded by the type of high-explosive force normally used to excavate quarries. Broken windows were all we needed to worry about, apparently.

"These are weapons which can penetrate sixty metres of reinforced concrete – and we're pelting them with hundreds at once," Humphreys said. "They can't hope to survive." Once a damage assessment had been completed, the same would befall the machines between Hayle and Godrevy's furthest tip to the north. It would be one of the more substantial bombardments Europe had seen since the Second World War, certainly the greatest to ever shake British soil, and the tripods would be eliminated.

"What if it doesn't work?" asked a journalist.

Came Humphreys' answer: "It has to."

An exact timeframe, given the growing traffic jam in the South West's airspace, was elusive. Once that was sorted out, Hammerdown would come – and not just from the sky. Warships and submarines, missile batteries and artillery, all would join in and "some" units would be British, it was promised from the Downing Street podium. From this very quayside, knowing now that Hayle would be spared the hellfire despite Dickens' warning, I'd have a front row seat to the performance. It was for this reason, ridiculously, that I dawdled in fleeing and, becoming so eager to watch the fireworks, eventually abandoned my place in the queue. Who would pass up the chance to see the aliens defeated? I'd seen science-fiction films; of course I knew about forcefields and deflector shields, but this was the real world – logical reality, rather than fiction, told me that those delicate looking beasts couldn't stand up to the world's assembled arsenal. Maybe I was a more optimistic person than I thought – or, perhaps, just a realist, and very occasionally what's realistic is also what's good. Doesn't happen very often – but it happens.

Finding something to do until the denouement, I helped an older couple – they were unaware of the ban on private transport until I told them, and then they acted like it was *my* doing, which is the sort of thing retail prepares you for – sort through their assembled packings until they could narrow it all down to two bags. It took a long time to explain that they probably couldn't bring the Bavarian grandfather clock.

"What's all that rubbish?" the husband fighting a losing battle with his hairline asked, gesturing back down the street towards the quayside, and I looked to see a mass of excited and noisy fugitives crowding along the river, more joining them each moment, dwarfing the queue which had been snaking for perhaps half a mile. So, the stampede had begun at last.

Small slices were being cut away from the great panting crowd, bit by bit, as boats took them away – from my own mental calculations, and the (very belated) realisation that the boats consistently returning meant no Death Rays were flashing from the hills, I imagined that the whole gritty exodus could be complete before the sun fell. Yet walking back down, ditching the oldies to their clock, I came to glean that all these new people were not, in fact, trying to hitch a ride at all – Hammerdown was imminent, the missiles now promised for two o'clock on the dot, and they were gathering to watch just as I had intended. And there I was thinking I was an individual. I checked my watch – it was 1.54.

There was a lot of shouting, with many nervous glances over the River Hayle, across which rolled fields that hid the more distant lands yonder, and it all appeared still and quiet and without any flashes of combat. No tripods loomed like overgrown black dandelions. One man pointed out there was no reason to worry about us being ambushed. Given all their surveillance the military would provide us with warning aplenty – "and if they don't, well, just listen to the birds and tell me when they stop singing," he said cheerfully.

As if it were a New Year's clock, soon all were counting down the seconds to Hammerdown's unleashing. None of us could quite imagine what its execution would look like, nor whether it would actually work, or even if we could be sure we were safe from heat or shrapnel. The phrase "if they bleed, we can kill them," was heard in the crowd, which I found funny, but I was also an absolute mess of jitters. I looked to the watch of the person next to me (mine had, naturally, dried out its battery) – 1.59. A few seconds passed. 2.00.

"Time's up," I whispered to myself.

"Yeah, it is, yeah," said the watch's owner, loudly, ruining my dramatic moment. A little girl near me was encouraged by her parents to put her fingers in her ears. A few moments passed, quiet, without disturbance but for birdsong, and then, in a growing crescendo, there came the pumping swell of unseen explosions in St Ives's direction. Hayle fell silent; faces turned in the direction of the hills. Behind them flashed great balls of red and orange light – Hammerdown, at last.

The muffled thuds grew greater and greater as unseen rockets and shells fell ever closer, to the point that I feared they may eventually sweep over us as well, but with a tense grip on the shoulders of two strangers I didn't do what my common sense told me to do and run. Instead, I kept my eyes fixed on the aggressive colours bursting behind the hills. I felt jealous of the cows, tiny specks on one of the distant embankments across the river, grazing unconcernedly amid the fortissimo.

Everyone stood arrested by the sudden stir of battle, so near us and yet invisible to us, and the ground trembled with each high-explosive blast.
"Nothing could survive that," I heard a woman breathlessly assure herself and, I'm sure she hoped, the others around him.
"What're those?" asked someone else in a frightful voice, pointing to the sky, across which a stream of orange cut fiery ribbons – a skipper butterfly, amber-coloured and easy to misidentify as a moth, frolicked between my eyes and the contrails. "More ships?!"
"Calm down," a soldier reassured her, artificial thunder tumbling like so many waves over Hayle, the powdery reek of cordite growing stronger, "looks like rocket artillery; probably M270s. All part of the plan, miss, all part of the plan."
"Are they *sure* they're just hitting them aliens?" somebody else asked, as I clambered atop a rusted mooring post in hopes of a better view over all the heads. "I left most of my things back there."
"Chill – we're ruining some aliens' day and that's all that matters," laughed a multi-chinned man with much certainty, but I sensed a collective trepidation – few were willing to believe the monsters vanquished until they saw metal bodies lying broken and beaten across the landscape.

All along the quayside, everything was quiet but for the low mumblings of boat engines, in vivid contrast to the river's opposite side – for past the hills, still, cracked the terrible cursing of high explosives.

"Thank Christ we didn't oversleep," I muttered. At last, after what seemed like an excessive and very expensive amount of time, the barrage faded until it petered out altogether. The horizon never, though, went back to normality – the flashes of light shifted into a humming red glow which stained the blue sky, entwining with a thickening mist of smoke. I walked along the quay's edge, closer to the viaduct, hoping to catch some loose news – in an Army Land Rover doorway stood a moustached captain, parked so close to the water's edge as to risk falling in, speaking rapidly into a handheld radio.

"Greybeard, this is Argonaut One-One; do you have a damage assessment?" he asked impatiently. A crackle of a reply, which I couldn't make out, came back. "Well, send it as soon as you know, please, I've got a lot of people here about to turn blue." Cordite poisoned the air, the stench so strong that children were complaining about it, and, as I noted all the terrified gulls passing overhead in flight from the bombardment, still having a terrible few days, so did I hear another, heavier sound carried on the air.

"Hear that?" asked a man in a mesh vest.

*"Greybeard, Greybeard,"* insisted a voice over the radio, *"we need an update – what's the targets' status?"*

"Something's wrong," whispered somebody.

*"Stand by, stand by, we're awaiting confirmation that the target has been destroyed."*

"Will you be quiet?!" roared another man at a yelping cockapoo. Then the sound came again, unmistakeably from St Ives, over the river and the fields, a muffled thud—a thud I'd heard before. A footstep. My guts turned to water.

Out from the smoke, one, two, three, four armoured Blight machines faded into view, taking shape one by one, far away over little trees which now looked even littler. It reminded me of the first I saw, stepping from the rugby club's mist, but now a whole squadron stood in line and looked down on Hayle. Black cowled figures backlit against the glimmering red – all the tools at man's disposal and they hadn't done a shit of good. Beneath his breath, the captain at the Land Rover muttered a curse. His radio spasmed to life.

*"Black Six, Black Six, contact, contact, contact,"* said the unseen operator matter-of-factly, as if he had been anticipating this the whole time, and then; *"initiate delaying action. Don't stop for nothing."* At sight of these strange, swift, and terrible creatures the crowd at the water's edge was so horror-struck as to be completely silent. There was no screaming or shouting – the fear snuffed out all noise. Then the quiet was broken – the tripods gave out a simultaneous metal honk, a warped battle cry, a shrill clarion from Hell. Hoarse murmurs turned to shouts and wails, a movement of feet, pushes and punches —suddenly the whole mass of people were surging in every direction. I slipped from the top of the mooring post and a man, lugging a bus-sized suitcase on his shoulder, swung round and sent me staggering with a blow to the temple. Crumbling to my knees, clutching my head, I looked up through the crowd and saw the Things appear and reappear in vanishing and reopening gaps. They were moving, now; striding calmly for the river, making rapid headway and entirely unmolested. Resistance was non-existent – I heard no gunfire and saw no further explosions. It was like our defences had just... given up. With powerful footsteps, they were coming closer – in moments they'd be on top of us.

Away. Needed to get away.

A woman, rushing past, shoved me aside in her hurry; still on my knees I stumbled backwards and fell beneath the surging crowd. Feet trampled painfully all over me, pushing air from my lungs, and for the finest second I was sure this was my undignified end. I wouldn't even get the glamour of death by alien! Then, from somewhere, a pair of hands took my shoulders and hoisted me back to my feet. I looked about wildly, still buffeted by the panicking crowd, but never saw whose they were. As I tried to see, through the gaps in the crowd I then saw the viaduct explode.

Each stone segment, one by one, warped and disintegrated as if grabbed and ripped away by an invisible hand. Rubble flew skywards and the support columns crumbled in turn. Stone crashed upon the town – I saw an ambulance crushed beneath a boulder, rooftops caved in, human beings squashed and maimed. Asteroids were raining on Hayle. Somehow, all I got struck by were a few pebbles – somebody near me took a piece of railway through the abdomen. Tanks, those we saw in the car park whose supermarket was but a vague shape within the grey dust billowing from where the viaduct once stood, at last remembered their responsibility and took up their part in the chorus. They fired heavily one after the other. Quayside clearing as the orchestra began, I stood rooted to the spot, alone now, and watched in dumb awe as shells exploded powerfully against the tripods. They didn't leave a scratch – more than one bounced off as harmlessly as an errant Frisbee – and in an instant I saw mankind's hopelessness.

Glittering in the sun, the menaces paused, the nearest perhaps weighing up their next move; then the Wickes erupted into a tower of flame which rose over the viaduct's dust and the commercial buildings around it. Those buildings, too, detonated soon after. The smoothbore cannons of the tanks fell silent as the car parks followed. Satisfied, the tripods continued their headlong advance upon Hayle in an irregular line, the nearest now wading into the river. With a flourish, the hot whips of the Death Rays swept invisibly across the town.

Heat burst everywhere, flashes of fire mixed with terrible screams, as one ray narrowly missed me but not those near me. They were replaced with light. Flames erupted over grass and

road and building all at once. The first explosion nearly threw me off my feet again but I rejected the physics trying to make that happen – to fall meant death and death was unacceptable. It's always better to be alive, probably, unless being dead is really cool, but nobody's let us know yet. So, too, did I refuse to run away because, the machines already close enough to tower over us, though I might be terrified and though more Death Rays were lancing the town all around me, I wasn't punting logic from my mind just yet. Running *away* was to go in the wrong direction – there was only one route of possible survival I could see and it was below the water.
"Not a lot of fucking options!" I yelled to myself, to the tripods, to the laughing universe, as the line of stone buildings behind me burst into fire. A blizzard of embers gushed painfully over the street. Flames licking my feet and breathing becoming tricky from the smoke, I sprinted down the quayside and toward the approaching Blight, whose metal tentacles were beginning to disgorge like ungodly sea creatures, then leaped from the edge. I thought of yelling "cowabunga!" and, out of respect for the dead, chose not to.

Falling towards the dark blue water, I had a second to see a crowded boat crushed beneath a Blight foot, and then I was under. Salt water invaded my mouth and nose, the massacre's din muffled, and a vague sort of peace reigned. That was until the splashes of others who had copied me sounded like thunderclaps. Slowly, willing myself to stay down here forever, I sank towards a murk of green seaweed, my chest rapidly feeling like it might explode, cursing my meagre lung capacity. Looking up I tried to tell with stinging eyes when the machines had passed overhead and so put their backs to me – but I couldn't tell. All I had to do was get behind them, I thought, then I'd be safe. They were busy with the rest of the world. They wouldn't turn for an anonymous bug like me.

My lungs were becoming incandescent. I'd read that drowning

was pleasant, once you got past the blind thrashing panic, but I wasn't keen to test that allegation. Accepting that, though I couldn't live for long up there I also couldn't live forever down here, I kicked with more reluctance than I can begin to explain and propelled myself back towards the murky surface. Please, I begged the universe, *please* let them have passed by.

Breaking the surface, I emerged gasping into a wall of heat. In the minute and a bit since I'd been gone it was as if night had suddenly fallen – a hurricane of ash and smoke blocked all but a few strands of sunlight. Fire, crackling in all directions, even upon the water, offered the brightest light. Those boats which had survived for this long motored all around me, still filled with people, going in either direction at speed and pushing aside bodies – some motionless – bobbing in the water or rapidly emptying as passengers jumped for the same safety I had assumed lay below. A Blight machine towered overhead scarcely a hundred yards away – as I stared at it, splashing to stay afloat, a tank flew through the air between me and it like a toy and vanished in the smoke.

"Oh," I almost whimpered, "I can't *believe* this is the best plan I could come up with!" Another member of the helpless armoured cavalry – one of the machines must have been flinging them about – came crashing into the darkened river. This threw up a huge wave of frothy mud which tumbled me around and capsized an escaping fishing smack.

In another moment a second machine was on the bank, feet sinking deep into slimy mud, and in a stride stepped across onto the quay. Now it straddled the river – had I thrown myself into the water but a few feet further upriver I would have been looking right up at its metal belly. With a stretch of its spindly legs, it raised to full height, surveying the mortally wounded town. As it appeared out of the smoke so came more shells from the other side of Hayle, or maybe more missiles from a distant aircraft, or maybe both. Three came, two narrowly missing altogether, but the third impacted with a great concussion, replacing my hearing with an obnoxious ringing. More followed. The Thing's body was replaced by terrific flashes of light. I screamed all the expletives I could think of, hearing none of them, and sank back below the water – I would have loved to stay there for the rest of time but Shakespearean words, "what pain it was to drown," haunted me and eventually, my chest on fire, forced me back up. Why couldn't I be born amphibious?!

Distantly through the smoke, as I bobbed in the nightmare, I saw blurry jets scream by, low in the sky and hugging the coast. One by one, they popped in mid-air like balloons. The end, now, was on my mind. A soldier's body drifted by me in the black water – when did it turn black? – missing everything below his waist, and from the radio tucked into a chest pocket I heard desperate yells.
*"This is the Hayle evacuation centre! We can't fit any more people! We're gonna have to leave some behind!"*

Realising its quarry's harmlessness, perhaps, the disinterested machine, now being ominously left alone by counter-fire, looked down and finally regarded those of us scrambling in the water. For a time it seemed curious, almost detached, before metal tentacles like spiny dreadlocks coiled downwards from its body and dived into the water. At its own leisure, the Thing retrieved struggling individuals and hoisted them screaming into the air. Sometimes it wouldn't bother grasping them but instead the tentacles shifted, on the fly, to become sharp lances which impaled people. Limp or convulsing, they would then be reeled in. It was entirely confident of its dominion – and, with the tendrils stabbing their way closer and closer, massacring all who had been stupid enough to jump into the river, so was I. Acceptance curdled in me – the cold realisation that I was at an end. This was the page I closed on. I only hoped Disco would be okay.

Then another shell burst across the tripod and exploded – and this time, somehow, so did it. Explosive force of many unsurvivable magnitudes ricocheted through its body, knives of red-hot shrapnel cutting clean through the Thing's unnatural armour, failing for no clear reason. The hood bulged, flashed, and burst open in tattered fragments of glittering metal. An arterial spray of scarlet liquid, maybe blood or maybe alien motor fuel, shot from the wound at an incredible pressure and doused half of burning Hayle. The river began shifting from black to red.

"Fuck my *mouth*!" I shouted, screamed, cheered. Answering shouts came from people in the water about me, from which I could have leaped with exultation, as a triumphant chorus sounded. Suddenly, for just a moment, it felt like we were going to win, after all. The maimed colossus reeled backwards like a drunken giant. By a miracle it recovered its balance, thick smoke and miscellaneous goo pouring from its injury, but after a moment's hesitation there came more shells. Each broke through the Blight machine's exposed innards and shattered its hull like a melon under a sledgehammer. The Thing whirled, hooted in anguished protest, then stumbled and finally collapsed with tremendous force into the water.

A terrific explosion shook the world – but it wasn't the machine which exploded. As its corpse hit the water, the river flashed brilliantly into steam, reacting to something extraordinary hot within the beast – what I suppose was the Death Ray's now-exposed generator – and it was all quite dramatic. Simultaneously, a bloody big wave triggered by the fall and composed of scaldingly hot muddy foam came sweeping over the lot of us – boats overturned and people struggling shorewards screamed and shouted faintly above the seething and the roar of the dying Blight machine, which slowly sank deeper into the River Hayle.

A fishing boat nearly collided with me as it was carried by

on the wave, while I splashed wildly to keep myself above the surface with the boiling torrent rushing painfully by. I came close enough to the riverbank that I could cling to an overhanging tree branch and pray the rushing water wouldn't take my clothes with it. It did take my backpack and, as I felt it slip from my shoulders, I realised that Disco's medicine was lost. This occupied my thoughts for far longer than it ought to have, given the circumstances.

Thick clouds of steam were still pouring from the alien wreckage, obscuring everything in a hot haze – but through the tumultuously whirling wisps I could see, intermittently and vaguely, gigantic dying limbs churning the water and spraying mud and froth into the air. Tentacles which moments earlier clung to human beings now swayed like living arms as if a wounded spider was struggling for its life. Gruesome jets of red fluid spurted noisily from the machine and into the sky, pouring down all around as rain, and I clenched my eyes nearly-shut in fear of some getting in and blinding me.

My attention was diverted from this death flurry by a furious yelling. I turned to see a man, knee-deep in the river's shallow edge, shouting to those of us still in the water.

"It's not over!" he yelled, waving like a conductor, "get back under! Get *back* under!" He pointed to the other Blights, two of which advanced with gigantic strides towards the riverbank, honing in on their wrecked compatriot. Hopeful potshots struck both, all unavailingly, but the Things were uninterested in everything except reaching their fallen friend. Staying alive somehow a possibility again, I abandoned my acceptance of death and ducked once more beneath the hot water. Breath held until my chest was agonising, I swam painfully downriver, away from the fallen beast and with bodies all around, under the surface for as long as I could be. The water was a bubbly tumult and rapidly growing hotter. I felt like I was being put on a simmer.

When I raised my head to take breath and threw hair and water from my eyes, the steam was a whirling white fog hiding the two Blights, turning black as it mixed with sulphuric smoke. I could barely see past my own nose as I choked on it. Whether above or below water, it felt like I would drown on something. Glowing embers were like firefly swarms. Only the painful noise of hooting and destruction told me They were still there. Somewhere. Then, dimly, I saw them; colossal grey figures magnified by the mist, stooping over their comrade's limp ruin, concerned and careful. A third and fourth machine flanked further afield and, as the mist to my right turned a faint orange, I sensed the whole town was now a firestorm. A deafening and confusing conflict of noises joined the mist to dominate the air – the Blight's clangorous din, the crash of falling houses, the hiss of trees, fences, boats flashing into flame, the crackle and roar of fire. Then I saw the church, steeple silhouette forcing its way through the mist, still standing and awaiting its fate, shadowy and faint in the steam. Fire reached up on all sides like desperate hands. From within, before I started paddling to the bank until my feet at last touched soft ground, I thought I heard singing.

My thrashing feet found something solid and for a moment I stood, up to my chest in near-scalding water, dumbfounded at what I was meant to do. Limp bodies were all around, like rotten lilypads, many indescribably lacerated or barbecued. Those who had survived this long were scrambling from the water and squelching through reeds and mud like little mice. Some ran right between the tripods' legs and went ignored. I couldn't hear gunfire anymore.

Then the Death Ray's white flashes swept across the river's surface towards me and the water in its track exploded into gushes of boiling steam. The Death Ray came no closer but the steam, drifting my way, did. I turned shorewards and struggled to wade out, thinking I might outrun it, but in another moment the huge wave of boiling steam barrelled over me. It hurt. I screamed pitifully, begging it to stop, but it didn't. Scalded, half-blinded, I staggered in awful pain through the hissing water onto the shore. Stumbling on something uncooperative, I fell into the riverbank, my hands sinking into mud all the way to my elbows. Crying seemed pretty appealing until a Blight's foot, with a great squelch, came down right in front of me. Few things silence you quicker. Had I not happened to stumble, I realised, I would have been under it. I watched the foot rise again and vanish and stared into the misty oblivion which took its place for quite some time until, slowly, I crawled again through the mud. Smeared all over, considering rolling about in the muck in some feeble effort at disguise, I kept going until I was out of the water altogether and crawling up a bank. I felt like a tetrapod. Breathing heavily, I finally fell onto my belly. There I lay, stripped of my upper clothes by the raging waters and my skin prickly from the heat, expecting nothing but death; it was like being fourteen again. But, slowly, keeping as low as I could, I returned to crawling up the bank until it levelled out and I found myself a hole dug by another Blight foot. A tank lay upside down beside it. Slipping into the hole, I sat against its wall trying to find my breath and then, if possible, catch it. Every intake of air hurt. I wiped my face and my hand came away bright red; soaked in whatever had gushed from the dead monster. Frantically, I tried to wipe away the rest until my face burned.

Slowly, as the world around me became real again, I realised I no longer sensed the machines presence, nor heard any nearby chaos. The sounds of disaster were growing more distant. Carefully, with scalded hands, I pushed myself to sit up and clamber up the hole to peer over the rim back towards Hayle. Clear then faint then clear again through the smoke's veil, I saw the tripods – they were growing smaller as they stomped deeper into burning Hayle. They had left me lying in the mud. Between them and me, a butterfly, perhaps the same one as before, perhaps not, danced and landed on a daisy. More machines, fresh from torching Godrevy, were advancing from the north, tearing into the town like a pack of dogs. And then, very slowly, I realised they had passed me by – and I had escaped.

# XIII.

With Hayle's incineration, along with a couple thousand young servicemen and straggling escapees, fire and smoke visible from many miles away, the worldwide presumption was that this marked the start of the Blight's great conquering advance upcountry. But it was not, yet, so – they were in no hurry. A profound reckoning, meanwhile, befell the government. The exodus' bungling, some said, was not just catastrophe but farce. How could it all go so wrong? The Defence Secretary resigned in disgrace, to be named Chancellor of the Duchy of Lancaster about two hours later, while a hangdog Prime Minister looked for where to place blame after having approved a fatally muddled evacuation located in a town so obviously pinned between Blight positions. Downing Street's special advisors eventually settled on the coach companies chartered to ferry out evacuees. These failed to supply the promised buses quickly enough, stranding thousands, not to mention slowed the evacuation by clogging up the roads with all the buses we'd just been told they hadn't supplied. These two allegations could, apparently, exist in harmony. There were plenty of loyal MPs who, dangled the prospect of promotion, would loudly agree. No amount of scrutiny would alter their commitment to what the whips told them to say.

The rout having taken place in full view of television cameras, some correspondents succumbing to the onslaught live on air, there was no hiding the reality that our weaponry couldn't scratch a Blight war machine. Stocks in armaments manufacturers, naturally, now plummeted where before they had risen, as did almost everything else besides gold. But there was some emanation of hope to cling to – for one machine had, somehow, come down. This was the one I had seen collapse into the river. There was, however, no clue how that happened. Nothing special characterised the tank shell which struck it. Many others had struck many other machines in just the same place. It made no sense to anybody that Hammerdown's explosive epic would fail and yet one anonymous little shell would not. Forensic examination of the plentiful footage depicting this denouement would yield, it was hoped and prayed, the answer to how the feat might be repeated. It would need to be repeated a lot. Of course the Blight, whose machines had seemed outraged at the loss, were surely doing their own post-match analysis – with the goal of it never happening again.

Parliament met that night, standing room only, and some members spoke as if they finally had their chance to play Churchill. Others scolded them, attacking the war fever, insisting this ought to be treated as "a public health crisis with a military solution." The Blight were no ordinary armed foe – they were more animal than man. Treat them as we would a swarm of sharks or locusts.

Sorrowfully, the House invoked the Civil Contingencies Act, and now Her Majesty's Government wielded all the executive power necessary to empty Cornwall of people and destroy the enemy. Quite how this latter task would be accomplished was a little bit hazy. Jeering voices reminded all of yesterday's promises regarding the so-called "ring of steel." Eyes turned skyward to Oumuamua, still dangling above us in that mocking way, a twinkle in the night. Maybe it was a control centre – without it, maybe every Blight machines would topple over without a word. It had happened in films, after all. Perhaps that was why the machine in Hayle had fallen – its mysterious defences, a skintight forcefield or some other dumb bullshit, remotely maintained by that watchful rock, only to crumble at the first connectivity issue. All that lay beneath was delicate metal skin.

Even if this were not the case, it was probable then that Oumuamua existed to guide capsules onto the Earth. Were it destroyed, no more could land and the invasion would at least be isolated to this tip of a peninsula. Plans hatched to blow it up – but launching any kind of strike against such a distant target would take months, maybe years, to assemble, cost billions, push other projects aside. It would consume the scientific world's attention. All that to repel an invasion which, so far, touched a tiny sliver of the Earth – and a part whose best economic days were distant history. The days when the world was so hungry for tin that Cornwall was to the Phoenicians what Arabia is to us had been gone for a while. Was it really worth it? In the absence of any stars falling beyond one fraction of one seasonally backwater English county it was tricky to convince the world that they, too, were in danger. For all not directly touched, this was a safely distant spectacle. Even people vox-popped in the Midlands hesitated to spend *too* much money putting things right. "Why can't they just move out?" one asked of Cornwall's hapless residents.

Issues arose, also, when considering that only powerful nuclear devices could likely dent the great rock of Oumuamua. These bombs, of course, had to be launched from somewhere. Were lift-off to fail, the consequences would be unpleasant – and the White House appeared quite unwilling to irradiate southern Florida beyond habitability for the sake West Cornwall. France, with its own South American spaceport, wouldn't even risk Guyana – I don't need to tell you how the tabloids took that. "Wait and see," the government realised with a mounting fury, was becoming the international community's great slogan; as if it had not recently been their own, too.

Help was, sort of, coming. I'd already seen French and American soldiers in Hayle and more waited just beyond the horizon. Belgian units were readied, loaded onto planes, then stayed home for fear of abandoning their motherland to an eventual Blight landing. The American Congress debated, at the insistence of one jumped-up senator, reactivating mothballed battleships to safely pummel tripods from afar. The Countryside Alliance warned all forces in Cornwall against endangering pristine ancient hedgerows. An urgent question was raised in the Commons concerning whether the Treasury would commit to taking the opportunity which destruction afforded to "start over and reinvigorate" the Cornish economy. In the meantime, a growing American force – answering to our General Humphreys who they routinely shut out of meetings – was unloading at Falmouth, Plymouth, Bournemouth, and lots of other mouths, eager to fight honest-to-God aliens, the Pentagon brimming with excitement at the thought. Rapid-deployment Marines rapidly deployed to get themselves bogged down in uncooperative moorland and wedged in narrow country roads. That the Second Battle for Britain, as the Daily Express demanded we call it, might be fought by Americans was humiliating to some – mainly those who didn't need the help.

But where, people asked as the Marines rumbled by, were all the tanks? Humvees and light armoured vehicles abounded but real power, of the type which conspicuously failed very recently in Hayle, was lacking. This was outrageous. Expecting vast armoured divisions the public, sudden experts in the minutia of mechanised warfare, were unnerved by their defenders prioritising speed over firepower. But after Hayle and Hammerdown's abject failure, what alternative was there? Delaying actions to slow the Blight's advance until the evacuation was complete, said those in charge, were now the strategy, for there was no conventional alternative. No *conventional* alternative. Everybody knew what that meant. Invocations of nuclear force began to bounce about the commentariat – no minister dared comment. It was rumoured, and never answered, that American bombers now landing in Bristol were loaded with enough atomic power to transform the whole Westcountry into glass.

While the authorities, now fully alive to their antagonists' tremendous power, worked with flurries of disconnected energy to establish a new defensive headquarters at Redruth's Blowinghouse Industrial Estate – abandoning, to much outcry, Camborne, for Redruth's superior transport links in the direction away from the Blight – so too did the enemy busy themselves. Everything west of Newlyn and the Towednack moors was cut off from the rest of the country. It was theirs, now. Helicopters both foreign and domestic – mostly foreign – shepherded the lucky among the trapped to the multinational fleet taking shape on the horizon's lip. Boats drove up beaches on all sides, crammed themselves with escapees who had learned of their coming online, and took off again. Cornwall emptied in every direction. Everything from Land's End in the west to Gwithian and Eastern Shag Rock in the east was property of the Blight. Everyone left inside either hid or died. More stars fell, all dropping into these three hundred occupied square kilometres, supplementing their forces with ever more tripods. Capsule followed capsule on interstellar flight; every few hours brought reinforcements which plunged into upturned fields, and the more that landed in Cornwall, the more the relaxing world mused this might only be Cornwall's problem. But developments came thick and fast. Slowly, and surely, a growing pillar of dense green smoke began rising from the Blight realm. Something else had fallen to Earth today. What were they up to in there?

Aerial reconnaissance couldn't hope to make it into Blight airspace without being slapped out of it, but low-orbit satellite imaging yielded some clues. The answer was soon pieced together – they were building. Royal Marine scouts, crawling their way through blackened Blight territory, concluded the same as they watched, perplexed, metal giants moving busily to and fro. Something quite dreadful, all were convinced, was being constructed on the moorland, hidden in that grim smoke – God only knew what. Now, surely, begged the Prime Minister's chief advisor, was the time to rain megatons upon the county lest Hell come marching out of it. The Prime Minister, indecisive, couldn't help but fumble – all he could do, eager nonetheless to play at soothing war leader, was wryly tell the nation he had "a cunning plan" to defeat the invaders. It wasn't, much but not all of the public felt, the time for that vibe. "He's doing his best," said one woman with a shrug. That was enough, apparently.

I, of course, was lying in a hole on the Hayle riverbank. I had no knowledge of anything beyond the mist, let alone the debates playing out around wooden desks and on radio call-ins, and I probably wouldn't have cared if you'd told me. With all the smoke, I barely knew the state of my own hands in front of my face. For all I was aware the tripods had marched on, far past Hayle, in unstoppable conquest. This was good news, in a way, for I was momentarily safe. But I was also then trapped, perhaps forever, behind enemy lines. Maybe a Blight tentacle would pluck me for mincing or probing as their fancy might take them – I couldn't have that. All I knew was that I had to choose a direction to walk. Lying on a muddy riverbank with my tits out in a vast cloud of smoke and steam, while a great pitch for a festival, would do me no good in wartime. With infinite pains and labour I climbed to my feet and plodded downriver, through burning vegetation and the choking smoke of burning Hayle, wheezing at every step. My goals, now, were just to get to a place where I could breathe.

Everything else would have to follow.

After a while, once the nightmarish daze of events had faded and my mind seemed a touch clearer, I remembered my toplessness and the modesty that civilisation insists on returned to me. Finding a corpse lying on the grass, his legs missing beneath the knees, white eyes rolled up into his head, I wrestled for his corduroy. Once I had it on, sticking to me with the wetness of what I hoped was the river, I went back to tramping through the muck and hot smoke. There was no sign of the tripods – neither sound nor sight.

Soon, the river yawned open into an estuary, mud turning to beaches with rolling dunes and porcupine grass on either side, and I sat there for a while, beside a half-finished sandcastle and a Coast Guard phone booth. Everything more than a few feet from me was obscured on all sides. Then, through a gap in the smoke, I saw an empty fishing boat drifting sideways into the open sea, very small with its wooden hull singed black, but still the painted-on name 'Wet Lady II' was visible. Bubblegum-coloured buoys dangled like Christmas tree decorations from over the deck and its sail-less mast stood like a pylon. Without pause or even thought I ran to the estuary, waded in, and swam, hoping to intercept it. This was far preferable than walking across open ground – anything was. It didn't even matter that I couldn't actually remember if I knew how to swim or not. It was a wonder I'd lasted this long in Cornwall.

Swimming furiously and not seeming to drown, I just caught the boat, grabbing one of the buoys and being dragged slowly along as it went with the current. Hands burning as they grasped the buoy's fibrous rope, I hauled myself aboard. I'd never done a pull-up before and felt rather proud of myself as I fell into the wooden deck. There I lay in the footwell, staring up at the smoke which beams of sunlight tried to penetrate, wondering if my brain would ever recover from the last couple of days. Slowly, having reached the sea, the boat rocked in the splashing tide and I felt the smoke clear as I drifted from the destruction and, very slowly, into the bay.

The boat had no oars – its outboard motor may have worked but I feared making a squeak of noise. With no other choice, I nested in the footwell with a sodden cigarette packet and crusty seagull droppings for company as we went, very tediously, out to sea. Despite risking a tripod spotting me, I peeked back at the town, which you'd need to be quite the prick to have a go at me for. It proved pointless, anyway – the smoke formerly known as Hayle, and the steam burst up from the river, had the whole bay in its grasp – with the golden Porth Kidney Sands on one side and Hayle Towans on the other I could see nothing but the nearest slithers of dune and beach. Perhaps something moved beyond, perhaps even people, sneaking about and watching me jealously, but I couldn't see them.

All sound, besides the rocking boat and the gentle waves lapping against the hull, was gone and, realising this, so too did I recognise that I was all alone on the water. That sense of isolation struck me across the head very suddenly – a realisation that no other little boats joined me, not one brave hero returning Hayle-ward as they had been doing all day, and a rippling dread filled my stomach. Through the smoke there emerged an orange lifeboat which lay on its side and overcome with flames. Bubbles gurgled around it. The deeper into the bay I drifted, the more the steam began to fade until, with desolate horror, I realised that St Ives Bay was a graveyard. The hanging steam was not the result of the Death Ray swept over the river at all, nor of the fallen machine, but of Death Rays slashed across the bay itself. The little boats which had marshalled such a courageous evacuation were strewn about either ablaze or shattered into floating archipelagos of debris, so thick that I could have walked across the water on them. Death Rays had burned them all from the Earth. Billowing on the pancake-flat surface in places were little islands of fire. Now the steam was really clearing and, further to sea, I saw what I now know was the Panama-flagged *Lightning Girl*, a bulk carrier which had spent its past fourteen years hauling aggregate materials from the Gulf of Mexico to Rotterdam and back again, and whose crew unanimously voted to answer the call and come to our aid. Now she lay on her side – black smoke gushed from a vast wound in her superstructure – sinking rapidly, her stern dipping lower with each passing minute. And all around, pushed aside by the Wet Lady II as it ventured into the carnage, were the dead.

Gulls perched everywhere, already feeding, and maybe, at one moment, a basking shark's dark silhouette passed obliviously under me, but I couldn't be sure. Bodies, of all ages and apparently endless in supply, bobbed motionless in the cold and bubbling silver surf. I checked several which came near for signs of life. None had any – just stared at me with glassy eyes. I looked for Harry and didn't see him – I didn't want to see him – and thought of how I would've been another in this crowd too, if there had only been one more space available, and for a moment wished I was.

"Hello?" I called over the silence. A gull, pecking at a corpse's head, glanced at me. "Isn't there anyone out there? Isn't there..." I saw a mass of flesh where several people had been melted and fused together by the Death Ray, so now they resembled a ball of burnt barbecue from which poked hands and feet, the kind of thing I would never think possible until I saw it. "...anyone?" My muscles failed me and I fell powerlessly back into the footwell, white dots on my eyes, the universe vanishing from sight.

After a while of drifting both across the bay and in and out of reality, I looked over the deck's edge again. The smoke and steam was thinner, now. Towards blackened Gwithian, a clanking tripod made it way along the Towans, kicking through campsites and dunes towards its brethren which had torn Hayle from the face of the Earth. I was sure it was the one which seared these rescuers away without a care towards their innocence. Yet I felt no hatred towards it – not to its ugly pilot. Mercy, pity, decency, all were clearly so far beyond its comprehension that it'd be like blaming a dog for stealing your food. For a moment the Thing paused and looked out over the bay, admiring its handiwork perhaps, and I thought it looked right at me, like it knew me, before it turned away again. My self-importance still insisted on being perceived in this cold world where I didn't matter.

For a long time I drifted, my whole body painful and weary after the violent escape, my ears ringing faintly, coughing fit after coughing fit retching its dry way up from all the smoke inhalation. Then, the hooting of distant machines carrying over the bay, my fears got the better of me. I finally accepted that I couldn't bob aimlessly among the dead forever. So I crawled along the deck and tried to operate the boat's motor. I guessed that a thin cable dangling from the plastic covering must have some relevance – my mechanics apprenticeship serving me well – but several tugs did nothing. I was about to give up and cry instead but, with one last heave, it spluttered to life, like in a film or a bad book. I almost cheered but thought the body floating near to me would find it inconsiderate. With care not to disturb the swimming dead, I loudly navigated with all the skill of a clueless novice over the increasingly tumultuous waves and around Godrevy Island and its chalk-piece lighthouse, past the headland altogether, eyes fixed on the charred headland and praying no tripod would appear and see me. I was taking this boat as far east as it could possibly go. Safety, suddenly, was in my grasp.

The furthest the boat could go, it transpired, was not far at all. After rounding Godrevy, Hayle and St Ives vanishing behind the yawning bite-wound cliffs of Hell's Mouth, the engine sputtered again and, despite many furious tugs of the cable until it snapped off, died just past the heathland of The Knavocks. With the last of its momentum, I guided the boat beachwards and into a tiny cove, superbly hidden from prying eyes. It was only a two hour walk from Hayle. All that swimming and traumatising imagery for nothing. Getting the boat hadn't saved my life – just a couple of hours.

The Wet Lady, a name I would have changed had I found safe harbour and been allowed to keep the boat, failed to reach the sand and began pulling back with the tide at the water's edge, so I jumped down – soaking myself once more – and waded onto coarse, damp sand. Deadly sick, I crumpled and lay besides an abandoned sand castle, again, its edges smoothed by the shallow waves until it looked like a video game graphic which hadn't loaded properly. On the cove's opposite end a fat grey seal with huge black eyes watched me with some concern. Tall cliffs cradled the beach, nesting seabirds in every crag, and, for a time, I thought myself trapped here until I spotted a worn path winding its way up to the heather. The time, by then, was about four or five – though my phone, like my dead watch, was a casualty of Hayle, so I had no way of knowing for sure.

Grunting and gasping my way up the path, my clothes wet and sticky, I found myself on a silent and empty road between silent and empty fields. Westwards, the landscape was a black carpet smouldering all the way to Hayle, a town entombed in smoke which blocked all view beyond. If it hadn't been there, I would have seen the green smoke further afield, though I doubt I'd have known what to do with the sight. Just like everyone else. I neither saw nor heard any roaming machines. Loneliness, sweet and worth savouring in these times, reigned.

After pillaging a holiday home – blue graffiti scrawled across the garden wall read "commit to net zero now you cunts" – of food and fresh clothes that magically fit me but finding no water, its taps eerily unresponsive in that "civilisation is collapsing, didn't you know?" sort of way, I walked down the two-lane road towards Tehidy Woods' distant green mass, where a childhood memory of being bitten by a swan resided. There was my water source. Maybe I'd find the swan, too. Get my revenge. Or go from enemies to lovers – anything was possible.

By hugging the coastline's very edge, sure I could scramble down a nook in the clifftop if a tripod came sniffing, I wasn't seeing any fellow refugees. Still not used to that word. If anyone else survived Hayle they must be taking more central and more developed and *much* more sensible routes east. Thirst was starting to get on my nerves, Tehidy Woods didn't seem to be coming any closer, and I was bitterly regretful that through the day I had drunk so little water and so much whiskey. In my parched state I even, for what we'll call intangible reasons, felt angry with Disco; I can't account for getting shirty with a cat who wasn't there to defend himself, however he'd do that (meowing, probably), but my impotent if aborted desire to find him – though, if he was alive, he was far better off without me right now – worried me enormously. At some point, I already knew, I would end up turning around. I had to find a way back to Penzance, aliens or no aliens, just in case. He might still be there. I wanted my cat.

Some time into my hike I must have sat down and fallen asleep – not that I remember it. I woke at a bus stop which was half-buried in a blackberry bush and, with one look to my left, I saw a strange, thin man sat on the sloped plastic seat beside me, close enough to smell the sweat. He was framed by a laminated advert on the bus stop's side for NHS jobs. His red polo shirt was smudged with soot, his face boyish and clean-shaven, brown hair neatly trimmed in a vaguely fascist way, and he stared at a faint flickering which danced over the sky. Rows and rows of faint down-plumes of cloud, tinted with the midsummer sunset, spread beyond it.

"Can I help you?" I asked warily, stretching my neck, which was strained from all the lolling.

"That depends on what I want, really, doesn't it?" he replied, not taking his eyes from the sky, and I noted the dark rucksack lying at his feet.

"Got any water?" I asked abruptly. He shook his head – hair lifted from his ear, revealing a silvery stud.

"Only literature. I think there's a river in that direction," he said, pointing across the fields facing us. "But I don't fancy going that way. Goodness knows what lurks."

"I can't disagree with you," I replied.

Turing to me with interest, he suddenly asked: "Are you saved? Have you found Jesus?" I grinned at his joke. He didn't smile back – my grin fell away.

"Are you fucking kidding?" He sighed.

"Some attitudes never soften." He looked back to the clouds. "You'd think today would be enough to change some minds."

"Of all the people I could meet…" I muttered, looking away from him and to the blackberry bush, its leaves brushing the bus shelter, hoping to find elusive ripe fruits among the hard nettles. The days of the hunter-gatherer had returned.

"Sorry to disappoint you," he said, looking both ways down the road, as if waiting for the bus. I wondered if I needed to tell him the services weren't running.

"Don't be. I shouldn't even be here."

"You-"

"Don't." I put a hand up to silence him. The other deposited a handful of sour berries in my mouth and I tried not to wince at their tartness.

"What?"

"Don't say what you're about to say," I said with my mouth full. "That we're all supposed to be here, that God's got a plan for us, just don't do it, mate, seriously. Not in the mood – at all." Blackberry seeds were stuck in my mouth's every cavity. He didn't say anything for a time, until…

"You look tired."

"It's been a long day." He didn't reply – he'd gone back to watching the sky, perhaps searching for God, and I took him in. He probably thought me a strange figure, too; my face blackened by smoke to the point of looking like a racist performance, clothes still dripping wet, ill-fitting corduroy that I definitely wasn't going to tell anyone I stole off a corpse. "And I'm gonna catch a cold." He nodded slowly, then spoke, vacant eyes still locked on the sky.

"I did *everything* right," he said quietly, looking hurt, a toddler betrayed. "Everything God asked me to do, I did it, and in return..."

"Please direct your concerns to the Book of Job," I said dryly. "I think they cover this issue there. Blackberry?" He stared at the offering for a moment then, with a weak smile, took it.

"Thank you."

"Don't mention it." Silence reigned for a moment then, feeling guilty for my snark, I kept us going.

"Were you in Hayle?"

"Connor Downs," he answered, then continued, obviously bursting at the seams to tell me. "We've been touring the South West, preaching, then everything went arse-shaped, and, well, you know the rest, I'm sure." He gestured to me and my general state.

"Yeah."

"I told everyone we weren't going anywhere. Stay put and we could do some real good. Never mind the God talk. People need food not Bibles; it's best to help folk when they're still alive, not once they're dead, you know what I mean?"

"I do," I said, wondering if I'd judged him too quickly – apparently that's God's prerogative, anyway, so maybe I should leave it to Her.

"Some of them went to Hayle, trying to help, in their own way – or going out into the fields to find anyone who got lost. We didn't know how badly they might be hurt and the police were no help. Nobody was any help. There was this girl, Anna, she'd just joined us, never seen anyone so eager to do good. She went on her own then the rest followed. Just trying to help. Never did anything wrong. Then I saw the smoke... oh, God, the smoke..." I stared at him and offered no answer. "Anna... April... Michael... Laura... all gone. Just kids. My fault. And now I'm looking at the sky and I'm hoping for answers and for the first time I know I won't get any."

"It's not your fault," I said feebly.

"You're just a thug," he softly told the clouds, though at first I thought he was talking to me and was ready to get incredibly defensive incredibly quickly. "I see it now. I wish I'd seen it sooner so I hadn't wasted my time." Silence, again, fell, and I scrambled to find something to say.

"Are we far from Camborne?" I asked, eventually. I couldn't think of anything else to ask; Camborne wasn't even of any specific interest to me. I felt exceptionally useless.

"We're certainly far from God," he spat.

"I get that it's hard to have your faith challenged and all," I said, "but... you know." Great. Wow – I was really helping.

He sighed: "You can't conceive, nor can I, the appalling strangeness of the mercy of God."

"That's Graham Greene, right?" I asked. He looked at me with surprise.

"Not bad," he said. "We'll ordain you, yet."

"Well, you're progressive then, I'll give you that."

"We're humanists," he replied. "We broke from our old church when they wouldn't disavow this crusty old bishop who said transgender people aren't put together right. We marched against Section 28, for climate justice, for Black Lives Matter, for every little piece of good we could find. 'Just do good' is written in big letters next to our altar. Our church has always believed in the total and undeniable value of every human being. Somebody has to." He looked, again, with growing rage towards the sky. "What are these creatures that he's sent?"

"What are *we*?" I asked, clearing my throat, thinking myself poetic.

"Let's not start with the 'humans are the real monsters' rubbish," he replied. "That's tired." Yet again, silence. It was becoming annoying.

"So..." I clicked my tongue. "Are we far from Camborne, or not?" Rather than reply he suddenly stood and marched across the road and into the neighbouring field. Not wishing to be alone now I had a taste of company, I hurried after him, God talk or no God talk, no matter how dangerous open spaces were these days. "Wait," I insisted. "Don't go being a twat!" But he was in his own place now.

"Is this what a loving God does?" he roared to the sky, beating his chest, voice cracking, while I stood aside and watched with pity. He didn't seem like someone used to shouting. "I was your servant on Earth – I spread your word and did your work. To hell with your punishments! To hell with *you*!" He took a few moments to regain his breath, though his composure didn't come with it, before he turned to me again, face flushed. "What now? These creatures are everywhere. The Earth belongs to them now."

"Maybe not," I said. "I guess we just keep walking until we find something. Maybe Camborne, I don't know, but it's a start." He rolled his watery eyes.

"There's no such thing as Camborne! Nor Truro, nor Devon, nor planet Earth!" Staring at me, his breaths grew heavy, as if the black smoke was invisibly rolling over us. "Don't you see it's all gone?"

"That's not true," I insisted; my own defeatism washed away at the sight of it mirrored, as I realised I didn't want to be that kind of person at this kind of time. Even if I didn't believe it I would tell him everything would be okay – that's what a good person would do.

"Yes it is, look around you!"

"There's always hope."

"Bollocks to your hope," he scoffed, then, seemingly liberated by his foul mouth, he continued. "Hope can eat my ass!"

"We killed one of them," I pointed out. "I'm sure we can kill the rest."

"Killed?!" he cried in wide-eyed disbelief. "Men can't kill the ministers of God!"

"Maybe it was a woman on the gun," I replied, tongue buried in my cheek. "I saw it happen – I was as close as you can get and I watched the wanker blown to kingdom come. Trust me – it's a handful of them versus seven billion of us."

"There's gotta be more coming"

"Then it'll be two handfuls of them versus seven billion of us!" I shouted, quickly hushing – we were still in an open field. "We'll just keep killing them! Ever watched the news? We've gotten pretty good at it." Interrupted by a distant rumble – artillery, maybe, or warheads launched from far beyond, falling on unseen targets beyond the smoke, still believing one might get lucky again – we looked as incandescent flashes rippled through the column of smoke once called Hayle.

"What's that?" asked the preacher.

"That's us. Thank your God for the military-industrial complex." He laughed. "Look – we're probably right in the middle of alien territory right now. We can hide for the night but I'd rather keep walking and find more people. Maybe there's still defences left we can get behind, I don't know, but it's better than a field or the scraggly woods."

"Well, nothing good ever happens in the scraggly woods. How far do you reckon they've pushed?" the preacher asked, not questioning that we were now, by the forces of desperation, companions. "Assuming they don't have everything already."

"Goodness knows," I replied, omitting 'God' for 'goodness' out of some sort of respect, "but they're definitely here and they might not be that way, so let's go that way."

"Alright," said the preacher with a deep breath. A maybeetle droned over the hedge and past us. High in the west, over the smoke, hung the faint and pale crescent moon. "Alright, no harm in trying, I guess. What's your name, by the way? I'm George. George Chertsey." I told him my name – I feel no great need to tell you, though.

# XIV

While George bleated at clouds, the Blight were preparing their offensive.

Unseen preparations beneath green smoke may have unnerved the world – but they gave George and I time to join the fugitives streaming over Redruth where, at long last, salvation seemed possible. Out of nowhere, passing hasty new defence lines and chaotic triage centres at petrol stations and supermarket car parks, seeing so many walking wounded stagger zombie-like with us from the Red Zone and slowed down by George constantly trying to help them, we came to realise we were never in Blight territory at all. They hadn't yet advanced. Once more they dawdled. Consequently, I was now safer than I'd been at any other point during the emergency; for the first time I stood in undisputed human territory. That knowledge was, to put it mildly, heartening. This was also when I first learned about the mystery of the green smoke – not that the news bothered me at the time. I was just glad to be away.

At a makeshift coach depot we managed to secure two seats while the worried looking driver debated with a police sergeant whether this was included in his contract. Anxiety tormented me that we may have stolen spaces meant for evacuating children. But, suddenly, reclining with USB ports in our armrests, we were rescued. Safe. Just like that. A paragraph and a bit was all it took. A volunteer just out of school confidently said we'd disembark at Saltash – then we'd learn where we'd be accommodated. Thousands had signed up to host a Cornish refugee – though most of us weren't Cornish. People up and down the land were throwing open their doors, preparing beds, pushing dinner tables together, for the helpless individuals streaming from an ever-enlarging Red Zone. A lot of people found the generosity of spirit quite emotional. Cynicism, of course, tempered my reaction. Had the good folk of Cornwall been speaking Sudanese Arabic or Tigrinya, I thought, things might be a touch different. I must be a very weary person to hang out with.

About eight o'clock, our defences, still digging fighting holes and draping what camouflage netting was delivered in time over vehicles, reported three tripods strolling from the green smoke. Advancing slowly, even cautiously, they were guessed to be probing. What did we have in store for them, they might have been wondering? They made their way through the Leedstown farmland towards the great (by Cornish standards) conurbations of Camborne and Redruth, just as George and myself were pulling away down the A30, putting ever greater space between us and them. Then they came in sight of the nearest Anglo-American company deployed to delay them – entrenched infantry and the twenty-five millimetre autocannons of infantry fighting vehicles took aim. The Blight advanced on them in a sweeping line each spaced a mile and a third apart. Sirenlike howls reverberated over the craggy landscape, running up and down the scale from one note to another, noises so painfully weird that even seasoned veterans plugged their ears in hatred of it.

New tactics, given the war machines' obvious technical supremacy, kicked into action as they moved on empty Camborne. Asymmetric warfare – out-thinking, not outfighting – was now the name of the game. Tregonning

Hill, once said to be the abode of giants, lay to the south – now it hosted a Royal Marines commando unit. They fired an ineffectual volley of rockets at the nearest machine as it passed obliviously by. These rockets being useless, as expected, the Marines then bolted down the hill and into a prepared trench hidden under a blanket of ferns. The goal had been to distract the Blight, perhaps even divert them altogether, for they seemed to pursue whatever attacked them, buying crucial additional minutes for the exodus just ahead, the exodus of which I was part. It worked – the targeted tripod turned its head and stomped south through Godolphin Cross. Death Ray silent, it serenely approached the ancient hillfort, unwittingly stepping over the hiding Marines, and made several circuits in search of its antagonists. A comical game then played out as the soldiers ran round and round the hill, just ahead of the tripod, just avoiding its direct eyeline. Maybe sensing a game was afoot the frustrated beast, apparently not happy to be deceived, then obliterated Tregonning Hill – it turned volcanic in an instant. Tregonning Hill was reduced to a smouldering hole – an inflamed pimple on the face of the Earth. The Marines, rather more important than a hill, were fine, if a bit warm.

This, of course, was just a sideshow.

Alerts ringing through all strata of the military command network that the enemy offensive was here, the resistance plan – Operation Pendrake – began. Anything sent to meet the enemy would be lost, as was known, and no military commander was eager to look cameras in the eye and say they sent men on suicide missions knowing there'd be no reward. The forces deployed to Cornwall, it therefore transpired, were never meant to face the Blight at all. Once the tripods came within a certain distance, a professional withdrawal would immediately begin, shooting as they went, moving north and south if they could, seeking to distract and harry and confuse the tripods. In doing so, their advance, hopefully, would slow. "There is an art," General Humphreys explained, "to retreat."

From a safe distance, aircraft bombed them constantly, and not once was a machine seen to stumble, let alone fall, as one had in Hayle. The miracle refused to happen twice. Clearly, the fighting retreat was the only wise option available. Only in one place did the line hold – at Helston the Royal Lancers stood firm, nothing more than bait to draw the tripods momentarily south, knowing they hadn't a prayer but staying in the knowledge that they might save a few more like me and George on the A30. Tracer rounds battered the tripods like fiery arrows until Death Rays turned them, and Helston, to ash.

All civilians not yet safely behind the lines were, for lack of a better word, ditched. Make your own way east, proclaimed posters hastily stapled to telegraph poles and fences by departing troops, only hours earlier welcomed as protectors. A few stayed – specialists, SAS or American operatives mostly, who quietly stalked the tripods and with laser pointers guided munitions fired from beyond visual range to their pinhead targets. Some remained for the sake of it – they just didn't want to run away from such a grand spectacle.

Within what might have been minutes, the first machines approached Camborne.

The lead machine stepped over old mining cottages with bombs flashing all around, shattering Tresvithian sixth form college as the tripod stalked through the recreation ground, before the missiles seemed to give up and try their luck on the second tripod behind him. For a time, as ever, nothing came of it. Agitated sighs all round. Then something happened: after a brief and perfectly ordinary bombardment this machine was seen to advance a few paces, then abruptly stagger and limply collapse to the ground. Euphoric cheers erupted in command centres and front rooms, footage of the fall reloaded and replayed in a frantic haste to identify what weak point must have been hit, rooms filling with the clap of high-fives. That was the Americans in the room. All the while, the overthrown Blight struggled pitifully, belly on the ground, legs like a dying cranefly. It set out a prolonged ululation, a near-animalistic wail; the third glittering giant, catching up, answered, crushing a pumpkin patch in its haste. The first machine just turned and watched with fire at its feet.

Dismay soon descended: the flailing machine hadn't been felled it at all. As the smoke cleared so was the truth revealed – it remained uninjured. A leg of the tripod, by pure luck, had fallen into one of the many long-abandoned tin mine shafts which pock-mark the Cornish landscape. The same ones which Harry had hoped to hide in. Now, it was stuck. Volleys of Hellfire missiles from Apache gunships struck the stricken monster but succeeded only in throwing up great mounds of earth and setting some brambles alight. In reaction, its companions – the first tripod had by now returned from its adventure at Tregonning Hill to make them four – brought their Death Rays to bear upon blameless Camborne. The stone houses blew up, the parish church and the School of Mines and the railway station and the Aldi and the charity shops flashed into fire, and in moments another proud little town had succumbed. Casualties, though, were only those too stubborn to leave.

After this dousing it would seem that the three still standing took counsel. SAS scouts hidden in vegetation watched, amazed, as they stood close and leaned near each other as if in private conversation. Eventually, the machines gathered around their fallen brother and, with numerous snaking metal tentacles far too long to cram into their hulls but fitting anyway, endeavoured to heave him from the shaft. The military coalition opposing them, scribbling notes on the clear effectiveness of such simple traps, poured everything they had on the three vulnerably clustered machines. Chemical munitions, for the first time, were authorised for use. Just in case. VX nerve agents sequestered from a Colorado stockpile, for years slated for a disposal always delayed, came flying in on artillery shells. Milky, sickly mist spread over the machines and half of dying Camborne – absolutely no effect was seen, to the surprise of few, but the deployment was of deep controversy nonetheless. Protests even took place – such weapons had been prohibited for more than a century. Aliens or not, surely some lines ought not to be crossed? Our glorified press officer General Humphreys, in defending the breaking of such a long-standing taboo, explained that the Geneva Convention doesn't apply to non-humans. The Chemical Weapons Convention, which was the treaty he meant, did, actually, but that didn't seem to matter. Besides, said many, the Blight did it first.

Napalm, white phosphorus, phosgene shells smelling of freshly cut grass, and cluster bombs came next. Observations of their results would always be followed by a matter-of-fact "no effect on target" over the military airwaves. All man had were toys against them, frustration at their trillion-dollar armoury's inadequacy deep and resentful, useful only in reducing another stretch of Cornish countryside to a blackened husk. All the while the untouched tripods stood, almost bemused, in the middle. Anything and everything was thrown at them that day – except the one thing that *might* work. The one last taboo. About nine, the darkness lit by still-burning Camborne, the trapped machine finally escaped from the pit. In a last piece of irony it wasn't hauled out by tentacles but excavated by the very munitions meant to destroy it, and was soon leading his brethren through Camborne's fiery ruins.

It was then that the nightmare truly unfolded. These four sentinels were just the blast front. No less than fourteen more emerged from the green smoke and strode to meet them. The line formation expanded – its intent was unmistakeable. To sweep eastbound, stopping for nothing and covering every inch of land, with total dominion on their mind. And they'd have the numbers. More tripods were stepping from the green smoke minute by minute. There was no reason to believe they wouldn't keep coming, keep emerging, sweeping in all directions, permitting the coverage of every parcel of terrain as they drove up England. Now it was clear what they had been building in there – themselves. It wasn't just tripods coming down in the capsules – so too were toolkits for manufacturing Christ only knew how many more. How many more would fall? No longer was there any safety to be found on the Earth, which they would swarm as they replicated, untouchable, at their own steady leisure.

The sight of machine after machine calmly strolling from the haze sparked delirious panic and, quite suddenly, passionate pacifists found themselves authoring online posts demanding the immediate release of atomic force. Protests in major cities called for Trident to let loose. Cornwall, it was insisted, must burn, or everything would.

As this drama played out, George and I were still comfy on our coach, having crept up the crammed A30 to somewhere between Truro and St Austell. 4G's wonders still able to be appreciated, we watched on his cracked phone as the tripods waded through a soup of evening fog congealing across the fields and rising to the ankles of their three-legged forms. A bleak sense of doom had come over us all. Commentators estimated that, at their current pace, it could be as little as ten hours before the first tripods stepped over the Tamar and into Devon, leaving little in their wake, and who knew where they'd stop?
"Cutting it fine, aren't we?" George said direly. Passengers were screaming at the driver to get a move on as if the carriageway wasn't bumper to bumper. A terrible slaughter was on the

horizon – we all knew it. At the realisation of their coming a woman aboard our coach erupted in noisy tears, while others disembarked to take their chances, sure we'd be overtaken no matter what. I stayed. After so many brushes with death it felt wrong to look the gift horse which was this coach in the mouth. It was no good to do anything but sit there as we drove up the crowded A30 far too slowly, hoping we could reach Saltash before them, knowing we probably wouldn't. Numbness reigned in me. Maybe I was a bit traumatised – afraid of the outside. I didn't know.

The Blight legions, first overtaking Redruth, then Truro, then St Agnes in their tsunami surge, met little resistance now besides the occasional spurt of distracting tracer fire from a distant, fleeing army. Acre after acre fell into their empire. The howling of munitions had ceased and, besides the tripods' stomping feet and ghostly wails, there lay absolute silence across the towns and roads and farms. The Blight were in solitary possession of West Cornwall beneath the darkling night, lit only by the slender moon, the stars, quiet Oumuamua, and the ruddy glare of what they burned. But just ahead of their moving crescent, which now overcame Perranporth to the north and the creeks and valleys of Roseland's heritage coast to the south, picking off every survivor it found, fumbled our evacuation. All who weren't quick enough were smited. Roads choked with traffic turned to cinders when the hunting tripods found them. Survivors scattered into the wilderness. It was an inevitability that, as death sprang across the landscape, the evening sky over much of Britain turned blood red from the great columns of smoke, so thick and so atmospheric it birthed flickering lightning storms. I saw it myself, a sky stained with horror, electricity waltzing unchecked through unnatural clouds.

Everywhere, in all nations, in Finnish bars and Turkish terraces, Chinese high-rises and Bolivian squares, people gathered around screens and stared at this inhuman metal army, awesome in its power and complexity, strolling without lasting challenge. A wave of fear swept all corners of the world – the lackadaisical "oh, well, we'll just see what happens," fell apart once the legions came pouring from the green smoke. No matter where they were they wondered when the Things would reach them, too.

Watching from the coach, live footage of the tripods transitioning to repeats from earlier in the day as camera crews were whisked away with the rest of the evacuees, my own inner armchair general had become vocal. Why not, he asked if not scolded, bury atomic bombs in the empty mineshafts and trigger them as a tripod walked by? Yes, they had all manner of fancy shielding, but what good were those shields if they were tumbled through the air, tripod and all, and buried beneath thousands of tonnes of geological debris? It wasn't as if Cornwall was wanting for empty shafts – a machine had just stepped into one purely by coincidence alone! If this was out of the question, the bombs too hard to transport, the situation too fast-moving, the mineshafts too narrow or too haunted, then why not nitroglycerine, sticks of TNT, even popping candy would be better than nothing! And how would the Blight know to avoid the shafts? They didn't have Google Maps!

Rigid anger gripped me that no effort to counter the enemy was being made right in front of me and so, of course, couldn't have been happening at all. On the road outside, along the hard shoulder, I saw military traffic – and it was all moving east with us. I raised my proposal to George, who I could barely see – out of an abundance of caution the coach lights had been extinguished and so we sat in our own little oblivions. Practice for what was to come.

"What good would that do?" he asked bitterly, the woman opposite him bleating into her phone that she was still getting

charged for a full holiday. "More'll come, and they'll just walk over the rubble, and keep coming forever and ever. I told you it's all gone. You'll accept it eventually." I just sighed.
"Oh, look," I muttered at his phone, "Pray For England is trending."
"Well, that's good, at least."
"I thought you hated God stuff now."
"No, I hate *God*, but I don't hate godly things. It's our responsibility to be merciful and loving now, since *someone* doesn't want to be."
"Whatever, mate."

The stuffy-aired coach lurched to a halt, again, traffic on the black A38 going in the same direction on both lanes yet backed up to rigidity There was much agitation inside and out. Genocidal enemies were approaching and we were in a traffic jam. In the disorientation of night and the chaos of rumour, everything became questionable; what direction were they coming from, at what speed, would they bypass us or fry us? More than one person, amid the relentless stops and starts, had demanded to be let off, even threatened to brain the driver or smash their way through the windows when this wasn't obeyed instantaneously. While buses and trucks and vans and cars quivered bumper to bumper, panicked officials running between them, hopping over the central reservation, in some vain effort to unclog the pandemonium, a hundred other questions struggled in my mind. I suppose I didn't properly appreciate that danger was again approaching, even after all I had been through. Maybe I'd run out of space to be scared – or just wasn't eager to abandon the comfort of a padded seat. Who knew when next I'd get one?

How much, if at all, I wondered as the anxiety around me turned to shouted panic, the coach feeling like a chaotic school bus, did the Blight understand us? Did they even *want* to? Did they grasp that we were afraid, that we were organised in our resistance, that vast societal constructs were in play to counter them? Or did they interpret the stinging of our weapons as we might interpret a disturbed beehive? And what was their ultimate aim? Half of Cornwall had been reduced to a lifeless husk, so it appeared, but still I wasn't quite convinced they aimed for our extermination. Why, after all, had they been plucking people alive from the Hayle River? Did slavery, serfdom, *waitressing*, await me? And above all, I thought as tracked Army vehicles trundled by in the wrong direction, where, exactly, were the government planning to stop them? Were they planning to stop them at all? What did I pay them for?!

All thoughts were dashed from my mind by our driver when, a dozen seats ahead, he rose from his seat with great suddenness, shouted "fuck this," and descended the stairwell to vanish onto the dark carriageway. Silence engulfed the coach, all staring in his direction, for just a moment.

"Did he just leave us?" someone asked.

"Oh my God – he ditched us," I whispered, a strangely plain attitude to my voice. "Wow – we're *so* dead."

"Is he coming back?" asked a woman, straining to look, but whether he did or not was immaterial – his flight triggered a torrent and, in a mad rush, the remaining passengers surged from the coach and onto the road.

There was now hysteria that the tripods must be upon us. Why else would he run off? I still had enough faith in the authorities, somehow, to believe that we'd get at least a morsel of warning were death approaching, even if it was just a PCSO running around blowing a whistle. There wasn't much point sitting on an empty coach, though, so I went, too, if only for the fresh air. Squeezing past those who wrestled bags from cramped overhead compartments, I made it onto the road into a maze of stranded buses from all manner of disparate chartered companies – one minibus bore the scarlet livery of

GWYNEDD HOLIDAYS AND GETAWAYS, another was clearly requisitioned from a special educational needs school, which felt a bit off – and saw a young fusilier screaming wildly at our runaway getaway driver.

"Get back in!" he yelled, with furious, frantic gestures towards the coach, spit leaping from his mouth. "Get back in!"

"No, I'm not having this!" the driver protested. "They'll be here soon! And you fuckin' know it!"

"Get back in your fucking vehicle!" the soldier screamed, begged, knowing the catastrophic knock-on, that one abandoned meant all would have to be abandoned, but still the driver refused. The fusilier drew his sidearm. "Get back in or I'll shoot you! I swear to God – I'll kill you!" Our driver stared down the barrel for a moment, then looked up at its bearer again in contempt, before turning and running, daring the young soldier to shoot. For a moment I was sure he would – until his arm lowered and, with a petulant scream of "fuck!" to the dark sky, he climbed into the cab himself. "How's this work then?" he demanded to nobody, for it was only him inside.

A river of people flowed down the carriageway, forsaking the traffic jam and in doing so contributing to it, as they abandoned vehicles in their haste. The crowd grew with each passing minute. Fresh news, or rumours, or nonsense, of the Blight advance circulated – several tracking apps had by now become available to download and, once your email address was registered and you agreed to share your data for targeted adverts, all said they were coming. None agreed on their speed.

Over the sounds of human fear I tried to look back westward, past the overburdened refugees and soldiers and emergency services, through the forest of coaches and buses, towards where we had come from. I expected to see smoke or fire, some evidence of the Blight's work, as the world we left behind was annihilated. But all I saw was a deepening blue sky against rolling and empty Bodmin Moor, which we stood in the middle of, and one solitary star that may actually have been Venus lolling above. White mist spread wide and low on the moors. There were no crashes, no explosions, no monstrous alien cries; only the soundtrack of this panicked road and the helicopters which swooped overhead, low and loud, in the same direction as us.

"Bet they're happy," I said, jealous and annoyed, pointing to a Chinook speeding by and probably crammed with far luckier evacuees.

"No doubt," answered George.

"Lads," interrupted a traffic officer, his fringe spiky with sweat, "this ain't no time for sightseeing. Get moving that way, please, right now." We did, further, between stationary buses. One, also emptied, was being deliberately driven off the carriageway – firefighters having chopped segments of the crash-barrier away – into a ditch to make room for those behind to pointlessly advance a few extra metres. As we walked, feeling like we should be running, we passed a soldier rendered anonymous like an eerily growing number of others by a camouflaged hazardous material suit. His gas mask was buried in a floppy hood, making him appear like an apparition, and I caught a voice from his radio.

"*Gas alert, gas alert,*" it warned. "*Substances now being discharged in the direction of Bodmin and surrounding areas. All personnel, seek open areas or higher ground immediately. Seek open areas or higher ground immediately.*"

Another voice: "*We are not evacuating civilians fast enough – repeat, we are not evacuating fast enough.*"

Another: "*Black Dawn. Black Dawn.*" At that I now pieced together, through the hurricane of rumours, just how close we were – at this present moment, here rooted to the A38, George and I stood in the heart of Bodmin Moor's open desolation. If the machines were in range of Bodmin town they would, in the time it took for me to cook toast without burning it, reach us. They were *very* near and I realised, with appalling horror, that yet again what had seemed like salvation – getting on that coach and thinking I was on an express to safety – was no such thing. That kept happening to me. Jumping from one frying pan into another frying pan. Stuck in the middle of a moor with the Things bearing down, that familiar sense of doom returned. Doom should never be a familiar sense.

All around me, people pushed by in their mad escaping rush and, as they did, I started feeling aware of myself as just one number in a great body of statistics. I'd never felt this before; to see myself not as an individual but as a bit of many, a great collective, soon to vanish in the eternal ether because one of these horrendous machines willed it. Well, though I was now ready to acknowledge this fate, I was nowhere approaching ready to *accept* it – not like in Hayle, when I'd practically accepted death, when escape had been impossible and then happened anyway. If it could happen on its own then I could force it to happen, too. Destiny isn't real, no matter what George's God Squad might say – what happens is just whatever ended up happening.

"George! George!" I shouted to my companion, who was trying to convince a soldier to let him conduct an impromptu sermon for whose who desired it, and was being told to piss off. "Fuckin' *George*!"

"What?"

"Get off the road!"

"What?" He gave me a puzzled look. "Why?"

"Just do it!"

"I wouldn't do that, if I was you," the soldier advised him, muffled by his gas mask, a surreal picture of calm. "That's the moor – people don't last the night out there."

"Oh, right, there's tigers and bears and shit!" I spat. "Get off the road right now! It's a fuckin' death trap!"

"But-" George said no more for, at that moment, an unseen tripod's haunting wail echoed over the moorland. Everyone fell silent, looking wildly for its source, before the torrent picked up again, running turning to sprinting, shouting

turning to screaming. Even the police were running now – not what you want to see. I just turned back to look at George.
"Any more questions?" I asked.
"Um, not really, no, you've made your point quite well there."

George joined me in jumping down the exposed embankment and – guided by the puny wattage of his phone torch – onto the rough moorland, stumbling in puddles and soft tangles of gorse, but making good progress, feeling the darkness slowly, almost lovingly, swallow us. This must be what it looked like when the gas ate you, I thought. A copse of elm trees, bulbous and expansive, were silhouettes against the indigo sky ahead and we made for them, all the while feeling growing regret that I hadn't encouraged more to follow us, though paradoxically glad I hadn't. By not doing so, I hadn't made myself responsible for their fate.
"That phone lasts forever!" I remarked breathlessly, the good type, at least compared to the other option the Blight offered.
"It never stops working for you!" George shouted back. "Like Jesus!"
"Is that a joke?!"
"Yes! I lost my *faith*! This is my coping strategy! The heck are we even going?" Sarcastically, he added: "Jamaica Inn?"
"Those trees," I answered, and his face plummeted; we passed a prehistoric line of granite standing stones, barely existent in the dark, and I realised that if George's torch were to fail now we'd be in quite a pickle. "You a good climber?"
"Is *that* a joke?"
"No!" I answered, picking up the pace, chasing the torch light, pain somewhere deep in my ribcage ordering me to stop sprinting and stubbornness somewhere deep in my skull refusing. "We can't outrun them, so we've gotta dodge them! It's the only way!"
"You're sure about this?" he asked.
"Not at all!" I said truthfully. "But it's all I've got!" Then, after what seemed like an interminable time, glad not to have

discovered neither tiger nor bear was in fact on the bleak heather, which wouldn't even have surprised me right now, we reached the little collective of elms.

"That tor's higher," George remarked, pointing to a growing incline which pushed its way heavenward. All around us was darkness, penetrated only by distant lights, like little orange pixies dancing in the void. "You sure this is good enough?" I considered for a moment.

"It just feels too obvious. Like, if you were a giant alien death machine, you'd probably check a big hill, right?"

"Maybe, but I'd also check a little clump of trees."

"Well, we're here now, and I'm scared to move again, so..."

"That's very fair, very fair. Good on you for admitting to being scared – they never do that in films. Takes me right out of it."

"You're babbling."

"I am," agreed George. "Also scared. Also trying to cope."

"Fair, fair, fair, fair, fair, fair..." I realised I'd said 'fair' too many times and stopped.

Slowly, against the distant hum of noise from the carriageway and groan of the last few helicopters, we climbed the elms – I went first, glad to be able to hide my face from George for, with each step higher up the trunk, I became more and more convinced that I'd made an unforgivable error. The ink felt wet on our death warrants and it was written in my hand. That knowledge was probably etched all over my expression – hence my desire to hide it. Because, of course, he was right – this was an appalling plan. The worst possible plan I could have come up with. Climb a tree? What the fuck? But what else was there in this barren expanse? Second thoughts weren't what was called for right now – hope, in the face of absurd odds, was. Gusts of glacial wind swept around our elm like water around a rock, knotted branches on all sides requiring dextrous navigation as we ascended, and, all the while, my second thoughts tried to tug me back down. That hill, or tor, or whatever, was sounding better with each strained step.

"Well, hope you like frostbite," I said, trying to bat away my fizzing nerves with humour, tree bark scratching at my cold hands, glancing for a good place to vomit, if I needed to, that wouldn't leave George's head drenched in soapy bile.

"I've had frostbite," George replied, heaving himself up beneath me, leaves whipping in the wind all around as they began entombing us in a motherly embrace. The wind, now deflected by a thousand little shields, lessened. "It sucked."

"Really?"

"Yeah; I've got eight toes."

"But you can still climb, right?"

"Fuckin' hope so." I heaved myself up, hand tucked into the crease between branch and trunk, praying I wouldn't meet a spider. I didn't think I'd be able to handle that.

"Was this a missionary thing, or…?"

"Geography trip. Year Eleven. Svalbard. Fell asleep with my foot hanging out the tent."

"And I'm trying to survive an alien invasion with you." Looking down, I saw his face between my knees as he clung to the trunk, and he looked up at the same time. He was smiling goofily.

"Yes. Yes you are."

Another alien hoot carried on the torturous wind. The leaves rustled. We both looked in the cry's direction.

"That sounded closer," I said.

"Possibly," George replied, as I realised I couldn't hear helicopters anymore. "But we're higher up – maybe it's clearer without all the vehicles and hills and things around. I don't know."

"Should you have gone first?" I asked. "Feel like I'm going slowly."

"You are – but it's fine. I'd go faster but I don't fancy putting my head up your arse."

"No, I'd rather you didn't, if you please."

Eventually, George came level with me and, sure his weight wouldn't permit getting any higher as the trunk narrowed, shimmied onto a large branch. He sat atop it, legs dangling, there being no apparent method available to safely lay on a branch this thin. Our only option, it seemed, was to sit there under cover of darkness and auburn leaves and hope for the best. I followed him onto the branch and sat, too, feeling like a schoolkid and looking at nothing – we were entirely obscured in the leaves with no view of the world beyond. Even if we had a view it would have been invisible in night's black soup.

"Got anything we can string a hammock up with?" I asked, semi-joking.

"I do not," George replied, then sighed, shivering with arms tightly crossed. "Some situation we're in. Up a tree on Bodmin Moor, at night, with no food, no winter clothing, no shelter, and… oh, yes, and there's an alien invasion going on."

"Sure is. This whole thing's felt like a dream from the start."

"Maybe it is. But *if* it is, only one of us is the dreamer. The other doesn't even exist." Silence passed us by, only the wind as companionship and quite unwelcome, and I wondered where my backpack had ended up. With a start I realised that, while sent downriver by the wave of the crashing tripod, it must have eventually drifted back upriver, back towards me. I could have gotten it. Could have retrieved Disco's medicine. Icy guilt took me – but I supposed I could ransack a Pets At Home. Still clinging to that fantasy of finding him, I suppose. Nothing wrong with a fantasy. Especially in a situation like this.

"What did you call that hill?" I asked.

"What hill?"

"The hill you want us to go up."

"Oh. Um… you mean the tor?"

"Yeah. What's that? Cornish?"

"No…" he said slowly, our shivering getting worse. My bones hurt. We'd have to huddle, soon, like penguins. Ugh. "It's, like, an outcrop of rocks. Maybe it's Cornish, I've no idea, but I think it's used in Exmoor too, so, who knows? When I was camping

there- *ow!*" He cried suddenly, recoiling his hand, and I flinched, having to grip the branch so as not to fall backwards.
"You alright?"
"Yeah," he answered, examining his hand. "Bastard splinter. That'll get infected and kill me, I bet, now the modern world's about to collapse and they're not gonna be making no more penicillin."
"Possibly," I said, taking his wrist so I could look but seeing little in the dark, his hand's silhouette barely perceivable even when right in front of me, so I did nothing but make a few encouraging noises.
"How do you think you'll survive?" George asked, shaking his hand vigorously once I returned it. "Assuming I'm right and the world's ending. Do you know how to live on your own? Without the comforts of civilisation, I mean."
"No," I said, "not really. I guess I'll learn fishing. My dad tried and failed but I'll need it now. Maybe that extra motivation's what I need."
"You'll just choke on a fish bone."
"Is that likely?"
"Exceedingly." Through the dark, I saw he was picking at the splinter.
"Leave it alone," I said. "*That's* how it'll get infected."
"I'm just getting it out."
"Leave it," I said again. "Your body'll just push it out when it's ready – it's got ways."
"I bet you think that's down to evolution, don't you?"
"I'm not having that conversation with you," I answered. "But *you* explain goosebumps."
"God did it."
"Course he…" my voice trailed away. "...did. Do you hear that?"
George snapped to alert and listened, expecting to hear the stomp of a tripod, but there was nothing. Only the omnipresent breeze.
"No…"
"Exactly," I said quietly. I could feel those goosebumps, now.

"We're next to a motorway. I could hear it a minute ago. Why can't I now?" Even in the darkness I was sure I saw George's face shift a ghostly white.

Forgetting my personal safety, I struggled to my feet, the branch a balancing beam, holding another above me for support, and, peering through the leaves and out across the moorland, I saw far-flung headlights like red and yellow stars, forming a long and stationary line through Bodmin Moor. Yet I heard nothing from across the way. The distant commotion had ceased. A minute or more passed before George, having precariously joined me, the branch trembling beneath us, spoke again.

"What's going on?"

"Fuck knows," I said. "Maybe nothing. I can't see any tripods."

"I can't see *anything*."

"Well, yeah, me either. Or hear anything. I would have thought *somebody* else would've come this way. We can't be the only ones who thought to get off the road – there must have been a thousand people." A bat flickered by and vanished. The night calm was unbroken and, straining to spy the carriageway through the leaves, I was about to give up. But then I saw the lights grow blurry, inconsistent, before they faded and disappeared altogether. It was as though the night had come down and swallowed them. I realised, in an instant, what I was watching.

"The lights…" whispered George. "The lights are all going out."

"Are they?" I asked softly.

"What do you mean?" he replied, looking at me, then back through the leaves. I heard a sharp intake of breath. "Oh. Oh, dear. Oh, dear, oh, dear..."

"Shut up," I hissed. My voice was shaky. Tears wanted to burst from my eyes. Apoplectic horror raged inside me. "Don't say a word. Don't even breathe." I looked down, through the leaves and branches below to the heather-dressed ground, but this wasn't visible in the dark. I couldn't remember if it had been when we first arrived. Was it, instead, now hidden by the same thing hiding those lights? By a common impulse, without sharing a word, George and I climbed higher, disregarding whether the tree could hold us, snapping errant branches out of our path to clear a way, each breath of mine taken with the anxiety that something new and very unwelcome would come into my lungs. I felt seasick, rotten, putrid with each step, with my nagging certainty of what was happening – never had I so badly wished to be wrong.

As it ascended, the trunk narrowed until it became a mess of twigs masquerading as branches, too thin for any of them to possibly hold our weight, and so the two of us simply stood there, clinging to the trunk if to a galleon's mast, craning to see through the leaves. Neither of us spoke. Through the myriad of gaps between the leaves, I saw nothing but black. Though the perfect Moon was out and as luminous as ever, nothing was revealed by its reflected light, as if the Earth rejected it. This lack of visibility spooked me in an awful and grinding way – there ought to have been a moorland out there which, though it was darkest night, I should have seen some hint of – the bumps and troughs of geographic features, defiantly visible even as vague forms lit beneath the Moon, but I saw nothing. It was like our tree drifted in space.

"What's going on?" George asked, at last.

"You tell me," I said, feeling very sick, still.

"Gas."

"Yeah. Me too." It was flowing over the moors, I was sure, our tree a little island, with the pair of us just high enough to be beyond the reach of poisonous hands. Far away, to the south-east, beyond now-unseen hills, we heard a machine hooting, then another answering, and by instinct, reduced to lowly animals, we stopped peering through the leaves and held ourselves tightly to the trunk, trying to somehow appear one with it. These hunters were invisible, and so far away, and we were just two little creatures in a tree who'd probably attract no more of their interest than a pair of unseen squirrels, but still we froze as if we mattered.

Eventually, accepting we couldn't cling forever with our hands as frigid as they were, we dared to venture lower, to where another branch could accommodate us. Hopeful that we were still safe as long as we could see what was below us, we again shimmied to sit on it.

"Don't slip," George whispered. "For God's sake, don't slip."

"Thanks for that," I muttered back. "I was thinking of slipping. I thought that'd be a fun thing to do."

"I was talking to myself – but I'll allow your snark, for now."

I said nothing – I wasn't anywhere near the head space for banter. At least on this branch we could rest – a second thoughtfully acted as a backrest. Maybe I could even close my eyes. What could dreams possibly do to me that was worse than waking life?

Feeling a tug at my sleeve, I looked to George and he silently offered me tangled headphones – he had a second pair, and was plugging both into a jack so we might hear something that didn't portend death. Gladly, I accepted, and endured his music tastes – they were far too tonally disparate for the deathly situation, especially the tracks from *Waitress*, but were far preferable to silence or forced conversation – to block out those alien calls.

# XV.

I don't remember when I was swept into sleep but I remember my dreams, of feeling what it was like to burn and running for water in corridors that never ended, of drowning in black mucus, of a pale-faced man in a tuxedo, red tentacles splitting from his back, grinning wide enough to split his bony face and whispering, "better wake up soon – before you forget how to." These visions clung to me even as I became aware of their unreality and shook myself out. I nearly fell from the branch I'd drifted off on. I looked around, realising daylight had managed to return, and the air smelled crisp and fresh. George dozed beside me, the headphones dangling from his ears but not mine (he must have removed them when I fell asleep). A robin sang from a nearby branch.

I'd anticipated spending eternity trapped on our little perch above the swimming death – we wouldn't even be the only ones feeling that way. I've read all about the St Breward villagers, who spent three days crammed in their church steeple with the gas flowing outside, miraculously surviving to a man – but, peering with anxiety through the leaves, I saw that only harmless grey mist, in place of sludge-like gas, drifted over Bodmin Moor's rough bumps. Everything was, by my half-awake reckoning, as it ought to be. Nudging George awake, I suggested with some urgency that we climb down and scout for food – I'd woken desperately hungry and strongly doubted that any carveries were open – if a tripod, or the gas, were to reappear we could just ascend once more. Trees seemed the antidote. Monkey mode never leaves you.

George agreeing, we began descending. I went first – the view to the bottom was obscured by greenery and so I couldn't see the ground. After the fewest of careful steps, batting through foliage, a putrid smell struck me. I gagged on instinct – and my guts turned to hot liquid. In a rush of panic, I thought I'd unwittingly lowered myself into residual fumes of the nerve gas. Yet, though the stink overpowered my stomach, tickling it to near-heaving, I noticed that I didn't die. Encouraged that this would keep being my situation – at least in the short term – I carried on.

With a few more perilous steps on branches too thin to take my weight – yet undergoing the strain regardless – I cleared the murmuration of leaves. I looked down to check my next step – and I went rigid. Surrounding the tree's base on all sides, I now saw, were corpses. The smell grew stronger. Clinging stock-still to the trunk, the bark's imperfections biting at my fingers, I stared with blank silence. They formed a clump, a messy pile, around our tree. Though they were each so different, because there were so many, dozens piling on top of one another like donated clothes, they were anonymous in their collective, like how I had felt back on the carriageway when I realised my place in mortality's scrum and tried to say no. Distributed in a circle around the tree, some frozen in the frantic throes of clawing their way up, then in irregular piles towards the carriageway, it was immediately clear that, just too late, they had attempted the same escape as George and I. The gas had other ideas.

"No use staring," I heard George say above me, nudging my hand with his foot, but, despite his urgings, I refused to continue. I'd seen plenty of death but this felt different – I didn't want to get closer to them and their eyes, bulging open like squeezed dog toys, black socks for tongues, dark blood and bodily fluids I couldn't name bubbling from around eye sockets and out of nostrils and ears.

"Just go," George insisted, "for God's sake, we don't have time for this." Eventually, acidic bile in my throat, I was goaded to obey.

Lowering myself with great delicateness in among the Hieronymus Bosch painting, there I stood, forced to stand on top of them as if a triumphant champion. I saw, at another tree some metres away, a kneeling woman still locked in her last action, sat against the tree and forever in the process of smothering her infant with a cardigan. She must have thought it a better death than liquidation of the lungs and I didn't fault her. I wondered if she succeeded in time.

With an aching slowness I picked my way between the bodies, seeking any tiny patch of space so I wouldn't have to stand on them, and back towards the carriageway. Oh, God, there were so many of them, more than I saw from the tree, more than I could comprehend even when they all lay there. More than made sense. A dreadlocked woman clutching at her throat with unnaturally twisted limbs, an elderly couple laying in each other's arms while others draped all around them, a man missing all his fingernails, implying they had been scratched away as he clawed at a tree, trying to ascend as he choked, others reaching for the trees or lying crumpled under them, having fallen when so close. Mobile phones buzzed from pockets.

Had any seen *us* up above and hoped to follow? I thought to call out as I had on the boat, to ask if any were alive in some improbable air pocket deep beneath the bodies, or if some had made it into the neighbouring trees like us. But even now, fearing the tripod responsible was near, I dared not make a sound. Shame lashed me; what a dirty and wretched coward I was, then and now, for all these failures. I could have warned more people than just George. I could have told others to jump into the river. I could have told people to get away from the machine on Clodgy. I could have taken more than just my fucking cat out of St Ives. But, instead, I just ran. All these times I might have saved one person, just one, and I didn't. Gutless. Looking past the colourful confetti of bodies, which to this day I find populating every dream like an unwanted guest you know is coming, I saw the carriageway – all the vehicles were where we left them, in silent stillness, coaches like beached whales and cars like dead beetles. Even in the crisp morning brightness I saw dim headlights still turned on.

"How'd they get this far?" I asked, at last. The smell was so overwhelming that talking wasn't easy. "The road's all the way over there."

"I guess it doesn't kill you quickly," replied George, blank-faced, stepping over a corpse. "What a waste."

"Is that it?"

"Is that what?"

"Is that all you've got to say?" I turned to him with sudden mounting fury, my horror and self-hatred finding its outlet. "They're all dead – we could've done something." In listening to music, I thought, we must have drowned out the screams.

"So why didn't you?" asked George. Maybe they hadn't screamed. Maybe they were silent, their lungs turning to froth with each gasp, *knowing* they were dying while we idly chatted a few feet above.

Those words came to me again: "What pain it was to drown." It must be so much worse to drown on yourself. Had we known what was below we could have done something, perhaps, or at least shouted some words of comfort to the dying. That would have been better than nothing. We should have known – we saw the gas come bounding in. Perhaps, with it being a distance away, some type of disconnection reigned – that as long as I couldn't see death happening, I didn't need to confront it. Here, then, was my punishment.

"Anyway, they'll be happier dead," George continued coldly, fist pinching his nose, drifting now into a weird and needless tangent. "Oblivion is peaceful. There's no hell waiting for them – this is hell, on Earth. They're the same thing. I thought long and hard last night about the point of life without faith and I realised that with nothing waiting for you outside life, no heaven, no hell, there's no reason *for* life. And if there's no reason then there's no value – better to be dead and free and peaceful. Imagine peace – you can't. But the dead can."

"Idiot – if there's nothing outside of life, then life has *total* value," I spat, still thinking of what comforting words I might have offered from the tree last night, and how something was always better than nothing, views totally inconsistent with his newfound repudiation of meaning. I couldn't think of anything I would have said. "And if life doesn't matter then what're you still doing here? Just off yourself." I shrugged.

"You've got no sense of logic," said George, a stammer creeping up on him.

"And you've got no feelings."

"How're feelings treating you now?" he asked, halting and staring me down. "They feel good? Stood here?" He gestured around us, to the anonymous bundles I was trying not to see. "Go on, tell me, does it feel good to be here?"

"I've never felt good in my life," I said sullenly. "Let's just go. I wanna get out of here. I don't wanna be around this."

"I don't think you'll have a choice from now on," George observed as we walked the moorland, barren but for the crumples of lost humanity, back towards the road. Then, in a voice which somehow sounded like his and yet not, he said, suddenly: "The end has come. They will sweep all away. Angels and spirits, demons and souls surround us. This is only the beginning. There is no way to avoid it. There is no exit. Humanity is no longer going anywhere. The World Body is exhausted." I didn't reply – I'm not sure I even heard him. I remember him saying it – yet I didn't hear it.

Our plan, if you could call it that, was simply to walk

along the carriageway, sheltering beneath vehicles if a tripod appeared – Bodmin Moor's vast and empty sightlines would provide us plenty of warning – and pray it would assume this area to be spayed of human matter and unworthy of closer attention. Raiding any houses along the way, we'd continue upcountry for as long as our legs carried us, all in search of... something. Neither of us were sure – I still wasn't clear why George continued at all since life apparently didn't matter. His spiritual collapse was, so far, very unimpressive.

We climbed back across the steel crash-barrier. A cadaver was draped over it, like a towel on a washing line, formless in a woolly coat. I thought about shifting him to a more dignified position but thought better of it when I realised that I might feel pressured to show the same generosity to every corpse I found. There were just too many, coiled up on the road or in their cars, many of them in uniforms, as if a great battle had taken place here. But it hadn't – just a slaughter. Police helmets and coats and the contents of bags scattered about the tarmac, while limbs dangled from the roofs of coaches – having hoped, I supposed, that this might be high enough to escape the black wave they must have seen spilling between the hills. I tried not to look as George and I walked through the carnage at pace, he panting to keep up with me, urging me to slow down, while I ignored him and carried on with a curdling need to be away from all this. But George was right – there was no exit. No matter where I went, I'd be seeing more. This was just what the world would be like, now.

After a time which I didn't measure, the bodies and traffic congestion began clearing – the gas had to have dissipated eventually. Either side of the road many, *many* vehicles, whether cars, vans or buses, lay in the fields and ditches, where they'd been shunted by the authorities. They stood motionless and orphaned and, with the carriageway clear and empty, the sense of ghostliness only grew stronger in this silent moorland across which horror stalked.

I was going to say something, though I don't remember what, when suddenly all the road and surrounding country came to be bathed in orange. It was like a gigantic light bulb had been switched on somewhere behind us. I turned and, through watering eyes nearly clamped shut by the light's brilliance, I saw that from beyond the western hills there emanated a tremendous, almost biblical glow. It quickly became so bright that I shielded my searing eyes – my skin began prickling at its heat and I cowered with some silliness behind a Morrisons lorry. George ran behind a car near me as the glow became so intense that it was as difficult to see each other as it had been in the tree last night. The light began fading as quickly as it had appeared and, with some gathered courage, I peeked past the lorry and down the carriageway.

Distantly, far beyond the fields and over the hills, an evil black cloud, no bigger than my thumb with arm fully outstretched, rose above the horizon. Slowly, soundless, it grew into the hideous, poisonous shape of a mushroom.
"Jesus Christ..." I whispered, at once attuned to what this sight meant. "They've done it... they've done it."
"Extraordinary," said George with mindless awe, stepping from his shelter to stare. "Where would that be? Hayle, maybe, or somewhere else?"
"That kind of area," I said slowly, my mouth dry, anticipating warm urine running down my leg like in that nuclear war film my dad made me watch "because you need to learn" and glad not to feel it. "Wherever it is, it's not there anymore. I didn't think they'd really-" The sky exploded. The blast's shockwave, a cacophonous pound, shattered the air with a great thump, like the roar of the Earth bursting open and Hell crawling out. Though it carried no wind at this distance, and so we weren't launched from our feet, the thunderclap was so severe it left my ears ringing painfully for minutes afterwards. Birds

scattered from the trees in all directions. Yet even in that sudden storm I couldn't rip my eyes from the black-veiled thing, rising into and blocking the sunlight, thinking of the towns now burned into oblivion and whether it had even done any good to the Blight masters.

"Are we okay?" asked George.

"Well, our faces are still on our... faces." I checked – just to make sure. "But we need to get out of here. I don't know the prevailing wind but there's like a twenty-five percent chance of it being towards us and, well, I can't handle fallout. I really can't."

"Why twenty-five percent?"

"North, south, east, west."

"What about north-west, north-east, south-"

"Mate, alright, so my maths sucks. I accepted that in GCSE and you need to accept it now. I am focused on other things." We hurried further down the empty carriageway, the forest not much further now, the birds still complaining and my ears still ringing. I'd spend a while worrying they were perforated until, a few hours later, they finally faded, though presumably lacking a few frequencies from this point on.

"You know," George observed, "for an incredible historic moment, you're very chill."

"I've had my fill of history." I thought I could taste metal.

Though I worried about fallout, having seen one of those old *Protect and Survive* videos on YouTube way back when, I dimly understood how it actually worked and consequently could only be so afraid. We still hurried, quite keen to avoid it, whatever it was. In fact, unbeknownst to us, the threat was practically non-existent – the ninety kiloton blast, delivered by an American stealth bomber as our own Trident submarine system had needed another half-day to calibrate its targeting, was an airburst; detonated high enough above ground to prevent the whipping up of radioactive particles. There would be no mutations in these parts. In any case, the American planners said brightly, such particles wouldn't have drifted over England regardless, but northward – over West Wales and Ireland where nobody lived anyway.

Stomachs grumbling until relieved by peanut butter cereal bars from an abandoned Volvo (I thought I was allergic but I guess I'm not), our eyes scanned at all times for radioactive ash. George told me about Hiroshima and how toxic black rain had followed the explosion – we watched out for that, too, when we weren't keeping busy scanning for tripods. Like the ash, it never came. The thought did appear in our minds that, given how widespread the machines were, another nuke might come falling on us, too. If that did happen, all we could do was hope it fell right on top of us so we could be vaporised nice and quickly. We were on Bodmin Moor – we could hardly shelter from ninety kilotons in a farmhouse or beneath the terrifying roadside billboard for Gnome Homes.

"I want a gnome," I sighed.

"Sorry?"

"Nothing."

Finally, after more walking than any one person should be expected to do, we came across a group of tall American soldiers siphoning a petrol station outside Polyphant, rendered into spirits by their full-body protective coverings. I was surprised to see that they were unarmed. Quickly, they ushered us further up the road, saying there were stragglers and then there was us, and we were hurried into the back of a stuffy Humvee. We were rushed away down silent roads and past emptied refugee camps dotting the fields like abandoned music festivals, my body pressed tightly between George and an American GI who kept peering down my top. The driver asked me if I liked *Rick and Morty*. Then, we rounded a corner, and were in a village still crawling with troops. Suddenly, out of nowhere, we were safe – but I'd let myself think that before and wasn't prepared to believe it until I saw every last tripod lying dead.

I sat there, head against the hard aluminium door, George and I saying nothing, sharing from a packet of Skittles pressed into my hand, not minding the Humvee's dreadful suspension or the stench of diesel, astonished that I'd made it off the moor. The soldiers seemed pretty amazed, too, and kept asking what the tripods looked like. After a while spent wondering what these soldiers' presence meant for the state of the war, our yokel-accented driver told us that the fighting machines had halted their advance in the early morning, not pressing beyond Bodmin Moor after dousing it in black gas. For a few hours I had, once again, been behind enemy lines. This was also, notably, the first time I heard them referred to as the Blight – a moniker they inherited for how, like the potato plant disease, they blacken all they encounter. The nuclear strike, too, we were told intimate details of – in this war, it seemed, 'classified information' didn't really exist. Operation Eternal Dawn, as the atomic assault was named by the American planners so we didn't end up saddled with Operation Mugglewump or something, had targeted a region south of Hayle. Ground zero lay just outside St Erth and, under all that green smoke, the vast Blight construction complex birthing tripods by the hour. Damage assessments were inching their way through the chain of command – we commoners still had no idea as to its success.

What we did learn was that another capsule—a brilliant emerald meteor—had fallen during the night in Polperro. The Blight line advanced with its fall. Fitful cannonades of airstrikes met it, without much thought given to little Polperro, before the machine rose into the air and sprouted legs. The sense of a slow, lumbering, cold, inevitable advance further up the nation was further roused. Hope, briefly kindled by nuclear fire, faded – they would need a lot more bombs. Maybe Cornwall really would have to turn to glass – to become a place only visited for gloomy documentaries, with ashen-faced film-makers pontificating about how "there used to be life here," the Tamar a contaminated swamp marked by "danger of death" signs.

Then, as the smoke of the atomic strike dissipated, it became clear that the Blight machines and their great foundry were still there. They had not just survived – they were untouched while all around them burned. The promised cleansing of the invaders with one swift stroke was gone. Panic erupted in all places.

At last our Humvee came to Launceston's motorway service station. After being ordered to strip in a white tent for fear of radioactive contamination and getting showered with a painfully high-pressure nozzle by a soldier who ignored my pleas to let me do it myself, I was let out and handed replacement clothes. They were an itchingly ill-fitting grey shirt, orange cardigan, men's boxers, and baggy jeans fished from a John Lewis whose windows marauding looters had long since ripped out. Apparently they'd run out of bras so I guess I knew what I'd be stealing next. I watched my previous clothes burned in the car park, which was probably the healthiest option since the shirt came from a corpse, and was told to forge an independent path to Plymouth. There, I was assured, I was *promised*, I might find a seaborne escape.

"Aren't any of you lot driving there?" I asked one of the American soldiers, whose name tag read MAITLAND. He had a huge whitehead on his top lip and I really wanted to reach out and pop it. I didn't.

"Nah, miss," came the reply. "Everything's either staying put or going east."

"So take me east."

"No room."

"Are you *sure* about that?"

"Pretty sure, miss." I laughed in frustration. "And we're the

ones staying put, anyway."
"Against those things? You won't last long."
"Someone's gotta be the bait, miss." He shrugged – he didn't seem bothered by the prospect. "Just get to Plymouth and you'll find something to get you to Europe."
"Do you promise that?" I asked, wondering if I might use his answer in a future lawsuit.
"No promises in war, miss." I sighed.
"I thought you guys were meant to protect us."
"I don't know where you got that idea from, miss." Some help these guys were.

During my invasive shower I'd been separated from George, who was thankfully marched to a different tent, and wasn't very sorry about it – I never saw him again and don't particularly miss him. I was soon following a British sergeant major through his WHSmith headquarters, soldiers going back and forth, nervous energy crackling as updates on Eternal Dawn's success (or not) loomed.
"Excuse me, sir," I insisted, "long shot, but you haven't picked up a cat at all, have you? Like, rescued one?"
"Are you being funny?" he asked, accent pleasantly Yorkshire-scented.
"No, he's called Disco – black, green collar, screams a lot?"
"I can say with certainty that I haven't," he replied, stepping outside into the car park, dotted with Land Rovers and Humvees, some daubed with red crosses. "If he's still alive he's probably doing better than any people." I didn't press the issue. He seemed like a man with a lot on his plate.

Hitching a ride with an outbound convoy of the 16 Air Assault Brigade (Maitland lied, the prick), news was filtering through – the tripods were on the move. Operation Eternal Dawn had done absolutely nothing – machines had been sighted walking unhurt from the burning mushroom cloud itself! Terror overcame the troops at Launceston, deployed on the expectation that they'd soon be sweeping through a liberated county, and though official reports record an orderly withdrawal, all I saw was hoarse fear. Outright mutiny could be found on some sections of the constantly-moving front, soldiers questioning then refusing their deployment against immortal giants, some packing up and simply vanishing. By Sunday night all organised opposition to the tripods was over as the brass underwent their own panic and headed off further mutinies with a hurried general retreat. The withdrawal, to defensive lines at the Tamar and then to the Exe, would be total. Said the forlorn Prime Minister to the nation that night, the ornate fireplace behind him ringed with Union Flags, nothing more could be done until the whole of Devon and Cornwall were evacuated. Perhaps all of Great Britain would follow. No real plan beyond the empty words of "strategic withdrawal" was offered. The only offensive operations left were the rightly celebrated efforts to lay mines at the tripods' feet, to delay or trip or trap rather than destroy, which didn't work. Construction equipment was spasmodic with the arson of digging great pitfalls all over Dartmoor. Some way, somehow, the instance of the tripod trapping itself in a mineshaft needed to be repeated. Again and again and again. Already, attention was turning to the coming battles further upcountry. Cornwall, it was undeniable, was lost to the enemy.

All the way to Plymouth in a doorless Army Land Rover, hoping to hail a final escape to Roscoff or Saint-Malo, I could myself barely ponder the state of the war. Pictures of what had played out below and all around me last night, and how much of that suffering had been, in some strange and indefinable way, at my own hand, wouldn't shake. I thought of those people's last moments; the sudden realisations, the swiftly spreading blackness advancing headlong, towering, twisting, turning the twilight to darkness, striding over its victims, running, shrieking, falling headlong, shouts of horror, choking and writhing on the ground, and the swift broadening-out of the smoke's opaque cone. And then night and extinction—nothing but a silent mass of impenetrable vapour hiding its prey. And me, up an elm, listening to music, ignorant and safe, with eyes only for the moon.

# XVI.

The paratroopers disposed of me in the grey Tamar Valley parish of Callington, for this was as south as they could go – they now turned for Tavistock and, from there, across Dartmoor to Exeter where our routing defence hoped to cobble something useful together. Cornwall had simply been a prologue; a rehearsal for the real battles to come. I would have argued my case for joining them but Plymouth was, by now, my only interest – getting out of the country completely, rather than carrying on with the pointless exercise of keeping a step or two ahead of the Things forever, was the only way to break the cycle and make an escape that might last.

In Callington, I saw my first proper signs that the social body was liquefying – along the roads, bisecting the makeshift jungle of camps which had sprung up in fields for those too weary or helpless to flee, the withdrawing military having too few resources to move them all, a foaming tumult of people beset and delayed every military vehicle with demands for transport. I saw an infant held high in the air in appeal for help and scarcely recognised my own country anymore. It was hard to believe that in just two days things had fallen so far.

Many screamed slurs of abandonment and treason at the retreating troops. All hoped for transport to the coast – the government had ordered them to get out of Cornwall by any means, while providing no means itself. The Red Zone, by now a term for the whole county, was locked down with volunteers forbidden from entering to ferry people out. The motorways were clogged to uselessness and the railways weren't running. Only the sea offered any hope of easy evacuation. A torrent of people, many briefly misled into thinking Cornwall safe again after the atomic strike and so further exodus unnecessary, therefore hurried by every available channel for Plymouth. Failing that, any seaside village would do.

As they did, as the rule of nature took over from law, official institutions and authorities were losing coherency – I saw countless police cars and ambulances lining roads throughout the valley yet vehicles were overturned, storefronts bashed open, houses on fire. It would only get worse. As news of the resurgent Blight there came with it the gutting of society. This didn't magically stop at the Tamar – it was the same across the whole South West, even as far afield as Bristol and Southampton, as whole cities packed their bags and made for *somewhere*. There was a great stampede, knowing the Things would soon be upon them, too; at Temple Meads station, people were trampled in the madness. Others were crushed as they swamped the M5, which was quickly becoming the world's biggest footpath. Soldiers, panicked and exhausted, guarding access to the motorway at Taunton and facing rioters who tried to tear through the barricade, fired shots over their heads. The "keep calm and carry on" entreaties that some posted to their social media began looking rather hollow. Wild and unproven allegations flew that the government was deliberately delaying evacuees so as to slow the Blight, busying them with slaughter, buying time to save those shires which voted more loyally.

After a fruitless struggle to get on the last bus out of Asda — the double-decker, an open-top once used for tours to Lands End, was chased by shrieking people for quite some time before it picked up speed – I followed the A388 south, pleasant green country all around, reaching St Mellion after an hour's trek with all the other dishevelled and hopeless ghouls. There, a man with a fluffy ginger beard, sitting on a postbox and shirtless but for a bow and arrow, suggested I cut east instead, into the valley itself, to the Tamar's riverbank. I could reliably follow it, he promised, all the way to Plymouth, instead of relying on street signs and hearsay and prayer. Water, he said cheerfully, was always one's best chance at life, after all. I admit I was tempted to do absolutely nothing; to, in some apathetic throe, give up and just commit myself to the harvest. Were I dead, I reasoned, I wouldn't have to do anything anymore. Maybe George had a point about nothing mattering. Then, while squatting to piss in the thickets, I had the fortune to uncover a bicycle buried deep in the undergrowth. The front tire was punctured and the seat torn like a disrespected body, but I'd already sustained enough injuries from my trek thus far – my feet were more blisters than skin, my hand was burned sore, my muscles ached all over, and, in my squatting, brambles had caused me great damage in various places – that the prospect of crashing didn't bother me. Maybe this find was a sign that I should keep going – not that I believe in signs, but I also didn't believe in aliens, so, whatever. Fuck it. The sodden woodland pathways to the river were barely passable but, owing to a gruesomely overturned horsebox, so too was the A388, which felt like another sign, so I committed to the archer-approved route.

I cycled out of the madness and, skirting the unpaved road to Halton Quay, saw nothing and nobody but two children staring at a dead and smoking crow. Soon silence, welcome silence, came and then I was through the trees and there appeared Halton Quay on the Tamar's muddy bank. I'd expected nothing and it still wasn't what I found – the river of dirty glass sailed by land overgrown with healthy weeds, the only structure a decrepit white hut which looked as if it had been on the edge of falling apart for fifty years. A metal staircase was bolted to its side, white plaster peeled like leprosy from the walls, and a black featureless cross hung above an upper window – this I took to imply it was, either now or once upon a time, a chapel. Scribbled on a wall in black marker pen were the words "something wonderful is about to happen," which I stared at for a while.

Ditching my bicycle I looked inside, hoping to stumble across food or maybe a massage parlour, but there were no communion wafers or bad wine to be found – only old pews and an old lectern and all the other old dilapidated things I should probably have expected to find in a clearly haunted church. There were better pickings further down the riverbank; a farmhouse of grey stone, the type to fetch a handsome fee at auction, half-nestled into a cluster of healthy trees with its paved driveway big enough for banger racing. Hens scattered in the garden as I hopped the waist-high fence, navigated around busy flowerbeds, and meekly pushed through the unlocked front door. Whoever owned this place had left in a hurry and taken almost everything with them – or lived in Surrey and hadn't been here in months. I found food in the form of a Smarties tube and wholemeal pitta bread, which I ate with lukewarm butter and jam from the dead fridge – the Smarties tube, I feel the need to clarify, I ate separately from the bread, and by that I don't mean the actual cardboard tube, but the Smarties within. The tube, after talking into it to see if my voice echoed, I left uneaten.

I stayed in the farmhouse for a long time, sinking into a richly brown leather armchair, not feeling ready for the effort of following the river after all of today's walking, studying from afar the family photos on the limestone mantelpiece. Their stark whiteness – the frames, not the family, who were more pink than anything else – stood at odds with the rustic lounge. Inclined to loiter in place, in some irritating life-or-death procrastination, I felt like those many hundreds along the road who, in absence of hope or sheer disbelief at their situation, had taken to immobility. Like a deer which, too exhausted to run, just sits down in front of the wolf. Without access to fresh news, the farmhouse having a desktop monitor and keyboard but the electricity long gone, I felt no strong impetus to move. However, there then crept into my head a thought which I didn't like at all – that this house had been left unlocked and unemptied because its owner remained, in some room I hadn't explored, and that he might find me or, worse, I'd find him. Maybe in the bath with arteries opened or swinging from a curtain rod in the bedroom. This I didn't want – sharing a house, even with a hypothetical corpse, was undesirable. University had taught me that I didn't play well with others – Raymond Watkins moved out at the end of the first semester just because of how many arguments over the washing up we were having. I was, of course, always right.

It was the idea of the house not being so empty after all which at last induced me to get out the leather sofa, difficult as it was given how it seemed to be swallowing me like some strange beast, and go outside to follow the Tamar to Plymouth. From the start, I worried I might mistake some stupid tributary for the real river and follow it in completely the wrong direction until I managed to end up back in Hayle. The mere idea of that happening made me so angry that I had to stop walking for a second.

Climbing over a stile, which swung open as I did like in a Buster Keaton film, and replacing it on its fiddly latch because that's what you're meant to do, I followed a narrow footpath between trees on the murky river's edge, alone but for the occasional reeking dog muck bin. Passing several cottages and farmhouses in little places which I assume had names, at last I saw a few other fugitives who had plainly pieced together the same strategy as me, but I kept my distance. People were not something I was in the mood for. The Tamar's wandering shape meant following deep, meandering bends which at times had me frustratedly walking north before swerving back in the opposite direction, but I stubbornly kept to my plan for I was becoming sure that any deviation would mean death. The tripods were close – so close – but so too was safety. Just over there, across the water, lay Devon – I could have swam, but I didn't trust the current, didn't want to get wet, and wouldn't have been any closer to Plymouth where the evacuation ships better be waiting for me. Crossing this little river, obviously, wouldn't put me beyond the tripods' reach. They had pretty long strides. This side or that side, I had to follow the Tamar, wherever it wanted to go.

Kingsmill Lake was where I became truly agitated, however, and got closest to abandoning my entire plan. Downriver, I could make out the Tamar Bridge's distant blur, the Royal Albert Bridge's iron trusses just past it, with Plymouth starting at their furthest toll booths. Yet, though so close I could almost hear the motorists arguing the injustice of paying £2 just to leave Cornwall, geography was conspiring against me. Following the river meant walking a good two kilometres back north, entirely the wrong direction, following a wandering tributary as I feared. This river had no concern for my priorities. It was a painful moment – I could *see* the bridge but couldn't reach it without walking back towards the tripods for God knew how long (I didn't, then, know it was two whole kilometres. If I did, I might have drowned myself). All this meandering would doom me – I'm sure it's easy for a reader to look at a map and point out my stupidity in thinking the river could just be followed, but I didn't have a map, did I, you unhelpful wanker?

I sat stewing on a brick wall at Kellock Mill, an old inn with a water wheel at the lake's edge, joined by a number of alternately plotting or despairing refugees. They, too, couldn't bear the thought of walking back north. One man ranted at length that the RNLI were too busy pulling migrants from the Channel to rescue *them*. Some, not weighed down by sentimentality toward all they had brought with them, were electing to abandon their bags, strip, and swim the four hundred metres to the golf course opposite. Saltash, then the bridges, then Plymouth, then escape, lay just beyond it. Those left behind were rifling through the ditched bags before their owners were to their knees in the water. I thought about following but I'd lost the emotional catharsis which drove me to intercept the boat in Hayle and, further, I was too shattered and sore to think I could. There were whispers of everyone swimming together as one, to support those too weak to go alone, but I didn't trust their plan nor their charity. Yet it wasn't, really, that I didn't trust them or my breaststroke – it was that I didn't trust myself. Guilt, mental exhaustion, and a quiet but increasingly intense hatred of what I was weighed me down. Part of me feared that, if I started swimming, I might just stop halfway across and let myself sink into the murk.

Realising that the longer I stared at the shimmering water, the worse I'd make myself feel, I put my masochism aside and began picking my way along the lake's edge and up the river which fed it. With each step I prayed it wouldn't take too long before narrowing to the point that I could comfortably swim or, ideally, wade. I felt an utter moron – why, of all moments in my stupid life, did I choose *today* to take advice from shirtless nutters? Now I was stuck on my present, practically pointless, course. I felt helpless to myself and the world. The two main things. If a tripod appeared over the treetops, I imagined, I'd forget my tiredness and be first to jump into the water – I was something of a trendsetter in that regard – but for now I kept to a sheltered footpath through bushy trees, like clumps of green mashed potatoes, along slimy mud banks, feeling sorry for myself. Even pouting. Then, just off to the right, past the trees, I heard a woman scream. Without a thought against it, I hurried off the path and in her direction, sensing a chance to make up for past failures.

Running up a steep hill resplendent with poppies and fighting my way through a tall flowering hedge, I burst onto a narrow road, hemmed in by the hedges on either side. At once I saw the commotion's cause – a silver Fiat 500, Sheffield University sticker in the back window, was halted, partly backed into the hedge, with an estate car blocking it in front. Three men crowded around the Fiat and, with difficulty, were dragging two young women out. Plainly, they'd blocked them with their car and set upon them.

One of the women, small and impish and dressed in flares with round glasses, was torn from her seat and thrown onto the road with a squeal; one of the men advanced on her. Her friend, a slender black woman with braids and dungarees, was having a leg pulled on by the other two. They tried to wrench her from the car but she, and her still-attached seatbelt, had other ideas. Her free leg kicked fiercely amid screams for them to fuck off. Grasping the situation, with the brainsick men's attention fully focused on the women, rendering me invisible, I knew it'd be good for my own well-being not to get involved. Yeah. I ran full-pelt at the one who stood alone.

He leered over the smaller woman, who lay on the road trying to scramble backwards, facing me side-on. He still hadn't seen me and his ribs offered quite the invitation for an outstretched elbow. I never thought I was the type of person to do a thing like this – but I did it, crashing into him with rhinoceros force, nearly snapping my arm and knocking all the air out of my lungs. With a bleat he fell against the hatchback's boot, winded, and his would-be victim scurried a few paces away to get to her feet, hands grazed by her fall, now standing against the hedge and breathing heavily, unsure whether to stare at him or me.

"Fuck!" spluttered the man, sprawled against the Fiat, clutching his side, outrage in his baby blues. I tried to ponder my next move and realised I had nothing. "You fuckin' bitch, you broke somethin', you fuckin' bitch!" His compatriots, distracted by my arrival, inadvertently let the slender woman wriggle free and clamber from the car via the opposite door. Hobbling, given her leg had been twisted this way and that, she faced them over the roof.

"Alright!" shouted one of the two men still standing, burly and big-eared, throwing up his arms and advancing on me, "you and me, then, come on!" Realising a fight was unavoidable, I suddenly became very aware that I had no idea how to fight someone. Those YouTube compilations of bouncers fighting drunks outside Salford nightclubs were about as much training as I had. Jabbing sounded simple enough – but don't you punch with all force in the *shoulders*, not arms? Did I have that right? Balls – couldn't remember and he was getting closer. Damn my delicate frame – ideal when your attack plan is a sharp running elbow, not so ideal when the power of an ultimate warrior is called for. Naturally, I took a few steps back, my body language as uncertain as it could be, which only encouraged him. Shit! It was dog eat dog and I was the dog! The second dog!

"Get away from her!" then shouted the braided woman, just as the third man rounded the car and came upon her – she was more ready for him than I was for my quarry. But not very. She threw a kick to his legs, which did little, before he had her by the collar and launched her into the hedge – its foliage was so thick that she bounced right off and back into him, giving extra *oomph* to the punch she landed on his throat. He doubled over, clutching his Adam's apple, and, unsure what move to unleash next, she thought it best to shove him with the force of her whole body behind it and another "fuck off!" for good luck. Almost obligingly, he went down.

His friend, still advancing on me, looked back and realised he was deserted – I hoped this would make him back off but, instead, he threw a sturdy punch at my face. It struck my mouth and, pain ringing all over along with a strange relief that I hadn't felt any teeth leave my gums, sent me tumbling onto the tarmac. He stood over me – I'd have little chance against his walking boot, if he brought it against my jaw as I anticipated, had the braided lady not gained his attention.

"Oi! Fuckface!" He turned and, seeing that she now wielded a long, black-hilted bread knife seized from her belongings in the car, backed away. He put distance between himself and us while his friends, writhing with pain, watched.

"You respond to fuckface?" I asked him, still lying on the road, held up by my elbows, tasting blood in my mouth. Nobody laughed, which I get. Instead, at the first chance, the woman kicked a second knife (this was already too many knives in any other scenario) along the road towards me and – though I had no desire to plunge it into anyone – I picked it up for appearance's sake.

"Alright, alright," he insisted, as she waved the knife threateningly – I don't know how she could have been friendly about it. He had a laugh lingering in his voice like this was all a big joke. The man I had bodied (let me have that) was already staggering back up the road. "We're going, see? Just chill out, love, just chill."

"Don't you tell me to chill out," she growled as he hauled up his other friend by the shoulders, still clutching his throat and spluttering in anguished pain at each step, dragging him back to their car. He glanced from it to theirs and back again.

"Don't suppose you could move your car?" he asked, awkwardly.

"Are you serious?"

"Fair, fair," he said, the three climbing back in, chastened. They reversed up the road – one of them made obscene gestures at us to soothe his bruised ego – undertook a painfully long six-point turn, and disappeared.

I climbed to my feet, rubbing my mouth, blood on my tongue, and the braided woman hurried to me.

"You alright?" she asked, looking surprisingly well made up given the circumstances.

"Yeah, fine, I guess," I lied, my face throbbing; we were all panting like thirsty dogs. "That was fun."

"Split your lip."

"Yeah, I bet," I said, putting my hands on my knees, the blood clogging my throat unpleasantly. "But I've still got my incisors. And you had that knife all this time?"

"Yeah, sorry," she said.

"Apologise to my lip." I sighed and glanced at the serrated blade still in my own hand. "I guess you'd like this back."

"Keep it – I'm not the type for dual-wielding. I'm not..." She thought for a second. "...Lara Croft."

"Fair." I laughed and tucked it into a back pocket. I looked at her friend; she was huddled against the hedge and eyeing me suspiciously. "You okay?"

"I'm fine," she snapped.

"She's been through it, don't worry about her," the slender woman said, holding out a hand. "I'm Cynthia. You?" I shook her hand, answered, and, after introducing her friend as Linda, Cynthia thanked me for my help. Linda went to the Fiat and checked the engine – the men's interception hadn't been delicate. They'd rammed them head-on – it must have been a spur of the moment kind of thing. Cold contempt simmered inside me – I half-wished they'd come back just so I could finish the job. Hopefully they'd wait until I caught my breath and took some extensive close-combat courses.

"Don't mind if I sit down for a 'min, do you?" I asked and, without waiting for a reply, pulled open the passenger door and sat sideways on the seat, gasping for air but trying not to be too theatrical in case these girls got unimpressed with me. "I swear I'm fitter than this."

"Want a tissue?" Cynthia asked. "You're bleeding pretty bad."

"Oh, cheers."

"Look in my bag," she said over her shoulder, having turned to check on Linda. "In the footwell. Might be some in there, or there's some McDonald's napkins in the other door, I think. Can't be that much mayo and snot on them." Not wanting to root through a stranger's bag, I chose the napkins – they came away from my face streaked with hot blood. I looked from them to Cynthia and felt annoyed at the contrast we were making.

"How do you look *that* good in these circumstances?" I asked her; she looked surprised by the question. "You too," I said quickly to Linda, who just shook her head.

"Genetics," Cynthia replied.

"I missed a trick, then."

Cynthia spent some time talking to Linda in hushed tones, and I tried not to listen, as I sensed she was in need of comfort and not spectators. Eventually, Linda and my lip having calmed, Cynthia came back to me.

"So where'd you come from?" she asked. "Reckon those pricks thought this'd be perfect for an ambush – ain't nobody anywhere. You're a bit of a lifesaver, ey?"

"I don't know about lifesaver, you seemed to have everything in hand," I replied, dabbing at my stinging lip. "And St Ives is where I'm from."

"Jesus," she said. "You've heard about-"

"Yeah, I know, I know," I said. "What can you do?"

"Nothing, apparently," she replied, looking west, over the fields. "If you can't kill them with nukes, what can you kill them with?"

"The power of the human spirit," I replied, and she laughed.

"We're not even meant to be here – just on holiday. Dad's a doctor so he told us to get back to Dorking on our own – only got a provisional license, you know, I shouldn't even be driving. He wanted to stay and help people."

"What kind of doctor was he?" I immediately regretted my use of the past tense – but Cynthia didn't seem to react.

"Burns specialist."
"So he's got a lot of work, then." Cynthia nodded darkly.
"Don't know where he is now – it's Cornwall, so, somewhere bleak, probably."
"Don't say that about my friend, Cornwall," I joked.
"Don't tell me you like it here?" I shrugged.
"Eh. It's home."
"That's fair – and it's usually not on fire, I bet?"
"Not all the time. I hope your dad's alright."
"Yeah, same. He said he'd find us at our hotel by nine and we've been waiting on the river for him all day but…" She shrugged, too. "He's still not shown."
"And then," said Linda, suddenly slamming down the bonnet, making us both jump, "*someone* thought it'd be good to avoid the traffic so we came this way. Great plan, right? Great fucking plan."
"Change the record," hissed Cynthia. "You want the Blight or you want those three? I know what I choose. Can go ask 'em to try again, if you like?"
"You're not funny," she said. "Can we go?"
"Wait, so is he both of your dads? I asked. "Are you sisters?"
"Half-sisters," said Linda matter-of-factly, not looking at me when she spoke.
"Ah, that makes sense."
"Why?" I couldn't tell if she was joking or if I was being a knob – imagine, *me*, being a knob – so I changed the subject.
"So, where you gonna go now?" Cynthia shrugged.
"Home. But reckon we'll be happy with anything in that direction," she said, pointing eastwards. "But some arsehole put a river in the way. We've got valuables – can't swim it. There *any* bridges at all closer than Saltash?"
"I couldn't tell you," I replied honestly. "But unless you wanna go *towards* the aliens I think Saltash is the only option at this point. The Tamar's been fucking me raw all day."
"Jesus Christ," Cynthia moaned. "I'm never gonna get out of Cornwall. I miss properly franchised coffee outlets *so much*."

"We have those," I protested playfully.

"Where?" she asked, looking around at the empty road. A pink-bellied chaffinch watched us from atop the hedge. "Where are they?"

"Come on."

"Yes, come *on*!" yelled Linda, and we both stared at her; it was always surprising when such a big noise came from such a small person. "Is this how we're spending today? There's great big alien death machines on their way and you two're just stood here flirting."

"We're not-" Through the hedges, flashes of noise burst the sky open. Bombs were falling on unseen targets. All three of us watched in silence for a moment, in eerie anticipation, as the sound fell away.

"This holiday sucks," Cynthia sighed. She looked me up and down. "You need a lift?"

"Oh, I would *love* a lift," I said. "Sure you've got room?"

"It'll be cosy – but we'll manage. Won't we, Lin?"

"What?" Linda asked accusingly, crossing her arms. "I don't mind if she comes with. I'm not a bitch; I know you're expecting me to be, but I'm not – if I'm not allowed to be stressed now, then when? Huh? *Huh*?"

"Okay, okay, relaxio," Cynthia said, as I climbed into the back – made as intimate as promised by the haul of luggage, including bags, a duvet, and a shower curtain "liberated" from their hotel, and we set off upriver, Cynthia driving at a snail's pace. With the power of modern technology – a built-in Satnav, for the Blight hadn't managed to take down our satellites just yet – it took little time to turn onto the main road which took us to the village of Botusfleming. Traffic, all equally overloaded cars, began to build up. Hitch-hiking, I realised, might have been an option all along, although I suppose most other drivers wouldn't have felt indebted to me like these two perhaps did.

Outside the village, beside a vast and empty field, we saw sappers putting up triangular signs which, beneath a skull and crossbones, warned 'DANGER – MINES.'

"They're bluffing," muttered Linda.

"Wanna bet?" I asked. We kept driving, south, until after a thousand tight roads and tighter bends we reached the A388's slow-moving traffic jam. Armed roadblocks and diversions everywhere, we entered the outskirts of militarised Saltash – at the vast retail park orbiting a roundabout like the TK Maxx and Domino's were moons around Jupiter, all manner of military equipment was assembling for withdrawal over the river. Tanks lined up as if in a showroom, plastic coatings over their cannons, and personnel loaded up lorries by the dozen. I even saw a Chinook picking up crates of supplies, hoisted by heavy-duty cables, and wondered what they could possibly contain that was worth the effort. Our ace in the hole had been used – and had failed. Another Chinook swooped low with a Humvee attached to its cable, like a conker, bound for Devon.

Through the journey, traffic at a crawl at least partly because of the growing crowds trooping down the road like it was pedestrianised, I told Cynthia and Linda my story – my initial escape, then foolhardy return and subsequent odyssey from St Ives and across the county, all the while mourning my beloved Disco, and all the close-calls which characterised my adventure. If you can call it that. Cynthia was sympathetic to my plight, Linda too once the cat and his wonderful fatness was mentioned, but less so to my conviction that seaborne evacuation was the only option left. They hoped to drive all the way home, clutched by the conviction that all would be fine once they returned to Dorking. Everything had always been fine in Dorking.

We traded stories and banter, Cynthia and I more than mostly silent Linda, but after a time the jovial camaraderie died away and made room for unease. Try as we might, we couldn't relax. There was still no information on what direction the machines were moving, nor how fast, and that inevitable sense that they could be on us at any moment wasn't made any more comfortable by the military's antsy vibes. Indeed, as we slowly rolled onto the standstill motorway where, ahead, a tunnel yawned open like the mouth of a colossal concrete worm, we just felt like targets. It didn't help much that through the alleys and avenues between each car there ran that boiling stream of people, rushing the bridge to which the tunnel led, their fear perpetually renewed by the grey and indistinct dust specks which had started falling from the sky. Haunted snowflakes. Were they radioactive or did they once constitute a human being? Best not to think about it. Cynthia, detached or ignorant enough for me to be very jealous, tried to clear the windscreen of the dust by spraying it with detergent and turning on the wipers. She only dirtied it further, smearing radiation or remnants of vaporised humanity across the screen, and sighed at her misfortune.

At the sight of a much-fatigued soldier waving forward the inching traffic, I rolled down my window with such hurry as to ache my arm.

"Don't break the handle," Linda snapped.

"I'm not breaking it," I hissed back, before returning my attention to the soldier. "Hey! Any news?"

"Any of you injured?" he replied with the vibe of a hungover student.

"No – how far's the aliens now?"

"If you're not injured, you gotta keep moving," he said, ignoring any further inquiries, so I hopped from the car with Cynthia's assurance that she wouldn't abandon me to the Blight and, fighting my way through the throngs, pursued answers from all around, starting with a man I saw tapping madly at his phone.

"Any news?" I asked.

"Nah, pet," he said angrily, "got no service – they've been knocking down the phone towers."

"4G should work here, surely," I said – bear in mind that I had

absolutely no idea how 4G worked. "There's gotta be a mast in Plymouth."
"Must be overloaded, or they're putting it all to military comms, or whatever – fuck if I know. Nothing worked before, don't know why it'd start working now. You can thank austerity for that!" You'd think at least one person would be more helpful but, no, everyone was useless.

I turned to go back to the car and, as I turned, bumped into another soldier. This one was young, with sunken eyes, and dressed only partially in his uniform. At once I knew he was a deserter and, by his eyes, hopelessly lost in the world and in himself, like a ghost only halfway possessing an empty body.
"You okay?" I asked, pointlessly, and he stared at me.
"It's all good," he replied, eventually, as I regarded him, worried it'd just take a nudge for him to launch himself at me.
"You need anything? Food? Water?"
"I lost three-fourths of my men out there," he said, gesturing limply over the hills, and he left. After a moment of wondering if I should shout something encouraging after him, I went back to the car. There the mostly unhelpful radio, prone to only brief spasms of information as it relayed old news for listeners far from danger, reported that the machines were being officially described as "meandering," and thought to be consolidating their positions again. This news, though, was bland and generalised, often going back to reports of foreign governments making their own preparations or volunteers welcoming refugees in Birmingham or Norwich or even Normandy, which was lovely and encouraging, but I wanted news relevant to me. It wasn't forthcoming – it was as if they'd forgotten that there might still be people in danger and in need of reliable information.

Explosive flashes were starting to pop from beyond the hillside. Another round of long-range bombings were underway, it was said, with the hope that constant harassment, even if not destructive, would at least inhibit the invaders in their business. With each explosion, we could be sure of how near the tripods were – near.

"Radio said every road's blocked from here to fuckin' Wiltshire," said Cynthia, hunched over the wheel, while Linda tore into a party pack of Revels – to her credit, she offered me plenty. "Half the country's on the move."

"The rout of civilisation," said Linda, as if she were reciting Keats. "The massacre of mankind."

"What are you, chief dramatist?" I asked. She glared at me. "This car won't get us anywhere. If I was you, I'd ditch it and come back and get it after the war. That's what I did in St Ives. Not like the Blight'll steal it."

"But it might get nuked – like yours probably did," said Linda. "You know how much this car cost me?"

"It's yours? You're not even driving."

"License got suspended."

"Why's that stopping you? Cynthia's just on a provisional."

"That's allowed if I'm in the car, idiot. Think."

"Yeah, alright, whatever," I sighed, not eager for another fight, though I did have the knife now – Linda had been stewing in stress ever since the traffic jam began and I couldn't say I blamed her.

"Look," said Cynthia, sitting back and staring up through the sunroof, looking at the clouds colliding into each other like suicidal battleships, "I'm not saying *no* to leaving the car, but what's the plan then? Why's walking any better?"

"We get a boat," I said at once.

"For fuck sake," Linda muttered. "That's not a plan. 'Get a boat.' In what world is that a plan? You sound like a dad who just turned fifty." Someone knocked on the window, demanding a lift, pointing out how many more could fit into our car if we jettisoned the luggage – silently, Cynthia showed him her knife. He quickly disappeared.

"We're right next to *Plymouth*, we can get on one, surely!" I said. "Plymouth's whole thing is having boats!"

"Yeah, and don't you think everyone else is thinking the same thing?" Linda asked, gesturing to the people all around us. She then shouted with some hysteria: "And if we don't get a ride, we're trapped! You know those things are everywhere, right? We're in a killzone! No, we're not going nowhere. You're not killing me."

"Nobody's killing anyone," I said. "But trust me – we're going nowhere fast unless we try getting out of the country altogether."

"The radio did say the EU's letting Brits in without any paperwork," said Cynthia, barely audible over the increasingly panicky beeps of the cars around us. "Which surprised me."

"Nice of them," growled Linda; I could see she was clutching her own hands to control their shaking. "I'm still not getting out the car. We're not wandering through the fucking woods or whatever. It's just not happening. We're getting away. Stop sabotaging us."

"Have you *seen* the Blight?" I asked Linda, suddenly. "I mean, actually seen them? Up close?"

"No," she said, staring straight ahead, anticipating what was coming.

"Well I have," I said. "More than most – and I've seen what happens when they gas you. Or burn you. Or *catch* you. Trust me – you don't want that."

"Clue's in the words 'gas,' and 'burn,'" said Cynthia. "Nothing good ever comes with those words."

"Except fish fingers, maybe," I said.

"That doesn't even make sense," muttered Linda.

"It doesn't, really, does it?" Cynthia and I both sniggered – Linda didn't. "Look, Linda, don't kill yourself over your possessions. Your life's more valuable."

"It's not that – I just don't want to do something I can't take back," she said quietly, as a pair of fighter jets screeched loudly overhead. "We're making progress – we'll be at the bridge soon. We walk – we're on foot and we're slow and if we're wrong we either burn or we choke or we get stomped on or... or a hundred other things. That's if they don't harvest us first – those things *eat* people!"

"That's a rumour," said Cynthia. "Don't be spreading rumours."

"Does this seriously look like progress to you?" I asked, doing the same as she had done, gesturing to the gridlock ahead of us. I felt my frustration build but I really didn't want to shout – I might find myself relying on her, some time soon, even if it was just to find a good Parisian hotel. "There's no good option. Come on – we haven't moved in twenty minutes. Let's ditch the car. Let's get out of here. We're so close now – the moment we're out to sea, we're safe."

"Until they start invading France," Linda said.

"And they'll surrender fast," Cynthia added.

"Then we'll go to Spain," I retorted. Cynthia snorted a laugh and Linda glared.

"Fine," Linda said at last, her face beetroot, her eyes watery, and I started to wonder, too, if a mistake was being made – but I had to believe this was the right choice. I just had to. "Fine. Fuck it. Fine. Just... put the car somewhere out the way. Don't just abandon it in the road. Don't fuck up people who wanna go this way and actually survive."

"That's more than fair," I said and, though I felt relentlessly impatient, I waited until we could reach a Burger King car park just before the tunnel to safely deposit the Fiat. The Burger King was still open – the queue was too long for us. From there, we were on foot, three more bodies in the crowd, vanishing into the tunnel, passing through its vision of dark claustrophobia. Orange warning lights flashed around us as if we were trapped in some nightmarish nightclub and, then, the bridge to Plymouth emerged from the light at the end.

With the sun high in the sky, the day had become unfairly hot and yet, with more flakes of grey ash drifting down by the minute, it also seemed to be snowing. I found myself constantly, uselessly, picking it out of my hair and off my clothes, only for it to be replaced a moment later. Everyone was finding the snowfall very disconcerting and I heard many anxious questions about whether this was fallout – no, said someone who looked like they knew what they were talking about (they wore glasses), just what happens when aliens and conventional munitions set half a county on fire. An increasing number of people were following our example and abandoning their cars, lugging great armfuls of belongings to the bridge, all towards what some seemed to imagine was automatic safety – the Tamar Bridge's grey towers, beyond the toll booth platoons, were now clearly visible over vehicles' roofs. Beacons for all to converge. Pushing through the crowd was like riding into the smoke of a fire, the air hot and pungent from all the bodies, while the mass roared like flames themselves.

Getting closer, I felt a murmuring grow stronger, spreading through everyone, nervous energy crackling – far up ahead I could just about see that, once reaching the toll booths, the crowd was stopping and collecting and advancing no further.
"Something's up," I said and Cynthia, gripping my arm to avoid being swept away in the tide, jumped several times to look over the heads.
"Definitely," she agreed. A man in smart but crumpled clothes passed by, eyes on the ground, pushing back against the crowd.
"Bastards, bastards, bastards, bastards, bastards, bastards," he muttered, almost wailed, loudly and quickly, one hand clutched in his hair and the other beating invisible things.
"Mushrooms, mushrooms, mushrooms, mushrooms," *I* muttered, which was so stupid, whether you get it or not, and I hope you don't.
"Everything alright, mate?" Linda asked, as Cynthia tried to collect herself from my joke, and he stared at her in an aneurysm of rage.
"They ain't letting nobody by on the bridge!" he yelled.
"Hold on, hold on," I said, Cynthia's laughter snuffed out at once, "take it easy; who won't let you by?"

"The Army!" he said. "I think they're putting mines up on the bridge! They look like mines!"

"Mines?" Linda cried. "On the bridge?!" With a start we looked back towards the toll booths and the simmering crowd. It was growing dangerously packed up there.

"Yes, mines!"

"Are they gonna blow it?" she asked with horror.

"I don't know!" he shouted tearfully, a jet screaming by overhead, causing all eyes to shoot skyward, "I don't know what they're gonna do!" He went on his way without once looking back. We pushed deeper into the crowd – it quickly became clear that soldiers in helmets with polycarbonate face coverings, many wielding riot shields and truncheons, were blocking anyone from crossing the bridge's span. By now I could see Plymouth, a grey formless mass, and the banks of the valley which the bridge crossed. We were *so* close.

"Oh, that's just not fair," I said.

"They better have a *fucking* good reason for this!" Linda shouted. A woman, stood beside us, shouted a reply.

"They think we're gonna stampede!" It was hard to hear her over the psychodrama of the crowd. "Reckon we'll all trample each other if we go all at once!"

"Are they thick?!" I shouted back, buffeted constantly as people fought for position, the air hot with breath, ash still falling, one flake finding its way into my eye, "this is the best way to *start* a fuckin' stampede!"

"Tell them! Tell them!" She threw up her hands in frustration.

"Your attention please!" A soldier, stood on a blockading lorry, was shouting down a megaphone like a town crier. "We are pausing all crossings over the bridge! Please be patient!"

"We'll all be patients at this rate!" Linda spat, as others yelled every curse under the sun. "Hospital patients!"

"You could've done that better, I feel like," I shouted over the noise and she shot me a look which I probably deserved – I considered telling her it made my lady parts tremble but, even if I had, I wouldn't have been heard over the repeated honks of

the plumbing van behind us.
"Maybe there's an alien near," suggested Cynthia. "And they don't want it chopped down with us on it."
"I don't care," whined Linda. "I just wanna go." Anxiety was palpable, both around me and inside me – I really wanted to get over that stupid bridge. I even considered attempting a Bavarian fire drill with the soldiers, hoping that if I pretended I had the authority, and acting really, really confident about it, I might convince them to let me by, but I doubted both my metal and my outfit.

"Make way!" I heard voices cry. "Make way!" Two men stormed past back towards the tunnel, hauling a surfboard improvised into a stretcher, on which lay a woman with a dirt-caked face – I supposed she'd been trapped in a crush. A goofy French bulldog followed, lead dragging on the floor, tongue lolling, seeming to enjoy the whole exercise. I wondered how bad things were in this crowd if people were dropping like that. Grabbing the shoulders of strangers either side of me, I hauled myself up to look over the multitude of heads behind us. Back toward the tunnel was a tumultuous stream of people, pent in between the crash barriers, their individuality merging into a rushing and indistinct multitude. How many, I wondered, were falling beneath feet or having the air pressed from their lungs? Few were coming aside from the flood – the hillside to the right was too steep for many to climb, though some still perched, but one could clamber over the crash-barrier on the left quite easily – there were side-streets leading downward into Saltash, but that was no sanctuary. Everyone, like me, saw Plymouth as the only imaginable place of safety. It had become the obsession driving this crowd. Suggest leaving the road, and losing your spot, and they'd look at you like you'd shit in their kettle. A tiny handful elbowed out of the stream but, for the most part, just rested for a moment before plunging back in – there was no route out but the bridge and the ships it led to, and any delay only brought their doom closer.

"This is insane!" Linda wailed, tears breaking from her eyes. "We're trapped!"

"Go on! Go on!" cried voices further down, and I saw that their owners were forcefully attempting to break through the barricade, soldiers beating them away with truncheons and hauling them off the wire fencing they tried to scale. In my mind I saw the crowd as some massive human battering ram against the Army's lines.

"Get back! Get back!" the megaphone-wielding soldier roared. People were pressed against me from all sides, hurting my chest, and I realised I hadn't enough space even to turn.

"Push!" someone shouted in my ear.

"No!" I shouted back, fearing the crush, my voice hoarse. "Don't!"

"They're coming!" came another scream. A rumour was now prancing around, gaining speed and energy and seizing the wretched crowd's mind, that the Army was stalling us deliberately – that we were bait for the tripods to gorge on while Plymouth safely emptied. Ahead, over shoulders, I saw missiles thrown at the soldiers. Misty white clouds of tear gas rose from the crowd's crunching front lines.

"They're coming!" I heard again.

In one car against which I briefly became pinned, there was a man in a Salvation Army t-shirt leaning from the window, ignoring me, and shouting.

"Eternity!" he bawled, meaninglessly and repeatedly. "Eternity!" After a few moments, with the crowd bustling this way and that, our little spot became marginally less congested and so I could breathe and move again.

"You guys okay?!" I yelled to Cynthia and Linda; Cynthia held up two thumbs.

"This sucks!" she shouted back.

"Just get to the side of the road and wait for me!" I replied.

"What? Where're you going?"

"I'm gonna find a way across!"

"There's no way across!" wailed Linda, hands on her head. "We're fucked!"
"We're fucked when we give up!" I shouted back. "Cynthia, get her off the road, *now*! I'll be back!" Cynthia took Linda's hand and led her through the crowd to the crash barrier, as I started pushing my way forward, trying to fight my way closer to the bridge. Ducking and weaving between the narrow spaces still existent between some in the crowd, the bridge's towers grew at each step. I was regularly deafened by people stupidly punching at their car horns and saw desperate fistfights over nothing which could have mattered, babies crying from several directions, resuscitation being attempted on a limp woman. Others had found refuge atop vehicles – each was an island of refugees above the vast crowd whether the drivers liked it or not – and some atop sat motionless, staring at nothing with miserable eyes; others held phones skyward in search of signal or used their height to waste time voyeuristically recording footage of those below. More than once I found a lifeless body pressed beneath scrabbling feet. The traffic was of all types – cars, taxis, buses, vans, a recycling truck, a streetsweeper marked CORNWALL COUNTY COUNCIL, an articulated lorry whose trailer read "Reynolds Heating & Bathroom Plumbing," all were crowded with swarms of riders. Dark and dried blood splashed the front wheels of a tractor.

I gained some paces down the motorway, closer to the soldiers; close enough to hear their young and panicked voices.
"Clear the way!" they cried.
"Get back right now!"
"I'm not asking – I'm telling!"
"Eternity! Eternity!" came echoing down the road – or was it coming from the soldiers now? – and my eyes itched as smoky tear gas drifted over me. I wiped at them with my (well, technically, someone else's) sleeves, still staggering through, determined to reach the barricade and at least confirm with my own eyes that it was impassable, at one point crawling

between a man's legs despite trampling's omnipresent threat. With every bump I feared tripping, going down, and never having a chance to get up. Sad, haggard women trooped by, away from the bridge, crying children clinging to their hands, faces smeared with tears and dirt. A tattooed man in a black tracksuit, clearly smashed, stood on a car bonnet and loudly lectured that we were lambs to the slaughter, that the tripods weren't real, that we were all hoodwinked, gesticulating with his Special Brew like it had all the answers.

I was now only a dozen people deep from the barricade. Bridge towers loomed over me like concrete giants and I saw batons waved in the crowd's direction, people spasmodically bouncing off plastic riot shields, heard screamed accusations of treason and murder. Black dread told me that I was wasting precious time – I hadn't a prayer of passing. Perhaps, I wondered for a moment, the neighbouring pretzel-shaped railway bridge could be an alternative but, remembering I'm not a train, I was quick to add that to my growing list of fool's gambits. A soldier, I noticed, was being led away from the roadblock and down the bridge with blood trickling from his head, and I felt relieved that some of the objects being thrown had found their mark. There couldn't have been a decent justification for shutting the bridge down – whatever it might be, I'd refuse to accept it. Stress burned inside me, oxygenated by my helplessness – and amid all that was said and shouted and screeched in my ear, one refrain ran clearest and most universal of them all.

"They're coming!"

Biting the proverbial bullet before the soldiers started sending real ones, I turned away and squeezed back through the outraged crowd to where I hoped Linda and Cynthia would still be. As I went, I noticed a little girl of no more than eight, all alone, soot-faced and crying, stood against the front of a van – she'd lost her shoes and her pink floral socks were stained scarlet with wet blood. I awoke in an instant and, without a word, scooped her up, carrying her as I went, having not an inkling of what we would do with her but certain that leaving her here wouldn't be it. I whispered encouragement into her ear but, since touching her, she'd become very still. I made it only a few steps before I heard shrieks.

"Ellie! Ellie!" A woman, the purest of fear in her voice, burst from the bodies and the child suddenly wriggled from my hands and darted to her and disappeared with her back into the tide.

"They're coming!"

Linda and Cynthia were, I was unimaginably relieved to find, where I left them – they stood on the other side of the metal barrier, free from the crush, agitated and ready to be anywhere else. A few had done the same but, as everyone could see, if you weren't on the road then you had no way over the river.

"Any news?" asked Cynthia. She looked resigned to her fate.

"Shit's fucked."

"You know, I thought it might be." I stared back out at the crowd, halted with no more room to push forward, and wondered again how awful it was to be trapped at the very front, pinned between riot shields and a few thousand desperate souls who didn't care if they walked around or over you if it meant getting to Plymouth. Plymouth, of all places.

"I'm feeling very lucky to have friends right now," I said.

"That what we are?" scowling Linda asked.

"Look," snapped Cynthia, cutting in, "this ain't happening – we're gonna have to cross the river some other way. Swim if we have to. It's gotta be done." I was stung with disappointment that the one thing I'd spent the afternoon trying to avoid was now unavoidable – the opposite of what I wanted – but to stay here was to join a suicide pact.

"Maybe we don't have to swim," I said, hopefully. "Maybe there's boats picking people up on the banks?" Cynthia shook her head.

"Everyone I've asked says there's been no boats for a while now.

They're all going to the beaches – there's thousands of people on all them, too. It's a nonsense. Yeah; swimming it might be our only chance."

"Great," sulked Linda, "first the car, now our bags, we'll be naked by the time we're out of the country."

"I can only hope," sniggered Cynthia, winking at me – I didn't know what to feel about that, but it certainly didn't have to be something bad. Once we were in France or Spain, presuming we didn't end up another pair of skeletons on the riverbed, I'd try getting to know her a little better – they had champagne in France, probably.

"I'm not much of a swimmer," I warned, as we hopped the embankment, passed something called a 'holistic soft tissue therapist,' and drove down a street leading to the Tamar. "I don't think I'm in any state for it. And are we sure the currents are okay?" A rustic mock Tudor pub, the Black Swan, appeared, sheltered under tall trees with chairs overturned in the beer garden. It was still open for business with revellers, including a traffic warden and a vicar, enjoying the 'apocalypse open bar' for, as the wooden board on the pavement said, it was "last call forever!" Tempted though we were, we carried on, hoping to get down the bank to the Tamar's licking edges.

"You'll be fine, don't worry," Cynthia reassured me repeatedly, then: "Linda's a lifeguard."

"Really?" I looked at her.

"Used to be. Only at the leisure centre but I probably remember all of it. It's only swimming."

"And a bit of chest compressions," added Cynthia. "Remember, when you need to resuscitate someone, you pinch their nose, put a sock in their mouth, and twist their nipples like you're revving an engine."

"I don't think that's true."

"It is true – I've checked," she giggled. With all the human tragedy around us, I still managed to laugh – humour, usually bad and unfunny humour, was definitely turning out to be my traumatised coping mechanism.

"I'm bigger than you," I said to Linda. "Would that be an issue?"
"Well, I'll drown before I let *you* drown," she replied, and her candour momentarily silenced me. I'd assumed she was rapidly coming to hate me, and was probably already there and setting off beyond the line of hate into something unexplored, what with all my shit jokes and meddling in the fate of her life – either I was mistaken or she took the oath she swore as a former leisure centre lifeguard very seriously. "Anyway, long as you lie on your back you'll just bob down the river and probably be fine."
"Probably?"
"Would you prefer a 'maybe'? I've got all kinds of qualifiers – take your pick. I'm like FIFA."
"What?"
"Forget it."
"Well," I said, "I hope I *am* fine. Or that we just find a boat. I'd be fine then. Nobody's less happy about swimming than me. Like, sure, *mentally* I've been face down in a river for years, but in real life..."
"You'll be *fine*."
"Unless I meet a rip tide."
"So don't meet a rip tide; that's my advice."
"And it's great advice." Cynthia stepped in.
"Let's focus on crossing the river first," she suggested, "before we worry about floating off into the big blue yonder. And if we do get carried out to sea, I'm sure the Navy's waiting out there to pick us up."
"Didn't even know we had a Navy anymore," muttered Linda; we were distracted, just for a moment, by two cars colliding at a distant junction. The drivers seemed fine – their subsequent fistfight attested to that.
"To be fair, I don't think you can account for alien invasion in the Autumn Statement," I replied, as we carried on past houses and a nail salon and a shop with no signage but a lot of naked mannequins.
"Don't be *fair* on the Tories, you psycho," Cynthia hissed. A pair

of jets raced overhead, perhaps in reply, fast and low over the bridge.

"You'd think the Tories would love the tripods," Linda said, watching the jets pass down the Tamar Valley, speaking under her breath as if someone near us would be offended. "Don't they count as non-doms?" I bit my lip to stop myself laughing – I'd already resolved to make her laugh first; that way, somehow, I would win.

Our party went on down a steep hill towards the river, the towers of the Tamar Bridge appearing and disappearing as we trod through thick woodland. Clearly, we weren't the only ones whose impatience had snapped, for we were joined by many others taking matters of the river into their own hands; a lady carrying a toddler and with two other children squabbling over a stuffed hedgehog, a man in dirty grey who navigated down the bank with a thick walking stick and a carer guiding him, patient even given the situation, a woman with an afro and thick headphones that made her look like an air traffic controller, and a few dozen more. We were all just random groups of people, a cross-section, some family, some friends, some united by circumstances, all with the same semi-hopeless goal in mind – to escape a force bent on conquering them. Sometimes a person would trip – and each time, if they didn't recover their balance quickly enough, someone would help them up.

We broke out of the trees and onto Old Ferry Road. Tightly packed multicoloured terraces guarded a car park and tarmacked jetty, and there streamed the silver river beyond. Plymouth, a mere five hundred metres away, watched. The bridge's thick concrete supports loomed not unlike the feet of the alien giants, unfathomably big this close up, almost psychedelic with graffiti scribbled across the reachable portions. The jetty was already crowded; a white motorboat was all that was still available the new arrivals were heaving it into the water – they appeared completely clueless even to the mechanics of unloading the boat from its flatbed, let alone how it might be operated.

"This'll float, right?" asked the 'driver,' wild-eyed with the lower half of his shirt unbuttoned, who had climbed up the pleasure craft's side and now stood uneasily on its deck. Others directed a bubbly Citroen Picasso to shunt the trailer – to which the boat was still attached – into the water. Our little threesome just watched, at once both amused and sympathetic to this desperate scramble, aware there were already too many people for us to fight for a spot. There was yet another plan fucked.

As of yet, nobody but the most confident of swimmers had lobbed themselves into the river – many dawdled nervously at its edge, waiting to see what happened to those first few to pit themselves against the current. I tried not to laugh as some neatly folded their heavier clothes and balanced shoes on top, as if it were all a day at the beach.

"No room for us on there," sighed Cynthia. "Is there?"

"Not a chance," replied Linda, sullenly. "And I don't wanna embarrass myself by trying."

"I could show them my tits," I suggested. "Might get us aboard."

"Is there much to show?" Linda asked, smirking, and I just looked her chest up and down in reply.

"So..." I said, finally, regarding the Tamar with trepidation, "we're definitely doing this, then?"

"The river looks a lot bigger now we're here," Cynthia mumbled, as the trailer was successfully shunted far enough to slip off the jetty and crash into the water. A cheer rang out and enough people swarmed aboard that it was clearly wise of us not to join in.

"Come on," someone was shouting, hauling a friend aboard the circus. "Just gotta push this out, then they can't catch us. We win!"

"It's true," I muttered to myself in reply to them, remembering the graveyard which St Ives Bay had become, as people started belatedly realising that the vessel still needed disconnecting from its trailer – which was now underwater. "Boats famously can't be caught."

"You think anywhere near here hires out wetsuits?" Linda asked, kicking off her shoes and peeling off bright yellow socks; now that we were in her realm of expertise – swimming – she had assumed authority. "Cause if not, we're rocking up to Plymouth basically naked. You can't wear *those* and expect to swim well." She pointed at my jeans.

"Yeah, I know, I know," I sighed; I noticed, across the river, pale grey smoke rising from a boxy terrace. A fire, as likely an abandoned stove as looters, was growing within. Nobody was tackling it. "I don't mind being naked."

"Me either," said Cynthia, fingers hesitating at the buttons of her top, "but I *do* mind the cold…" The valley upriver suddenly cried out; tongues of red flame leapt over the hills against the hot, blue sky, causing all to scream or otherwise duck – except me. I didn't react at all.

"Well," Linda said, staring as the fireballs bloomed from the Tamar Valley like time-lapsed flowers and the ground rumbled with it, "you can either burn to death or you can freeze to death."

"Or choke," I added. Heat swept over us.

"Or choke."

"Maybe the bridge was a good idea," Cynthia mumbled, people pushing past us and further onto the jetty's edge, seeking a better view of the hinted destruction. For many it was their first direct experience of the Blight – and, now they were so close to escape, after all that running away, they stopped to pull out their phones.

"That's not *them*, right?" asked Linda, with a cracking voice to match the crack of artillery fire from some distant field. "Right?"

"No, you can feel the ground shake," I observed. "They just set stuff on fire, they don't blow it up – that's *our* weapons." This

was a complete guess, a blind stab in the dark, designed to put her at ease – my survival was definitely at least somewhat dependent on their keeping it together.
"But why're they so close, then?! They wouldn't be falling that close if there wasn't a target!"
"Well... that might be true," I admitted.
"It's alright!" someone was shouting, to no avail, the panicking crowd balanced on the jetty's edge, others swarming about the boat trying to get it going. Its engine was refusing to turn on – maybe there was a reason it was the last one left. "It's alright! Calm it down! It's friendly!"
"They aren't half taking their time," said Cynthia. "The tripods, I mean. I'm not complaining but, well, fucking hell."
"Of course they are," I said, "we can't hurt them – so no harm in going slow. Being thorough. There's a lot we could learn from them.
"Yeah, well, we'd better be quick," Linda replied.

Embracing the inevitable, I moved to unbutton my jeans – but I paused as suddenly some of the crowd, thrown into terror by the explosions, began leaping into the river and trying to swim across to Plymouth – only to be swept away, many wailing or thrashing against a current much stronger than it looked and much stronger than them. Submitting myself to the river's mercy was not, as I feared, the smartest option.
"Shit!" Linda screamed, and suddenly she was running along the concrete bank, roaring instructions, ordering people to swim perpendicular to the current, or at least not to flail about; float, she cried, accept that the water was in charge now. She used fewer words than that. I saw at least one person, caught in two intermeshing currents, slip beneath the surface and not return.

Unfortunates vanishing from view behind the bridge's legs, to a destination we didn't know, Linda returned to us, panting, eyes watery, the sounds of battle closer now. Swearing emanated from those still failing to get the boat going, now trying to simply unlatch it so it might drift safely out to sea.

"Well, what's the next great plan?" Linda asked me accusingly, death in her eyes.

"I don't know..." I said indecisively, staring at the river – I suddenly realised that I couldn't bring myself to jump in. I had to be in control of what happened to me – the moment I was in there, I wouldn't be. Seeing those people drift away, to be drowned or dashed against rocks, only told me I would be making a very silly mistake. Social pressure wouldn't be enough to push me in. Have you ever eaten food you *know* will make you vomit, but done it anyway, all for appearances? I was at the gagging stage.

"For fuck sake, make a decision!"

"Why me?! You've been useless since the start!"

"Fuck off!" Linda shouted. "We're only here cause of you – and now you're choking!"

"Fine!" I shouted back. "You guys swim if you want to. You'll still make it – I can't, but-"

"Don't be a moron," Linda spat, grabbing me by the collar and trying to shake me from my stupor. "Not ditching you."

"You're the moron, clearly," I retaliated, driven just a bit mad by the awful sight on the river, prying her hands off me, "just fuckin' get out of here – I'm nobody. I'm just a stranger. You don't even know my name!"

"That's *your* choice."

"I thought you said your name," said Cynthia, puzzled.

"What's your deal?" Linda asked darkly, considering me, looking me in the eyes yet seeing a lot deeper than that. "You don't *want* to leave, do you?"

"Guys," Cynthia interrupted, "there's gotta be other ways. That boat's not going nowhere; look at it! It's a death trap! Can we go further south, maybe, and get to the sea? There's probably boats at Torpoint, still; my mate used to do Sea Cadets there."

"*That's* the death trap!" said Linda. "They'll catch up with us! Let's get back to the bridge and get across! Then we can get a lift back to Dorking. It's the only way!"

"All that'll do is keep us ten minutes ahead of the tripods," I argued. "And eventually something'll slow us down enough to get caught. The sea's the only way!"

"*This* is the fucking sea!" Linda shouted, pointing at the river. "So get in it!"

"Are we living on the same planet? You saw what just happened! We'll just get washed away. We have to find a…" I tried to think. "…a beach, or a harbour, with actual boats, and go from there!"

"What, so, you wanna go south, too?" Linda asked, exasperated.

"Maybe!" Did I?

"It's too risky!"

"Risk versus reward," I said. "If it's the only way out to sea then we take it – we spend a bit more time ten minutes ahead, and that'll shrink, and I'll hate it, but if we get abroad then we've got a fighting chance! They might never land anywhere but England. You think Dorking'll be safe forever? Fucking *Dorking*?!" Linda paused to reflect on my statement.

"I don't like it," she said, suddenly quiet and dour, and I knew I had her.

"Well, the alternative is I very quickly learn to swim against a rip tide."

"Oh, no you don't," Linda snapped, "not making myself responsible for you like that." She was, I saw, coming to accept my reality – which was nice, considering that ordinarily reality is full of shit.

"Let's just go back," Cynthia said, putting herself between the two of us.

"Go back?" demanded Linda. "Back to what? The bridge? The car? Where?"

"Any-fucking-where," Cynthia shouted, pale to the point of queasiness, "but we can't stay here! This is Hell! This is literal Hell!"

We panted back the hundred yards up the hill, leaving the fighting crowd, now busying itself raiding nearby homes for flotation devices. Even a loveseat was being tentatively dipped into the river. They disappeared back behind the trees. Returning to the dual-carriageway we plunged into the human congestion – a dying man sat against the crash barrier, face deadly white, shining with sweat – hoping to reach a street which might meander south towards Torpoint. Any such street must first break off from the carriageway – and so the carriageway, clogged with desperate people, had to be negotiated.

"Alright," I told the others, "we've gotta go that way." I pointed back down the carriageway, through the tunnel we'd come from, deeper into Cornwall, over many hundreds of bobbing heads.

"Christ, of course," said Linda.

"I think there's a river between us and Torpoint," I said, ignoring her. "We could go through Saltash and then loop round it but the fastest route between two points is a straight line. So we go south. We can get across the river, I'm sure, it can't be worse than the Tamar."

"Why're you fine with that river and not the Tamar?"

"The Tamar's a killer and that's about it," I told her, tiring rapidly of explaining my preferences towards water bodies. This isn't how I imagined an alien invasion playing out. "The other one's probably just a stream – the current'll be way calmer and we can live with that."

"We *maybe* can live with that," Linda corrected. I really wanted to punch her in the jaw quite a lot of the time.

"The alternative is death."

"Well," huffed Linda, buffeted by a stranger, "it's a nightmare getting ten yards in this crowd. Any more bright ideas?"

"Um..." That was trickier – there was a solid wall of people between us and the southbound lay-bys off the carriageway. I turned to Cynthia.

"Wave your knife around!" I told her. "Just go completely

mental!"
"Gladly!" she laughed. "Out of the way!" she bawled as we went, towering higher than most; down the road I saw a police car turn into a southward lane and knew that to be our route.
"You're really proving your quality," I joked as she slashed the air, scattering those few who actually noticed her, mostly bemused rather than intimidated – which was enough to clear a path to thread through.
"Fuck yeah I am."

Eventually, we managed to push our way down the side-road and onto a high street replete with Specsavers and independent property managers and Christian health foods. Handfuls of people with the same ideas as us, which kept happening because nobody's that unique in their thought processes, were also here and also heading south. Soot still fell from the sky like snow. It gathered on the clipped privets by the bus stop – there I saw a row of stretchers along the pavement. Several people, crushed on the carriageway, were being gently lain there. We hurried past this line of suffering. A volunteer on his knees, hands caked in dried blood like icing, looked up at us.
"You guys got any water?" he asked. "My friend here needs water. I'll take Sprite." He gestured to a middle-aged woman, hair clipped short and breathing softly, who lay on the street beside him, gently stroking at her own beaded necklace.
"Aren't there any taps?" Linda asked.
"Don't work," he said.
"Wait," said Cynthia, "I swear I know-"
"Who this is? Yeah, I thought I recognised her – our local MP. Wouldn't leave until everyone else had – even refused to take the helicopter. Put kiddies on it instead. Guess *some* of them are alright, huh?"
"They're coming!" I heard again and – though I'd started blocking out that refrain as useless white noise – we hurried along, leaving one of our few water bottles, as Cynthia

sheepishly explained to us that she had mistaken the MP for somebody else and Linda ranted acidly at the injustice of sending a helicopter for one person while leaving thousands stranded at the bridge.

It took us some time to pass south through Saltash, at one time hopping across a railway embankment and then an empty football field, its rusted goalposts empty of netting, ash still falling, All the while I tried to mentally measure if its volume was increasing or not – but I couldn't tell. It was at a chalk-grey housing estate, traffic slowly moving as motorists came back from the Tamar Bridge, hoping to find an alternate route for their precious vehicles, that my attention found something new.

A bearded, eagle-faced young man was on the opposite pavement lugging a wheeled travel bag which, the moment my eyes rested on it, fell open like a book – it disgorged a hurricane of banknotes, presumably gathered from a number of trips to abandoned banks and shops and houses, which were collected by the breeze into a cloud of money flowing down the street. Some notes shaved us and, fearing paper cuts, I swatted at them like they were midges. Linda grabbed at several, to find herself staring at a fistful of twenty pound notes.
"What you gonna spend that on?" I asked her pointedly. She considered them for some time before stuffing them into a pocket.
"Never know."
"Oi!" shouted the man, suddenly rushing across the road toward us. "That's not yours! Get your hands off!" Then, when about halfway across the road, he was struck on the hip by a braking silver estate car. It sent him reeling with a shriek but, impressively, he kept his footing and didn't fall.
"Fuck you playing at?!" cried the driver through his window, just as the man stumbled into the path of a Humvee coming in the other direction.

"Stop!" Linda screamed. I just watched as he went under the Humvee's wheels. I wonder now how accustomed I was to death and associated catastrophe that this sight didn't bother me – I'd stepped over crushed bodies and seen people drown just minutes earlier and only been worried by how it applied to me.

The man made an animal yelp as his back snapped under the off-road tyres. The two and a half thousand kilogram vehicle didn't brake until it had entirely passed over his broken body. Perhaps the manual said that was the best recourse – like how you should speed up if you're about to hit a deer. A muscular American sergeant stepped out, more outraged than sorrowful, to run round the Humvee and find the man writhing among scattered banknotes.
"Jesus Christ!" he exclaimed. "You damned fool!"
"Should we help?" stuttered Cynthia.
"Do you know spinal surgery?" I replied.
"Dawson; help me get him off the road," the sergeant commanded an inferior, who had stepped out with hands on head, and both dragged him to the pavement by his shoulders. Uncooperative to the last, he thrashed about like a drowning man.
"Fucking civvies, dude," the Staten Island-accented underling complained as they did, in the melee losing his helmet which bounced a few paces down the road, the man pathetically clutching after the money they pulled him through.
"Go! Go!" A driver demanded – the angry backlog behind the Humvee was irrepressible in its impatience. They could all see what was happening and had no time to care. One car mounted the pavement and overtook through a front garden, bouncing over the lawn, knocking over a ceramic anthropomorphic honey bee.
"Could get a bus through there!" someone else yelled.

There was then further commotion as the man, rambling

about his money and that nobody better take it, twisted his head round and bit the sergeant's wrist. The soldier let go and, as the man fell into a seated position, landed a fierce kick against the base of his neck. They deposited him on the pavement and left him there without another word. He began to writhe ever more violently then, a clump of black clothes, lay still as the Humvee pulled away. Linda, I was surprised to see, covered her eyes. Yet most people passed by with nothing more than glances. Nobody else seemed to notice the money which blew along the road.

We remained part of the dusty rout, sweeping through the rest of built-up Saltash with rumours of the chasing Blight unerring, and though it was din and confusion indescribable I was at least glad to be walking. The sense of forward momentum relieved some stress – but I was looking over my shoulder as often as I wasn't. I didn't feel that was excessively paranoid of me – even now, I still do it from time to time and I still don't feel that way.

At every opportunity, wherever roads or paths or gardens or parks let us, we struck south. Dizzying frustration took hold whenever forking roads forced us to meander in any other direction, no matter how briefly, the same frustration I'd felt whenever the Tamar had done the same thing.

As grey conurbation turned to green fields we at last came upon the Lynher River. It was reassuringly narrow and still and unthreatening; at least by the standards the Tamar set. At once I knew I could swim it – I was seized by disbelief that it could actually be as easy as I dared hope. Nothing about the world was easy! Others were on the banks, some drinking from a stream, and on the water a fishing smack rowed its way across to the farmhouse on the opposite bank, loaded with people, its hull low from their weight.
"They coming back?" I inquired to someone. Maybe I wouldn't need to get wet at all.

"I bloody well hope so," was the helpful reply. He did come back, for everyone, and I realised civilisation still lingered within me when I fretted whether he'd accept contactless. He didn't – for he was, to my surprise, just being a good person and not monetising his efforts. A side-hustle this was not. So it was that we crossed, knowing Torpoint and rescue to be desperately near, but it was now falling dark and all three of us were exhausted by hunger. Cynthia's stash of cereal bars and squished bananas had proven unsatisfactory.

From other refugees, we learned that the tripods weren't in pursuit after all. Allegations of "they're coming!" were, yet a-fucking-gain, false alarms – the machines were, once more, pausing and consolidating. The Tamar Bridge was back open and we stared at news footage of crowds streaming across. We had rushed for nothing and all those people had been crushed for nothing.
"That could've been us," said Linda blankly; but she didn't gloat. She probably didn't have the energy.

Safe for the moment but dying on our feet, we agreed to pause and sleep. But the night was stiffeningly cold and none of us could drift off even though we so wanted to – the nearby barn being chock full of refugees, and the farmhouse and pub too, dismal images of them being suddenly struck by the Death Ray and all burning and melting together took hold of our minds. Distant explosions disturbed the peaceful night. We much preferred to stay outside and suffer the cold if it meant a better chance of escape were the worst so happen; the tripods could move quickly if they wanted to. So we took shelter in the beer garden, beneath oversized umbrellas with beer brand decals, wrapped in layers of clothes brought in the half-sisters' bags. All night, the northern sky was a murky scarlet. Through the evening more people came hurrying across the river, the boat still doing its thankless rounds – I've heard that the sailor, a retired engineer from St Just, is now in line for the Queen's

Gallantry Medal. This has caused some anger; it was the George Cross he was recommended for.

# XVII.

What, Linda asked that night under taunting stars, the fuck were the Blight waiting for?

It was assumed, understandably, that the invaders aimed only at destruction – so it puzzled many that they hadn't already annihilated the entire British populace. Instead, constantly, they dawdled, almost teasing the human world. A campaign of rapid dominance, of shock and awe, this was not. There was a tinge of disappointment in some voices, those who expected a little more from Earth's conquerors, anticipating blitzkrieg but instead receiving the careful thoroughness which only a patient hyperintelligence was capable of.

The aliens might pause but the humans didn't. Though you could go as far west as Plymouth and be safe, in a sense, still the west of England busily emptied itself. Not only was the M5 into the Midlands a sea of deserters, one big trek to temporary safety, but so too were the roads eastward through Cranborne Chase and the Cotswolds, and all along the South coast to hail shipping at Exmouth, Bournemouth, Southampton, Weymouth, and a hundred little seaside resorts. Military vessels unloaded their wares, jostling for space with civilian ships both volunteered and requisitioned, steaming for emergency centres springing up all along the Northern European coastlines. The same frantic rout poured in all directions away from Cornwall.

From above, aircraft beamed pictures of every northward and eastward motorway stippled black with streaming human traffic. Fields and market towns either side were flooded by black dots as people abandoned vehicles and trusted in their feet. Each dot represented some individual distress, some unique story, all lost in the blizzard. It was hard to appreciate the scale of those swarming black spots. Never in history had such a mass of our population moved and suffered together. It made the legendary evacuations of 1940 look like shit – and this exodus was spontaneous, taking our nervous wreck of a government by surprise, waved on by soldiers and officials unsure if their orders even permitted them to do so and not deigning to care.

Without any discipline, the authorities so overwhelmed all they could do was hand out water to those passing by as if it were a marathon, it took on the nature of a stampede; six million people, unarmed and unprovisioned beyond what they looted along the way, with no goal except ever greater distance. The New Forest became one vast campsite for those seeking to flee abroad, certain the capsules would come falling closer and closer until the whole realm was besieged, waiting for their turn to set off from Poole and find salvation.

Drones streamed aerial footage of the places left behind; whole busy motorways now empty, like a cut artery finally drained of blood, shopping streets cold and lifeless, and at ghostly Okehampton an exploring Internet journalist found the town colonised by a foreign race – deer. They had made themselves at home in a car showroom. This was the new character of the South West, far and wide, whole towns then cities left derelict, places like Bristol and Exeter empty but for patrolling soldiers, while those unfortunate places further east were inundated far beyond their capacity. The National Trust opened Dartmoor to refugees and great camps, almost favelas in scope, began to form. Even if the Blight vanished tomorrow, it was said, the economic cost of returning to normality might take years to recover from. Scarring would not just blight the countryside – but the balance sheets, too.

Meanwhile, beyond, over the Tamar Valley's deep wistful hills, the glittering Blight machines went to and fro, happy to let the nation flee as they calmly and methodically spread their poison cloud and took possession of conquered Cornwall. A very considerable number of people were still trapped in the county, as crushing phone calls and messages attest, hiding in attics and caravans and churches and the Homebase flooring section. Many suffocated – few, now, burned, for the Blight weren't needlessly destructive. They didn't demolish communities if they could avoid it. Instead, their Death Rays were reserved for electrical substations and solar farms, while their tentacles tore down every power line, punched huge holes in motorways and bridges, and peeled up railways or burrowed beneath ground to sever water mains. The Bude listening station and the Scilly ferry terminal in Penzance were among those few selected for particularly fiery demolition. They seemed in no hurry at all to extend the field of their operations and didn't step a foot beyond the Tamar's natural boundary. It was soon the case that, for all intents and purposes, only the slither of Cornwall south of that river's estuary – the Rame Peninsula, where we happened to be sheltering – was free and unoccupied.

It's frustrating and very inevitable that a mere few hours before we reached Saltash the river had been an astonishing scene. Boats of all sorts engaged in a grand and noble rescue of the sort I saw in Hayle, chugging back and forth under the great bridges, ferrying away all they could reach. Had we gotten there sooner maybe we'd have made it aboard one. They were eventually driven off – shunted downriver by a machine which appeared between the valley hills then vanished without a sound. Despite its lack of hostility and relaxed disappearance, for its interests were far outside this motley flotilla, its presence triggered mad confusion and fighting. For some time a multitude of fleeing boats jammed between the Tamar Bridge's supports, and the sailors had to fight savagely just to get free to set out for the Channel. People even threw themselves from the then-open bridge into the river, fearing it was about to be cut down. It wasn't – yet. While I and my new friends tried to sleep in the beer garden, a Blight machine, perhaps the same one, finally waded down the river. Nothing but debris and bodies floated between its feet. It looked one way, then another, then tore the iron bridges down in a waterfall of concrete and sinewy cables.

That morning, the day still dark and the Sun not yet warm, we woke to another capsule breaking through the cumulus clouds, its green flash illuminating the northern hills. It crushed a McDonald's at the very Saltash roundabout I passed the day before. Awake and energised by this sight, we made our way through the swarming country only to see yet another emerald star fall ahead of us, onto Torpoint itself. It shattered half the HMS *Raleigh* naval training site and had such a vantage point of the estuary that it successfully wiped several ships from existence even before its machine floated from the crater, sprouted legs, and strode to a nearby oil depot for customary burning down. The wind drove the thick black smoke east and over Plymouth – upon seeing it coming, panic erupted as many thought it the Blight's nerve agent.

This tripod's presence forced the last of the evacuation vessels to retreat from the Tamar altogether and out to sea. Only the southern coast itself was now available as a place of transit. Our route seemed blocked by the new machine until it made for the depots. Unsure of where the nearest coastline would be, we opted to squelch out way across the mud of St John's Lake – the tide was out, revealing many hundreds of suspiciously spherical rocks which turned out to be ancient cannonballs now coated in seaweed – and keep driving south until we hit the sea where, surely, rescue might still be possible. If not, well, maybe cave life wasn't so bad. It was a fait accompli – the Blight landings were overtaking us now and, if we didn't press ahead with what had rapidly become our only option, so too would their black smoke.

As we walked through fields approaching Millbrook, the news that the Blight were now in possession of the whole of Cornwall was confirmed by a ragtag group of soldiers. They had been seen tramping about Plymouth, and even, it was rumoured, beyond that, moving at speed towards Exeter. Capsules were falling in Cardiff and the Brendon Hills – allegedly. Someone even said they'd started landing in New Jersey. But we didn't see any, not even the Torpoint machine, and, in a strange way, that was worse – the uncertainty of where they might be, near or far, was a pounding anxiety. To feel as though titanic monsters are somehow sneaking all around you is an uncomfortable state to be in. It's even worse when you can't be sure if the world's ending all around you or not.

While resting in a barn to eat, envying the oblivious dairy cows in the opposite field, a man happened by, interrupting our brunch of baked beans cooked by lighting a pile of dead leaves. With a smug grin he told us that all his expectations of human nature and society's frailty were being proven true. Linda asked, with no patience in her voice, what he was babbling about and he explained that the scattered multitudes, all driving east across the Westcountry, had at last figured out that, eventually, they'd need food. Civil order itself crumbled wherever the ravenous refugees stepped, it seemed, with warehouses and shops looted. There were reports that a Somerset farmer had shot two teenagers helping themselves to his hens. Some were already so hungry they were actually coming back west, hoping to pick over what leftovers they could find in all those inviting abandoned cars, and the hunger was spreading across the furthest reaches of the nation as all inbound freight and shipping screeched to a halt. Nobody wanted to come near this burning isle. It was said a fleet of container vessels twice the size of the ocean they sat on were waiting just beyond the horizon's lip for instructions. Government guarantees were issued that, by lunchtime, C-17s would be parachuting food parcels for the desperate masses fighting to get east – no more was heard of this promise.

Perhaps they were too busy saving themselves; already, it was claimed and hotly denied, Whitehall was packing up and readying to evacuate for Brussels. Recently renovated offices had been found for them in the European Quarter. The Monarch refused to leave their post – the Royal Family was shuttled to Balmoral anyway, many too frail to put up much of a fight, with a plane to Ottawa standing by with engines running at all times of day. Demands were mounting for the Prime Minister to resign, or to form a National Government, or to do *something*; but even now, with his unfitness obvious, there were many who, seeing how he ignored advice, then invited advice, then ignored that advice, then insisted the advice had told him to ignore it, simply regarded him as trying his best in difficult circumstances. I didn't think that was an adequate answer to mass death. The man in the barn, however, was enthralled – he always knew civilisation was made of paper and ready to crumble at the first hint of pressure. He delighted in being right, as if he were an untouchable observer even as the crisis ate him, too.

Enormous quantities of high explosives whose nuclear nature nobody would admit to, we also learned, were being buried along the River Exe without a care for its precious mud flats or medieval bridges. If the tripods got too close... there goes the neighbourhood. The man, whom I was starting to worry would never leave us alone, didn't laugh when I told him they stole my idea. He also told us, though we couldn't trust anything we were told by stragglers with as little Internet access as us, that the militaries of a dozen nations were transforming the fields of the Westcountry between here and the Exe into one giant airstrip – helicopters bearing every flag were airlifting any survivor who came near. These claims were ten a penny – rumour spreads faster than disease. He even showed us a rather unconvincing image of a machine tearing down the Eiffel Tower. Though I pointed it out, again and again, he just couldn't see that the tripod was clearly superimposed onto a still from *Mars Attacks!*

Still driving south for the coast, where if there was no rescue to be found I'd demand to see the Royal Navy's manager, we reached Millbrook. Another star fell into the valley behind us as we arrived.

Amid winding streets and old cottages, a small body of wide-eyed idealists, two old and two young, calling themselves the Public Committee lectured on the main road outside a dog groomers. They'd "triumphantly seized" the parish council and were talking about what a grand opportunity the Blight's emergence – their reign blasting away the corrupt rule of capital and monied interests – presented for "real, honest politics, for the *many*!" After all, they explained with giddy excitement, now that the old world was being torn down, a better one could be built, one with justice and hope for all. As part of their victory, they insisted on appropriating all vehicles and any clothing thought too luxurious for the coming egalitarian community. Their success at this, being four in number, was limited, and they were hamstrung by rumours of Blight machines already bearing down on the village; someone, a lookout in the church tower, reported a machine visible against the hillsides not far beyond. While we ran they denied this, being inconvenient to their dreams, as the hoots got louder. We left Millbrook behind us. Soon, the

Public Committee must have scattered, I'm sure, with the rest – especially when they inevitably found that their brave new world still required hard labour. I'd heard them chatter among themselves about their roles in the coming Better Society, which the Blight would presumably let them set up – one proudly said he would write music, another hold communal seminars on something called "anarcho-green theory," a third would paint murals and gather stray animals to care for. None mentioned anything about growing food or setting a broken leg.

Speaking of food, with that tripod sounding closer by the second, I, Linda, and Cynthia agreed that, rather than waste time scavenging like some of our fellow runaways, it was best to ignore hunger as much as we could and just keep pushing. The sea was so close. By midday, having stupidly followed Maker Lane for a while before realising we were moving perpendicular to the sea, we were rounding the edges of a hill and high enough that we could see for miles over grey Plymouth and peaceful Devon. It was a world of green encasing a big grey blob – I didn't spot any trooping Blight machines and made a mental note to assume all future allegations were full of shit until proven otherwise. Then, we looked back and saw Cornwall to be an appalling mass of fire and smoke, some deathly black and some grey, as if a volcano's evil outburst were tobogganing over the landscape, lightning blazing through the clouds like the synapses of a maddened world.
"This is gonna be terrible for the economy," Cynthia sighed; I wasn't sure if that was a joke or not.

Crossing Mount Edgcumbe's manicured estate grounds and climbing a gritty stone path angling uphill, the silver sea suddenly came in sight, spreading further across my field of vision with each step. All day, I'd worried that it'd be empty – that we'd been abandoned. But at the hill's pinnacle, with nowhere left to go but down towards the water, we halted in amazement, for instead we saw that an extraordinary crowd of shipping had assembled at a scale difficult for me to enunciate. It appeared that, contrary to my fears that the world was just as cruel as the Blight, that it would kill us with apathy, anyone who could come to the rescue was quite keen to do so.

In a huge sickle-shaped curve vanishing into the mist towards unseen France, I saw every type of vessel I knew to exist and a fair few more that I didn't. They came from all over – every port and harbour in England and France, then further afield as Spanish, Belgian, Dutch, Swedish, American, Russian, Korean ships, most of them flagged in Liberia or Panama or Uzbekistan, crowded the waves. The whole Atlantic trade network had shattered as captain after captain turned to Cornwall – Linda, cynical even in salvation, remarked that this vast assistance would never be forthcoming had calamity befallen some wretched Third World territory; as it often did and with a much higher body count.

Close inshore were the fishing smacks, yachts, sailing boats, making the shallows appear a great regatta; a Scottish trawler had come from the Firth of Clyde on the off-chance it might render assistance – only to later get in trouble for sneaking a cheeky catch in French waters. Beyond, in deeper sea, were ships of larger burden; a multitude of container vessels, oil tankers, passenger boats, LNG carriers, a "hyper-efficient cube-boat" dispatched by an eccentric billionaire social media star, cross-Channel ferries, hovercraft from the Solent. I even saw the *Queen Mary 2* balancing on the horizon, in amongst angry, glowering warships. I knew at her sight which one I hoped to be evacuated to – had ever refugees so many waterslides to choose from? Across Plymouth Sound, I could make out a dense swarm of boats chauffeuring people from the beaches on Jennycliff Bay. A long jostling line of hopeful getaways even lined the breakwater and crowded its lighthouse.

Of all the shipping, it was the light grey warships (I bickered for some time with Linda over whether they were blue or grey until Cynthia intervened in my favour and Linda made the stunned realisation that she was colour-blind), sleek and angular polyhedrons, which emanated the most character. I could sense their frustration – built to deflect all manner of sensors and weapons yet helpless against the Death Ray, built to destroy anything yet powerless against the tripods. But, for appearances' sake, they had to be here. The blue sea was a dead calm and they hovered in an extended line, vigilant and impotent.

"Well," I said, "we'd better find ourselves a beach, I guess. Mind your step." We picked our way downhill, through trees and uncooperative terrain, cursing the good fortune of the refugees opposite who had beaches while we would have to make do with sheer drops and barely navigable rock formations. You may be thinking it's not a good look to keep getting jealous of refugees and, well, yeah, sure, maybe.

Some way down we came across a trail and gratefully followed it through the trees, the hill so steep that one trip would have sent me rolling to the water. I thought about it. A clearing soon opened to reveal a vast and alien stone building at the water's edge which, with its turrets and watchtowers, looked like old castle renovated into a prison renovated into a tycoon's folly. This, a brass plaque told me, was Fort Picklecombe. Many people were already here and we found our way around the building to discover another just beyond it – a horseshoe-shaped fortification, long since transformed into prestigious luxury accommodation, which sat so close to the water on uneven rocks it was miraculous it hadn't yet slipped in.

"You know," said Cynthia suddenly, as we navigated around this strange building for the promised ocean, "I feel like this trip shouldn't of taken so long. It's really not *that* far."

"I have been saying this for *hours*," Linda grumbled back. "It's been like running the wrong way on one of those horizontal

escalators they've got at airports."
"Like trying to run in a dream," I suggested.

These musings didn't have time to flower any further for, at that moment, from behind the cliff we had just descended there came the haunting metal groan of a machine. We all froze and listened as it reverberated across the Sound. Birds scattered from trees en-masse, becoming white sprinkles across the sky. I thought even the beach across the bay became quieter.
"That sounded close," I said, softly.
"Too close," said Linda. "Can we go?" Everyone had a similar idea – or, rather, the idea had already existed but was now becoming something more akin to an insistence. A stampede of sorts developed towards the two curling piers which protruded from the fort like a set of pincers. A man, tidily-dressed if a bit muddy, was the only one who didn't move; instead, stood rooted in the car park, he watched me.
"They're not that different, you know," he shouted as I hurried by, itching – I hadn't changed my underwear since Launceston and it was causing issues.
"Sorry?"
"The aliens and the immigrants. They're very similar; you'll see." I stared at him for some time before, with the next hoot somehow even closer, Cynthia dragged me away, assuring me that we didn't have time to deal with *that*, and towards the nearest pier.

One boat was chugging away and I saw others approaching. This *felt* like the end – and yet no relief or excitement appeared inside me. I was just waiting for something to go wrong again. We joined the queue snaking off the nearest pier, whittled down with each new boat, and it was so busy and crowded that more than one person tumbled into the water – all, being unhurt, were soon abashedly back on the pier, but the roar of the machine had horrified all, not least because we couldn't place it. I felt a great thumping in my chest which was probably my heart.

While we waited and congratulated ourselves on our patience I studied Fort Picklecombe with no interest – it was exquisitely ugly and I concluded that it deserved a spot in my growing list of places and things and entities that I wouldn't mind making acquaintance with the Death Ray. There it joined Idless Adventure Park's very disappointing haunted house, the interface of most streaming services, and the concept of batteries being sold separately.

After one too many hoots and the sudden absence of any new boats coming our way, Linda, in spite of all her assurances throughout the day that she was "totally fine," gave way to panic. So did a number of others who were becoming sure we'd been left to rot. One woman's grand idea was to turn back and go home to Newquay, having given up any hope of ever getting away – someone else replied that he'd seen the Blight busy themselves with the town's airport and singing as they went. Delusion was clearly running rampant.

With the greatest difficulty, the assembled masses were calmed by the slow, gradual approach of a ship – the *Magni*, a white Channel ferry, like a glacier mint with funnels – which we began realising was steaming towards us. It took some time just to accept this as fact, given the cynicism which comes to people when they're marooned at a Napoleonic fort and hunted by alien robots, but when the ship at last sounded its horn, rivalling the fighting machines for volume, a great cheer rang out. Linda even put her face against my shoulder in relief.

A pair of motorised dinghies skimmed the water toward us and then, slowly, the grateful crowd were unloaded from the pier by burly Royal Marines and shuttled back and forth to the *Magni*. All the while the call of the tripods drew nearer. We three were some of the last to leave – even now not daring to push into the politely assembled queues – by which time the *Magni* had turned its bow back out to sea and was readying to withdraw from the shallows. After a bumpy dinghy ride we were, one by one by means of improvised winches, hoisted onto the deck towering several storeys up. After clambering over the guardrails and falling over the side, I lay on my back and stared at the sapphire sky, before looking over to see that some of those rescued were now insisting to any staff who'd listen that the captain withdraw at once. After all, *they* had been saved, so why were we still waiting? Once all three of us were aboard and marmite sandwiches had been pushed into our hands, I asked a crewman where we'd go now.

"We're picking up more people from down the coast, then it's Santander for us," he replied, as a jet screeched low over the water, then burst skyward as it approached Plymouth. "I think. We're the UN's problem now."

"The bank?"

"No… the city. In Spain."

"That was a joke.

"Brilliant." He left me with my sandwiches – I'd never tasted anything better in my life and I hate marmite.

The engines murmuring and the horn again sounding, which agitated me enormously, the three of us sat against a wall on the crowded deck (we weren't yet mentally ready to go below) and made an effort to come to terms with things.

"Well," said Cynthia, "that's sorted, then."

"Is that your big statement?" laughed Linda, her tension broken now we were aboard. "Inspirational, really. I can see my book about the war now – I turned to Cynthia as we realised we'd escaped and she said, well, that's sorted, then."

"Fuck off," Cynthia laughed.

"What you guys gonna do now?" I asked, mouth full of sandwich – I'd managed to swipe some more, and I had it on good authority that there were cardboard boxes full of Walkers down below.

"Become an asylum seeker, I guess," said Linda. "Wonder how much sympathy we'll get when it's aliens. Not like that's *our* fault."

"Well, hurricanes and genocides aren't usually the fault of those they displace, either," I observed, and Linda sulked at the thought. "Still, Spain's nice. I've been to Seville – I'm sure Santander's good, too."

"Until the Blight get there," said Linda.

"Hopefully they leave Seville's plaza alone."

"Touch wood," said Cynthia.

"Are we moving yet?" I asked – we weren't. The humming engines were just keeping warm – the dinghies were fetching yet more people from neighbouring beaches and headlands, and I saw one returning on their latest trip, leaving a foamy trail in its wake. Another metal hoot came from over the hills.

"For God's sake..." whined Linda.

"Do I detect a moral quandary afoot?" asked Cynthia.

"What you on about?" Linda quizzed her, her anxiety resurrected at the realisation escape wasn't yet underway. "Why aren't we going?"

"So it's okay for them to not just stop but get closer for *us*, but now we're onboard-"

"But you can hear them!"

"You could hear them before we got on."

"I don't give a shit," she spat, "I don't want to die when we're this close to getting away! You feel the same, I know you do, but you'd rather make me look unreasonable than live! You're always like this, ever since we were on Nickelodeon!"

"No, I'm not," said Cynthia.

"You guys were on Nickelodeon?" At that, a flash, then a rumble of explosions beyond the woods behind Picklecombe Fort – the sky in that direction lit up, shifting orange to yellow at each burst, as if a firework display were taking place just past our visibility. The deck fell silent as many stood and crowded the edges to watch. People never learn.

"How far you reckon that is?" asked a passenger.

"Could be near St Germans," said another. "There's a couple of them walkers over there; it was on the news."

"What news?"

"Facebook."

"That's the news, is it?"

"Shut up," hissed a woman, "listen. It's getting louder, innit? I'm not imagining that?" She wasn't – the bombardment was tracing its way across the landscape toward us. Following a moving target. I found myself surprisingly calm – I just sat there, watching between the heads, waiting for whatever happened. Blow me away if you have to, I guess, I thought. What more could I do than what I'd already done to live? Perhaps I'd reached the point where bland acceptance was now my first response not just to the death of others but even myself. This wasn't universal; nerves darted across the deck, renewed demands that we make haste away from the coast coming with them, and then there came a shout which rose above the others.

"Look! *Look*!" someone was screaming, a special kind of fear in his voice, and heads turned down the coast – for small and faint some mile and a half to our south-west, a Blight machine had appeared, balancing on Penlee Point with its spindly insectoid legs, looking out to sea and either unaware of or ignoring our ferry. Sensing, or just assuming, that it was too distant to be a threat, many crowded to the *Magni*'s starboard side and stared at that distant shape, dark yet gleaming against the sky.

It was the first machine either Cynthia or Linda had laid their own eyes on, and they too leaned over the deck more amazed than terrified, until I pulled them back, watching this Titan dawdle at its domain's edge.

"I didn't realise they were so tall," mumbled Cynthia.

"It's too far away from us, right?" asked Linda, looking to me as if I were an expert. Given all my up-close experience, maybe I was.

"I don't think it's interested in us," I replied. "It's…" My voice was snatched from me for, at that moment, I happened to look away, back toward Fort Picklecombe. Above it, atop the hill, there stood a second machine. It stared at me. Not us. Me. So distracted was everyone by the one at Penlee Point that only I was staring back. But slowly, then very quickly, my fellow passengers noticed its presence too. Heads turned and silence fell – apart from my whispered "ah, fuck." We awaited its next act – then, after several sweeping glances over Plymouth Sound, it belched its awful metal shriek. All aboard ducked and the screaming began. Then, in a leisurely parody of a human stride, the tripod tiptoed down the hill and plunged its feet into the surf. Behind it came another, striding purposefully this time, without a care thrown to admiring the scenery, knocking down lines of trees.

The first advanced purposefully towards the *Magni*, wading deeper, pushing great waves of bubbling seawater aside, intent on intercepting us. In spite of her engines' throbbing exertions, propellers flinging up torrents of foam, the *Magni* fled with terrifying slowness. Aboard there was pandemonium, all pushing and shoving to get below decks or toward the bow – I and Cynthia did the latter, but in the sudden chaos I lost sight of Linda.

Running past the orange lifeboats hanging either side of the superstructure, feeling the growing presence of the machine behind me, I willed the *Magni* to go faster and knew it was already too late. At first I feared the Death Ray but, with each additional wading step the tripod took, I feared it less, for this approach must mean it had different designs for us. Maybe I should fear that more.

Another metal hoot – I looked landward and saw a third tripod atop the hill, watching passively, a jet of green smoke bursting from its hull. Then the sky split open – the noise of a roaring buzzsaw came from above and the ground around the beast shattered in plumes of violent smoke, explosions bursting harmlessly across its body, as thick yellow tracer rounds poured from the sky. Some bounced off its invulnerable hull. With a great roar, a Thunderbolt bomber from Moody Air Force Base in Georgia – recognisable for its straight wings and turbofans resembling gigantic hairdryers – dived upon the machine like a raptor with nose cannon spitting death. At the last second, it pulled up and away, followed by two more, snarling warthogs painted on their fuselages. They shredded the clifftops but to their target inflicted no injury. As it broke from its dive and veered skyward the third jet, I saw, suddenly erupted in blinding flames. Its corpse careened over the headland and into Whitsand Bay. I was so fascinated by this sight that I stopped altogether, clinging to the guardrails over which many were throwing themselves, and then the ferry lurched and I found myself on my hands and knees wondering how I got there.

Pulling myself to my feet by the guardrails I saw, not a hundred yards behind the heeling, pitching *Magni*, what had caused the lurch. Metal tentacles had unsheathed from the advancing tripod's vast bulk – they were now violently carving into the stern and dragging the ship back as if reeling in a tuna!

The ferry's engine chugged furiously but the alien was, somehow, stronger and slowly pulling her in. Straining metal and shattering glass filled my ears, along with the crash of lower decks beneath my feet collapsing and burying those below, tentacles shearing through walls and supports, and the horn sounding in protest or alarm or a desperate cry for help.

Clutching the guardrails to keep my footing on the heaving deck, slowly making my way to the bow as the ship shuddered in its mutilation, screaming metal like tortured violins, I couldn't take my eyes off the three leviathan machines now towering over the *Magni*, preying on her. They were deep enough in the sea that their spindly legs were submerged to what might have been the knees. The one in the middle, our first antagonist, gripped us tightly with its many tentacles, straining to keep hold of the *Magni*. Her engines still refused to quit. The rest of the hunting party only watched, uninterested by anything else on this vast sheet of sea, observing their helpless catch and maybe not quite knowing what to make of it. To their intelligence this giant was no opponent at all but just a curiosity. They may have wondered why so many specks of mankind swarmed on it, as we might when seeing flies on a crocodile's hide, and even meant no harm in what they thought was just an innocent study.

Then, the stench of acrid smoke filling the air, the machine gripping us let slip an unfamiliar, pained yelp. The other two reacted suddenly – they disgorged their own tentacles which slithered about the *Magni* and penetrated across her hull. Many made fatal incisions below the waterline. Somehow, while rooting about inside the ship, the first machine's own appendages had become trapped. It wasn't taking this well and the other two were now trying to free him from his ludicrous situation. I realised, with something which might have been hope, that he was in genuine danger – but so was I.

Wildly, I looked about the hysterical crowd for Linda or Cynthia but I couldn't see them. I called out their names but was drowned by the shearing of metal belowdecks – and that was when I could speak at all with all this smoke choking me as it gushed up from all around. Shapes, barely people, were visible in the increasingly dense haze. I sensed that my new friends were lost.

"What if they aren't? Are you going to run away again? Leave them to die when they don't have to?" I tried, I really tried, to see them but it was hard just to see my hand in front of my face. And all the while, buffeted by the running and the injured, the machines screeched and the ship screeched with them. Wherever they were, if they were still aboard they were either dead or wouldn't be aboard for much longer – the *Magni* bucked this way and that, making it impossible to stay on my feet, and after the fourth time of landing on my face I realised it was going down. Either side of me, this conclusion being a common one, people vaulted off the deck.

With it becoming the new and trendy thing, I climbed the blue guardrails and without much thought on the matter I threw myself from the ferry, too.

I plunged past portholes and snaking metal tentacles and the cloverferries.co.uk livery. The churning sea got bigger and bigger and my stomach rose higher and higher in my body. Splashes lit up the water all around – wreckage and people were coming down with me in great numbers. Regret flashed behind my eyes as it does for all who leap to their death – the realisation materialises quickly that, actually, they could have solved their problems quite easily. That clarity was with me now. For starters, I suddenly remembered that I wasn't so sure about my swimming skills right now. But, also, I became suddenly certain I'd left Linda and Cynthia behind. Shamefully, I hoped they were dead – only then would my escape not haunt me. Hitting the sea with legs tightly pressed together and vanishing beneath, the noise of the attack shut away by gurgling water in my eardrums, the same black thought that kept appearing appeared once more. It was running out of ways to enunciate itself. How many more times – just *how* many more – would I try to escape only to be thwarted? There was the sense of a curse hanging over me.

When, with all the energy I could muster, at last I broke back above the surface I found the sea more human than water. Many had followed me off the edge and were now thrashing about like the man with the broken spine. It was a miracle none had hit me on their way down.

I stared, splashing to stay above the surface, at the gaunt

metal figures standing over the ferry. Water bubbled furiously where the *Magni*'s engines stubbornly yanked at her still-trapped attacker, as if sensing an advantage, and, behind the lower decks' windows, I saw a sudden flicker of flame. Then, the windows exploded outward, showering us swimmers in burning debris and red-hot glass, as Death Rays sprayed across the ferry. Its innards erupted in fire – the tripods were trying to burn away whatever trapped their friend! White smoke turned black, mixed with the licking flames, and the ferry's chimney crumbled downwards as the floors beneath it melted away. It was like watching a giant and intricate wedding cake fall apart.

Yet, somehow, cantankerous *Magni* was still alive – by some miracle the Death Ray hadn't severed the connection between her engines and propellers and so, on fire and collapsing from within, she kept pulling at the self-ensnared war machine. Tentacles still trapped despite its comrade's efforts, as if a rancher holding back a charging bull with a rope he couldn't let go of, the tripod leaned back, straining. I saw a leg buckle. Unable to hold any longer, it stumbled, then fell forward. The monster's heavy body crashed atop the burning ferry's deck, crushing it, vanishing as it penetrated all the way to the burning cabins, and with its weight pushed the wreck's stern downward. Water rushed into the wounds stabbed across her hull. The stern, with the tripod slowly dying on it, kept going down and the bow concurrently upward, out of the sea altogether, its bulbous ram rising above the waterline.

Inarticulately, I started yelling in triumph at the machine's collapse. So did all those around me, a sudden spontaneous celebration, frantic cheering in defiance of the invaders, all across the water. I thought I heard distant ships sound their horns in acknowledgement or appreciation.
"That's what you fucking get!" a man next to me screamed, splashing to stay above water, blood streaking down his brow, the widest grin I've ever seen plastered on his face. His teeth

were red as the blood trickled into his mouth.

Our delight, of course, couldn't last – as the *Magni* went increasingly vertical and water gurgled all around her, the smoke cleared enough that the two perfectly active and invulnerable and very vengeful tripods which still stood over us came back into view. That appeared as good as any time to swim away – everyone around me seemed to agree – but I couldn't. The dive had winded me to the point of immobility. Combined with my sore limbs it took all of my effort just to stay above water and now I thought I could out-swim these things? Halfway out to sea? No – *this* time, it was over. Jumping had been pointless – back at the Tamar, Linda had offered me the choice between burning to death or freezing to death and now I saw the choice was elusive.

"Hey! Hey!" someone was roaring in my ear and I turned, brushing wet hair from my face, to see the bloodied man addressing me. "Grab on!" The Reaper stood over him and still he offered me his hand. Endlessly repeating my gratitude I put my arms around his neck and, with great curving strokes, he swam from the sinking *Magni* and the two machines.

With every moment there wasn't water splashing into my eyes – these moments were very few – I looked around desperately for Cynthia or Linda. But everybody was anonymised, just swimming nobodies, and those who weren't were the dead. Corpses bobbed everywhere, thrown from the ship or maybe having drifted here from some other site of slaughter, and my rescuer had to push more than one aside as he went. Some were little more than blackened skeletons. Heat cooked my back, coming off the burning *Magni*, now sinking fast, water gurgling wherever it found a hole left by the tentacles. More than one person was sucked in.

Arms fastened to this man, I then heard a great hiss, and with it came screams. I turned to look in their direction. Steam was geysering over one unfortunate lot of swimmers as a Death

Ray scythed across them. A burning wall of steam swept painfully over me. I tried to let go of my rescuer, to unclip my fingers so I might sink below the water and into what had been a safer place before, but I found them paralysed. Try as I might, I couldn't move them, my brain refusing its own orders. I was trapped on his back as he swam, unable to do anything but swim, knowing it wouldn't save him but still choosing to swim. Anticipation gripped me, awaiting another sweep, almost willing it, which would come my way and *finally* end me. Release me. Come it did. Tightening my grip around this stranger for some unattainable comfort, clenching my eyes shut, I heard the water behind me, then around me, leap into steam, felt its burn, heard the mortal shrieks all around, and awaited the pain and liberation of death. Then, silence fell and, safe in the blackness of my closed eyes, I refused to open them.

When, at last, I did open my eyes, I was shrouded in hot mist. Red and scalded bodies lay all around. That included beneath me. My rescuer, whose name I never knew, was dead, burned to a crisp, and I lay on top of him as if he were a flotation device. Spasming with horror, I slipped off and crashed back into the water. There I sank. How warm it had become. Almost pleasant and Mediterranean. I could drown here quite happily, I thought – but I didn't. I ascended with clumsy strokes and my stomach still in knots.

Floating there, adrift, nothing moving in the silent mist besides me, after repeated checks of myself I was sure I was entirely unhurt. This was beyond understanding. I'd been at the heart of the tripod's maelstrom and not just lived through it but not even felt it – not at all! Even when *between* the Death Ray and one of its victims I was still untouched. Waiting for another sweep to come, to pick me off, to correct this last loose end. I felt myself almost willing them to try again. Put this absurdity to bed. Set me free.

It didn't happen.

The tripods were neither visible nor audible through the steam and smoke coming from the invisible, probably sunken, *Magni*. They must have withdrawn. So I kept trying to swim, to head further out to sea, where I knew more ships waited beyond the steam. I went nowhere fast. Against the tide and too tired to really start let alone keep going, having been on a very low-carb diet these past few days, it was a hopeless endeavour. Delirious with relief to find a red life jacket bobbing nearby, I strapped myself in.

"Don't betray me," I warned the jacket as I tightened it beneath the water. Kicking to propel myself even before I'd finished, instinct overpowered me in a blind, almost blissful single-mindedness to be away from all of this. But after some time kicking, pausing to take deep breaths now the smoke had dissipated to the point where I could taste fresh sea air in amongst the carbonised humanity, I realised I wasn't travelling in the direction I was kicking myself at all. In fact, my effort strangulated by the current, I was being swept parallel to the coastline and back west towards Cornwall. The idea of returning, even when it was one of many directions away from the *Magni* and my last experience of near-doom, was a horror – and, worse, a piss-take. I struggled helplessly against it.

I was so tired, now, and not just because of the swimming but because of how fucking unfair all of this was – the apocalyptic realisation had come to me that my options were to either drown, be eaten by a mako shark, or be washed ashore at the one place on Earth you didn't want to be washed up. Drowning, with my lifejacket, would have seemed the least likely were it not for the fact that much of what had once constituted the *Magni* (and what had once constituted its passengers) drifted in the same direction as me. An indeterminate piece of plastic, melted into a point at one end, floated nearby. Despite several efforts to splash it away, it pierced my jacket which quickly deflated. Such a device, you'd think, would have compartments to avoid this – but that would have made sense. Can't have that. So I tugged myself out of the jacket, now just a heavy coat, and managed to clamber aboard a blackened piece of driftwood.

Laying there at least permitted a chance to take stock of my whole body, while the raft wobbled at my every movement. In the shipwreck's carnage I'd lost my shoes, my jeans, one sock, and had deep and bloody scratches all across my bared legs from kicking about in debris-filled water. Infection loomed as high as the tripods, which was fun, but I wagered that if I could survive the Death Ray then I could survive sepsis.
"Maybe the saltwater'll heal me," I sighed, lying flat under the burning Sun for some time, waiting to see what the world would do to me next.

When I eventually turned my head to look where I had come from I saw that the mist was gone – the two remaining tripods had indeed vanished, waded back to shore, while the third tripod and the *Magni* were replaced by a thick bouquet of rising smoke. Slicks of oil smeared the water like an ink blot. Wreckage burned merrily. I wondered, watching and unwisely scratching at my wounds, how many survivors had been caught in that firestorm, how many had been dragged underwater by the sinking ferry, how many stepped on by the two tripods. Most of all, I wondered which fate had been Linda and Cynthia's. I was at least enjoying imagining the tripod's metal cadaver on the seabed, lying atop the ferry like a dead lover, the Thing inside hopefully drowning and not understanding how.

Towards the horizon's edge, I saw that the fleet I so desperately wanted to reach was coming no closer. Instead, they beat their way France-ward and left me and Cornwall behind, growing faint then passing into the thickening haze of evening as the war went on without me. There was no rescue boat, not even to check if I existed, so there I lay. Many, it transpired, had stood on the decks of their ships applauding us as we went down rather than come to our aid. Our suffering had been their cosy heroic sacrifice. They'd probably remember us of the *Magni* as doomed heroes, who distracted the machines long enough for the rest to get away, as if it had all been some plan we courageously voted on with nobody voting against – posthumous baubles would be in order, kind words spoken of the captain's gallantry in staying to pick up every last person he could, then the inevitable "was he such a hero?" reassessments two generations later, a newfound insistence on telling the passengers' stories, then an Oscar-nominated dramatisation where two lovers die to buy time for the evacuation fleet, the screen fading to white as the Death Ray lands on them mid-kiss.

Bobbing there, laying on my back, I felt the presence of corpses all around. I didn't look in case one turned out to be Linda or Cynthia. I didn't even learn their surnames – and wouldn't, I supposed, until they were chiselled into a future granite plaque at Rame Head. Again, I wondered whether by some absurd fortune resembling my own they had made it – I so wanted to believe that they lived but, really, I think I just wanted their death not to be my fault. Hell had come walking up to me and I'd run away, the most logical choice, the choice everyone made, but I couldn't run from the guilt. So perhaps it was best, in this new world where death came so freely, to avoid others. The faces of the dead, of all those whose fates I might have better influenced, were knives in my mind, intruders in my eyes even when they were shut, and I didn't need any more added. There was no more room – even for those already there. With each passing second, Cynthia and Linda were more entities than people – their voices, their mannerisms, even their faces became unclear and forgotten and replaced only with a powerful sense of shame. They were shimmering, imperceptible concepts as everything – the escape, jumping from the ferry, surviving what should have been my end a thousand times in ways which no longer made sense – came to feel dreamlike, a living vagueness, and I found it hard even to comprehend myself or the water cradling me as I drifted back to where I had started and sensed in the warm air, with a golden sunset blooming on the unreachable sky's furthest reaches, that this was all a person like me deserved.

# BOOK TWO

# I.

By now, I'd wandered through so many near-death experiences that I ought to be giving them high-fives as I passed. After a frigid night drifting on a dark and murky Channel, wondering if freezing to death was my lot after all, certain that every shape beneath the surface was a shark or Blight submersible, I finally fell into something resembling sleep just as the Sun woke and threw beams across the indigo sky. It wasn't until a wave overturned my raft that, with a cry of "I'm up! I'm up!", I tumbled underwater and was dragged by an unerring current to a beach, paddling as best as I could.

Washed ashore at Polridmouth Cove, just west of Fowey (you pronounce it "foy," as I keep having to tell tourists), deep in enemy territory with no hope of ever leaving it, I shambled inland half-naked and half-starved. Exhausted, in need of food and water and fresh clothes and proper sleep and probably stitches, I paused first to sit on the sand and stare at it falling through my fingers. I did this for longer than I can now remember. Crying, cackling gulls watched me. I thought about crying with them but didn't want to waste the water.

There was a stone manor house, once administered by the National Trust, near to the tide's highest reach – I put a rock through its window to climb in. It was fruitless – just a museum full of Roundhead waxworks I couldn't eat and all wearing clothes too rigid with starch to change into. I thought about taking a claymore from the wall but sensed that my arm would get tired from carrying it so, after consuming their gift shop's remaining 'Death by Caramel' fudge, I just enjoyed a cathartic session of swinging it through some pottery before leaving.

So, as if still on the water, I drifted east, carried by a current I couldn't swim against, through an empty gravel car park and woodland and fields, following a sign for Fowey. Mercifully, I found elastic-waisted trackies and a DUKE BASKETBALL hoodie on a washing line before I found another person. Yes, I'd been swinging a sword around a National Trust house and smashing expensive pottery all while dressed in a shirt, thong, and one sock. Dreams do come true.

My leg scratches itched with every step, the tracksuit rubbed unpleasantly, my joints were sore beyond words, but I coped. As I crossed a field, keeping to its edges so I might duck behind the bushes, from the near-distance I heard a tripod's growl. I ignored it.

I came upon a housing development, the Thrush Meadows estate, on Fowey's outermost edge. The homes were little more than square piles of jet-washed sandstone bricks, so new that signs were up encouraging prospective buyers to "be at the start of exemplary," and with nobody around I hurried in. Forcing my way into the nearest abode, a five-bedroom semi-detached monster with perfect lawn and perfect driveway and no heat insulation, I drew all the curtains and made myself at home while keeping away from the mould crawling over the living room wall. Asthma would be the cherry on top right now.

There was neither electricity nor plumbing but, intermittently chattering to myself, I scavenged cans of spaghetti hoops and with a novelty Spongebob lighter set a careful fire in the downstairs bathroom. Being mostly tiled, I assumed it must be the least flammable room. Tissue paper and cardboard toilet roll rescued from the pedal bin were all the kindling I needed – I wasn't yet at burning books.

The fire made me feel a little better, as if I were a tiny island of light in an expanding darkness, and with the hoops I had my first sit-down meal of the apocalypse. After careful organising of the remaining cans – the only other food had spoiled in the dead fridge – I calculated that with some light rationing I had two days worth of supplies before my stomach would force me back outside. I could simply go next door into the house attached to this one but, finally being inside, the desire not to was overpowering. In the meantime I laid bowls, including warped ceramics sat on the mosaic coffee table which must have been a school project by the kids who once lived here, just out of the backdoor under the drainpipe to gather rainwater. I was relieved to hear them pattering that night.

Two weary days passed and I did nothing but wait in aching inactivity. Cut off from a world whose existence I could no longer be sure of, with no company except the family's sizeable collection of popular wartime history and murder mysteries, I at least found comfort in being able to brush my teeth using bubblegum-flavoured childrens' toothpaste and an index finger. The house, its windows single-glazed, was bitingly cold at night and I wrapped myself in strangers' clothes and duvets to keep warm. Again I thought about next door, and the door after that, and so on. Another house on Winfred Road, a street so young the foxes hadn't learned to come at night, might have been warmer, I thought. But, though hungry and cold, I dared not step outside – I knew whose territory I inhabited. They might be hungry, too. Cornwall, and by now surely half the continent if not the world, was under the Blight; I resided at their pleasure.

By the time I woke from my second real sleep in days, bar the nightmares and profuse sweating, the mental numbness had, at last, faded and settled into an omnipresent but manageable background hum. Vague semblances of acceptance pushed at the boundaries of my mind; it was hard to tell if it was trying to push in or out. With little else to think about, I was now occupied by renewed anxiety for Disco. I simply don't care if this annoys you. God knew what had become of him in a world where Men dropped like flies – I chose to believe that he was inheriting the Earth in his own buoyantly individual way, climbing trees and chasing sparrows, safe from the Blight by virtue of not being human, ignorant to the earthquakes around him. Cats can flourish with or without pylons and hydroelectric dams and supermarket distribution centres.

I paced the house, which I'd nicknamed Disco Hall in his honour, imagining how he might be enjoying this new world. An end to felling woodlands and paving over meadows might mean a rebounding of songbirds and voles and so plentiful breakfasts for him, I thought, until I then wondered what the Blight might build atop our rubble. That was hard to fathom – I'd only seen their tools of destruction, not of creation, and couldn't imagine what form a Blight colony might mould into. From the litany of experiences I'd been through I dared believe myself capable of surviving any emergency, to be the sort to realise danger quickly, to rise promptly, but I didn't know how long I could last once they started terraforming. I, like most people, require oxygen.

Hemmed in by my anxieties for Disco, for myself, for the burned land I'd have to learn to live in, I put aside more and more time each day to pacing. My lacerated legs seemed to be scabbing over nicely. Septic shock would have to wait for a later date. Life, though, was now a tightrope regardless – it was only the amassed forces of modern society and a thousand years of knowledge which kept you from dying from the easily preventable. With that society gone, and all that knowledge with it, I was as likely to perish from brambles or undercooked meat as the tripods. Probably more likely. Everything was an enemy now. This thought made me stop pacing on my sensitive and painful feet, lest I inflict an incurable injury, and I sat on the foot of a stranger's bed, weary and irritable. My perpetual nerves, intensified by the cabin fever of this woeful house which would feel empty even if full, refused to shut up as though they had anything left to contribute in a dead human world.

A coping mechanism began developing, of a type which any school counsellor would be proud of, where I'd imagine my negative thoughts given physical form as black scribbles, clustered in the room where they first materialised. I'd try to do all my negative thinking in assigned rooms and, once they were done propagating, move into some other room where the black musings couldn't follow me. My favourite spot to hide from them was a child's bedroom overlooking the empty garden and neighbouring cul-de-sac past the bronze fence. In one corner was a big plastic globe; its batteries still had enough life for the toy to cheerfully recite geography trivia when I tapped an attached pen to a territory. Sometimes, I'd stare at the minute sliver once called Cornwall and try to calculate how long at their pace the Blight would need to conquer everything. They must have already gotten quite far – I'd seen and heard nothing of the atomic detonations allegedly planned at the Exe, so either those had failed, been cancelled, or the Blight hadn't yet reached the terminus.

Then, whilst pondering these things, I noticed my nervous heart and sweating palms and realised the manic anxiety had followed me from the room I'd locked it in. Hurrying to the landing, I pulled stairs down from a trapdoor and bolted myself in the stuffy-aired attic. Surely it couldn't follow me up here. Moments after the door closed and I was bathed in darkness, I heard heavy footsteps outside, a machine walking by, and as the roof rattled I curled into a tighter ball. At least I'd been right not to leave.

All that day and the cool morning of the next, I was hopelessly hemmed in by the Blight, hearing more pass by than I could ever have dreamed existed. Eventually, as evening came and my stomach forced me downstairs, I scuttled about, avoiding the windows even with the curtains drawn. When eventually I gave in to curiosity and peeked, I saw them going to and fro beyond the rooftops, busy with alien errands. There were signs of people, too – a dark face at an opposite window, the slamming of a door, and I even thought I heard murmuring dance music emanating through the adjoining house's wall. It was this, as much as the Blight, which kept me indoors – I didn't want to inflict my curse on people. Being near me never seemed to end well.

I thought regularly about that machine which swept its Death Ray over us in the sea and yet left me unscathed and still I wondered – both internally and aloud when I was far from that wall – if there was something not entirely correct about me. Whether I'd imagined the events or if something else, something past my understanding, had happened. Something which spared me. But why? What good was I that anything would save me?

I heard and saw nothing of the possible neighbours the next day as machines strolled by all through Monday (I think it was Monday) morning, each seeming nearer and nearer, kicking aside chimneys and conservatories, sometimes driving along the main road right outside the house that hid me, sinking deep footsteps into the asphalt. One, perhaps sensing activity like how we sense a wasp in the room, about midday began treating the streets with jets of sickly black smoke – I scurried upstairs, back to the attic, listening in the darkness as the kitchen windows smashed inwards at the high-pressure jets making contact. Downstairs, the house flooded with oily gas, and I felt the machine's presence right above me, separated only by the roof's thin veneer. Thermal imaging would see me so easily and it was a wonder the roof wasn't torn away like a Tupperware lid. When, after an hour of awful stillness, I crept across the room and peeked through the skylight's shuttered blind, I saw that the country northward looked like a black snowstorm had passed. Switching to the south-facing skylight, where a gull I named Bertie had earlier been pecking in recognition of me as one of those animals which once provided such bounty and had now mysteriously vanished, I looked over the fields I'd crossed to get here. Surprise followed – an unaccountable redness had replaced the grass, as if the Earth itself was blistering, making this bit of the world look far too alien for my taste. The infection spread towards a beach further afield, fading away as it got there, but grew stronger at a nearby woodland where it crawled up tree trunks like nasty rashes.

"Not going back that way, then," I muttered.

Increasingly confident that the Blight, through some silly oversight, lacked the rudimentary thermographic technology to see me behind a roof so thin it rattled in the breeze, I kept peering from the skylight to watch for more malignant machines. Eventually, with no more passing by, not even a distant rumble of footsteps, I was ready to believe that the herd had passed. Now I had as good a chance as might ever come to flee – I should take it, especially with the last of the spaghetti hoops gone. I couldn't stay here.

As soon as I realised that the way of escape was open, and with the black smoke dissipated, I almost bounded down the stairs to the front door. My dreams of action, which had been with me through so much of this adventure, returned. It was as if with the smoke fading so too was the cloud in my mind – I can't reasonably explain this surge of energy. Bounding wasn't my normal mode of travel. Yet, inevitably, the cloud returned.

My mind was lethargic, unreasonable, prone to rashness and swings in attitude; once at the front door it refused to let me take the final step and open it.

"I'm safe here," it made me say aloud, projecting images of corpses and clanking tripods and the accusing eyes of Linda and Cynthia. Their scalded bodies, maybe in several pieces, must now be washed up at Polperro or the suntraps of St Austell Bay, scarcely recognisable, their giblets eaten by birds or buried with bits of someone else, a stranger's arm or jawbone misidentified as theirs. All those horrors I'd found outside – and none inside. What more awful things waited for me out in the Blight's world? As long as I was indoors, and as long as I kept my eyes open, even if I had to use sellotape or clothes pegs, I couldn't see them. "Safe here."

I wished I could leave my mind in the living room and set off without it. This being impossible, I dawdled, procrastinated; I sorted the house's empties, folded and refolded and arranged the clothes I'd appropriated, cleaned the kitchen, then rearranged the clothes, all to leave the place in the condition I found it for owners who were surely dead or shivering in a refugee camp never to return. With this busy work I eventually coaxed myself, on nervous energy's coattails, into stepping outside, even if my stupid brain did everything it could to drag me from the door.

All being quiet in the brightening afternoon, I trudged through the estate until I reached a field and then the barely paved A3082, two lanes hemmed in by hedges and gaunt wildflowers, towards St Austell's grey cobweb sprawl. Food must be in greater abundance that way. The dead lay contorted at intervals along the road, like dolls posed by a sadistic toddler.

"Oh, good," I muttered. "More corpses. I was starting to get worried." One was bent double against a car door at such an acute angle that his forehead grazed his chest – I thought his fingers twitched at the tap of my footsteps, and I quickened my pace. Cars littered the road as corpses of plastic rather than flesh – overturned, crunched between each other, some cindered and skeletal, all blanketed with thick black dust which, the further I walked, covered not just the road but the landscape all across. Bodies turned to skeletons. This place was a charnel house. It made me think of Pompeii; indeed, I even saw human forms obliterated into featureless ash figures, cowering or curling fetal where the Death Ray had found them. That could have been me, I thought. That should have been me.

I got to Par, a small town along the way, without misadventure, avoiding the smouldering wreckage once known as Polmear. At Par I was relieved to find some green had escaped suffocation – the world sprang back to life as I left the A-road. I went through a playpark, made up of orange swings, monkey bars, and a roundabout, marvelling at how strange the town's emptiness felt. Nature was endeavouring to address this. Roe deer went by under the chestnuts just before the steel gates, a brown-winged hawk circled overhead, and to my amazement some people were milling about the thatched River Oak Inn on a street corner. These were the first people I'd seen since the *Magni* – I kept my distance and ate a packet of mini Mars Bars from an abandoned car.

Away across the roads, past the A390 bisecting the fields like a great concrete snake, the trees and countryside were still a great mass of fire which dyed the sky orange. I presumed the Eden Project, its bubbly glass biomes just beyond sight and where as a child I had suffered the worst allergic reaction a person ever could, was sharing this fate. There was a man coming in the other direction down the road, wearing hiking gear, hands in pockets, and I presumed he was like me and taking advantage of a lull in the Blight's presence to shift his quarters, like mice guessing at the absence of the owl. I managed an awkward nod as he passed, keeping his head low, and it felt as strange as it sounds. Hoping to elevate this sense, I asked his back if he had any news.

"Do I look like someone who knows what's going on?" he replied over his shoulder in about as weary a tone as I'd ever heard.

"Have you seen any of them?"

"Any of what?"

"Seriously, mate?" He sighed and shook his head.

"Not today." Then, he stepped towards me and the world felt cold. "But last night, when I was walking in the woods, I stumbled across one of them. It was resting – and I stopped and watched it because I'd never seen one doing that before. They're always walking or making war but never resting – I'd started to think their species evolved beyond the need for sleep. And then, from behind, there came a second one – it ignored me completely and joined its friend. And then the funniest thing." He sighed and shook his head in wonder. "They started talking. It was some nonsense, gibberish language, all synthetic and warbling. Until, suddenly, with these inhuman accents, they broke into English. Just for a moment. Four words, taking it in turns to say each one; "cretins, fools, morons, lunatics." And then they said no more, for a while, until they said just one more thing, one going first, then the other repeating."

"What did they say?"

"Your name."

"What?" I laughed. He didn't.

"I'm not asking you to believe me."

"Well, go on, then. What's my name?" He smiled.

"Don't you know?" He turned and carried on and, after watching his back and trying to understand the joke, so did I.

A half-installed sandstone suburb, just like the last one, rose on one side of the road. Excavators stood vacant at the undeveloped far end, just a fallow field without a brick yet laid, reminding me of petrified dinosaurs. A large sign announced the identical development as "Crystal Tree Meadows." One of the excavators lay on its side, bucket dangling onto the road like a limp limb, and a tractor seemed to have been flung straight through one the houses, leaving a comically tractor-shaped hole in the roof. I wondered how many people were watching through the windows as I passed by, too scared even for flight, and I felt some vague satisfaction at having the bravery to at least be outside.

It felt like a flight of fancy to think that many could have survived – past Crystal Tree Meadows, butchery again became abundant along the road. I remember most vividly three cars smashed into a heap, pounded into the road by marching machines until they were just one jagged piece of matter, like separate pieces of chewing gum mushed into a single ball. With some grotesque curiosity I scanned them for mangled bodies. I saw nothing.

A stream, no wider than one of Disco's whiskers, trickled alongside the road soon after and I noticed, floating down it, a number of gooey red growths, some big enough to clog the stream's progress. They were the same shade as the red I'd seen the fields turning to from the attic. At the time, though, I didn't make this connection – I put a much more horrible interpretation on these masses; that giblets were washing down from the site of some massacre, which discouraged me from investigating.

St Austell getting closer; black dust which had once been black smoke covered everything, probably giving me undiscovered cancers with every inhalation. I saw no dead bodies, now – not human, anyway, but rotting corvids and gulls and one fox littered the road and surrounding fields. I wondered aloud if they'd learn how to cope with the Blight, the worst invasive species since us, in time to save some of their number. Were the invaders were bothered one way or the other by the survival of the crows?

"I'd better shut up," I muttered. Talking to myself, as my Spanish GCSE teacher told me, was a fair way down the path which led to madness.

As I came into St Austell, crossing a roundabout with its fresh flower arrangements and abandoned Army Land Rover and courting magpies, down the road I chose to follow I saw three people bearing heavy shopping sprint across from an Aldi Road to a home improvement warehouse opposite. This was no ghost town. Maybe no town was – we just got good at hiding quickly.

Black smoke – which, from its vertical stream, I knew to be from flames and so not worth panicking over – rose from various places far beyond the rooftops. Past some swaying, prickly palm trees there was an ugly grey high-rise offending the tightly compacted cottages around it, unfortunately uninjured by the invasion. I added it to the list of things I wanted the Blight to demolish until I thought of the residents – by virtue of their altitude, they probably survived the gassing, too. Maybe they were stranded up there, right now, forced to watch the surrounding country's ravaging. It'd make a great play. That was, of course, if a few tripods hadn't surrounded the building and, with a hundred curling tentacles, fished out every last resident. That cartoonish nightmare sat in my mind for a while. Then, as I clambered the wall separating road from Aldi hoping scraps might remain, even if they had to be picked from the floor or a discarded mop, I saw a person down the road. They were running right towards me, faint and tiny with distance, but growing quickly. Suddenly, the upperworks of a Blight fighting machine loomed into view from around the high-rise, barely a hundred yards away, black against the sky. Stood stupidly on the wall, visible from all angles, I shouldn't have lived to see the next five minutes – had that machine just looked down my story would've concluded pretty disappointingly right there and then. Maybe. I was, annoyingly, finding myself quite tricky to kill.

Rather than run, fearing any quick movements would only heighten the likelihood of being noticed, I elected to just slowly crouch then lay prostrate on the wall, keeping still, watching ants run under my hands and refusing to stir until the machine had moved on, kicking aside houses as it went. If it was good enough for dealing with a tyrannosaurus then it was good enough for the Blight. Somehow, ridiculously, it worked, and the Thing did pass by with great Earth-shaking footsteps. But then it stopped and paused, looking around, maybe searching for someone. Perhaps the man I'd seen running. When it looked away, just for a moment, another plume of smoke rising where the Blight's feet had crunched and ignited a petrol station, I hurried from the wall sprinted far beyond what my low caloric intake allowed into the Aldi. Its automatic doors were long since without power but had long since been smashed wide open. After weighing my options, I hid in the toilets. There, after bolting a cubicle shut, I sat on a lid and stared at the framed poster on the back of the door appealing for me to get my breasts checked and listened as the fading thump of the machine's footsteps rattled the building.

For the rest of the afternoon I scoured the shelves, worried that others might come and challenge my lordship of the store, but none did. The place was trashed and I found little to eat besides what had rolled beneath the shelving units in the mad rush of earlier, slightly less apocalyptic days. Brushing woodlice from a can of sliced pineapples with my sleeve, realising what currency can openers would become in this new world, an idea sprang fully formed into my head.

I would, I decided with little real internal debate, go back to Penzance and find Disco, fetching fresh medicine from a vets on the way. He had probably lasted this long without it. He was strong. But I'd find some, somewhere, surely. If not – there was a bit left at home in St Ives and it could last; at least long enough to be with him a little bit longer. Thoughts of Disco, hungry and without his medicine, wouldn't let me rest, and in the twilight I went out into St Austell again. Being not entirely sound, as my sudden mission to find a cat might indicate, I thought about starting a fire, just burning something down for the sake of it, but a colossal beacon probably wasn't what I needed right now and so I kept it peaceful. With a goal in mind, though, to find Disco no matter how stupid and pointless and impossible it was, I felt something resembling peace – the world could rot but I could survive, for I had a task and people need tasks to justify their lives.

There was more noise at night with indistinct voices drifting from the streets – and, after hearing that man's story, which had stayed with me despite my disdain, I couldn't even be sure they were human voices anymore. Keeping off the roads for fear of running into whatever spoke, I went through the hedges dividing people's gardens, tripping on weedkiller bottles and children's toys and battling the temptation of a trampoline, thinking I'd left my anxiety at Aldi. As the dark twisted into deeper blacks, though, it soon came hurrying after me.

Soon, I saw a far away scene across the fields in the direction of the Lost Gardens. A dozen little black figures were running across the green-grey of a fallow field, barely visible with twilight wrapping around everything, some gang of friends which might have formed this morning or known each other for years, each one with their own story. Then, from the trees behind them, burst a pursuing machine. In three calm strides he was among them and they ran radiating from his feet in all directions – two held hands, a connection severed as they separated to flee in opposite directions.

I expected the Death Ray to burst among the rabble but, instead, as I peered from around a delivery van, for even from this distance I feared being spotted myself, the machine distended a number of metal tentacles. In this low light they appeared the deepest of black. Robotically, it scooped the dozen up one by one, ensnaring and retrieving them. The tentacles extended far further than could have been possible. I'd seen this happen before – but, again, it was bewildering to see. They stretched so far that they seemed to defy physics, for the hull surely couldn't accommodate them, and yet there they were, these long black metal arms snaking between trees and snatching stragglers. With each catch they retracted back into the body and took their prizes with them. Instinctively, I plugged my ears with my fingers; I didn't have much interest in hearing the inevitable screams. Quiet filled my head. Once the machine was done, slowly, I released my fingers and the silence was still there. The monster stood alone in the field for a moment, as if considering its next step, before turning and meandering back through the trees.

I watched it go and again pondered whether the Blight might have some other purpose than decimation. This sight gave more heft to that word Linda had said – harvest. What else had Linda said?

"Those things eat people."

I stood for a moment petrified, not at the tripod but at the thought, and then, for seemingly no reason at all, the Thing stopped in its saunter and began turning back. It was a moment or two from looking in my direction. At once, I turned and fled up a driveway, down the side of a house, into the garden, and over a rotting wooden fence which fell apart under me as a dog barked from an upstairs window. Having expected another garden I instead tumbled down an embankment, flattening daisies as I crashed onto an allotment, narrowly missing a little greenhouse. I lay there, half-covered by manicured dahlias, not daring to breathe as the stars glared at me. It was getting dark faster, and earlier, than the summer

I'd gotten used to. For some reason, I just didn't move; I stayed lying there until I fell asleep.

God only knows when I woke but it was still dark. After several failed attempts return to sleep I got up to groggily carry on with the business of survival. Those voices were gone but they still worried me. Never again, I decided then, would I venture onto the road, which was definitely a realistic plan. The Blight were chiselling away, bit by bit, at my characteristics, I thought jauntily – once, I'd been all about being on the street. Street walker, they used to call me, and now they wouldn't. The fuck am I talking about?

Trying to keep to my strategy, I was sneaking across gardens and trampling flowers and looking for country lanes to wriggle through in place of paved roads, watching keenly through the darkness, right to left, left to right, for the Blight, who seemed to stomp all about. I was ready to believe that all I had to do to assure my safety was put barriers, whether buildings or hedges, between myself and any machine. It was only a couple of steps away from adopting the psychology of the baby; if I can't see them, they can't see me. This, though, couldn't last forever, not when I was getting as hungry as I was – I had to find real shelter, something stocked and far outside of St Austell, where so many machines seemed to roam.

Hungrier by the minute, I started daring to scavenge whenever the tripods seemed far away enough. One house in a line of retirement bungalows was scorched and blackened, its porch windchimes still gently windchiming, and I blundered through its cooling charcoal ruins. Near to what might have once been the lounge lay a number of tiny scattered bodies; old Victorian dolls, burned horribly until they appeared like villainous hobgoblins. All that had survived the inferno was a china elephant – its trunk just had a few cracks.
"Who *are* these people?" I muttered aloud, picking my way through the ruins and finding nothing worth salvaging.

Eventually, I surrendered to cruel reality and returned to the street; the bungalows made it almost impossible to shelter from something which towered like a tripod did and the gardens were separated by fences too high to climb. I kept close to walls nonetheless, climbing fences where I could, eyes scouring for tripods. There was a dead dog in the road, devoured down to the xylophone ribcage on which rooks balanced, and next to it was a machine's footstep – it had left a hole in the road deep enough to sever water pipes, and a muddy puddle had formed in the crater while a smashed transit van teetered on the lip. So too did half a human corpse – the other half, I assumed, was in the crater, pulped when the foot came down. I wondered if he'd been alive or dead when it did.

Overall, however, it seemed St Austell had escaped outright destruction. There were few corpses to be found, though the night was too dark for me to see down side roads where they might have crammed in futile flight from the black smoke.
"What am I doing here?" I grumbled. Feverish naggings told me I was going in circles and I was becoming more aware of my tiredness and thirstiness. Having gotten no decent rest from passing out in an allotment, I decided to find a place to sleep properly – it said something about me, I thought in my exhausted daze, that the only house I'd thought worth my attention until now had been the only one burned to the ground.

The first semi-detached anonymity I entered, scrabbling through a utility room window helpfully left ajar, noting the cylindrical wicker basket still overstuffed with washing, had been picked clean of anything eatable. Anything left was decomposing. They had emptied the cupboards, the fridge, the freezer; the latter was surrounded by a pool of warm water. This, with some vague shame, I cupped in my hands and drank along with the dust it brought with it from the floor. After a time of resting against their kitchen unit, weighing up the benefits of swishing my unhappy feet in that same water, it occurred to me to check their bin – there, sat atop an empty packet of Wiltshire ham, was a moulding cheddar cuboid. I took it and, with a steak knife, carved away the less tasteful bits before sitting at their unfurled sofabed and gnawing. Afterwards, I went back to the bin – but the smell emanating was so strong I didn't dare try digging deeper. For all I knew they'd put their cat in there. Before leaving, I checked for goodies under the stairs – next to a cardboard box of family photos I found a hand axe which I stuffed into a backpack. You can solve a lot of problems with a hand axe.

I carried on down the road, strangely serene now I had a backpack, checking house after house and eating my fill and wondering how long I had before everything rotted and I'd have to start fishing. The road soon widened and became the A390 towards St Mewan. Alone near a great stretch of farm, where dairy cows lay dead and dried out in the sun, stood a white townhouse behind tall iron fencing, its porch held up by columns, a great stretch of garden between me and it. I walked up to the fence and peered at the alluring house. The sun rose just past a brick chimney. Disoriented, I tried to remember how long *that* had been out – I thought it'd been night but I didn't remember when that changed. Had I slept at some point? I went into that first house intending to sleep – did I? An alien hoot rumbled me out of these wandering thoughts.

Squeezing between the bars of the fence, I went to the door. The axe helped me through, making itself useful both through utility and by making me feel cooler than I probably looked as I blistered my fingers on the rubber handle. Stepping through the wreckage I heard a hoot and, far away and almost hidden by the corner of the house, I spied a distant Blight machine standing near a patch of trees – it was facing off against a pylon and, with its noodle tentacles, slowly tugging the structure down. Quickly, I went inside and, in the pantry adjoining the marble kitchen with its island and dangling pans like teeth in an alligator's upper jaw, I nearly cried at the sight of a great store of food. Fridges still hummed; they must have been running on batteries, or maybe the house had a generator, or something else. Who the fuck cared? Food!

The house had what felt like everything; seeded brown bread, which I had to remind myself not to turn my nose up at, tightly wrapped in its plastic bag and still fresh, packets of pink chicken breast, carrots, bottled milk, peppers the colours of traffic lights, bottles of spices and independently brewed ales, eggs of an unknown animal but hopefully poultry rather than reptile, *five* different brands of cereal, tins of various assortments (this household clearly had a fondness for kidney beans and lentil soup), rotting salmon which I threw from the nearest window, packets of oaty hobnobs and shortbread, and a collection of green things I identified as cabbage, cucumbers, spinach, iceberg lettuce, and God knew what else. I didn't know how long the fridge's batteries would last or how long much of this would keep – I assumed the eggs would be fine until they hatched, which seemed the natural expiry date – so drew up a rationing system with a notepad I found by the toaster. It was a good thing I did because, as it turned out, I was destined to subsist on this store for quite a while.

That evening was spent sat in an expansive and nearly pitch-black lounge with leather chesterfield sofas and tasteless cedar coffee table. The darkness was comforting. Had I been able to, I'd have extinguished the moonlight which pried through the blinds over the casement windows. I ate lettuce sandwiches and tried to bear in mind that peasants of yesteryear would have killed for something to put on bread – and they often lived four or even five years longer than I'd so far achieved. They did lose all their teeth, though – I'd need to figure out a toothpaste substitute once Aquafresh supplies expired. I couldn't handle going toothless. I'd rather lose a limb. But in the deafening silence and absorbing blackness, my senses became confused. My mind became timorous and restless and I regularly felt the urge to push on from this vulnerable house – but I couldn't leave at night and I had to eat, I insisted over and over, for it was one of life's few pleasures left available. Viral husky videos, *Fast and the Furious* releases, and online pornography had faded into the black mists of time.

As I ate, gag reflex threatening to activate with each swallow of the brown bread, chasing every mouthful with a shot of whiskey, the moonlight seemed to shift from white to green, ever so slowly, so slowly I barely noticed at first. When I did, now bathed in a strange emerald, I turned my head to its vividness with more annoyance than fear, the whiskey doing its job and dulling me.
"The fuck's going on now?" I asked, just waiting for whatever was about to happen to me to happen, everything in the lounge leaping out, green and black in the night. Then the light, on the precipice of blinding, suddenly vanished. Darkness returned. A quarter-second later, there came an almighty concussion from outside, a rolling boom, crashing onto the house like a steel wave. With it came the shattering of glass, the smash and rattle of falling masonry, and the ceiling plaster poured onto me like a waterfall of dried frosting. I tried to get to my feet to avoid it – but I'd sunken too deeply into the sofa, so I just flailed like an overturned tortoise, before finally heaving myself up only for a fragment to smash across my head. It knocked me onto the coffee table, which I overturned, and I fell onto my ribs in the rain of stucco and plasterboard, out cold.

I must have lain there for a while before I was woken up, the room now pitch black with the Moon chased away, by something wet and slimy caressing my sticky face. Mental clearness slowly returning, like lemonade losing its fizz, I remembered my first encounter with a tentacle. Panicked, I reached out to grab it only to feel something else – something reassuringly soft and warm. Several pats and another wet feeling upon my fingers in reply told me even in the gloom that it was just a dog. He'd found his way to me and was trying to lick me back to consciousness. I had a boyfriend like that, once. That's sick. I shouldn't have said that.

"Good pup," I mumbled, patting his thin snout, trying to guess at the breed, my other hand pushing off the larger chunks of ceiling which had come to half-bury me in the middle of the lounge. Reaching for my forehead, which stung terribly, I felt an assertive bruise and tasted blood trickling down my face – suddenly, the dog's reasons for licking became a touch more suspicious. For some time I couldn't recollect what had happened; my memories stopped after exploring the pantry. I hoped I wouldn't have to fight the dog for the food because I'd probably lose even with an axe.

I stayed lying there beside the overturned table, the dog whining at me as if I were refusing to throw a tennis ball, until memories of the crash came to me slowly and then all at once. Gradually, head stinging, I pushed myself into a seated position.

"You're finally awake," came a whisper. I stared at the dog's vague lineation in the darkness, just perceptible now as a longhaired pointer, and silently dared it to talk again. "No, over here, love." I looked away and saw the shape of a man sat on the lounger, itself caked in white dust, having brushed off the larger debris and deposited himself there. In answer, I gave the shadow a weak thumbs up.

"How long was I out?" My mouth was full of dust.

"Not too long. But we can talk later," he whispered, voice gruff and heavy. Now I looked closer and saw his form in the dark, he appeared heavily built, like a rugby player or a bookcase. "Keep your voice down. And don't move, neither. Place is a mess and you'll make noise – and they're outside."

"Who's outside?"

"Jehovah's Witnesses."

"Seriously? They're still going?"

"Joke. It's the aliens. Remember them?" I looked to the window, an empty frame since the crash, and there was nothing but empty darkness outside. I sensed no movement. Looking up, I saw the wooden boards and copper piping which were all that remained of the ceiling. Most of it had come down straight on top of me.

"What the fuck happened?" I whispered. "I don't remember."

"Dunno, but it woke me up," he replied, seemingly forgetting his own command to keep quiet.

"What's your name?"

"What's yours?" I replied.

"Raymond and, yes, everybody loves me. You know, I *thought* I heard someone breaking in, but I just went back to bed." I couldn't believe I never bothered to check upstairs.

"Yeah, that'd be me. Probably wasn't the dog."

"Couldn't have been – dog's with me. He's called Jasper, if you care." I did – I reached over and scratched his chin, which he appeared grateful for. "Found him with a mallard in his mouth, out by Tehidy – still well-trained enough to bring it over when he saw me! All those fake dogs – your Chihuahuas, your pugs – they're dying out on their own. It's the proper dogs that're inheriting the Earth."

"And the cats," I added, eyes on the windows. Still I heard nothing and I questioned whether *they* really were outside. My head hurt.

"Oh, I've seen plenty of cats. Cats're doing just fine."

"I certainly hope so."

"Cat person?" he asked.

"Long as it's not human, I'm pretty fond."

"Edgy," he snickered, and I shook my head, dust falling from my hair. "You'd get on with them lot." He gestured outside.

"You sure they're out there?" I asked. "I can't hear shit."

"That's the thing about them – sometimes you can't. You ever noticed? Sometimes you hear them coming from miles away but other times it's like they just show up out of nowhere. There's something wrong about all this."

"Well, obviously something's wrong about all this," I replied, my voice still as low as it could be, despite being only half-convinced of the threat. "It's an alien invasion."

"Nah, not quite. There's something else going on."

"What's that supposed to mean?" Then, outside and very near, came a metallic screech, like a banshee, tearing through the house and me. My bones turned to goo. I nearly curled into a ball.

"There we go," Robert whispered with some triumph in his voice, as the awful noise faded. It was becoming very unnerving, how I still couldn't see his face, and I thought about nudging closer but didn't dare move after the screech.

"What the fuck was that?" I muttered with crawling skin and liquid stomach.

"That is them," said Raymond. Again it sounded, a hideous wave of noise, and went right through me, like nails on a chalkboard, like needles to the eyeball, like plunging into cold metal water, like your friends dying and disappearing around you and you could have done something but you ran away instead and you should just fucking kill yourself you fucking asshole.

"The Blight?"

"So we *are* calling them that," he remarked with an eerie calmness. "That's one of their newer noises. Other times I've heard honks, barks... and one time, well..." His voice faded. A strange chuckle came out of him instead.

"What?"

"You'll laugh."

"Try me."

"I heard them singing." Through his voice, I could hear his smile.

"Someone told me he heard them speak English, too."

"Wouldn't surprise me. Not anymore."

"They're just aliens," I said, as quietly as I could, desperately hoping Jasper wouldn't start barking. For now, he was too busy licking my hand. Maybe he was used to all this now. "Just big blobs with tentacles."

"We're just aliens – and we sing." I didn't answer – just looked back to the black window. "Personally, I reckon they're actually demons, which I guess is a type of alien – but each to their own."

"Not another Christian," I sighed.

"Non-conforming spiritualist." I was in Hell – which he probably didn't even believe in. That must have been nice.

Again I looked to the window – out there, everything was deathly still, only broken when some plaster or broken brickwork slid off the shattered wall. And, again, came that screech. I cringed until it went away.

"How's the house?" I asked eventually, just waiting for the noise to come back, looking for any excuse to leave and not finding it. Why would I go outside with that noise?

"Uh, fine, I guess. Bit too rustic for my taste. I'm a minimalist kind of guy."

"No, I mean is it still safe to be in?"

"Oh, right." Raymond was busying himself with Jasper, who had jumped onto the sofa demanding strokes. "I don't know; I haven't looked. But it took a beating, I'm sure. Can't be looking too hot. To be honest, I'd prefer to just not know. If it collapses on top of us, well, woopsie-daisy." I found this man so strange and incomprehensible that I was happy not to speak to him again until dawn came and I could stumble from the house and leave. Human contact was *not* what I craved. I knew what happened to people unfortunate enough to be caught in my orbit.

Morning light, eventually, filtered in – but not through the window. Instead, it poured through a small triangular aperture in the lounge wall's exposed brickwork. Greyly, I saw the newly trashed lounge for the first time. Debris lay

everywhere – it couldn't have been more everywhere if it tried.
"This place is a disaster zone," I sighed.
"Still habitable." Wondering why the window itself wasn't letting any light in, I reached through a shattered frame – only for my hand to touch something solid. I pulled it away to find my skin coated with fine, powdery dust. I realised, then, that it must be completely blocked by wreckage which had fallen from the outside of the house, and so the view remained entirely black. This meant that, having been craning to see outside all night, all I'd been doing was staring at an impenetrable pile of rubble.
"Sounds about right," I muttered.
"So," said Raymond, "tell me, what did you do before everything kicked off?"
"Um..." I didn't get his refusal to obey his own orders of silence. "I worked in a surf shop. You?"
"Little bit of everything," he replied. "Tiling, mostly. Bit of podcasting. Thought about doing some vocational degree thingy but they wanted me to do it at my old college and they can fuck *that* to another planet. Been honestly tempted to find the college just to make sure it got burned down. And my school. Maybe even my nursery – that's probably where all the problems started."

While he blabbered, I crept back across the dusty floor towards the window frame again. Keen to get out of here, I was thinking that I could maybe dismantle the rubble, or at least carve a porthole and figure out my situation. Raymond didn't want me opening the curtains of any windows and, frankly, neither did I – but a little hole might be discreet enough to safely spy. As I got close, my hand suddenly sank into something hard and cold and grainy which tinkled around my fingers. By the light I could tell it was glass but, being round without any sharp edges, like beads, it couldn't have been from the window.
"So that's what you look like," Raymond said, suddenly, and I

looked back at him. The light growing, we could see each other, now. He was older than I realised, heavily set, unkempt brown hair balding rapidly and prematurely, a dumpy expression on his pinkly round face, in shorts and a t-shirt which read "The Kinks." Handsome he was not; I was, slightly, disappointed.
"How did you picture me?"
"Black."
"Sorry to disappoint."
"It's not a bad thing – it's just a thing. It's your voice."
"I've got the least black voice in the world; what the fuck are you talking about?" He smirked and I turned back to the window.

Reaching it, with proximity and better light I could see that it wasn't being blocked by rubble at all. It was soil. I looked and realised that was what I'd gotten on my hand – not dust. Mud, manicured lawn blades, and dirt freshly petrified into glass flowed through the empty frame and over the carpet. Earth, it seemed, was banked high against the house and blocking any light from getting in. Abruptly, the right interpretation dawned in my mind.
"Are you fucking joking?" I said quietly.
"What?"
"I think one of their ships came down right outside. In the garden." I scooped up a fistful of dirt from the wall to show him, beads of glass mixed in with the dandelion roots, and with the daylight I could see how the expensive floor wasn't dark but just half covered in this. "See? This has to be part of the crater. I'll bet you anything there's a machine on the other side."
"Well, that's no good," he said. Casual as you like, he picked up a lager can I hadn't previously noticed and cracked it open.
"That all you got? This is serious!"
"It's fine – relax and have a drink."
"It's the morning."
"Morning, afternoon, time's different now. We can do what we

want." Jasper jumped down from the sofa and wandered out into the kitchen – nervously, I watched. "Don't worry about him. I've seen him *barking* at them and they ignored him. It's not dogs they're after."

"And yet here you sit," I observed, "completely unphased."

"Love," Raymond said, "we dropped a nuke on 'em and it didn't do nothing. So what can *I* do? We're fucked, fine, great, let's just accept it and get on with things."

"Well," I said, looking back to the blocked window, "I can't accept anything until I know what I'm accepting. I've gotta find out what's going on out there. I'd go outside, but..."

"What?" My hesitancy lit his face up in a smile. "Scared to look?"

"Scared to be seen," I corrected him.

He shrugged and regarded his drink for a moment, before taking another prolonged, savouring gulp.

I wasn't going to drop this – I wanted to know what was out there. The other wall had a window, sure, but I agreed with Raymond on keeping that curtain drawn. And, besides, it was in this direction that I was sure a fresh pit had been dug. So it was this direction that I needed to look.

Scanning the wall for a better option than trying to climb up what I found was a truly busted and impassable staircase, as I still had no clue on the Death Ray's mechanics and presumed it could strike me from any angle, I hit upon that triangle high on the wall. Were the Death Ray to spot me peering through it, at least it could only scorch away my eye – I had a spare. But, with the hole more than halfway to the ceiling, I couldn't reach it.

"You need a hand?" asked Raymond; he must have seen where I was looking.

"I'll use a chair," I replied, taking hold of a leather armchair's backrest.

"No you won't," he answered, heaving to unsteady feet. "They're all too heavy; you'll make a racket. Just stay there." He picked his way across the debris, keenly watched by Jasper who had sauntered back in, to me. "Do I have consent to touch your body?"

"Yes – and would you *please* keep your fucking voice down?" I hissed.

"This is my quiet voice," he sniggered.

Raymond placed both hands beneath my armpits and hoisted me with unnervingly little effort upward to the triangular hole. Planting my hands on the wall to steady myself, his hands digging painfully into the soft flesh under my shoulders, I hurried to look – already I felt his biceps straining and arms trembling. My eye went to the triangle.

Once I was done being blinded by young sunlight, through the minute gap I could finally see over the great pile of earth and across the tattered and upturned lawn. There, in the very centre, was a steaming crater of brilliantly gleaming silver glass. In it, as expected, sat a familiar Blight capsule, glowing red-hot. But there was something else. Through my tiny porthole I saw a dark shape splitting the garden view in half, so close that it was nothing but a blurry and indistinct mass. Only after a moment of thought did it dawn on me that I was looking at a tripod's leg – a second Thing was standing sentinel right over the house! Were we to exit from any direction, whether across lawn or redbrick patio, it'd see us – we'd be in reach of the Death Ray if we were lucky and the tentacles if we weren't.

"Can I put you down now?" I heard Raymond ask, voice pained, below me. "Don't need your arse in my face; not in a world without plumbing."

"You can't talk to a lady like that," I muttered.

"Ladies don't smell like this." I thought I saw the tripod's leg quiver and, quite suddenly, I didn't want to be at this hole anymore.

"Alright, yeah, yeah, put me down," I said quickly, and I was lowered back to the ground, out of the light and back into the gloom. My feet trembled and I nearly fell from them, as I looked up at the beam of light piercing through the triangle like a solar sword.

"Well?" Raymond's fuzzy shadow asked, crossing his arms. "What terrible news do you have for me?"

"I think we're in a bit of a pickle." For some reason, it was this which provoked the first grave tone I'd heard from him.

"Shit."

"Oh, so now you go all serious."

"Because you've gone all not-serious," he remarked. "You shifted – something really bad must be up."

"Don't try to figure me out."

"So go on, then – what's out there? What kind of pickle are we in?"

"There's a ship – I can see it. It'll sprout legs soon enough but it didn't look like it was doing anything for now."

"Okay, well, we already knew that's true, so what?"

"There's a tripod, too. Right on top of us. We're trapped as fuck."

"Right," sighed Raymond.

"If we leave, it'll see us. It's open fields all round and you can't outrun them."

"Yeah, I know," Raymond replied, staring at the triangle, the beam of light cutting onto his face. "That's how I lost my wife. Except it was a beach – not a field. We got all the way into the shallows then the boat we were going for blew up and there's one of them coming at us. Hard to run on sand, I told her, but I guess she didn't have much choice. Run and die or don't run and die – better to run. Nice to have something to do before they mince you."

"But you survived?"

"I made it to a cave. She didn't."

"I'm sorry."

"Not your fault, is it?" he sighed. "So, trapped, huh? Fuckin' radical." He stepped his way back towards the sofa and grabbed

an upturned bottle of whiskey which lay halfway underneath it. Jasper whimpered to himself as I watched Raymond ready two shots.
"I'm still not drinking." He shook his head.
"Well, here's to the vanquishing of humanity." He necked both then fell back into his sofa, which wheezed as he sank deeper into its leather, as if it was slowly eating him. "It was bound to happen sooner or later."

I went to the other sofa and sat there, arms crossed, trying to figure out what to do. I closed my eyes and listened to Raymond gulping whiskey – as long as he did it reasonably quietly I didn't care what he got up to. For my part I scarcely breathed, still being so unclear on the tripod's hearing range, and fixed my eyes on that light bursting from the triangular hole. Outside, there came a renewed metal screech.
"Give us a fucking break," I whined, putting a floral pillow over my head, feeling its metal zip digging into my cheek, wondering if Raymond would smother me if I asked. In reply came a violent hooting; so loud that it rattled the building and shook free dust from the demolished ceiling. We both sat in silence, listening, with myself put in mind of stories from the Great War where soldiers would hear the whistle of approaching artillery and consider it the worst torture imaginable for they could never know if it would land on them. Until it did.

After a quiet interval there came an industrial hissing from outside, like a steam engine's boiler, which went on and on until it was hard to feel tense about it anymore.
"Still reckon you can sleep?" Raymond asked. I smiled weakly.
"Unlikely. This is bullshit – I need to get going. I've got someone waiting for me."
"Oh yeah? Who's that?"
"Just... someone."
"Fair enough." He offered me his whiskey. "While you wait for

your chance, drink yourself to death." This time, gladly, I took it.
"Anything to get rid of this anguished sense of doom, I guess," I said. I heard him resist a knowing laugh. I took a mouthful of whiskey of such great volume that my cheeks strained before, with three controlled swallows, I forced it down my gullet. There followed a pleasant warmth in my empty stomach.

As we swapped the bottle, the noise seemed to shift from one direction to another. Sometimes it came from directly above, sometimes from the north, sometimes from the south, and sometimes from several places at once. Other shudders, probably the footsteps of additional tripods, came and went. A whole army was on the move outside. Curiosity willed me to go to any other window and open the curtains, desperate to know what surrealist visions were unfolding out there, but, petrified, I was able to ignore my altogether unhelpful brain, with whom my relationship was as strained as my cheeks. They must not see us.

After a long period of time I found myself becoming used to the noise, just like I'd grown used to the fear. Looking at Raymond, I saw that he'd long since been guided out of consciousness by the whiskey and whatever else he'd been drinking. I sequestered the bottle to help myself down the same path. It took a few more urgent swallows but my tired attention, finally, failed, and amid all the awfulness outside I fell into the bliss of sleep and dreamless ignorance. Waiting for death was boring.

# II.

When I found myself awake I also found myself hungover. Of all the many states I could be in during an alien apocalypse, this was probably the worst one – my hangovers don't fuck around. They grip me tight and they don't let go until I've gotten eight hours of sleep and eaten several curries – and I didn't anticipate any of that would be part of my life anymore. There'd only be one time you'd get food and sleep, now – when you could.

Given the brightness of the light bursting through the triangle, it must have been the height of midday – I must have spent the greater portion of the morning asleep, I realised, which wasn't a system I could keep up if I wanted to keep living. *If* I wanted to keep living.

"I feel like shit," I declared, rustily.

"So do I," Raymond murmured from the sofa beside me, on his back with a Radio Times over his face. "So does everyone."

"I've gotta eat something or I'll die. Can that dog hunt? You said he caught a duck."

"You don't just want to eat the dog?"

"I'm not a monster."

"The end of the world will make you into one eventually – believe me."

"Well, until then, can he hunt?"

"Probably."

"Can he find us a grouse?"

"Probably."
"Can we cook it?"
"Probably not."
"Well, what's the fuckin' point of being alive, then?" I moaned, shutting my eyes. "I can't do raw meat. I refuse. Of all the things that make up civilisation I'm ready to give up, that's the one I won't!"
"Calm down – you'll get used to the tang of a living thing's blood after a while. We'll go feral soon, then all will be well, and you'll find yourself crouched in a bush eating a rabbit before it's even dead. And its death throes will just make you hungrier." My hangover twitched in my head and the back of my throat. This condition – which is what I'll refer to it as because it wasn't *technically* my fault, for Raymond had inflicted the whiskey on me – was so insistent that it moved me to action. Doing nothing wasn't making me feel better – doing something might.

Slowly, I rolled off the sofa and got to my feet, aiming to pick my way towards the pantry.
"Where you going?" I heard Raymond ask after me.
"Food. You want some?"
"I've eaten."
"What? When? What did you eat?" Suddenly, I expected to find the pantry empty. Corpses no longer made me cry – but that might.
"Calm down; just did a sandwich, that's all. I've been up for hours. But now I'm thinking about food again and especially that chicken. God knows how long that fridge'll last and I'm not ready to go raw just yet, neither – thinking of starting a fire in the cupboard under the stairs. We can cook shit then – there's no windows so, long as we're careful, I reckon we'll be alright. They won't see the light. It'd be fun." I considered this.
"Might not be the worst idea in the world," I replied, nursing my poor head. "But I'd wanna sketch it out first. Be back in a minute."

"Make sure you have a balanced meal. Remember the food pyramid." I was halfway from the sofa to the pantry before, after pondering that we call it a food pyramid despite being 2D and so, really, a triangle, I realised that, in this new midday light, there came from outside a thudding vibration. It's persistence was wearisome and no tonic for my headache.

It was my first time in the kitchen since the capsule fell and I found it trashed. One of the walls was outwardly collapsed – the outside was, consequently, completely visible. Jasper slept on the floor, bathing in sunlight coming through the hole, while I looked out on a clear and unmolested rural landscape. Pretty as it was, I knew better than to run after what I'd seen through the triangle. Indeed, I tried to keep my distance even from the hole's edge, in case the tripod outside saw an errant foot. If the tripod was even still there – once I was sure it and its friends were gone, I'd be gone too. I wouldn't waste a second in this place.

The moment I began eating, opening a tin of pineapples and guzzling, I heard Jasper stir then wander into the pantry with me and watch. I handed him some rotting meat which, hopefully, his constitution could handle.

After eating, pineapple juice dripping down my chin and pineapple skin stuck between my incisors, I crept via the lounge to the hallway bathroom where, with crusty eyes, I tried to see through the frosted window. I couldn't make out anything in the front garden. Instead, I fell back onto the sofa and slept, more exhausted than I'd ever expected.

When I came to, I found Raymond was gone – immediately I assumed he'd done a runner. I then considered whether, if I'd seen a chance to do so, I'd have done the same – then I tried to stop thinking about it.

Slowly, I crept across the lounge, unsteady on my feet as sleep still whirled around me, and repeated the increasingly familiar journey to the kitchen where I was surprised to be relieved that I wasn't alone, after all. Across the breakfast bar, Raymond sat on the floor against a kitchen unit, Jasper at his feet, breathing softly in slumber, a bottle of white whine tightly nestled between his thighs. Noises, many in number, were coming from outside, and the house rocked with the beating thud. God only knew what the capsule, and its guardian tripod, was up to, and I was frustrated to find myself without the courage to go to the triangle and find out again. The kitchen window, above the sink and half torn out with the shattered wall, was no help – all I could see was an overturned tree, its leaves still touched with gold as they perished, and the warm blue of a tranquil evening sky.

"What a wasted day," I sighed. My stomach rumbled as my brain, desperate to continue the journey to find Disco, urged me to clamber over the units, climb through that hole, and run out into the evening. I'd have done it if I could bet the tripod wouldn't inflict some grisly end to me. I'd come much too far to die now.

For a good half an hour, instead, I watched Raymond snore and did little else. Then, something just changed inside me. I don't know what it was. Advancing on him, stepping with extreme care through the broken crockery and glinting shards of glass littering the tiled floor, something hot and angry pounded in my head. Nudging his foot with my own, trying to wake him, I failed to gain a reaction, and so I started kicking instead. Jasper growled with a nastiness which escalated at each strike, but I didn't let up, not for anything. Eventually, I kicked Raymond's heel with quarterback force – at that he started so violently that his other leg shot out and sent an empty fruit bowl spinning across the room, cutting a path through the glass and snowflakes of plaster. We both stared as it went, terrified, until it smashed against the skirting board.

For a long time we were motionless, looking up, waiting for a metal tentacle to come roaring through the ceiling, but there was nothing. Slowly, I looked back down at him, and he looked up at me.

"You want some wine?" he asked.

"No, thanks. And you've probably had enough."

"Have I?" His legs tightened around the bottle enough to risk exploding it, which I didn't think would be to the benefit of either of us. "Sounds like they're still hard at work out there."

"Yeah..." I sighed, not wishing to tune into the alien hum but now forced to. "Not what I want to hear right now."

"Or ever." I nodded – he didn't seem bothered that I'd just been kicking him. "Wanna take a look? I've got liquid courage going on. Might even be Dutch courage. Now's as good a time as any."

"I don't think we'll like what we see."

"I've never liked what I see. The world's ugly – and getting uglier."

"Eh, maybe," I said. "Fire and ash have a certain quality to them. Not to revel in the apocalypse or anything."

"No, no, Breaking Benjamin, of course not." Raymond tried to get to his feet and, wine making that problematic, needed help. I pulled him onto his worn out boots, his grip cracking my phalanges, and then we dared peek around the gap in what kitchen wall remained. Peering with the most extreme of caution past an exposed beam and down towards the house's front, I saw what had once been a quiet country lane, a busy meadow on one side, bespoiled by vast smatterings of dirt. Little else was visible. How safe it appeared. But then, looking now to the house's rear, I realised that things can, in fact, always get worse – a second cylinder had fallen there, too.

The capsule had crashed in the back garden; now we had one both front and back. Flower arrangements, the manicured lawn, a shed turned artists' studio, all had vanished; completely smashed, pulverised, and dispersed across the grounds by the blow of the capsule's fall from orbit. The angle of impact meant most debris was launched away from the house but there was still plenty of dirt and detritus near the kitchen – whether a chewed up tennis ball or clumps of mud with worms crawling inside. All around, the earth had splashed under that tremendous wallop and lay in heaped piles that hid everything behind. A giant sledgehammer might as well have been driven into the garden. The capsule itself lay still in its crater, so great in circumference that half of it spilled out of the garden altogether and into the adjoining meadow, looking like a massive dead black beetle. Severed plumbing poked through its crater's furthest wall like the Earth's cut veins.

In the fading light, I saw that we dangled on this great circular pit's very edge, the house nearly toppling over and in, staring down at the metal beast within. Soil, turned to glass, glinted across the garden.

"*BOOF*!" I jumped back, nearly slipping before Raymond caught me – the heavy beating sound had suddenly burst from the pit, then repeated like a drum solo, in some demonic performance so loud it shook those windows not yet shattered. Through the archway into the lounge came a bright green light which must have been the work of the other crater.

"We're in a lot of trouble," I whispered.

"I know," Raymond replied, the lack of concern in his voice heightening my own. "Came to the kitchen to find water – found this, so went on the wine. Want some?"

"I might need all my senses pretty soon," I said as politely as I could, before quietly insisting we go back to the lounge where, with the holes in the walls a little more minute, we weren't so exposed. "I can't believe you didn't tell me about this."

"It didn't feel relevant," said Raymond, shrugging.

"But when did that happen? I never heard it land."

"I told you – sometimes you don't hear 'em." Raymond flopped onto the sofa and spoke into a cushion which muffled hus voice. "Guess you don't even hear them land, sometimes."

"But look how violently it came down!" I almost squawked.

"That's not possible!"

"And yet..." He threw up his arms in the universal 'how should I fucking know?' pose.

"And what're the odds of *two* landing on top of us?" I asked his prone body.

"I don't know."

"Where's Jasper?" I looked about and saw no dog-shaped shape.

"I don't know."

"Hope he's okay."

"I imagine he is doing better than us." While he grumbled into the cushion I sneaked back to the triangle and, precariously stretching off the back of a sofa to reach it, checked on the pit which I had until recently – back in the good old days – thought to be the only one outside. Maybe the tripod was gone. Maybe there was some pathway out of here. Maybe there was *something* to cling to.

"Easy does it," I whispered to myself, praying my feet wouldn't slip.

"What're you doing?" With one hand supporting myself against the wall, I held up a finger, hoping it'd silence him.

Through the aperture, things had changed. The capsule was cracked open like a cartoon egg and, on the Pit's farthest edge, over the gravel-heaped driveway, I was disheartened to see a machine's legs stiff and tall against the purple sky. What was this? I'd been led to believe the capsules rose into the air and sprouted legs – so what had happened here? A resupply, maybe? A number of tentacles, springing from the tripod's unseen hull, rooted noisily about underground, busy in excavating the rest of the capsule. It was such a strange creature to behold that it was hard to notice anything else; even whether I was still, slowly and painfully, breathing.

"There's a heap of mould here." I jumped from my skin, nearly falling from the sofa, and glared over my shoulder at oblivious Raymond, who was examining a corner of the ceiling. "Not so upper-class, this lot, ey?"

"Would you shut up?" I hissed. He glared back.

"Doesn't matter if they hear," he said, shrugging. "We're already dead. You might think you're alive right now – but you're not. Accept it and it won't hurt." He turned back to his sofa and his wine. Keeping up my spectating, I went back to the hole as if it gave me purpose – I was reminded, as I heard Raymond yank his bottle back open, of what he said about needing something to do before you died.

This time, through the hole, I saw what I took to be another of the tripod's legs. Yet, craning, I saw there was another, making four, and at once I realised that this was no tripod. This was something different. Desperation seeped into me; a raw need to know what this new thing was in the evening dark. I even considered stepping outside where I would be mortally vulnerable – but at least I'd know. I needn't have bothered – the beast shifted and suddenly I could see its underbelly. It was indeed not a tripod, but more like a crab, of the same dark metal as the rest of the fighting machines. Six jointed, angled legs, three on each side, jammed into the ground, while reaching and clutching tentacles emanated from its body.

Most of these tentacles were inactive, waving absently in the air like anemones, but with some, tangling together yet never seeming to get stuck or obstructed, it was digging out all sorts of machinery from inside the cylinder. These, as they were extracted, were deposited on the lawn with such speed and deftness that it reminded me of an old teacher of mine, Mister Fallow. He was ambidextrous and delighted in writing sentences on the whiteboard two-handed, one hand at the beginning and the other at the end, converging perfectly inwards until the sentence was complete and not a flaw could be found. The crab did the same thing, knowing every step of its weird construction before it began, and its work was fascinating to watch even if I had no idea what I was actually watching. I wondered if this was how new tripods were built, the capsule delivering them, but why build what was already arriving fully formed?

Being able to watch them from so nearby, I was also struck by how weird the tentacles actually were. There was no fluidity to them, as I might have expected, but a strange, stilted, not-quite-natural stiffness about them. They were like stop-motion figurines. I saw a documentary fairly recently in which a computer generated recreation of one such crab machine stalked the landscape. Despite the great abundance of archival footage to which we have access, they either didn't pay attention or were rushing their animator. The tripods and the crabs alike were suitably haunting and menacing in their brooding stance but the tentacles, when the crab retracted them, were shown like liquid in their movements and flexibility. In reality, they were actually pretty slow, never much faster than a man can run, for they moved with total confidence that whatever they chased they would reach.

In spite of the tripods' metal sheen, and the tentacles' mechanical movements, I barely saw them as machinery; their coordination and animation was so otherworldly, so beyond how I expected things to be, that they took on an indefinably living quality. I thought about when that tripod had gone down in Hayle and all the red liquid had gushed from it, and I wondered again – had I thought it before? – if the machines could themselves be alive.

Watching the sluggish motions in the dimming sunlight, noting each strange detail, I suddenly felt a drunken tug at my ankle. I looked down at a scowling face.
"What's so fascinating?" Raymond demanded.
"Never you mind." I snapped. "Get back to your wine." I guess he took offence because he yanked my ankle again, much harder, and I fell. I had just enough time to fall backwards onto the sofa, which cushioned both me and the sound of my impact, before rolling winded and gasping onto the floor.

Raymond climbed up to peep through the hole in my place.

"Wow," he murmured while I clutched my ribs, stunned. "They're busy, ain't they?" I didn't reply, instead crawling through the detritus to his alcohol, hoping to pour it on the floor in front of him. Before I reached it he reached me and in his drunken state thought he was being playful as he laid a crushing foot on my hand.

"Get off!" I whined, the bones of my palm and knuckles cracking, not yet able to process this sudden shift in circumstance, trying to pull off his foot with my other hand. I failed.

"Say please," he taunted, a flash in his eyes I hadn't seen before, and I realised he was enjoying this.

"Fuck off." He put more weight on my hand, which screamed, my own eyes watering.

"I didn't quite catch that." I gripped his bony ankle.

"You're really hurting me." Outside, a metal hoot, and he looked towards the triangle without much concern.

"Really need you to speak up," he said. More weight flowed down his leg and onto my hand.

"Please," I said, ashamed, and with a hideous giggle, like the sounds I'd heard from the tripods, he relented.

Clutching my hand, I scrambled to a seated position against the sofa and watched him pick up the wine and wordlessly leave for the pantry – I heard nothing sloshing in the bottle as he had emptied it himself, into himself, already. The possibility of somehow provoking the crab outside into relieving me of Raymond entered my mind but I didn't want to be so brutal so quickly. He'd sober up, eventually, once there was nothing left to drink but the rain and the mould. Nonetheless, I was shaken by how quickly he'd revealed himself to me. Was it my fault? Was there some clue I missed that this would happen? And, now that my reality had really crystallised, how much worse things about to get while I was trapped with this psychotic prick?

After a while, with Raymond not having returned, I climbed with ribs and hand aching and looked through the hole again. Even with the constant peril I drew from without, and now within, it was irresistible. The busy crab had already assembled the pieces from the capsule into a shape uncannily similar to itself and from the woods a clanking tripod was coming into view, emitting jets of green vapour and working its way towards the Pit. This it inspected – I wondered how many more must be swarming just out of sight. Then, as it turned away again, its 'eyes' passed over me and it froze. It stared at me. I stared back, through the hole, quivering. Then, without so much as a whistle, it continued on its way and I realised that the Things had been aware of us all this time. They just didn't care.

# III.

Now that I knew the monsters weren't bothered by us, I was in a conundrum. I thought about leaving, just strolling right past them, but unpredictability was the Blight's greatest characteristic – they might spare you with one glance and strike you down with the next. They were similar to humans in that way – it was best not to play games with their mercy. So I decided to stay.
Time, as it can do, passed by, and a part of me began to doubt that the Thing ever looked at me at all. It seemed unbelievable that these genocidal slugs would let us shelter so close to what must have been a place of importance to them, as they assembled fresh tripods right outside our window, but the memory of being seen, even tolerated, persisted and haunted me.

Even after that, the slightest suggestion that another machine was coming would still drive me from the hole in heart-throbbing retreat, while Raymond laughed at me for being such a scared little mouse. Now that they knew we were here, I thought, it was best not to remind them. Then, a new sense began pulling me back to the lounge – for, terrible as the danger might be, the peephole's attraction was irresistible. It was my one source of knowledge on the comings and goings of the outside world and I was ready to risk all to keep it. I recall now with a weird sort of wonder that, in spite of our infinite danger trapped between starvation and becoming food ourselves, I still struggled for that horrible privilege of knowledge. It wasn't like I enjoyed what I saw – but I looked nonetheless. Racing across the lounge with grotesque eagerness whenever the noises outside changed, all for a glance of what I'd already seen a hundred times prior, my biggest obstacle was fast becoming not the creatures outside, but Raymond.

After he'd attacked me, obviously, there was no coming back – but I'm sure things would have devolved regardless. The plain fact was that we were absolutely incompatible, our personalities and attitudes completely opposed, and this incompatibility was only made more acute by the danger and isolation. Cabin fever, in short, had us both.

Raymond's useless comments and stupid jokes, always delivered with a heightened volume meant only to put me on edge, and the stupid rigidity of his self-radicalised mind, were driving me insane. I'd sit in the darkness unable to keep my mind off him for the worst possible reasons – he was a tool, and a violent one, so it wasn't just that I was annoyed by him, but I was afraid of him. He ate far more than me while fulfilling himself with drink which he now refused me access to, which wasn't his worst crime but still said plenty about his character, and I slept little with all the noise of his crashing about like an alcoholic elephant. Even Jasper was avoiding him – that should tell you everything. His endless and unhelpful mutterings about our situation's hopelessness sabotaged my every effort to plan a way out and drove me almost to the verge of craziness. This was especially so when he started calling me a "silly woman" whenever I exhibited any emotion – he, of course, was perfectly entitled to be as emotional on any subject he pleased. You should have seen when, in a rare spirit of bridge-building, he insisted we play a scrounged-up *The Big Bang Theory* edition of Cluedo. I won and he couldn't handle it; I thought he'd weep for hours.

As the days wore on, we shared fewer and fewer words – and when we did talk, it would be unrepentantly hostile. Raymond hated me, that was clear, and I didn't have much joy for him, either. My ribs still stung enough to remind me why. Rooms turned colder when he walked in; his shadow on the wall grew with each day and sometimes seemed to leave a few moments after him. He had no right to his hostility – my hand hurt and his didn't. More than once he shoved me out of the way but would ask the *dog* to excuse him, or denied me food and I meekly obeyed for fear of his fists, and once took out his anxiety by waterboarding me with a bottle of rainwater while I slept. His sudden flashes of temper were escalating so much that I hid the hand axe beneath the sofa; not out of any desire to use it but out of fear that he might.

It came to a head one dark evening when I happened to be peering again through the hole, spying a machine on a distant hill, its tentacles busy hauling down a motionless wind turbine, thinking back to childhood when I thought they were built to knead bread. I heard his dark voice behind me.

"How long you planning on keeping us here?"

"Keeping us here?" I asked into the hole, a chill coming over me. "Since when was I keeping us here?"

"It's the energy you've brought to the house; it's got me tweaked." I heard the further sofa wheeze underneath him as he sat, and I turned to look at him, still balanced against the wall with both hands.

"Hey, look," I said impatiently, my patience strained to the edge of snapping, "if you wanna leave, go ahead. Go on, piss off and get yourself zapped, see if I care."

"Love that, wouldn't you?" he sneered back. Quickly, I hopped down from the chair in case he meant to push me off again – I was still waiting for an apology for that.

"What?"

"Love to have all the food and drink for yourself, ey? Bet you've already picked the knife you'll do me in with, too, ain't ya?"

"I have, yeah," I replied unhelpfully, "I'll make sure to put it in your front so you know it was me."

"Nice!" he laughed; but his eyes didn't. I chose to push a little harder – it was unwise but I was too tired and angry not to. Maybe I did hate him, actually. Maybe I wanted to do things to him. Maybe I wanted an excuse.

"You're acting like such a prick."

"Am I?"

"Yes."

"Am I?"

"*Yes*!" I had to steady my voice lest it rise to hypocritical heights. "We need to actually be getting on and working together-"

"Working together!" I cringed at his shouted words. "That's glorious! To do what, build a better world from the ashes?"

"I don't fucking know!"

"No, you ain't got a clue!" he spat. "There's nothing left – the world's over! It's a husk. I can feel a wisdom tooth coming through, you know – it'll kill me when it does. Imagine that! We can't rebuild or grow anything or even treat a fuckin' headache – I should fuckin' know, with the one you're giving me! We're just chimps in the forest."

"I'm just trying to live," I said. "It's better to be alive than dead."

"How do you know?" he snarled back. "You've never been dead."

"Neither have you."

"I've been dead for a while – you have, too. We've talked about this." Bored, I turned away, climbing up the sofa and back to the hole.

"I'm still not keeping us here."

"I didn't mean 'here' the house, I meant 'here' the spirit."

"What?"

"We were having a good time before, me and Jasper, then you come in and bring it all down. Even the luck – you show up, then *two* ships fall on us! Coincidence?"

"Yes!"

"Your spirit's rotten." I whipped back round, seeing he was now but a few feet from me.

"Don't you say shit about my spirit."

"That's where you're keeping us – on the wrong bit of the cosmic wheel of action."

"Fuck are you babbling about?" In reply, he grabbed the hem of my shirt and yanked me from the sofa. I tumbled, just keeping my balance as I landed feet-first on the cushions, spinning to face him, holding the backrest tightly, grateful not to have toppled onto my face instead. I opened my mouth to protest just as my nose caught the punch. Under his tightened fist, it crunched.

"Oh, no, look what you've done," Raymond said passively, watching me crumple off the sofa and to the floor, clutching my gushing nose, trying not to writhe *too* much.

"You hit me," I spluttered pathetically, mouth filling with the taste of hot iron, eyes watering, firecrackers of pain streaking up my nose and into my skull.

"Did I?" He smiled and leaned against the wall, arms crossed, admiring his work, blurry as I stared at him. "Yeah, go on, squeal. Women don't have it so good *now*, do they? You think you're protected – not anymore. Back to being property for you, I think." He cackled throatily.

"You're a fucking dickhead."

"According to you," Raymond said, loftily. Jasper sheepishly licked at my cheek. "This is fun – I should do this more often."

"Fucking stinking fucking coward," I said, unable to think of anything cleverer, blood dribbling between my fingers and onto the dusty carpet.

"You're lucky I went easy on you – I do martial arts. My whole style is I just crush guys. I just win. I take you into the deepest depths and then I take your soul." Oh, he was so nuts. Had to get out. Had to get out now.

"I thought you were better than this." I didn't – but it might be a good thing to say.

"You don't know what's possible from tortured men," he

replied, all giddy. "Especially once they're under the shadow and go down to elemental things."

Slowly, I pushed myself to my feet and stumbled without poise to the kitchen, praying he wouldn't follow.

"Bastard," I whispered, pinning a handful of thick kitchen roll to my screaming nose. "Bastard with shitty poetry."

"I bet you think I'm a menace to society!" I heard him shout from the other room. "But guess what? That doesn't exist no more! I'm king now, bitch!"

"You go outside and tell *them* that!" I shouted, stomping back into the lounge, shooting blood from my top lip, pointing past him to the triangle from which poured pitiless moonlight. Raymond was already back on the sofa, legs open, drinking. "Tell them you're king!" A hoot came in answer and I fell silent as he loudly chugged. Eventually I spoke again, quieter: "Just stay the fuck away from me. Once they're gone, I'm gone too, and I'm taking my half of the food with me."

"Sure you are."

"I am. And I hope you never make it out. I hope they get you. I'll help them, if I can." He turned his head to look at me over the sofa. Even in the dim, I saw the glint of his bared teeth, and it made him and Jasper look so alike.

Gradually, then all at once, I got as tight a grip of my emotions as I had of my nose and, sat alone on the toilet lid, realised that even after this awful experience I couldn't just run away. Growing certainty that the Blight had ceased to see man as a threat, and so were no longer distracted by the sport of hunting us, had pushed me to make a dash from this house, and Raymond had become just as great a push factor. But, I thought mournfully, I couldn't just run off into the darkness. That was the way to doom. There was food and drink here and I didn't know where else it could be – and then there was the question of exposure. I needed to figure out a strategy and not let myself be killed by a sudden surge of emotion. Broken noses make it difficult to think straight – but I simply had to. These machines might tolerate me but would the ones over the next hill? Take the risk, you might be thinking, so what? It'd probably be fine. Easy for you to say.

So, sat against the wall in the porcelain bathroom, holding back emotional tears and letting flow ones of simple physical pain, my head brewed with ideas. It was clear Raymond had gone quite mad, or perhaps always was, and I'd pander to that as best as I could until the time came that I could ditch. I only wished I knew how long that'd take – we could, theoretically at least, be trapped here for years with nothing to eat but each other. But, one way or the other, I had my decision. Escape would come once the sun rose. Raymond could have his poxy kingdom – I chose to have the world.

After a long time, with Raymond safely passed out on the kitchen floor with his head in the round dog bed, I ventured from the bathroom. Where else would I go but back to the peephole? Outside, my nose hurting as I had to press it against the wall as I peeped, I saw no fewer than three fighting-machines. These stood in an orderly manner around the Pit, above which the crab-machine was now completed and stood showroom still, and were injecting their tentacles into its inert metal body, servicing it in some way which I didn't much want to speculate on. It was a strange sight, almost like a ritual, and I pulled my eyes away from the clumsy beasts, feeling weirdly voyeuristic. My nose hurt.

Raymond was sat against the peephole's wall when I next saw him, myself having napped in a bath lined with towels, as if guarding it. He read some history book he'd found about curling and looked unnaturally intrigued. An hour or so had gone by, passed with fitful sleep thanks to my nose, and the urge to peek was immense as ever, like an addiction, but the fear of telling him to move was stronger. Instead, resembling an insect larvae wrapped up in my duvet, I huddled up against the wall beside him. My pandering, though it'd take a lot of effort to pretend I liked him, began now.

"I picked a hell of a time to get into curling," he remarked blandly, and I didn't answer for literally why the fuck would I? Oh, I couldn't do this. I couldn't pretend to like him – no matter how necessary it was to keep me uninjured. Silence it was, then.

There was no sound to be heard through the wall. Even if there was it'd have been drowned out by my own agonising stomach. Raymond eventually announced he was "taking a massive shit" and meandered for the bathroom – with no plumbing, we'd developed a 'disposal system' using a couple of saucepans from under the kitchen sink. It wasn't ideal and I don't recommend you try it. He first fetched a wine bottle from the hallway, disappearing from view for a moment, when there came a sudden movement – at once I hoped he'd been seen through the window and snatched and my heart was in my mouth with delight. Its thumping hurt my nose. Instead, annoyingly, he came bursting back through the doorway, inarticulate, gesticulating, and for a moment I shared his panic until my self-consciousness restored order.

"What?"

"Just look," he insisted.

"At what?"

"Don't you 'at what' me," he bleated, "you've spent all your time looking out there, and now the moment I want you to suddenly you don't wanna! Honestly! I can't believe-"

"Wait," I hissed, "did you look out the window? You pulled the curtains back? What're you thinking?!"

"Holy shit, just-"

"Alright, alright," I snapped, deliberately taking my time to climb the chair to the slit, having no desire to fully expose myself via the windows, "if it's so frigging important. Don't get all heavy and uncool." Raymond, huffing and puffing, slipped from sight and crept back to the hall to peer through a corner of the double glazing. I didn't press my eye against the slit – it would mean pressing my broken nose against the wall, which I didn't want to do again, and so I could only get a more limited view than normal. That didn't end up mattering.

Twilight remained, the stars little and faint, yet all was illuminated by a flickering emerald glow from the Pit. The whole garden was a mosaic of green gleams and shifting black shadows. Over and through the glow went disinterested bats, busy with their own little business, and the sprawling Blight machines were no longer to be seen. I broke from the slit, my squinting making my brow ache terribly, and stretched backwards to see through the doorway toward Raymond – he sat at the base of the broken stairs, legs contracted and crumpled, face pressed against the window. His sudden interest fascinated me – if he cared, whatever was out there must have been good. Clangours of machinery ricocheted over the house. My face darted back to the slit, considering whether to pick it a bit wider open with my fingernails, and, amid that noise, like backup vocals in thrash metal, came the suspicious drift of human voices.

I let my whole body rest against the wall, watching closely, as a fighting machine ambled into view, bats chasing each other between its legs. The green glow was so strong that I could only see the machine's armour by its shimmering. Suddenly, I heard a yelp, as a long tentacle reached over the machine's shoulder. Then it came back and something – struggling violently – was lifted high against the sky, a black, vague silhouette against the starlight. As this black object came down again, I saw by the increasingly bright green that it was a man, like a jewel in the light.

Stout and ruddy, he was an older man; balding, dumb-faced, big-nosed, and with a bottom lip fat as fish bait. Before all this began, he must have been walking the world, thinking himself of considerable consequence, probably in property or finance and bellowing at cyclists from his car window. Other machines began gathering all around the Pit. Through their legs and appendages I could now barely see the man, but in my snatched glances I glimpsed his staring eyes, rendered into green orbs by the blinding light from the crater he was dangled above. When the gathering had commenced around the glow, the machines seeming like witches around a cauldron, the tripod which held him made some strange sound. Somehow, I knew what they'd do before they did it – but I couldn't look away. The machine dropped him into the Pit. He vanished noiselessly – and that lack of protest is what stays with me – into the burning green void, and for a moment there was silence. And then began a shrieking and sustained and cheerful hooting from the Martians. It continued, drunk on the occasion, and I realised it sounded not like their ordinary metal soundtrack, but laughter; even singing.

The sound shattered my head. Slipping from the sofa I fell knees first onto the ground, pain shooting through my legs, and as I struggled to my feet with hands clapped over my ears, I bolted from the lounge and towards the bathroom, the furthest part of the house from the sight. Raymond and I met each other's eyes as I passed the doorway; I'd never seen his so wide.

"Oi!" he cried, and came running after me. I thought he was going to attack me, for unclear reasons, and so I ran faster, skidding into the tiled bathroom, to the shower cubicle where I closed the fibreglass door as if the resultant capsule would provide any safety. Raymond stopped at the doorway, his breath heavy, and stared at me with furious suspicion.

"You better not be making a break for it!" he hissed, burning hypocrisy in his newly discovered fear, as if hypocrisy was something to be surprised by when it came from him. "They'll see you!"

"Do I look like I'm going anywhere?" I asked him, banging my fist against the shower door, suddenly realising how ridiculous

I looked. He took a moment to collect his breath – all the while, outside, the laughter subsided then started again in a regular and uncanny rhythm.

"What... the *fuck...* are they doing?" Raymond whispered urgently, suddenly remembering the need to do so. He sure picked his moments.

"I have no frigging clue," I whispered back, suddenly forgetting my hatred of him, so supplanted was it by hatred of the noise. "It's like a black mass."

"Make room." For some reason he, too, was odd enough to regard the shower as a place of safety and so we both crammed into its tight space, pressed uncomfortably against each other, knocking over bottles of exfoliating scrubs and eucalyptus two-in-one shower gel with our feet.

"This is a bit farcical," I admitted.

"Get out, then," he snapped back, but I didn't want to, so I stood there with Raymond pressed against me and fingers plugged into my ears. The metal cackling was only heightening. I wondered how many more people were being sacrificed to the Pit – and why. I dared believe this meant the Blight had religion – or, even worse, games.

That hour crawled by as we lurked in the shower – with each ticking minute I became more desperate to get out, away from Raymond, but I was far more desperate not to make noise. Yet, so too did I want to know what was happening – I had to see. Tightly balanced between horror and a terrible fascination, I felt hopelessly hamstrung, but I did at least break through the mental barrier of getting out of the shower. Instead, I sat on the toilet lid while Raymond stayed put in the shower, sitting among the shampoo bottles.

"I wonder what they're doing now," I said after some time, legs drawn up and held tightly.

"Who knows?" snapped Raymond, pouring the contents of various gels onto the floor next to him, mixing them with his forefinger. "Who the fuck *cares*? Oh, God, I need a drink."

"There's gotta be a way out," I said, more to myself than to him – he was too useless, and untrustworthy, to incorporate into any escape plan. "They're not watching the house. I bet we could slip out if-"

"Will you shut up?" he groaned, throwing a bottle at me, which I pawed narrowly away from my still pained nose. "I bet there were loads of people like you in Nine-Eleven, you know, coming up with ways to escape."

"And I bet some of them made it." He shook his head so energetically it must have given him a headache.

"Stop trying to outrun the tsunami," he demanded. Another round of laughter reverberated through the house. "Just stop. You're driving me *insane*."

"There's a way out," I insisted. "I'll find it. I'm gonna find it."

"I told you to shut up," he hissed, his voice raised, and, as he was too impossible to talk to, I decided my interests were best served by not provoking him into raising it any further. Instead, I gripped the toilet roll holder with both hands and pulled myself to my feet. Slowly, I sneaked back in the direction of the kitchen, ignoring Raymond's protests, peering fox-like around corners to ensure no Blight infantry had billeted in what they thought an empty house.

With the dead washing machine far better company, I tried to consider my position with just a bit of clear-headedness, if I could just fucking handle that for just a fucking second.

"Okay," I told myself, "you're fine, just don't go *completely* nuts, not just yet, afterwards it's fine. They've gotta piss off at some point." But I'd been saying this for I didn't know how long and it just wouldn't happen. Why, of all places across the world they owned, would the Blight make a permanent encampment right outside my front door?! Digging a tunnel through the upturned soil and in a direction away from the Pit seemed an option, but the chances of collapse or detection or some other fuck-up were far too great – as were the chances, I thought with a glance back to the bathroom, of doing all the digging myself.

Nonetheless, with not a lot of frigging options and needing something to do before I died, I stepped into the tattered kitchen. Jasper eyed me suspiciously – he'd slept through outside's nightmare. I went to the broken down wall, fell onto my belly to crawl through the beads of glass, and, hoping with all my heart that I wouldn't be spotted, with my hands I tested the strength of the compacted mud which had been thrown up from the second Pit. Maybe I could make some sort of trench. Some cover to sneak to the nearest field and escape. Jasper had followed me but soon grew bored and went back in the house to sleep while I spent some minutes digging with my hands, silent as I could, each handful of mud a chance to get away. When I had made a hole about a couple of feet deep, the loose earth crumbled, and all my work was for nought.

For a while I stared at my failure. Then, not so much losing heart as having entirely lost it and buried it many days ago and miles away, I crawled back to the house, sat against one of the counters with Jasper beside me, and stroked his spine. He purred gratefully in response while I, having no spirit even to move, abandoned the fantasy of escape by some silly trench. Something else would have to materialise.

Having drifted to sleep without realising it was coming, I woke with a start to the sound of what must have been crackling gunfire way off in the distance. My neck ached from the awkward angle at which I'd slept, but I ignored it and crept back to the hole in the wall – the Moon, with the sky to herself, was shining brightly over the copse of trees and, I now realised, that awful green glow was gone. In moonlight's pale gown the fields beyond looked serene. I saw no machines. Then I heard, quite distinctly, a pyrotechnic of thumping explosions past the hills, in six separate intervals. And that was all.

# IV.

Explosively frustrated at our imprisonment, I went back to the lounge and peeped again, having nothing better to do, just in case the machines hadn't gone. Maybe this time they had, I thought, as I always thought, as I'd keeping thinking until I died because I didn't know any better.
Instead of keeping close to me and trying to ruin what little remained of my life, Raymond had stayed in the bathroom and so I could feel something akin to freedom. Left eye tightly shut, careful with my nose, I peered through the slit and was delighted to see nothing of interest – the birds, the green glow having momentarily tricked them into thinking it dawn, had fallen silent again. Maybe the time had come.

Then, still intimately focused on the dark universe outside, I was struck by a sound behind me – instinctively, I span round and, from my elevated position atop the sofa, kicked out. My kick burst into the darkness and my shoe caught a bottle of Bucks Fizz which Raymond – stood directly behind me – was holding. In a carousel, the bottle span from his hands and smashed on the floor. Both of us stared at it before he took, instead, to staring at me.
"That was the last one."
"Sorry," I said, shrugging carelessly, hopping down from the sofa before he could pull me down. "Should be more careful."
"Yeah, you fuckin' should," he snapped, shoving me painfully

against the wall. Dust fell from the ceiling.

"Don't touch me," I warned him, but he was elsewhere.

"Sick to the back teeth of you," he grumbled, looking me up and down, evaluating me.

"Oh, well," I replied mutedly. "I'll live." Raymond shoved me again, harder, and I thought I might go through the drywall – instead I bounced off, and had to twist my feet about to prevent falling against him and into his clutches. Yet, still, I wouldn't retaliate – that was probably exactly what he hoped for, and I knew my strength compared to his. "Stop fucking doing that."

"You wanna take my drinks, I'm taking your food," he announced, turning away to the kitchen.

"You what?" I followed, my pace quickening with each step.

"Only fair," he said, turning through the archway and out of sight. "You need some discipline, clearly, and I can't put you over my knee, so I'm doing this."

"I didn't *take* your drink, you prick, it was an accident!"

"Oh, yeah, I bet! Just a little silly accident that you *definitely* weren't planning all this time!"

"Will you grow up?!"

"No!" I couldn't help but snigger.

"You laughing at me?" He reappeared from the gloomy archway and took a few steps towards me – I stood my ground and felt quite proud of myself for it.

"Little bit."

"Right, you fucker," he said, jamming a finger in front of my face, before turning back to the pantry, "I'll show you."

"Are you kidding me?" I asked, following as he vanished again, exhausted already. My back hurt. My nose hurt. Everything hurt. I found Raymond in the pantry, as he said, pushing our food about the floor with his foot.

"Everything on *this* side is yours," he shouted, "and everything on *this* side is mine." It took a moment before I realised everything was moving towards his side.

"Right, you can pack that in," I said, grabbing his forearm, trying to pull him away – he span round and, with an open palm planted on my face, pushed me backwards again with such strength that I slipped and tumbled over.

Sedentary, I watched helpless as he carried on, the movements of his feet getting stronger and stronger until, instead of moving our food, he was madly kicking it to death. Cans were crushed and burst open, packets popped, glass smashed, and in a few moments all our food was gone. I saw a man insane. Climbing up the wall back to my feet, Raymond muttering curses at our food like it had wronged him, I grabbed him with my arms around his waist, trying to pull him backwards and out of the pantry.

"Get off me!" Raymond protested. A tussle began; he thrashing about to escape me, and I clung on with all the stubbornness I could muster, not entirely sure of my endgame, feet slipping on a floor coated by tea bags, apricot conserve, and easy bake yeast.

"Just stop!" I shouted back. Elbows tried to connect with my head.

"It's your fault! It's your fault!" Hysteria, more than me, gripped him.

"I didn't do anything!"

"Get off me!" He pried my hands apart and, tightly gripping them so I was trapped against his back, tried to headbutt me. I ducked my head below, sheltered between his shoulder blades, my hands finally slipping out of his. Clawing at his shirt, I still tried to cling on, stop him from turning towards me – he still managed it and grabbed me by my hair. At once I let go, hands held up in surrender, terrified that he might wrench a fistful from my scalp.

"Okay, okay, okay," I repeated breathlessly, the two of us panting, staring at him, eyes pleading not to do what I knew he wanted to do. He let go and I scuttled backwards into the door frame.

"You think I won't kill you?" he asked with ice and fire on his tongue. I rubbed at my head where a clump of hair ought to have been missing.

"I'm sorry," I said quickly, diplomatically; I decided then, at last, that with the coast having looked clear, I'd be gone in the next few minutes. To hell with waiting for the Sun. The outside could have looked a lot worse and I'd probably still have made this choice. Keeping Raymond calm until he left the room and I could make my move was now all that mattered. "I'm just hungry."

"Like I care." He barged past me and back into the lounge, out of sight, and I could rest for a moment against the wall, catching my breath. Every force in the universe conspired to keep me right there, to stop me moving for fear any sound would provoke his return, yet I tip-toed to the kitchen against the universe's bidding.

There, watched by Jasper, who also hid from Raymond's ravings, which continued indistinctly from the lounge as he kicked and threw about everything in sight, I stood at the precipice of the hole in the wall, the thin separation between shelter and sickly darkness, and steeled myself to move on. I knew nothing, really, of what was out there and I had no wish to be sacrificed to the witch's brew. But I knew what was in here and what could be in here in the future; one way or another, there would only be one living person in this house by the night's end.

Gingerly, I stepped over the fallen masonry and into the cold night, which felt *so* much colder than inside even when there had been no barrier between the two, mud squelching under my soles. After two steps I felt a hand on the back of my collar. This ripped me from the night, crunching my trachea, and back inside – I fell onto the kitchen tiles clutching my bruised throat. Raymond stood over me; his eyes were a wild inferno.

"The fuck do you think you're doing?" he demanded, bubbly spittle in his beard, but I couldn't reply – my throat burned so intensely that I could either breathe or speak but not both.

“Answer me! Speak! Open sesame!”

“I’m going!” I coughed, panting dry breaths, and he punted my ribs. Pain shot through my body and I curled into a ball, arms protectively bent over my head, ashamed at what little of an action hero I was.

“You’re gonna bring them here!” he roared.

“What?”

“Don’t you ‘what?’ me, you know what I mean!” He kicked me again, this time my shin, and I did all I could not to whimper. Just wait, I told myself, wait until he stops and then scramble and run and never stop running. What a prick I’d been to wait this long – but the tripods had been right outside, cooing, singing, pretending they didn’t mind me, luring me out. No choice had been a good choice.

“I didn’t do anything!” Jasper was barking now, at Raymond, but otherwise being entirely useless.

“You want them here!” Raymond roared, his intelligence entirely overthrown, and when I looked past my shielding arm I saw he was in a flood of deranged tears. The ground trembled. “You want the house for yourself! They’ve been protecting you and you work for them! You want them to eat me!”

“I don’t!” I cried, although I wanted to simply tell him he was fucking insane – but the problem with the fucking insane is that they won’t hear that they’re fucking insane. That’s one of the key symptoms.

“I saw it in my dreams,” he babbled, leering over me, far too close to risk making a break for it. “But you made me ready! Your weakness! It braced me, you know. Made me want to be better and now I am! Now I’m ready to unlatch the gate!” I stared at him through my forearms, eyes bulbous and watering, trying to think of something clever to say.

“Eat shit!” Again, the ground trembled and, immediately following that, came the unmistakeable hoot of a war machine. It was close, so close I thought it might be standing over the house itself, peering down one of the chimneys. We both looked up in its direction, before Raymond fixed me with a terrible stare, leaning down close to my face, his own sticky with sweat.

"I'll show you, you *bitch*," he growled, hands gripping his knees as he leaned over me, veins popping across his neck like purple vines. "I'll fuckin' show you." And then he stood back up, straight and almost formal, appeared to ready himself, and walked through the open hole out into the night. I stared after him as he half vanished, the darkness wrapping around him, shouting his presence to all who might hear.

"Come on then!" he yelled. "Where are you? Let's be having you!"

Scrambling to my feet, my bruised body protesting, I heard another metal hoot sound in reply. Again, the ground shuddered, as if some great subterranean beast was waking up. Bits of loosened masonry fell from the wall. Jasper whimpered.

"Stop it!" I shouted after Raymond, out of no concern for his own safety; I was still here, still trapped, and I'd go with him if he carried on.

"You want them, you can have them!" he bellowed over his shoulder towards me, mouth so wide he might have split his lips, then, back into the wilderness, pounding at his chest with a fist, "you want us, come get us! Let's do this shit!"

"You don't know what you're doing!" I cried. Then, in no mood to approach him again, I reached for a discarded mug, its 'this girl runs on coffee' slogan broken by cracks and chips, lying encrusted in dust. I threw it at him – it sailed over his head unnoticed and vanished into the dark, shrinking into a ball of white before it faded from existence altogether.

"I know!" Raymond cried back like a fanatic preacher. Another hoot. So close, now. "I know! It's a test!"

"You've gone completely mental." Talking hurt my stomach – clutching my ribs, which were bruised at best and broken at worst, I had to steady myself against the wall. I might have found the injury which, in time, would kill me in this new world.

"My whole life's been leading up to this!"

"That's how life *works*, you prick!" Another hoot, closer, and more shudders of the Earth. "Be quiet!"

"I've been quiet for too long! It's time to give ourselves to them!"

"Shut up!" I wailed in mounting terror – boiling tears streamed down my cheeks. This couldn't happen. He wouldn't kill me. "For God's sake, shut up!"

"No!" shouted Raymond, at the top of his voice, his arms extended, stepping deeper into the dark. In three strides I was out of the kitchen and in the lounge, fierce with fear, fumbling beneath the sofa. "No! Come on! I want you! Come to me and take me! I'm ready!" He heard me behind him and turned to look. "Aren't you?" His eyes widened.

Now I was stood behind him, outside at last, with nobody to pull me back, my mind empty and my hands not. In a flash, one last touch of humanity drifting from my fingers and my eyes, I struck the axe down on his skull. Raymond's neck buckled, eyes narrowed in confusion, and in a strangely bloodless motion he staggered two steps further into the dark with the blade jammed in his parietal roof. The axe slipped from its new sheath and out of my sweaty hands to plonk onto the grass. A slick of red smeared the blade and gleamed in the moonlight. I looked up – I hadn't realised the Moon was still out. Raymond stared at the blade for a moment, then at me, before closing his eyes as if in exasperation and slumping face-down onto the upturned turf. I fell onto my backside and sat, watching his body twitch until, after a few controlled breaths, my ribs hurting with each, I slowly pushed myself away and back into the kitchen. There I rested against the counter next to an upturned saucepan.

"Axe me tomorrow." I burst into a cacophony of inhuman giggles which soon evolved into me retching on the kitchen floor. When that subsided, still on all-fours, I stared at my grey reflection in the saucepan's sheen. In the metal sat some old woman with a broken nose and blood across her face and I had no idea who she was.

From above, there came a sudden crunch. Slowly, mechanically, I looked as plaster slipped and smashed from the ceiling. The moonlight cradling Raymond's little form darkened. Then, the ceiling burst open like a sore, the smoke alarm fell between my feet, and a single metal tentacle came curling slowly in. Its structure thinned to a needle point, plastic and copper piping crashing down as it penetrated with the ease of a knife through jelly. Jasper barked frantically at the slithering thing while I merely stared, numb – the long metal snake seemed not to notice or care for either of us, feeling its way downwards, now halfway to the floor and curling towards Raymond. I thought I saw him quiver.

Fascinated by the thing's slow advance and knowing I couldn't persuade it to leave, I just sat there. Watching. The tentacle was now some way into the room, twisting and turning with creepy sudden jerks; it put me in mind of a huge metal pipe cleaner being jammed through the roof. Jasper stopped barking, reduced to faint and hoarse whimpers, and he too only stared at the thing until he stepped forward to give its sharp point an innocent sniff. Naturally, I feared the worst for him, yet the black worm seemed unbothered. It curled around the kitchen units and back outside through the hole in the wall, towards Raymond. It was, surely, now aware of me – and, like the machine I'd made some sort of presumed eye contact with, it didn't care. I came to wonder if any of them would ever care about us. Were people now completely reduced in their vacant eyes – or, I thought in a flash of main character syndrome, was it just me?

Trembling violently, I pushed myself up the counter's side, barely able to stand upright, looking from the inhuman machine to the former person it approached. Slowly, I stepped away from the kitchen and into the lounge, disappearing into the darkness like that mug I threw, and stood in the oblivion staring across the room at nothing in particular. Had the machine seen me kill him? What might it think, if it thought anything at all, of me, a former person, just like Raymond? Other tentacles, I guessed, could be heard moving to and fro outside; they tapped against the walls or scraped like keys on metal. A whole army of appendages were pawing at the house, feeling it out, examining, with curious machines at the other end. In my mangled brain I think I remember trying to speak to them, appealing to their nature, somehow, not to tear down the house, but I was just talking to myself – that was all I ever did.

Irresistibly attracted, despite everything, I made for the glaring peephole but before I was even halfway that wall burst open too and another tentacle invaded. Then another, through the window, bringing with it dirt from the crater wall and the window's glass and wooden frame, then another through the same wall as the first, widening the newly poked hole.

The tentacles snaked about through the air, through interior walls, along the floor and burrowing beneath it, ripping up pipes and sawing through half-rotten foundations. The whole butchered house shuddered and I stood there, silent, one of the snakes curling around my legs but not ensnaring me, only passing by, the ceiling caving in all around. I wished the lights still worked so I could press my face against them and burn out my eyes. Instead I returned to the kitchen to see the first tentacle now scrutinising Raymond's head. It would infer from the wound what kind of creature I was, and so I kept going, to the bathroom, where I shut the door to banish the last vestiges of moonlight and cover myself with the darkness again. The grind of the tentacles' exploration through the house filled by ears. All I could do now was wait for those already here to either leave or come to me – it felt like waiting for a bus in the rain.

Then that faint metallic jingle, of scraping against the wall, returned, from the opposite side of the wall which I leaned against. It traced, slowly, nearer to the shuttered bathroom door. Then – silence. Intolerable suspense. The quiet a screeching needle in my ear. Something fumbled at the latch. It had found the door. The panicked handle shuddered up and down for a few dire moments and, then, the door opened. In the darkness I could just see the thing, like a black elephant's trunk, waving rigidly towards me, turning to examine and touch the wall, the floor, the ceiling, the sink and the shower. Blind head swaying back and forth, it pressed deeper into the room and disappeared into the same darkness which concealed me. I could only see that part of its body which protruded through the doorway, with no clue where the rest was. How close it was getting. At one time it clipped my foot. I bit my hand. Tasted blood. Wanted to scream. Not at the tentacle, not necessarily, but all of it. All which had become.

For a time, the tentacle was silent in the dark. I expected to feel a grip on my ankle or around my waist at any moment. Then came a clunk, a scraping on the ground, and the intruder's presence lifted. Thinking it of greater interest, it was examining the plastic pedal bin instead of me. Cramped, I dared to shift my position, still listening, whispering passionately for Jasper's safety. I forgot to think about mine – he was, after all, just a puppy. All dogs are puppies.
"Just don't kill him," I went. "Don't kill him. Don't kill him. Don't kill him." This I repeated for a long time. Then I heard that slow, deliberate sound creeping towards me again from the other side of the wall. Slowly, slowly, it drew nearer, scratching, tapping. Then I saw that tentacle shape in the doorway vanish, withdrawing from the room – after a moment's pause, it returned, reaching for the door, and I saw that its extreme point was now a human hand. Attached was not a metal tentacle but a pink, freckly human arm, far too long to be human but human nonetheless. It took the handle

and pulled the door shut between me and It. Darkness enclosed me again. Outside came a series of heavy bumps and then passed an infinity of silence. They were gone.

Burying myself in that bathroom, curled between the wall and the toilet, I stayed, not daring even to crawl out for the pantry's water no matter how much I craved it. All I could think about was that hand. Even the absurd had stopped making sense.

# V.

When my bodily needs inevitably forced me from the bathroom, my first act was to dive on whatever stores of food were left. Imagine my despair when I found the pantry completely empty; every scrap of food was gone.

At first I suspected Raymond – then I remembered what I'd done. It was unlikely to be his ghost. Either someone had sneaked in and somehow hauled it all away or else the Blight took it during the night. But why? That's weird. They had no more use for my food than I had for theirs. Why take that but not take me?

At the discovery, once again, I despaired in my familiar way until I accepted hunger. How much must I now be deficient in? Desperation was pushing me towards viewing the growing cobwebs in the ceiling corners as a valuable protein source. There was little else available; I couldn't eat the Jenga blocks scattered about the lounge floor, regardless of their potentially rich nutritional value. Then, when I went to the kitchen, something distracted me from all this talk of food. It was pristine. The holes made by the Blight tentacles were gone – as if never there. As if last night never happened. Wandering about, I tried to find some evidence of last night's invasion and found none. Even the triangular aperture, which I had seen explode, was still there in a wall which ought not exist.

Reconciling all this with my memories of the attack proved impossible; I couldn't decide what to trust. Only the now, I decided, eventually, could be believed – the past should be cast into the same oblivion in which I myself resided.

My mouth and throat were parched, as if coated in sand, and I felt my strength ebbing with each passing moment. Sat in the lounge's darkness, wondering how you're meant to know when hunger shifts to starvation, I'm embarrassed at how wretched I must have looked. My mind was practically animalistic, focused entirely on those twin thoughts of eating and survival – it was a burning dagger in my head that one couldn't be gained without risking the other, for only by venturing outside might I find food, and if I went outside then all bets were off. But if I didn't go soon, I might become too weak to ever go, and then that would be the end of a little story called me. Alien noises were not to be heard that night, though I didn't take that to mean I was safe. Being free of them was so strange that at times I thought I'd gone deaf.

After another day without sustenance I finally broke, my stomach too painful to bear, and took the chance of alerting the Blight to my unbelievably continued presence. I stepped outside into the cold morning air and made along the wall for the drainage pipe, which lay severed on the ground. In what probably wasn't my moment of greatest dignity, I licked it for traces of rainwater. Blackened and tainted and partly composed of dessicated moss, I was nonetheless somewhat refreshed. This wasn't the time to be picky. No enquiring tentacle followed my gurgling, which emboldened me, but as soon as I was sated I hurried back inside.

In a rambling and inconclusive way, I thought much about Raymond and his death. At times the axe would land on his skull without my hands on its handle, as if guided there of its own will, and I'd half-believe this was how events had played out. Perhaps it never happened at all – the house hadn't, so it seemed, actually been ravaged by tentacles, so maybe I hadn't killed him, too? I pondered, also, whether murder continued to be murder if laws no longer exist – as Raymond said, there was no society. This land was certainly not under the jurisdiction of any government besides the natural law dished out by the Blight, and so had I violated any crime? Raymond would have had an opinion to offer.

Urges to venture back outside, even beyond the property and into the big wide world, became overwhelming at times. I slapped them down whenever I could – 'wrestled' is probably the better word, for they certainly fought back. Sleep was elusive, having forgotten me as well as anyone else on Earth, and my most demanding activity was climbing onto the kitchen unit and reaching through the window, bending the plastic drainpipe in, so that any water would now collect in the sink and I wouldn't have to leave. Vague, impossible plans of escape taunted me all the time but I knew what waited beyond even if, for now, the enemy remained silent so as to trick me. Raymond was right; it was a test.

If I did sleep it was to be greeted by horrible phantasms of Raymond's death. At times they'd be supplanted by vast dinners in cosily lit settings. My mind knew what it wanted. Asleep or awake, a keen pain urged me to drink again and again, as I had no food. You couldn't live off water but that didn't mean I couldn't try. All the while, the light sneaking in through the hole in the lounge wall which shouldn't still be there was shifting in its hue, from grey to the gradually deepening red of blood.

Looking closer, I couldn't see anything through the hole. Nothing but that fuzzy red. Then, with two cold fingers, I reached in and felt something wet and slimy on the other end. Pinching tightly, I tugged it back through – red weeds, unnaturally sodden, slithered from the hole trapped between my fingers. They had grown over it, turning the half-light crimson.

It was while examining the weed and mentally measuring the risk of tasting it that I heard a familiar snuffing and scratching from the kitchen. Investigating, I saw a dog's nose peering in through the hole in the wall – I jumped at the sight, momentarily thinking it some other alien contraption, until the rest of his dumb face appeared and I realised it was Jasper. At the sight of me he barked excitedly, hurried over, and jumped up with muddy paws.

"Happy to see me, ey?" I asked, hoarsely. "Even when I topped your master? How loyal." He kept jumping, happy as a dog can seem, while I thought about the best way to kill him. Raw flesh was acceptable at this point and, after all, I'd killed a man and looked him in the eyes while doing so – what was a dog? Crouching, I had my hands on his neck while he tried to lick my face and was ready to tighten – but Jasper's eyes were so different from Raymond's, trust implicit even at the moment of strangulation, and my hands soon crept away again.

"Good dog," I sighed softly, scratching his chin. Perhaps realising I hadn't any food to offer – dogs are just as transactional in their love as any human – Jasper withdrew back through the hole, stepping through ankle-high red plants I hadn't previously noticed, and vanished. Presuming the coast clear if Jasper was happy, for a moment I stepped outside to join him, my feet submerging in the red weeds, and I heard the flutter of a bird's wings. I felt a deep and yearning jealousy towards the both for being able to survive out here when I couldn't, and went back inside.

For a long time I lay on Raymond's sofa. I thought again of the red weeds. Slowly, I rose and went back to the peephole, and with two fingers again pulled through another sinew of the strange wet matter. For a while I stared at it, unable to imagine anything less appetising, until, just in case, I prodded it with my dry tongue – it bolted back into my mouth at the first contact. It tasted like its colour. Outside, I heard a faint pitter-patter – probably Jasper going hither and thither – but nothing more. My stomach twisted with hunger, again, and with all quiet outside the pain finally jolted me to action. For the first time since I'd arrived, I stepped towards the collapsed staircase and yanked open the front door. It resisted me, more of the wet red plants having crammed into the crevices between it and the wall. They squelched at the door's opening as if I was messily removing an organ.

Sunlight crashed over me and so too did the full sight of the Pit for the first time – all of it under a carpet of red foliage. There wasn't a single alien beast around. No machines, no Blight, no nothing. There were, however, plenty of dead – black skeletons, stripped of flesh, stacked like exuberant Halloween decorations, the weeds tangling around the bones. A multitude of crows, or maybe they were jays, hopped and fought over the skeletons, balancing on decayed ribcages, poking beaks into eyeholes, while I stared all about, scarcely believing that the monsters had really left. The storm had not just passed but been gone for a while.

Slapping away the red weed dangling from the doorway, I climbed the rubble forming the Pit's lip. From up here, I could see in any direction save behind the house, over which weeds climbed, and saw no Blight. My way was clear. Leaving this place wasn't so frightening now I was outside – but what poor fool would I next murder through the curse which accompanied my company? By leaving, by taking this curse with me to roam the county, I surely endangered others. If there were others. But, in a gust of desperate resolution and with a violently throbbing heart, I shook away this moral dilemma and fucked off down the side of the Pit and into open country. Pushing into the red fields, I looked back. The house, still somehow unhurt by all those tentacles I was still sure I'd seen, was welcome to shrink from view.

When I last saw this part of… was it St Austell? Par? Some orbiting commuter village? I forgot exactly where in Cornwall I was. Wherever I'd put myself, when I had last seen it in daylight it had been a straggling street of comfortable and unaffordable houses, interspersed with the palm trees which London and Birmingham holidaymakers were often surprised to find we had. Now things were transformed – a multitude of red cactus-shaped plants, knee-high, were bursting up everywhere like the Earth had some ungodly STI. Even the grass was red now. Our flora was no challenger to these new arrivals – the nearest trees were dead and brown. Their trunks were criss-crossed by networks of red, pulsating wet threads which dripped with an unpleasant mucus.

Further down the road, I saw, the neighbouring houses had all been wrecked. The red weed grew everywhere, from every nook and cranny, and in its growth pushed apart the sinews of buildings and burst them apart like whiteheads. Far away I saw a gaunt cat sat on a brick wall, watching the scene with a detachment I liked to imagine it had applied to the pre-Blight world. This sight, strangely, gave me some tiny joy – if one cat could survive, so could another. Traces of people, there were none. At least the fresh air felt nice. Enjoy it while it lasts, I thought.

# VI.

Entombed in the house, my thoughts had been intense but narrow – focused just on my immediate security. Not for a moment, I think, did I wonder what was happening out in the wider world; whether the Blight had reached the Thames, or the Danube, or now happily ruled over the planet and were makings designs on the Moon. But I thought I could at least imagine what lay outside – tripods and pits and maybe some odd new constructions as the Blight settled in. I never considered, though, that the world, conquered or not, might ever look different. Dogs would still bark, waves still roll, grass still grow, geese still chase me. I was ready to see civilisation in ruins, but not the Earth itself. But now, having left the property, I saw that the world had gone all weird. Everywhere I looked, the red weed reigned. Fields were scarlet patchworks, trees suffocated under its encroaching vines; from the forests to the roads, in some places the weeds had already reached neck-height in an extraordinary burst of growth, like great alien corn fields. Lurid tarpaulins of red overtook everything. If I found a particularly tall spot, I was sure that from one horizon to the next I'd see no other colour. I knew of course, what all this meant: the terraformation of the Earth was underway.

With that realisation I touched an emotion beyond a person's normal range – one the animals we dominate know only too well. Rabbits, returning to their burrow only to come across a dozen busy excavators digging the foundations of a JD Sports, would sympathise. Inklings morphed into certainties; I'd never thought myself an overlord by virtue of my species, but I did feel that position taken from me. Dethroned, I was no longer a master, but an animal no different to those crows which danced on the skeletons and scavenged the Blight's litter. Man's imperial hold on the Earth had faded – the reign of the Blight was here.

Philosophy, though, can't hold your attention if it's competing with hunger. Dismally, my dominant motive again became food – the animal in us is buried very close to the surface – and so I hurried down the footpath's bank and into the red weed, which I could barely see over, to reach the houses, a struggling swimmer in this alien sea. It was wet and smeared my clothes red, a hot stench of copper from its sickly petals, but in its density I felt reassuringly hidden – and even thought about rolling about in the plants, turning myself a matching shade, so as to better blend in. I didn't.

At a T junction I chose the nearest garden wall and, hopeful that food remained in some of these houses, climbed its six feet – or, rather, I tried to. The weed was all over and made the brickwork far too slippery. So I went along the side, pushing through the Blight flora, until I found the creaking front gates. Here, at least, the junction's tarmac wasn't yet inundated by red and so provided a clearing – though already I saw young scarlet saplings breaking through where before they would have been dandelions. Struggling in my hunger, I reached a front door buried in weeds and, too weak to kick it down, clambered through an open window. Inside, I found onions and half-dessicated baby carrots and tins of rice pudding and sweetcorn and mushy peas, all of which I ate without a moment's hesitation. All this did was tease my stomach – I was no less hungry than before. With my pain whetted not eased, I went on my way, eager for more.

"Should have eaten that fucking dog when I had the chance," I muttered to a crow watching me pass by. Then I threw a stone at him – I missed and he flew away, cawing.

All along the two-lane A390, passing Sticker and approaching Truro (the street signs were still intact, though with weeds crawling all over them), I foraged while walking. Scarlet and crimson trees leered over me throughout my walk – it was like trekking through an avenue of gigantic blood clots – or I should probably say limp. My ribs still stung from the clashes with Raymond, the pain mixing with hunger until the two were essentially impossible to separate. Sharp equalled ribs, dull equalled hunger, I thought, as I came across a group of mushrooms in the undergrowth. I devoured them. Guidebooks, I dimly remembered, had told me that one type of mushroom which looked exactly like these was perfectly safe to eat and even bestowed blessings – another, which also looked exactly like these, would kill you before you could swallow them, I didn't die but neither did I feel blessed, so perhaps I made a mycological discovery. Pier Andrea Saccardo – which is a name I always knew yet never had an excuse to cite – ain't got nothing, as they say, on me.

Elsewhere, I came across a red sheet of flowing shallow water – a stream turned to what might as well have been blood. Nourishment wasn't to be found here – the Blight must have been poisoning the waterways to feed their invasive plants. I wondered if the oceans were still blue.

After pressing through an overgrown dairy farm, I was surprised to find that I could suddenly look down on Truro, the county town, from the valley's steep bowl. Its mighty three-spired cathedral was almost lost in a tangle of red weed, which grew so high as to be unbelievable, and so too was the rest of the city from one end to the next, urbanisation gobbled up by a great red swamp. Much of Truro's desolation was concealed, the Kenwyn and Allen rivers propagating the ravaging weeds, so I had no idea how badly damaged it actually was beneath all that alien matter.

At once, I knew there'd be no point in trying to scavenge Truro – what could I hope to find in an alien jungle? Fauna, I thought at all this teeming vegetation, might soon follow flora, too. Would I be competing with alien wildlife once the Blight introduced them? Was I a red squirrel? Even that was optimistic – competition would only be possible at all if the air stayed friendly to my lungs. If the world's forests were choked to death and the oceans' plankton poisoned by the red weed, which so far as I could tell offered nothing besides a constant metal stink and probably cancerous exhalations, I wouldn't last long enough to greet any xenomorphic pandas.

Orbiting the outer confines of Truro instead, ransacking houses and finding little which hadn't by now degraded into mould, I gathered enough to subdue my hunger. Cider, which I found in cans at one place, was drunk in great quantities, which was nice. Insulated by alcohol, again I tried gnawing on the red weed, my nose very painfully pinched. It was no more appetising than before and it took some effort not to vomit the cider back up. The weed was spreading and expanding at such a speed that, if I'd looked closely, I'd probably have seen it moving, as if in a time-lapse video.

Taking a country lane to bypass streets rendered impassable by thick weeds I found a stream, tracing the edge of the overgrown River Road, trickling near me. Though it was poisoned red I tried looking for fish like George had warned me against when we sat in the tree together. I wondered how he was doing. Sufficiently shallow for me to wade, I stood barefoot in the murky redness, but of course there was nothing and the weed was growing in knots below the surface which, like nets, would have impeded anything coming downstream – ensnaring my feet and ankles, it even came close to impeding me.

When there came the distant hoot of a Blight machine I paid it no mind but a second hoot sounded closer and so, reluctantly, I gave up on the water sports. After untangling the weeds from my ankles and pulling my shoes back on, I slowly made my way around Truro. The commuter suburbs along the A390 towards Threemilestone might bestow better treasures.
"At least I cleaned my feet," I sighed.

Highertown's suburbia, long stretches of bungalows and prim front gardens slowly becoming cheaply made estates on cul-de-sacs or winding streets, shifted the scenery from the nightmare of the strange to the wreckage of the familiar. Highertown looked like it had been visited by a number of tornadoes, roofs and walls torn away and scattered impassably over roads, other buildings burned to black shells. The Mercury Theatre on Irving Road, an art deco multiplex whose posters still promised plenty of Hugh Jackman and big-eyed animation, had taken a machine's foot through the roof and I explored its ruins in some wonder at the screening rooms now opened to the cold outside light. Yet give it a few yards and whole streets seemed undisturbed, houses quiet, curtains trimly drawn and doors locked, cars sat untouched in driveways and disabled bays, as if it were just a normal sleepy morning. Normality seemed an inch away. This was, of course, only the case after disregarding the red creeper – though less abundant here than Truro, it was still snaking over lawns and up walls and tree trunks, infecting cars, ensnaring the pumps of a petrol station, and making me want to keep walking lest it wrap around my ankles if I stayed still for longer than a few moments.

I hunted for food in house after house after house after house after house after house after house after house, breaking into them one at a time, and with each crumb I gathered I grew slowly satisfied – there were no roast chickens or secret wine cellars, but I made do. Once the time came to genuinely hunt or forage, I knew, then I'd really be buggered – I tried not to think about that too much, and slept in someone's unmade bed through much of the afternoon.

All this time I saw neither human nor Blight. Two hungry-looking dobermans patrolled Lancer Crescent near the primary school's towering wire fence but both hurried away from me at the first sight – I was glad, having feared they would come bounding the other way, a petite ape with bruised ribs being quite easy prey. At Treliske I found the Royal Cornwall Hospital, a concrete fortress whose maternity ward had been carved out by a machine's appendage. Military vehicles and equipment sat abandoned in the grey car park and, still dressed in green fatigues, I saw two skeletons – not bodies, but skellingtons, picked clean and lying under a streetlight. I considered pinching a firearm but quickly disregarded the idea, as I wasn't a teenage boy who thinks himself something of a semi-automatic weapons expert because he plays *Call of Duty*, though making a mental note of their presence in case my situation ever became just too much.

The hospital, surely, had been emptied. I wandered the Outpatients and Radiotherapy corridors in blind search of medicine or maybe an attending physician until I came across the adjoining pharmacy, half hidden by weeds, and was stunned to find it untouched. I filled an Army backpack with painkillers, Berocca, supplements, bandages, and whatever else would fit. They would, at the very least, prove an appealing currency to other survivalists. That was assuming I ever met one. It was certainly preferable to sex.

In the road which separated the hospital from a smashed retail park I found the crushed and scattered bones of what must have been cows. Either they had wandered here, freed from their paddock, before death or been flung through the air by the Blight. Grim as it is to say, I examined the bones for meat but what was left couldn't be seen for all the flies. Guess I could have eaten the flies, but I'd have plenty of time for that when I was dead.

"Well," I muttered to myself, "at least I'm holding onto my dry wit. That's good."

After sunset, feeling safer in the dark, I left the house I'd hid in and struggled on along the road towards Threemilestone, raiding as I went until the night scared me into hiding again. The Death Ray must have been used liberally here or, with no firefighters, one spark had been enough for quite the chain reaction – swathes of streets were charred ruins, not at all worth picking through, though I tried anyway from time to time, feeling vindicated when I unearthed a packet of mints in an upturned car or rescued a bottle of Fanta from a half-melted fridge. Those houses which survived were dull and grey, and the landscape would thank the Blight for getting so many out of the way, but how desolate the place looked in the dusk – blackened trees, blackened ruins, yet everything red-tinged with the weed. There was still birdsong.

As time went by and still I didn't bump into another soul, it was easy to believe that mankind had been swept from existence, and that I stood on the Earth alone, the last woman left alive. It took some effort to remember that Cornwall wasn't the world. But as I proceeded, coming across another skeleton missing its arms besides the In Cod We Trust chippie, I became more and more convinced that the extermination of mankind was, save for such dumb stragglers as myself, at least accomplished here. The Blight, I thought, had gone on and left the country empty, seeking food in more populated places, in the Tokyo Metropolis or Uttar Pradesh – compared to them, Cornwall must have seemed slim pickings. If only Oumuamua arrived in February, when the population wasn't quintupled by tourists, they might not have thought us worth the bother at all.

# VII.

Standing a little out of the way from Threemilestone, snuggled in the trees at Chacewater Hill, there was a thatched inn with a good view of a Screwfix opposite, its roof like bear fur and grey doves nesting in the chimney, called the Worm and Buck. It was where I tried to sleep away the dark morning. A lot of people, I noted with appreciation, had made their twin mattress beds before fleeing. How many, delayed by their own politeness, now sat dead at the wheel on the A30 or blew as dust on the wind, when if it weren't for making the bed they'd have escaped? Not all of them, surely. Even when Hiroshima had its bad day, the great majority of residents survived mostly intact – man is a hardy insect.

Needlessly, I took the trouble to kick down the inn's thick front door – the key turned out to be under a stone beside it – and ransacked every room for food, finding only pork scratching packets behind the bar and the beer barrels either spoiled or empty or looted altogether. The place had already been turned upside down. This must have been the thousandth property in which I'd found nothing worth taking; I was on the verge of despair before, in what must have been a bedroom for a very small dwarf, I found some cans of Pepsi and a packet of grapes in the mini-fridge. I don't like grapes but I was willing to like anything at this point – and I welcomed the processed sugar more than I can explain.

Trying to drift away, breathing lightly in case some Blight machine came beating through this part of the world in search of midnight snacks, I just couldn't escape consciousness. It was frustrating – my sleep schedule was by now confined to intermittent, dissatisfying spurts and I needed to make the most of them. Certainly no seven and a half hour disappearance from the living world, which safe civilisation had made possible, seemed to exist in my future. There's a strange type of despair that comes over you when you realise that a good night's sleep may never happen again. Prowling from window to window, I peered out for some sign of the monsters, like a child checking under their bed, until at last I forced myself to lie down and stay there.

Laying on the bed, staying on top of the covers in case I needed to get out quickly, I stared at the dark ceiling. Since leaving the house, my mental condition had been a hurrying succession of vague emotional states and little else. A sort of stupid receptivity. But in the night my brain, reinforced, I suppose, by the grapes and Pepsi, grew clear again and I gazed upon my navel. Don't pretend, this deep into my story, that you're surprised. Three subjects struggled for territory in my mind like feuding kingdoms: the death of Raymond, the whereabouts of the Blight, and, most importantly by far, the possible fate of Disco.

Those thoughts of Raymond carried no sensation of horror or remorse. It was just an infinitely repeating image – was I numb or had I run out of room to put all my guilt? In night's mocking silence, I stood trial for that moment of wrath – and of fear. Maybe there was some other way – but maybe I didn't want a different way. Maybe I'd been waiting for an excuse. All I can say to a reader who might condemn me is this – my crime went unseen. Raymond's body was taken – probably mulched or sacrificed or whatever else the Blight did with us. Nobody would ever cry foul play at the death of one among many thousands in those days of the apocalypse. The world knows Raymond was murdered only because I admit it here – go for it and judge me, if you want, but remember that.

When, by a great effort, I set aside mental pictures of split skulls and a body resting almost peaceful in moonlight, I faced the twin problems of the Blight and the fate of Disco. For the former I had no data points to extrapolate, no information to interpret, no nothing – I was just one tiny, pathetic little creature sat on the skin of the Earth with no greater capacity for knowledge that the foxes I could hear fighting over the bins next door. And, for Disco, it was the same – I knew nothing. When I realised that, the night became more terrible than if I'd turned and seen a tripod tentacle coming in through the window.

Sitting up in bed, staring at the dark, wishing to see Disco again, I found myself praying that the Death Ray might have suddenly and painlessly struck him out of being. Better that than some slow decline – like the skeletal cat I'd seen on the wall – in the absence of birds or voles, which I knew he could catch, because he was not just a smart cat, but a good one. I didn't *actually* pray, of course, that would be ridiculous, plus I didn't know the direction to Mecca, but believe me when I say I came close. Strange night.

The bright morning was fine, I guess, the sky glowing pink to the east, fretted with little golden clouds. For a moment it was hard to believe the world had ended – that moment passed when I left the Worm and Buck and pressed to Chacewater. Crammed all down the road were vestiges of the panicked torrent which must have poured Devonward when the fighting began. A Sainsbury's delivery van, missing a wheel, lay on its side in the ditch, a poster for a local production of *The Gadfly* stuck to the undercarriage. Cars were scattered all over the road, overtaken by gas, decomposing figures behind the wheels or lying on the potholed tarmac. A policeman's hat was trampled into the glass shards swamping the road and, as the road lurched up a hill, I also found a brown lorry on its side, windscreen smashed and bloody. The footprints of a Blight machine pressed through the fields either side, the owner having uncaringly stepped over this carnage. My ribs didn't hurt so much anymore, at least.

My plan – why I was going where I was going – couldn't have been vaguer. Grasping it was like grasping at smoke. I still had that ridiculous idea of going to Penzance, scavenging all the way, on the off-chance that I might find Disco. Then, at least according to my exhaustion-fuelled daydreams, we'd establish our own little commune, just me and him, and he'd catch birds which I would pluck and roast while learning horticulture from stolen library books. Maybe we'd find a boat and go to the Scillies. The Blight probably didn't land there – if they did then, I don't know, we'd go back.

This all presumed I ever found him – and I knew I had no chance. If death, whether by Blight or by accident, hadn't escorted him from the Earth to cat heaven, also known as dog hell, then the woman whose care I'd left him in must have fled with him. Either that or he himself had fled into the wilderness and gone feral. I didn't enjoy the idea that, returning to nature, Disco might have forgotten all about me, but I steadied my emotions with the knowledge that he'd be far happier this way. My heart, nonetheless, ached for Disco and the world before when I'd be woken by him screaming three inches from my face. Wherever he was, if still alive, it was far away. Given that finding a working car, and so becoming the noisiest non-alien in the county, was off limits, Cornwall felt very big. Distances between neighbouring towns could become painful journeys – and what of the irradiated wasteland which must exist where the atomic bomb had fallen? That, if not the blast then the fallout, must surely have been the end of Disco. Every five minutes I seemed to think of another way he must have died – it didn't do my motivation to find him any favours.

Feeling vulnerable the longer I passed through the wreckage of humanity on this road, I withdrew down a steep ditch, where I belonged, and into the trees to go from trunk to trunk under cover of scratchy thickets. The dark expanse was lit in patches by yellow gorse and broom and as I prowled it occurred to me that I saw no red weed anywhere. The trees came to an end at a row of half-rotted wooden fencing keeping me from an empty pasture, and so I turned back onto the road, went to the opposite ditch, and hurried down it. Far, far away, across the fields and up the hills, I thought I remembered there being a towering radio antennae whose red light would blink at night. If it ever had been there, it wasn't anymore, and I carried on – the sun was rising, flooding the road with light, and I came upon a stone bridge traversing a twin pair of brown railway tracks which cut between the trees. Halfway across, I glanced down at the tracks and froze.

Trudging out from under the bridge's arch beneath me there was a man, hood pulled tightly up, and it *was* a man given his clumsy way of walking without care for the world around him, as if he still owned it. Dressed in a black waterproof coat which squeaked with every movement, he walked down the middle of the rails with his back to me, blissfully unaware of the eyes on it.

Silently, I leaned over the bridge, regarding him, thinking about throwing a rock to oust this rival for food. But, eager for company, I shook that nonsense from my head. I had a yearning need to be alone, yes – but, right now, the need to know that I wasn't burned so much brighter. I could already feel the regret getting ready to jump onstage.

"Oi!" I cried. He froze in place before slowly turning around, a large butcher's knife already brandished from inside his coat. He stared ahead, through the bridge's archway, then looked up at me, and I realised that he could climb the bank and give chase if he wanted to. I couldn't outrun him – not with these ribs. Was I so naive to think nobody had yet turned to cannibalism? I probably would, eventually; though I hear it's quite salty.

"Where'd you come from?" he shouted back, voice full of suspicion and echoing down the arch beneath me. Red, greasy hair fell over his eyes, and even from here I could tell how dark and dirty and sunken his face was.

"Back that way." I gestured, truthfully. I hadn't realised until now that my voice was hoarse, but it was. "Been stuck in a haunted house for God knows how fuckin' long. What's the date?"

"Hell if I know," he replied, knife withdrawing back into his coat – I was glad to see it leave, though I wasn't about to forget he had it. "Does it matter?"

"I feel like it'd help." He took some steps back down the railway, much closer to me, so I might have spat on him if I was so inclined, craning his neck to keep eye contact.

"Well, my watch broke a while ago, and I haven't been counting the days. Calendars aren't good for anything if the world's ended. There's no festivals on no more."

"I guess so," I conceded. "I guess so."

"If you're looking for food, you need to go looking elsewhere," he added, crossing his arms. "This whole place is *my* country now."

"Oh. Really?" I feigned genuine curiosity – this was somebody whose mood could turn on a dime, I was sure, and I didn't want to provoke him. Not with that knife. Raymond had been my big lesson.

"Yeah. People used to call it Chacewater but I'm colonising this whole valley. It's my little kingdom now. I'll be an enlightened despot – don't you worry."

"That's how I like my despots," I joked.

"Well, there's only food for one person, and the despot gets first dibs. So I hope you're just passing through."

"I am."
"Where to?"
"I don't know," I answered slowly. "I'm still getting my bearings."
"But you're definitely not staying?"
"I don't want to," I replied, and he looked at me doubtfully. "I don't want to be with someone else anymore than you do. I've been trying it and it's never worked out."
"Tell me about it. My squire got eaten – that's not a sentence I ever thought I'd have to say, but here we are." Then, suddenly, I recognised his boots – Army issue. And his red hair, sneaking out of his hood, one strand at a time... I shot out a prosecuting finger.
"It's you!" I said suddenly, making him flinch again. "The soldier! We walked to Hayle together!"
"What?" Confusion. Then, suddenly, realisation spread itself across his face. "Oh! Shit! Yes! You're that girl from St Ives, right?"
"That's me!" I was breathless with excitement. "I assumed they got you in Hayle."
"I assumed they got *you* in Hayle! Aw, well ain't this nice? Hey, forget what I said, you can stick around – but only you! I know you're cool. You wanna come on down?" Common sense begged me not to, but I scrambled down the bank to the railway anyway, too delighted at the familiar, and friendly, face to heed it. He was now ensnared in my story – and to think he had once escaped.

"You'll have to forgive me, but I've forgotten your name," I said once I arrived at his side, glancing down the tracks, keeping some of my attention on his hands in case they went back into his coat.
"Did you just check if a train's coming?" he laughed.
"Maybe." I smiled and he laughed harder.
"Oh, no bother about the name; I don't remember yours neither. It's Drake."

"No, it fucking isn't," I sniggered.

"Hey now, we're in a magical new time where you don't have to keep any paperwork on you," he said urgently. "So I can have whatever name I want."

"If that's what makes you happy-"

"It does."

"Then I support it."

"Well, thank you very much." He laughed again, slapping me on the shoulder. I winced. "Good God almighty, how mad is it that we both made it and then run into each other again? Fancy that."

"How'd you manage it?" I asked. As if in reply there came a metal wail through the trees – distant enough not to be threatening, yet, but close enough for me to use the word 'yet.'

"Walk and talk?" asked Drake, if I must. "Don't worry – there's nothing to be worried about. They're not looking for people anymore, I don't think. Keep your wits about you and there's no trouble." I nodded and we strolled down the railway tracks as if on a grunge album cover. "I didn't survive in any spectacular way, believe me. Back in Hayle the aliens, they blew everything up, obviously, including the roads. Exposed the water mains – so I crawled in a pipe."

"Brave."

"Yeah, it didn't feel brave – it felt like I was being a fucking moronic gimp. But I lived and nearly everyone else didn't."

"That seems to be happening a lot nowadays."

"Yeah. Happened to your nose, by the way? You look battered."

"I got battered."

"Need to toughen up." I stewed in those words. "Anyway, they left Hayle eventually, then I figured I'd go to the coast. See what I could do. Then that nuke went off."

"I saw it," I said. "It looked... pretty wild."

"It felt pretty wild." He reached under his hood and, with a quick motion, pulled out a clump of thin red hair. He held it out for me to stare at; it was as if he had dragged his hand across the floor of a barbershop. "And it's feeling wilder by the minute."

"Jesus," I said quietly, as he sprinkled the follicles along the ground. "Radiation sickness?"

"I'm not a doctor, but, well, probably. It's definitely something. Maybe I caught something off those red plants they're growing everywhere. Breathing in spores. Don't suppose you got any iodine?"

"Sorry." I'd mention the medications in my backpack when I could be sure Drake wouldn't beat me up and take them. Suddenly, he looked over his shoulder. "What?"

"Nothing," he said, relief in his voice. "Just a rook. Or a crow. Or a jay. I don't know the difference."

"Long as it's not a magpie; then we're buggered," I offered lightly. "Unless we salute – you're probably good at that. Army and all."

"I never noticed birds had shadows until these last few days," Drake said, ignoring me, still looking over his shoulder with eyes scanning the treeline. "Let's get off the rails; it's too open for me. There's a pub not far from here – let me buy you a drink."

"That's a *great* idea. You sure know how to treat a lady."

"Hope you like your booze warm and stale."

We hurried through the trees; the pub he spoke of, the Hammersmith, wasn't far beyond, alone between fields with a big car park and promises of Sunday carveries. Entering via the spookily empty kitchen of grimy stainless steel, I sat at its musty bar while, after throwing his coat over a stool, Drake perused the drinks.

"I'm going to more pubs in the last week than I ever went to as a student," I remarked.

"What did you study?" he asked, finger pausing over the gins, and I wondered if I should lie. Like he said, we could be what we wanted to be.

"Criminology. Then I dropped out and did English Literature like I should have from the start. And then I dropped out."

"And now you work at a surf shop."
"That's how the economy works."
"Oh, I know. I studied Physics. And now here we are at the end of the world and none of it matters. Kinda freeing, really, innit?"
"Have you seen any Blight?" I asked. "Since I crawled out-"
"Blight?"
"Isn't that what everyone's calling them?"
"What, the aliens? I don't know, maybe; I just call them aliens. That's what they are."
"But have you seen any?" He unscrewed a bottle of Famous Grouse and poured me a generously large honey-coloured shot. "They've mostly pissed off." He drank my shot – then poured another. I'd let him have as many as he wanted – I wasn't in the mood to threaten a man's whiskey ever again.

As Drake spoke, he became very animated, almost theatrical, delighting in the chance to finally talk to someone.
"I guess they've got bigger fish to fry now," he said, finally pushing a shot (the third one) towards me, "but they had a huge camp off near Redruth, I heard from this guy, and it was still there after it got nuked. Like a city – he said you could see the lights at night, like all the stars had fallen out of the sky. I bet they'll be building more all over the world."
"Like termite colonies." I downed my shot and felt warmed.
"Apt." He copied me. "But I haven't seen any of them, not for… like… five days? Four? But fuckin' hell, they're up to some stuff. They're building ships, now, it's not just the weeds."
"Ships?"
"Spaceships. Starships. Whatever."
"Starships…" I whispered.
"Another drink, squire?"
"Lock and load," I sighed, and Drake poured me another, bigger shot, which I also downed. He leaned against the bar, getting close enough to my face that I could smell his unpleasant breath. I needed to find some toothpaste.

"Tell you what, you can't even tell a nuke went off anymore. That whole area's completely red now. Like an alien planet. I guess they're turning Earth into their new home. Fact is – we've been full-on colonised. This must be how the Red Indians felt."

"Native Americans." He shrugged. "It's really all over, then, isn't it?"

"What, the world?"

"Yeah." He nodded.

"Aren't you relieved, a little bit? Humanity had a good run but now we're done and beat and I'm kinda fine about it." I stared – strange as it may seem, I hadn't arrived at this fact until now, yet it was so perfectly obvious when he spoke it. Total extinction, as opposed to reduction and the return to an animal way of life, hadn't really occurred to me, not as a definite thing. I kept thinking that I'd plumbed new depths of fatalism and defeatism, but I kept surprising myself. Like a yo-yo, I'd acknowledge our doom, then forget about it, only to be reminded again later. I couldn't wait to see what other neuroticisms I was capable of. I repeated these reflections to Drake.

"It's your mind's lifelong habit," he said with conviction. "To think you're still superior. You're not; we lost. We *lost*. It's all over. Not even the nuke could stop them – they lost *one*, just *one* of those tripods, and how much did that cost? Right now they're in America and China and all those places and crippling them. Walking all over them. New York fell as easy as Hayle."

"But we killed one in Hayle-"

"By accident!" Drake interrupted. "And these are only the first. They'll keep coming. How many showed up just in Cornwall? How many do you reckon will fall on the rest of the world? Every inch of the planet'll get covered sooner or later. It'll be theirs so easily it'll amaze you." I gave him no answer; I just sat staring past him, at my reflection in the dirty mirror on the wall, trying in vain to devise some counterargument which wouldn't come and which I wouldn't believe.

"I need to wash my face," I muttered at the crusty blood above my lip. "The war's getting in the way."

"This isn't a war," said Drake. "It's as much a war as there's a war between us and the ants. Ants build their cities, live their lives, have their wars and their revolutions, until we want them out the way. That's how it goes."

"Oh, I don't know," I complained. "There's no point dwelling. It's just the way things are now and we've gotta make the best of it. Even if we are just ants."

"Edible ants." We sat looking at each other.

"What do you think'll happen to us?" I asked. "In the end? Extinction?"

"I've been thinking about that a *lot*," he said. "A lot. Haven't had time to do anything other than think. It's the people that think who survive, you know, who consider, and really think about stuff, they're who make it. Everyone's so scared of death – I was in Afghanistan, I've been pretty close to death and it's just death, it's not that bad – but I think they're more scared to think. They've got all these big institutions, you know – governments, companies, everything, all designed so they don't have to think. They can just be told what to do. I was with this group and someone told us there'd be food one way, and they all went that way, and I ignored it and went the other way. And I'm alive. That's when I knew I was special, when I was the only one walking in that direction, toward the aliens, because I've got a head on my shoulders and they've just got receivers. Their heads are just things they hang their hats on. Just dumb sheep hoping someone else'll save them."

"You don't think much of people, do you?"

"God, no, not anymore. It was nice to see so many of them get trampled, or burn, or just plain starve..." He saw my face and halted awkwardly. "Sorry, sorry, that's not what I mean. I just mean... still being alive means I'm doing something right. It's good to know I'm doing something right when nobody else is. I never had that feeling before."

"I get you," I conceded.

"Well, obviously, there's plenty of food left lying about, but it'll go. And we can't start up camps or farms again, cause the aliens'll just find us. All we can do is hunter-gather, like Stone Age times, but we've gotta get enough people together that we can breed and sustain our numbers, you know? Otherwise there's no point – we'll just wither and vanish. That's the first certainty, right?"

"Right, but if you say the words 'let's set up baby factories,' I'm leaving."

"Oh, no, no, not a chance of that," he said quickly, laughing, a certain uncomfortable edge to his laughter. "I'm not just deserting my morals. I'm a really big feminist. Hell, I still bet we can cling onto a bit of democracy if we try really hard. Maybe we won't keep the Westminster model but, well, you know, baby steps."

"This'd all be so much easier if we were as small as ants," I sighed. "I should've been a bug."

"We'd have to start worrying about bees." Drake laughed again before returning to his tangent. "But once the aliens are done smashing everything up, they'll still be hunting us, feeding on us, all that nice stuff. I saw one, the other night, out near St Austell, breaking up houses with its tentacles and rooting about for people to eat." I realised he may well have been watching my own living horror from a distant hill, when tentacles had invaded the house after I offed Raymond, the damage somehow healing the following day – I said nothing and hoped my flashback wasn't obvious on my face. "But I don't think they'll keep doing that once they've grown their own food and they're raising their own animals here. We're a stopgap – we'll be competing with their cattle, soon."

"Will the nightmare never end?" I asked coldly, scanning the bar for my next drink.

"Oh, no, not at all," he grinned unpleasantly. "We've just been stupid so far. Getting on their nerves by shooting them and nuking them and all that silliness. We should've stayed quiet from the very start and they'd of left us alone, I reckon. They don't *really* want any bother, they just wanna build their civilisation here and figure out what to do with us after. We've gotta stop being all reactionary and start being sensible. No more bombing them and thinking that'll do anything."

"You want people to make friends with them?" I asked, cautiously.

"I want people to accept the situation. You can't change it anymore than you can change the weather – you moan at the rain but you don't think it'll help, do you? So you get an umbrella. We've gotta start getting umbrellas. That starts with us accepting..." He slammed his shot glass onto the bar, like a judge bringing down a gavel. "...that we've gotta live like this now. We have to live without cities or countries or science or any of that. That's in the past now."

"But when you say 'live like this,' what does that mean?" I asked. "What does living look like now? Because I don't know how long I can just wander around the fields looking for stuff to pilfer off shelves. I don't see that lasting forever and I don't know what I'd do instead. Thought about growing food or catching fucking boar but, like, one screw up and I'm dead. And is that *it* now? Just... eat and sleep and wait for death?" Drake looked at me for a moment.

"Was your old life really that different?

"My old life had video games." Drake smiled.

"It's hard to say what'll happen."

"Great."

"If you're hoping for fun, I reckon you'll be disappointed. There's no more BRIT Awards, or Eurovision, or FA Cups, or Bella Italia." He said it with a certain sense of wonder at all these things disappearing into the ether.

"Oh, no, not Eurovision, anything but Eurovision."

"But I'm dead set on living." He clapped his hands together. "Even if I have to do it without *Would I Lie To You?* I don't wanna be exterminated and I don't want them to catch me, neither, and make me their fuckin'..." He took a deep breath, thinking up his next words, "...budgie in a cage. And I'll tell you what, sooner or later, you'll have to show what *you're* made of, before it's too late."

"Maybe I already have."

"I suppose you have stories aplenty, too, don't you?" I didn't like the look of his smile.

"I might."

"Well, you can tell me all about them. But I'm telling *you*," he jammed a finger in my direction, "I've got it all planned out. I've thought it out. We're done. We're too stupid. We've gotta learn and we've gotta stay alive so we can learn. That's what we've gotta do!" I stared, astonished, and profoundly stirred – because Drake, I realised, had absolutely no idea what he was going to do. He had plenty of wishy-washy rubbish about adapting, living, accepting the reality, but this was all the opaque media trained non-speak of the football interviews and political party conferences he thought the Blight had banished. But, no, they weren't gone; he was keeping the spirit of PR speak alive. I heard no actual ideas, policies, concepts, identified problems and suggested solutions. He had only feelings and platitudes. I needed to find Disco – at least *that* was a plan. Or a goal. Or something. But perhaps I could bring Drake with me – an extra pair of eyes and hands, at the cost of an extra mouth. Again and again, as I thought about this, Drake muttered that he had figured it all out.

"If you don't want 'em to catch you, you've gotta get ready," he was saying. "I'm getting ready."

"Uh-huh." He swigged a drink.

"I'll tell you what though; it's a different kind of person who'll survive in this new world. You've gotta be a proper beast to survive."

"I wouldn't call myself a beast," I said. "And I've done okay."

"Yeah, I've got my doubts about you – you're slender."

"Thanks?"

"But you can think and that's what matters. That's why you lasted, I bet – or maybe you won't last much longer, who knows? Give it a year and then we'll know who had the mettle. The rest'll be buried. I'll tell you who won't last, who'll get done in first, is all the little busybodies."

"The who?"

"Oh, you know the sort!" he cried. "The useless ones who think they're useful! All those people who work in offices eight hours a day and talk about sales reports and 'have you got my email?' and work to live and live to work and all that shit. They've got no spirit, no dreams, no nothing. They decompose while they're still alive."

"All those people who work in glass towers," I said.

"Plastic towers, not glass," Drake replied. "You need a bit of ambition to get in the glass ones. These lot who live in all those prefab suburbs all choking up the greenery round every town, who get the train to a job they don't understand, who tell you they vote tactically, who wear corduroy, who read the books they're told to read and watch the films they're told to watch, go on their holidays to Tenerife or maybe have a walking holiday in the Brecons..." It occurred to me that he could have been describing literally anyone who wasn't him at this point. "...they're just the worst. You know, people like me, we're meant to be 'common,' aren't we? But it's the people you find most often who're the common ones and we'll see how long they last without their car insurance and their central heating and their microwavable curries and their Horlicks and their iPlayer and their kids who never come downstairs." He slammed his fist against the bar, making me jump. "Every day of my life I had to see 'em in their hundreds going to work like brainless little fucking insects, all these little cogs, and now I get to see what happens when shit gets bad for them. When they have to live like humans are meant to live – scared, and nasty, and with very short and brutal lives. It'll be grand! Give it a week of raiding empty Tescos and looking for berries in the hedges, I guarantee their empty stomachs are gonna lead them straight to their masters. They'll *give* themselves to the, what did you say, Blight?"

"That's mad," I said. "Give themselves to them? What, like, offer themselves up? People aren't gonna do that."

"Oh, it's already happening in some places, I just bet. Everyone's a Quisling if you starve them. They'll be grateful after a while. After a generation or two they'll wonder what people did before there were aliens to take care of them. They'll just add a line to whatever they tell their kids – 'ah, well, back in the olden days, we didn't have mobile phones, or Internet, or Xbox, or alien overlords!' I can imagine them. I can *imagine* them." He spoke with a sombre gratification. He'd been waiting for this vindication his whole life.

"Do I detect some satisfaction in your voice?" I asked. Drake looked at me.

"You do." He smiled and licked his dry lips. "Sick little game, innit?"

"I always thought it was people on *this* side of the bar meant to spill all their feelings."

"Well, the world's changed, hasn't it?" he laughed. "You know, up that way somewhere-" He pointed in the direction of a nearby window, "I heard church bells. Either they're automated and the battery's still going – or someone's risking it and ringing them still. They still think there's worth in doing it."

"Brave of them."

"Religious of them. Makes me wonder how long all the religions will last, once we're all slaves. Will the Muslims last longest, do you think? In Afghanistan I found them to be pretty resilient." He laughed again, scornfully. "Maybe the Sikhs. They've all got swords."

"I don't think that's true."

"Just hope the Christians go quick. Can't be doing with any more carollers." He paused, lost in thoughts, like lights bouncing off a disco ball. "I bet they'll start keeping people as pets. Put little chips in their heads. Teach them tricks and tell their kids the little pet girl had to be put down."

"The Christians?"

"What? No – the aliens."

"That makes more sense."

"And maybe they'll train us to be their soldiers, too. Help crush any resistance, just like any other occupation. Let them try and get me, though. I've got a whole arsenal at home, now. Plenty of goodies got left behind. I'll annihilate the lot of 'em if I have to. Until they annihilate me. Rip and tear."

Grim meditation settled. Drake moved from behind the bar with complaints of aching feet and went to a stool near to the window. There, he sat drinking and quietly contemplating the rustling trees and gravel car park and a nightingale chirping from a red branch. I too sat, just thinking – there was, I found, little reason to doubt all his wild opinions. He might be an ever so slightly psychotic ranter – natural given the pressures of surviving in a hellscape like this – and I couldn't be sure I wasn't in some way the same, but a phrase about a broken clock came to mind. People probably *would* submit in return for safety – it wouldn't surprise me to see it. What would it take, I wondered, for *me* to do it? I might be closer than I realised. You had to laugh at this scene, the two of us like Marx and Engels, discussing the future shape of all life with absolutely no means to influence it. In the days before the invasion nobody would have thought either of us any authority on the world's trajectory – I a lowly shop assistant overactive on Twitter and he a FIFA-loving soldier. But we were the only ones left – the authority fell to us.

"There's probably a generator somewhere," Drake said suddenly. "If you fancy playing the fruit machine."

"I'm good."

"Fair."

"You still haven't told me what you're doing – your actual plans." Drake hesitated and I wondered if I'd stepped too far, become too challenging, precipitated a crisis by forcing him to reckon with the fact that he *had* no plan. Only vibes.

"Well, it's like this," he said, steeling himself for another monologue. I steeled myself, too. "Whatever happens, we've gotta figure out how we keep sustaining the species and all that."

"No baby factories?"

"No baby factories, I promise, and no cannibalism neither." Those were my two biggest fears eased – so why did I still feel nervous? "But, look, all those tame and useless people, they'll go the way I said; dead, slaves, pets, anything but free. They'll get three meals a day off the aliens, yeah, but that's about it. They'll still have to live in a cage – but your average London flat isn't far off one, so maybe they won't know the difference. As for us, well, there's one option left for us, I reckon."

"And that is?"

"Well, they clap eyes on us, and we're dead, right?"

"Right."

"So, we need to make a new life – where they'll *never* find us. You know where?"

"Go on."

"Under*ground*!" I could have leaped across the bar and punched him in the mouth – he must have seen this coming, because he hurried to an explanation. "Look, when I was in that sewage pipe, it got me thinking..."

"There's a sentence." I leaned back on my stool. I was so dead. We all were. This guy just would not drop his fantasy – I remembered how he'd been banging on about about hiding in the mines when I first met him. But, then, I worried I was being hasty. Drake had a solution, at least in his own mind, and what did I have besides some contorted scheme to find my cat and forage in the bushes?

"Everyone thinks sewers are horrible, but that's only when the cities on top of 'em are full of people shitting into them. And they're not anymore. Soon enough they're gonna be washed out by the rain and the Blight'll never think to look in them. Probably don't even know they're there. But they're big and airy; good enough for anyone to shack up. You know half the homeless in Las Vegas live in the sewers?"

"I don't think you know how to pitch an investment." He held up a hand to silence me.

"Irregardless – every house is above the sewers, every building, every basement and cellar and vault and store and everything else. Then there's railway tunnels, subways. Right? Are you starting to see it?" In my mind, a diagram was opening up – a vast network of underground tunnels, like corridors, so complex it looked more like a map of the nervous system, with free access upwards through all sorts of compartments to the world above.

"I'm seeing something."

"What we need to do is get to London, or maybe Paris, where the sewers are the biggest. Form a band of people; all the fit and smart ones. All the rubbish stays on the surface. The sewers won't be for filth anymore."

"So you want me to come along, then?"

"Well, obviously; we'll need women, too." Few words can be so adept at making me take a step back. "Not like that, I just mean... ugh, you know what I mean. Having kids and all that; it'll happen on its own. You don't need to force it and I don't *want* to force it. As long as everyone's strong and nobody's weak, I'm happy. Life's real again – the world's got no room for pipsqueaks now. In the before times, they'd just keep popping a new kidney in you. That's gone – you've gotta work hard just to keep yourself going. Anyone who ain't strong dies. They have to die. They just have to. In fact, they should *want* to die – it's basically treason at this point to stay alive, keep being weak, making everyone else weak."

"Yeah." I nodded quickly, imagining him pushing the wheelchair-bound down flights of stairs and calling it progress. Was this a society whose flag I wanted to wave?

"Once we're organised and set up, we'd probably find things easier than you think." He was exciting himself at every idea pouring off his tongue – and the more he spoke the more it sounded like he was making it up as he went along. We were both learning his plan at the same time. "We could set up greenhouses in all the abandoned buildings, nip up there when the Blight aren't looking; set up basketball hoops, even keep the Premier League going in some form. Have one-man teams, each is the club they support, and we play football like that until we've got enough people for a full starting eleven. Keep score on stolen office supplies and in a few thousand years when society's put together again they'll be able to look back and know if Chelsea or Arsenal won more titles." He laughed with delight.

"I've always preferred rugby."

"League or union?"

"I don't know what that means." He shook his head. "Look, I'm just not certain turning into sewer rats is the way to save humanity."

"Well, it's better than just sitting there, waiting for it all to blow over. We've gotta do more than that. And, for someone like you, especially, I've got just the job for you."

"Oh?" I waited – and wondered if I'd need to form a union.

"You've got brains."

"...cheers." Did I?

"You've got brains and you know how to use them. We've gotta make sure no matter how bad things get, we don't forget science – we've got to get together every science book we can find, every single one, and we've gotta learn everything and keep teaching it, generation after generation, forever. If we forget it, we're fucked – we'll never have a base to learn again. The Blight'll never let us. Just one chance. That's all – just one chance. It'll be the new religion. And we'll be able to, long as we don't annoy the new masters – they've got brains too, they won't do us any harm if we don't get in the way. You don't go looking for ants to spray with chemicals 'til they infest your house, right?"

"I suppose not, no. But you've been saying how we're done for – I don't see the point of learning science if we're dead anyway."

"Well, maybe we're not dead forever. Imagine this – you're looking out the window and you see four or five of those tripods marching around, blasting everything in sight, but there's no aliens in them. We're in them!"

"You what?"

"We could learn how to drive them. And then we could fight! They'd never see it coming. Oh, it could take an eternity, but with enough time we'd figure it out – as long as the right people are in our new society. People who won't sell us out. Who've got the patience and who'll see the big picture. We'd have the wit for a smash and grab like that, eventually, I just know it. See, you think I think humanity's over – I don't. Just the current iteration. But the new one, the better one, the one we could make – that one could start and it could take over the world just like the aliens did. Cause that's the thing about ants – you try, and try, and try, but you can't get rid of them." We were all about ants today, I thought.

For a while, Drake's daring imagination – all that courage and talkative, kind of babbling, assurance – managed to dominate me. Excitement crackled in my blood. I was almost ready to believe in him and his forecasts. Maybe building utopia in the sewers, playing football, and stealing alien death machines really was a realistic expectation. Oh, man, I wanted to believe in it. I really wanted that faith – I was coming to understand how pyramid schemes ensnare people with their 'get rich quick' promises – so I might have something to keep me going forward. But the dark clouds were always there. I wasn't blind to where I was – crouched in an abandoned pub with a broken nose and horrors all around. My power was non-existent even before the Blight. What had it been reduced to now? And I was expected to build a new society. Hope in a better future was a hard thing to keep your hands on back when we had running water – try clinging to it these days.

Yet, still, I let Drake babble his mad stories about what wild escapades we could look forward to, simply because I'd rather hear something positive for once. Maybe that's weak of me – or maybe I just needed a bit of optimism, no matter how batshit, and could dare to believe, just for a moment, that there was something left to believe in. And even if I couldn't buy it, why argue? Why take it away from him? He only had himself to hurt.

After a while Drake must have grown either tired or overexcited and he invited me to his lair – his words. After scanning the sky for Blight craft, as he insisted they were even patrolling the skies now though I'd never seen any, we hurried to an old stone schoolhouse nearer Chacewater which had become his personal citadel. Several petrol-run generators were assembled around the perimeter, powering a substantial collection of video game consoles, flatscreens, and Blu-Ray players inside. It felt like walking into a Curry's – at the sight of this man cave, I had my first true inkling of the gulf between Drake's dreams and his powers. All the objections and doubts I'd been pushing down clawed their way up the wall again. When I voiced them there wasn't a sentence Drake would let me finish. He had a van, he explained, which he'd been using to ferry his goodies to the schoolhouse, and therein lay his big and bold strategy. We'd load the van with ill-defined "equipment" and somehow drive it all to London without attracting any Blight attention. Holes, one by one, gaped open in his grand plan, not least that it would mean ditching all ideas of finding my cat – but still I tried to cling to the weird semblance of hope which insisted on sticking around. Drake, and his dumb ideas, were all I had. What still surprises me is how little convincing it took for Drake to shrug and promise that we'd go looking for Disco first then go to London. And so, just like that, he had me onboard.

In the van's cabin, under the protective canopy of swaying trees, we drew up a list of needed supplies if we were really going to settle London's sewers.

"Hold that thought," Drake said before I could even put pen

to paper as he stepped out of the van. He was gone for a few moments, before returning lugging a metal stepladder from around the side of the schoolhouse. "We'll need it to get into the tunnels."

"I suppose so..." I agreed, watching through the wing mirror as Drake awkwardly loaded it, before he unexpectedly slammed shut the van's rear doors.

"Well, so far, so good. Reckon we've earned a break." I stared at him. Our eyes met in the mirror.

"We haven't even done anything."

"We've done plenty," he said and, without waiting for reply, marched back inside the house, all relaxed shoulders and limp arms. I followed to find him flopping onto a beanbag in what had once been a classroom and was now one of many, many dens. A generator in the corridor hummed as he flicked on a black brick of an Xbox.

"We should go upstairs," I said, stood hesitantly in the doorway. "Check if there's any Blight near us before we start turning on generators." With a lot of poorly disguised reluctance and much huffing, he admitted my idea was good; I flicked the generator off again and we went upstairs.

In an empty classroom, its walls still covered by laminated posters of a Geography trip to the Icelandic lava fields, we peered through a window speckled with condensation. There was little to see past the nearest beech treetops – it seemed to me that the schoolhouse was a poor choice for a headquarters and attracted Drake more for its grandiosity and the resultant sense of status rather than out of any practicality. I'd have set up in the unglamorous surroundings of an industrial estate – then we'd be right on top of supplies and not facing all these roundabout trips I already saw us making – or perhaps a nice farmhouse. Oh, wait, I'd done that. Hadn't gone well. Shit.

"Well," Drake remarked sullenly at the difficult view, arms crossed, "you can hear them coming. They're big. Don't need to see them."

"You'd be surprised," I replied. "They're pretty light-footed when they want to be. We should find a better vantage point – past those trees, so you can actually see the area."

"Completely unnecessary," Drake objected. "No footsteps, no problem."

"Well, maybe they can hear us before we hear them," I suggested, on the cusp of pleading. "At that point, seeing them first is all we've got – otherwise they'll hear us working and drop on us unawares. We'll need to learn this quick if we want that new civilisation of yours." Drake appeared to roll my words around in his head before, finally, he relented.

"Alright, but let's hurry it up," he said wearily, dripping with reluctance, and we went back downstairs and into the pleasantly crisp outdoors. Birdsong flowing through the air, we were soon following a muddy footpath which wound around a hill like a serpent.

"What were you on that railway for, anyway?" I asked suddenly, spotting a rotund bumblebee busying himself on the brockweed and trying to enjoy the sight while I still could.

"Getting some fresh air. Are you gonna take long on this scout of yours? I wanna put some mushroom soup on before it goes off. Swiped the *Mad Men* box set from HMV yesterday, too – still haven't got round to watching it. Got me some lovely headphones, now. Kind I always wanted."

"We've still gotta work."

"You can't spend your life working." With that, finally, I saw Drake for what he was – though I wasn't entirely without sympathy. When life gets tough, sometimes all you can do is chill and eat soup.

Suddenly, the path ended, fading into vegetation, so we went together through the wilderness, following the terrain wherever it pushed higher and puffing our way atop a decently sized hill with a reasonable view to the north.

"Christ," whispered Drake, as our ascension completed and the view opened up. I nodded.

"On the cross."

There were no machines to be seen but they would almost have improved the sight of a countryside flooded red. Stretching across everything, that colour stencilled the landscape as if a giant had been bleeding to death, making all we could see appear like an apocalyptic oil painting. In hillier parts, like ours, the red weed hadn't quite reached – the Blight, in seeding the rivers, must have ensured the lowlands would succumb first to the weeds' choking wrath, at least for now; soon, I was sure, where we stood would be buried too. Down in those lowlands, the red creeper strangled an old Methodist church's steeple and swarmed up shrivelled trees, their branches stretched gaunt and dead and set with leaves sucked dry. Where a little stream trickled down our hill, it grew ever more red as it progressed, throttled by a bubbly mass of living red weed. Going underground hardly seemed like adequate shelter – how long did Drake plan on fighting off the weeds as they broke into the sewers? – but I didn't break Drake's heart by saying so.

"Weird, right?" I asked, instead.

"That's one way of putting it."

"Interesting how much it depends on water. I guess a desert's the place to be. Maybe we should go to Egypt instead of London. Or the Arctic. I saw it fading away before when it got near the beach – maybe it only likes freshwater. Maybe some biomes can be saved."

"Either way, we've not got much time to appreciate what's left," said Drake, looking around our feet where the weed hadn't yet gained a foothold. Among the wild grass, green and brilliant in the sunlight, dense flowers bloomed. And, from deep within the red beyond, curdling smoke was rising.

"Maybe someone's trying to clear it away," I said hopefully.

"Maybe. They'll need a lot of paraffin – that shit's slimy."

"There must be more than just us two still left, after all – I bet some of them have their own insurgency plans, just like you."

"Oh, there's plenty of people left – but I don't know about them having plans. I ran into this guy a couple days ago, he'd been hiding in an attic and was looking for other survivors. Didn't know what to do when he found them, so I left him. He's one of those weaklings I told you about."

"I see."

"He did tell me something funny, though."

"It's amazing we can still find funny stories," I said, gazing out at the mutilated country.

"Apparently a lot of people started drifting to Falmouth once it all came falling apart, all thinking they'd find a boat or something, I guess. Didn't find any, obviously, even the shitty little canoes were gone by that point. The smart ones got there first. So they had nothing to do and nowhere to go, so what do they do?"

"Go mental?"

"They went mental." He laughed. "He said it looked like if we'd won the World Cup – but were depressed about it. All night they're partying, getting sloshed, like there's not an apocalypse on. Orgies in the street, he said."

"Get real!" I laughed.

"Hey, I believed him – but here's the best bit. This goes on all night, then the Sun comes up, and when it does they realise they've had a tripod stood there just watching them the whole time!"

"No way."

"Yes way. Might've been there all night! They all scarpered, he dove in, and scooped up like a hundred of 'em." He smiled wickedly. "A tasty treat."

"That's grotesque."

"Yeah, hell of a way to go. Bet the history books'll say they were just poor, desperate refugees!" He laughed again, then slapped my shoulder. "Come on, let's get back – ain't no machines anywhere. Told you."

"Maybe it's alien bank holiday," I said, as we made our way back down the hill. "Man, I'm gonna miss Christmas."

"We'll keep it going in the sewers, don't worry."
"Don't get me *too* excited." We laughed.

Throughout our trek back to the schoolhouse, knees pushing the reddening undergrowth aside, Drake returned to babbling about his grandiose plans – these were much less focused on the humdrum details I might have liked to debate and more on what he'd do once he was behind the controls of a tripod. Apparently that was no longer centuries in the future but a few weeks away. I noted, with trepidation, that a minority of his plans involved repelling the Blight themselves – he seemed much more focused on imposing himself on everyone else. Eloquently, he told me how he'd sear away all those "idiots" who would have "only just" relearned how to domesticate horses. Walking through the muck in a world where I lacked even a hair straightener, it was hard to imagine seizing a tripod and leading humanity to revolution; harder still when Drake, our esteemed leader, was so giddy with excitement at having a second player for his looted Xbox.

"We should eat something," Drake declared as we returned to the schoolhouse, or what he was now calling Drake Hall, and having already guessed that we were done with physical labour for today and needing to eat more than I could ever have imagined back in peacetime, I agreed. Through some exceptional wiring – he could work hard if only for his stomach – a cooker in the school kitchen had been restored and we could sit at a long plastic dinner table as if it was Year Eleven again.

The pair of us worked on what I think would be a vegetarian jalfrezi together – I chopped the peppers and onions while he fetched alcohol. Pouring it out onto two plates felt like emptying a box of treasure – meanwhile, Drake assembled packets of Doritos and salsa and shredded cheese and all sorts of things. It was very over the top. I didn't care.

The food was, if I'm honest, utterly wonderful in ways I can't quite describe. Transformative, regenerative, life-altering, use whatever words you want – and I just know that, in normal times, I would've thought it was shit. I felt spirit return to my body. The salsa *was* too hot – how quickly I was ready to complain again – but premier Burgundy wine in a school canteen was a novel and very welcome experience.

"Holy shit, I needed that," I gasped, having filled myself, feeling like I was partaking in some great national holiday. Carried away just a smidge, we'd made enough for a whole classroom – I'd need to find some Tupperware for our journey west.

"Just wait," said Drake. "It gets better..." He hurried away, around the corner, and I watched nervously until he returned with an expensive looking bottle of champagne in one hand and a wooden box of cigars in the other.

"Oh, that's just ridiculous," I laughed.

"I know!" he cried in delight, placing both down between us, then putting his feet up on the table. "Sixth Form was never *quite* this good." We lit the cigars together – I had no idea how to smoke, or rather I didn't know how hard inhaling could be, and so yacked it back up. The curry nearly came up, too – I was grateful that it didn't.

"The wine's probably enough," I said, once I had my trachea back under control and once Drake was done laughing at me. "We shouldn't get too drunk – we've still got things to do, right?"

"Hey, you're a guest," Drake insisted, pouring golden champagne up to the rim of my glass, letting it overflow out of sheer merriment until I pulled it away. "How many more chances for this will you get in your life?"

"Not many, I suppose."

"Not many!" He glowed with optimism. "Besides, I'm in the mood to celebrate. It's a great occasion, you turning up out of the blue."

"You taking it as a sign, huh?"

"Something like that. I've got myself a trusty lieutenant!" He slapped my shoulder again then, wincing, examined his hand. "Shit, those're *some* blisters."

Holiday spirits abounding, once we'd eaten Drake then insisted on playing video games – *I* insisted that we wash up first, it feeling wrong to leave things for the dinner ladies to clean if they ever came back. As darkness fell, with thick curtains drawn over the tall windows, he taught me to play *Call of Duty* in the classroom turned lavish gaming room until, conscious of the bombastic noise, we switched to *Little Big Planet* and I sprawled on a beanbag, half-cut and my stomach gurgling with happiness, guiding sweet cartoon figures through manic obstacle courses, while our species sat on the edge of extermination and the red weeds inched ever closer.

Amid many hours of gaming, during which Drake finished the champagne and threw the bottle from an open window in a moment of abandon, we went back to the cigars – I was starting to get used to them. The night got dark and darker and found ways to get darker still. Drake, drinking without stopping, followed its lead. With each puff his optimism and crackling energy, like a brightly burning candle, faded. He spoke rarely, about this vague idea or that vague idea, until eventually we were playing in stiff silence. Bodily needs roused me to break the quiet.

"I'll be back in a second," I said, rising and hurrying to the door.

"Where you going?" he asked urgently.

"Gonna piss."

"They can't take that from you!" he shouted after me as I went down the corridor, through a door, and into the stairwell. Halfway up the stairs, I stopped and looked through the wall of frosted glass. Past the trees I could see moonlight blazing across the valley. The northern hills were shrouded in darkness; the nearer ones glowed ghostly, their treetops shimmering in the Moon's gown. All the rest of the landscape was black – but I knew what colour lurked underneath. Then, feeling the cold, I reached to close a window and my hand brushed something sticky on the frame. I looked down closer and saw that the weed was climbing in. I stared, first at it, then at my hand with its unpleasant red tattoo, then out of the open window, across the darkness and to the harmless stars.

Dreams are harder to shake away when we're awake than when we're asleep. Drake, I'm sure, would wake up eventually but, looking at outstretched Cornwall, I was suddenly there. To think I helped him load up a van and thought of going to London without my cat! I'd let a mental fantasy overcome me and my stupidity crashed into me all at once. This was idiotic – I'd only kill myself by staying with Drake, who had no idea what he was doing and who would have to be dragged kicking and screaming towards any kind of hard work. And, surely, he'd die soon enough – he was in my company. It was inevitable.

The day had been wasted. I felt a violent revulsion towards myself and, drowning in remorse, which sounds like a melodramatic glam rock song but bear with me, felt like a traitor – to my kind and to Disco. He might be waiting at his food bowl this very moment while I wolfed curries and humoured nonsensical plans. Did I seriously think we'd get across the country and build an empire of the sewers? Would I really be allowed to first spend weeks searching for Disco? Drake would give me a day, maybe two, and then it'd be time for a new voyage while my cat wondered when I'd be home. And he still needed his medicine...

Turning back, I hurried down the stairs two at a time, spirited my backpack from the makeshift bedroom I'd been given, went through the front doors, and vanished into the darkness, leaving Drake to his dreams.

# VIII.

I jogged through the dark and down the nearest hill, looming trees watching me go, taking Station Road towards the empty Blackwater Bypass. Red weed was tumultuous here, overcoming the trees and roads to the point where it felt like I'd been shrunk to microscopic size to explore somebody's intestinal tract. Squelches burst underneath my shoes. But, by the light of the moon, I thought I saw that the weed was changing colour. It must have been the moonlight's trick, I thought, but it really looked as if its spongy fronds were turning white.

When the bypass became the A30 and skimmed Redruth's edges, where whole buildings were invisible under scarlet bindings, I hopped the crash barrier, still ditzy from the champagne, in search of new lodgings. Most houses were impossible to consider entering, given that they looked less like dwellings and more like grim red seedlings, and I feared that wherever I slept I'd wake to find weeds growing down my throat and into my ears. This had already befallen the bodies which littered outer Redruth's streets, many stripped to skeletons with the alien flora for clothing, so I kept walking even with my stomach gurgling ominously from the curry. It was clear that my best bet was to find my way to the coast, if I could figure out what direction that was, and hope like hell that the weeds still didn't like it there. If they'd gotten used to the beach, though, I'd happily float away because this place was impossible. In places I was barely able to tell where stood buildings and where lay streets for all the weeds; they grew and enlarged like slimy circus tents everywhere they sprouted. At one point I saw a house's roof crumble under the weight of its weeds, brick chimney toppling in after it. The noise of the collapse, breaking the hideous silence, was almost a relief.

At the street corner, where a mostly consumed road sign pointed towards Redruth Station, there lay on the ground a corpse less rotted away than the others, weeds growing into his open mouth and across his face like a bloody balaclava, still clinging to a steak knife. Thinking it was more useful with me, I pried it from his hands – and he spluttered awake with wet breaths. Punched by shock, I staggered backwards. Stupored, drunk on noxious chlorophyll, he was shuddering alive. With every breath I could hear the weeds rattling inside his lungs. Fixing the black sky with helpless eyes, skin eaten away and flesh conquered by the weed, I saw in him – and on him – my future.

"Ellie?" he gurgled. With watery groans he attempted a furious lunge at the strands clinging to him, but they pinned his arms to the ground and so he writhed slowly, alive but trapped in his sarcophagus, and at the sight I speechlessly turned and ran. I could, should, have stayed with him – comforted him, maybe even tried to free him, but his brutal voice terrified me so badly that all I wanted was to get away. That was the way of things for me. And what good would I have done had I cut away the weeds? I knew what I'd be saving him from; but I didn't know what I'd be saving him for.

The pestilence somehow grew even thicker the closer I got to Redruth, to the point where it was wholly impassable, reduced to a Blight lair. Was this what their cities looked like? Did they simply nest in the organic mass and feed from the slime? Seeing the town as a lost cause – to the long-standing agreement of many a Whitehall department – I returned to the red-tarmacked carriageway, leaving footprints in the sludge and practically asleep as I walked, happy to remain so, for I couldn't stop moving without fearing the haunted weed finding its way up my nose and binding my brain. I feared that more than I feared the machines. The whole landscape was, still, horribly quiet.

Snacking from my backpack as I went, I wondered if the weed could become more amiable when cooked. No doubt some culture, somewhere, would master the art of frying this stuff – they wouldn't have much choice but to try. Maybe with rice, fried prawns, and soy sauce, it could end up almost agreeable. Of course, that was if rice, prawns, and soybeans could survive in this new world where the red weed gobbled every inch of space it found.

Some way further north, I saw in the moonlight the landscape becoming clearer of the weed – it was the Portreath coast and I was right! The weeds did dissipate when they approached the sea! I hurried that way, thinking I could sleep on a beach if all else failed. Elements were a threat I could actually comprehend.

Drifting sleepily through Illogan towards the coast, I passed a weed-overgrown cottage from whose every window spewed black smoke. The air smelled, briefly, of relieving soot rather than metal and death. Going on towards Portreath and the clifftops, no longer able to countenance the misery of remaining awake, my head pounding with tiredness and alcohol withdrawal and seeing the weeds now fading away all around, I broke a window at the Sapphire Seals Bed & Breakfast and, with my coat beneath me to shield against stalagmite shards, crawled in and fell asleep almost immediately on a worn down cream sofa. The aquarium next to it was murky and alive with weeds – the good kind. The Earth kind.

I woke a mere couple of hours later, the dawn sky a

magical burning orange, and was glad to hear at least one bird warbling. The red weed hadn't found its way inside the cottage, yet, either held back forever by the soil's greater salt content or just dawdling. I wasn't about to wait for it – I left and tramped the rest of the way to the coast. It would take longer but I would get to Penzance one way or the other, the plan being to visit St Ives first, fetch Disco's medicine, then blast south to Penzance. Getting from one town to the other, I knew, would be tricky – the land between was surely utterly overgrown but unless I wanted to hike the whole coastal path around the peninsula then it was my only option. Tired legs were going to define my future for quite a while.

Once I found Disco, and in my strange mental state I no longer doubted that I would, it was off to the Scillies for us. I came to think that, given how small the islands were, maybe the red weeds would never establish a foothold on such hostile ground and we could survive quite well. Maybe the community there was untouched by the tripods and would welcome us – they certainly would when they saw Disco – before a fisherman adopted me as an apprentice. The whole idea exploded in my head and I grinned stupidly at the thought of safety becoming so sudden and so secure. I had to get there first, of course. Rationing what I carried, I reckoned I could last a couple more days and there was plenty more to be found for someone as increasingly well trained as I in the art of plunder. The transition from digital tech-wizard to hunter-gatherer had come so quickly I barely noticed its passage.

When, at last, I reached the cliffs, having somehow still not seen nor heard any tripods despite my increasingly vast sightlines, there was no sense of joy at the sight of the sea as I thought there might have been, not even at the discovery that it was still blue and perfect. I only felt more trapped and more impatient to take to the water. I must have come onto the very same footpath I'd walked after escaping Hayle, only the opposite way. Others, in the first days, must have thought these cliffs protection or perhaps been driven there until the only escape was to jump into the predatory surf. Dead bodies, a dozen or more, lay scattered along the path, some on the very edge of the cliffs. Their white, bulging eyes like gelatin candies told me that when faced with suicide or the gas, these ones had chosen to choke. They escaped becoming food for the weeds, at least, which wasn't growing here, but not for flies or dogs. I didn't peer over the edge to see how many took the other option.

With the red weed absent it felt like any ordinary early morning hike – the wide open fields criss-crossed by ancient hedgerows and wooden gates, signs threatening walkers into keeping them shut, great meadows of dark heather and spindly bracken, dodging the odd puddle breaking up a path of stones and dried mud. Skirting the cliffs, I saw they became sloping – I could easily pick my way down to the narrow rocky beaches below and the caves which would make ideal shelter from rain or tripods. Instead, after some three hours of walking, the path taking me through Gwithian and Godrevy where the fields and meadows were singed and burned black for miles all around, I came within view of St Ives' old harbour across the bay. It was an odd sight, home – as if I'd been away for years rather than a few weeks. I'd had periods that lasted longer than this whole rotten mess (and, assuming my implant kept working, I'd never have one again. Yeah, that was happening… I'd need to cut it out of myself eventually. Best not to think about it right now). There was Smeaton's Pier with its fat and thin lighthouses, the fishermen's cottages at this distance seemingly stacked on top of each other, the little chapel atop the Island; and all of it free of red weed. Though this was where the nightmare began it looked, somehow, untouched. I could half-believe the town might spring back to life – or that, when I arrived, it would already be alive with noise, cars and people coming and going, like the cataclysm had never happened. Like it had all been a dream.

Stood besides black Gwithian Beach on a terrain of dunes like a pock-marked golf course, the spiny grass burned and crusty, I stared at all the wreckage which had slowly washed up since the war began. Hayle's exterminated evacuees, which I once drifted through, were now scattered as broken boats and indefinable debris all along the beach. Slowly I meandered onto the black sand, fused to fulgurites under the Death Ray, which crunched as I walked among the carnage. Ashen skeletons lay in boats resting on the mutant sand. The tide, inextricable, was coming in, and would soon sweep everything away just to return it in twelve or so hours. Then, for the first time since God only knows when, I happened upon some good news – you don't often find that in a field of skeletons. A cobalt boat, happily stood upright, which appeared fully intact – she was a small vessel by the standards of some of her contemporaries on the shoreline with a cabin no bigger than a garden shed and empty lobster pots dangling off a hull whose every crevice was diseased with rust. Across the blue bow was emblazoned in white the name *EXCELSIOR II*. With some effort I clambered aboard and sat in the cabin, examining the controls, delighting that the keys were in the ignition and delighting that boats had keys – I don't know what I'd thought they had instead. I tried them and the engine spluttered to life; but she was still stranded on the black sand. With one look to the tide, crawling nearer then retreating, crawling nearer then retreating, I doubted that would be a problem for long.

It wasn't a problem for long. Napping in the cabin, I was woken by the boat's gentle rocking in the surf, her keel still grinding in the sand, the water not quite deep enough yet to permit movement. I sat and waited, watching the gulls and occasional cormorant pass by overhead. When at last the water became deep enough and the boat slowly rode the little waves away from the black sand, cautiously, carefully, as if this would make it quieter, I turned the key and, again, the engine rumbled to life. Water was thrown up by the outboard motor chugging behind me – I felt the momentum of the *EXCELSIOR II* press forward and back towards the beach from which it drifted. Turning hard on the steering wheel, I was able to course correct and with acrid diesel in my nose scraped the boat's side against the sandbar. Then, remarkably, I was labouring through the swell of young, unbroken waves and making for St Ives. This whole driving a ship thing was pretty easy!

All the way I kept my head low, eyes scanning the empty cliffs and beaches, but still I saw no tripods anywhere. Their absence was almost becoming frustrating – I needed one every now and then to justify my anxiety. Hayle's bleak ruins became visible as I skirted the estuary's mouth, the viaduct's great stone apatosaurus legs still standing though the span was long gone, much of the visible town an incomprehensible mass of rubble and charcoal. Jellyfish, pink and slimy and translucent, glided all around the *EXCELSIOR*, which I grappled with as she tried to veer left and aground. I wanted to aim for St Ives and stubbornly fought to stay on target for a while but the appalling steering made me fear overshooting such a small target and dashing myself against rocks instead. The swell of the turquoise sea, too, was becoming unnervingly bold as clouds grew on the horizon.

So it was that I ran aground at Carbis Bay beach instead. Overlooked from the steep hills by tall Victorian hotels, I headed into the town, passing under an arched railway bridge and newer, uber-modern hotels. It was an uphill climb past small and expensive plastic and pebbledash houses until things levelled out. Carbis Bay was just as I'd left it – shops closed, houses locked up, blinds drawn, the town a picture of desertion and stillness. In some places plunderers had been at work but rarely anywhere other than the newsagents and a specialist wine shop – this I couldn't hugely fault. Burlington Jewellers had been broken into but the thief must have been disturbed – gold chains, opal-infused rings, and watches you're never meant to wear outside lay scattered on the pavement, one of the more expensive looking of the latter dangling off the edge of a drain's grate. I gathered them up, being human and thinking they could be useful in the coming barter economy.

Further on was a stone church, upper edges of its steeple grazed off, and against a black marble tombstone was a tattered woman in a heap. The sleeves of her rusty brown dress were pulled up past her elbows and her forearms deeply gashed. A smashed bottle formed a pool of shards at her feet. She seemed asleep – but she was dead. I'd gotten good at telling the difference; at sensing their coldness without touching them.

The more I penetrated towards St Ives, the profounder grew the stillness. It was not the stillness of death – it was the stillness of suspense, of expectation, that gnawing sense that a sword was dangling above my head, held by a single quivering thread. The destruction which had already taken the rest of the world, the destruction which started here, had only me left to claim.

It was on Trelyon Avenue, trees to one side and a looted BMW showroom to the other, that I first heard, creeping almost imperceptibly upon my senses, like a spider you become aware of long before it reaches you, the howling – a sobbing, high-pitched alternation of two indefinable notes.
"Uuuuuul-la... uuuuuuul-la..." it moaned. "Uuuuuul-la... uuuuuuul-la..." Perpetually, it kept on, a river of noise flowing through every space. Cutting through the grounds of Belyars Castle, keeping to the trees for cover, it grew in volume with every step I took. Houses and buildings deadened or cut it off, then gaps would open and let that strange, remote wailing again come forth at full pitch. When I emerged through trees

and hopped down a wall onto the road along which stood my shattered old comprehensive, it came in a full tide.

"Uuuuuuuul-la... uuuuuuul-la..." I stared in what might have been its direction, down the increasingly winding lane which would eventually lead to my house, wondering at the cries. It was as if Cornwall herself had found a voice for her fear and solitude.

"Uuuuuul-la... uuuuuul-la... uuuuuul-la... uuuuuuuul-la..." wailed the superhuman notes. Waves of sound swept through the trees as strong as the wind and the sway of the branches and the rustle of the leaves seemed entirely from the power of the cry.

Continuing down the lane I passed the bowling green, where a tripod's footprint had carved its mark. Water collected inside and toads obliviously ribbited within. But where were the red weeds? St Ives seemed pretty clean. I had half a mind to climb a hill and scope out the town before I dived straight into it, but that meant exposure – the lack of tripods so far didn't indicate a lack of tripods in the future. The trees still made hiding possible so I stuck religiously to the narrow lanes.

All the houses here, gated mansions with gravel driveways the size of tennis courts, were empty and still, and my footsteps echoed eerily down the lanes. When the houses faded away and, breaking the monotony of development, became fields, I found a baby blue camper van, vintage, lying on its side in the middle of one such empty field. The skeletons of several Shetland ponies were picked clean all around it. Herring gulls searched for morsels between the ribs and fought when they found them. They looked well fed. I puzzled over this sight for a moment and then carried on into town to find my house Disco's medicine, and, perhaps, that haunting voice. It grew stronger and stronger but I couldn't see anything past the hedges, save for a haze of smoke rising from some uncertain point further beyond and mixing into the low clouds like an

unappetising smoothie.
"Uuuuuul-la... uuuuuul-la... uuuuuul-la... uuuuuul-la..." cried the voice, coming, I now felt sure, from the same direction as my house. I was *so* tired – and, with that desolating cry working its dark magic on my mind, I started thinking, which I should never do. Just for a moment, lucidity returned.

What was I doing wandering this town of the dead? With all the world lying in state here I was, still clinging on, the final rat on the ship. A black shroud wrapped around me, starting with my neck, and the quiet which dwelled all around the distant alien cries felt like the louder of noises. My mind ran through old friends that I'd forgotten for years, then on the people I'd met in these past few weeks but who were now gone forever – Drake, George, Raymond, Linda, Cynthia. Most might still be alive – but did it matter? They were people turned to street signs, just marking a place in time for me, coming and going like leaves on the wind. And while all fell or gave up I kept walking. Where? This cold world had no room for people anymore, yet I persevered in crawling about on it. I wouldn't find Disco, would I? I wasn't even sure I could find myself.

I came onto the main road by the dentist surgery and here, at last, lay the bloated masses of red weeds again. I'd almost missed them. They crawled on walls and garden fences while lifeless bodies rotted to formless gristle, their metal stench mixing with an evil, ill-meaning smell wafting from some of the houses. Thirsty after the heat of my long walk, happily, I found that the Costcutters which had taken a Range Rover through the roof – the automatic doors had shattered outward in the blast – and had a crashed fighter jet on the road beside it still, somehow, stood.

So, tip-toeing over the carpet of shattered glass and around the upside down SUV and numerous overturned shelves, I tore through several bottles of water. Microplastics were the least of my concerns. No matter how much I drank my head still

hurt – I found some sacks of compost in the storage room and tried to sleep instead. It wasn't much different from lying on an airbed. But that dismal howling, invading my ears, held me away from sleep like a meat hook in my back.
"Uuuuuul-la... uuuuul-la... uuuuuul-la..." Frustrated to the point of tears, I went back out into the store, took packets of Ginger Nuts from the biscuit aisle, and launched them one by one at the wall. They exploded against it in a mist of crumbs. Nearer the door was a freezer – it had long since lost power and the fish fingers and beef mince packets writhed with maggots like rice.

I wandered on down the silent main road past battered houses and wrecked cars and picked-away skeletons and a peeling billboard for Sky Atlantic's new Australian spy drama. I then ascended a familiar hill, street sign obscured by weeds, and, suddenly, found myself in front of my house.

Somehow, though untouched, it looked different – it wasn't the weeds which climbed up the lower walls, but something else, something not quite within my conception. Has it always had this many windows, this coloured door, this satellite dish, I asked? I couldn't remember.

Slowly, I tried the door and found it still locked – I'd lost my key some time ago, I think, though I couldn't remember when. The spare key, handily, was still under a plant pot and the door still opened for it – I don't know why it wouldn't have but I was ready for all forms of disappointment. It was desperately cold inside but, even with it clawing at my skin, I felt giddy to be back – until I realised Disco wasn't at my feet, greeting me, mewling for scratches and food. The stairs didn't seem to be where I left them but I went to my bedroom and, after a pause to steel myself, stood at the window. Over oft-broken rooftops, towards the rugby club with its solitary remaining floodlight and against the blue sky's glassy clearness, there I saw the hood of a Blight giant. And it was howling.

"Uuuuul-la... uuuuul-la... uuuuuul-la..." I wasn't afraid. Maybe I was too tired to be. Watching the thing for some time, I saw that it didn't move; it just stood there and yelled (which reminded me of Disco) for no reason (which also reminded me of Disco).

"Uuuuuuul-la... uuuuuul-la... uuuuuul-la..." That perpetual sound confused my mind, so much so that I wondered if it was a sonic weapon, clouding the brain and eroding judgement, but after some time with my fingers plugged deep into my ears I realised it wasn't – because I realised what I wanted. I was infinitely curious why the Thing was crying – I was sure it was crying as I understand the word – and I needed, not wanted but needed, to know. So, I left the house again, taking care to relock the door, and struck into a lane which wound round the rugby club.

Crawling through dusty rubble which had once been a line of council houses called Maybury Road, I got a view of this stationary, howling Blight through the chicken wire fence. It staggered like a drunk in the middle of the pitch, seeming entirely unaware of itself, wailed, and little else.

"What the fuck are you doing?" I whispered.

From another lane in the direction of St Martin's Church I heard a yelping chorus and saw, first, a dog with a strip of putrescent red meat in his jaws coming headlong towards me, and then a pack of starving mongrels in pursuit. The first dog saw me and, after a moment of locking narrowed eyes, turned ninety degrees and burst down a different alley, as though he feared I were a fresh competitor, his pursuers following. Yipping dying away down the silent road, the wailing reasserted itself in its place.

"Uuuuuuul-la... uuuuuuul-la... uuuuuuuul-la... uuuuuul-la..."

Bewildered by whatever the Thing was playing at and feeling increasingly naked and, by my proximity, playing with fire – a tricky combination – I crawled backwards out of the rubble and sneaked away down the lane from which the dogs had come, the expansive tree cover proving very inviting.

Intending to loop back around and return home, where I could fetch Disco's medicine and change clothes (I'd die before I wore another thong), I pushed aside an old gate to enter the St Martin's Church grounds. There, among the old, often overturned tombstones, I suddenly came upon one of the crab machines I'd seen in the house with Raymond – it was clearly dead. Its body was settled on the ground with legs splayed out at uneven angles, one of which had penetrated straight through the stone church all the way to the nave. Others dug deep into the soil. Trees were severed all around, making the grounds appear like a timber yard, and half of the thing's body crushed the hedges and adjoining housing estate. It was motionless as steam gushed loudly and uncontrollably from gaps in the armour. Even from here I could see parts were smeared with blood and the Blight pilot's gnawed entrails, torn from the wreckage by the dogs, lay gleaming red in the grass. Cautiously, I approached the mechanical corpse, the hissing steam growing louder, and for reasons I can't explain began to climb up the metal hull. I guess I just wanted to know what was inside. To touch it with my bare fingers sent indefinable emotions rippling through me. As I climbed I found a limp scarlet tentacle dangling from a crevice and twitching unpleasantly. After a moment of staring, it then drifted towards me, almost reaching out, and having been on the Internet long enough to know where that was going I jumped from the machine and ran to the bottom of the church grounds and away from the dream I must have been in.

Wandering, in a confused, almost drunken daze, I pushed on, eager to be back home and in the passingly familiar. At the bottom of the church grounds, far away through a gap in the trees, I saw a second tripod, as motionless as the first, standing on a hill in the ruins of Penbeagle and silent as a sea without tide. At the main road below, which I hurried down to complete my loop, I came upon the red weed again. It was spreading from the edges of the trickling Stennack River. The spongy mass of dark-red vegetation was everywhere. But, as I looked closer, I saw that the weeds were changing – they had turned white, just as I had seen the previous evening. It wasn't the moon at all.

Crouching down, I scooped up a handful and at the touch the weeds dissolved into powder between my fingers. I realised then that I was in silence – the alien cries had stopped. A chill broke over me. Only now did I realise that while that voice had sounded, the solitude, the desolation, had been endurable; by virtue of it St Ives had still seemed in some vague way alive and that sense of life had upheld me even if it was the worst possible type of life. Now suddenly a change, a passing, and then nothing but gaunt quiet. At this, some part of me snapped. After all I'd been through, it was the silence which pushed me.

I looked around – at the dying trees, the empty yet full sky, the wrecked road, everything. Cornwall gazed back at me spectrally. The air was composed of death rattles. Windows in the white houses were like the eye sockets of skulls. Surreality invaded my mind and sang insane hymns. My brain was laughing at me. I came to understand what was happening – I was in purgatory. None of this was real. Everything around me was *for* me, every inch of the Earth, in some vile test I couldn't understand. A thousand noiseless enemies swarmed, projected by my imagination, and terror seized me. Black shapes moved on the road and on the walls. Birds laughed at me. I couldn't bear the stillness any longer and, my mind broken, not even caring if the world was a sphere or a disc or a cylinder or a trapezoid because I'd just fall off regardless, aware that I'd never, never in my *life* see either Disco nor any other human being again, I sprinted back home with bile

burning my throat. Locking the door behind me, hiding from the approaching night and deepening silence, faces of the dead flashed with accusing fingers in front of my eyes.
"I'm sorry," I whimpered, slamming my head into the door, begging them to go away. "I'm sorry." This I repeated, my own uuuuul-la, for so long my throat ran dry and itchy, until a new resolve possessed me. With it came an unfamiliar comfort. I wanted sleep. I wanted escape. I wanted death. It was the only way left for me. Slowly, I opened the door again, into a bright and warm mid-afternoon, the night gone, and marched back towards the rugby club.

As I drew nearer, the sunlight so great I squinted most of the way, I saw a swarm of black birds circling above me and clustering on the rooftops either side. My heart gave a bound and I began to run. I hurried through white weeds choking a road which burst into dust as I waded through and emerged on the rugby field's grass before the falling of the sun. I felt no fear, only a wild, trembling exultation, as I ran towards the motionless monster.

In another moment I'd scrambled up a bank of overturned earth which half-buried the pitch and stood upon its crest, feet sinking into the mud. There was the gigantic tripod, stark and silent and staring back at me. Seagulls circled the hull. I was so close I heard the machinery whirring inside.
"Come on," I whispered, then shouted, then screamed, thumping my chest so hard my ribs screamed back. "Come on! I'm here! I'm ready!" I thought I saw something in its eye. Something new. Then, at once, its whirring stopped. The hum of machinery ended. The tripod shuddered, dipped its head to the ground as if in prayer, and went rigid. It was dead. All I could think to do was stare with bulging eyes. White powder, what had once been a forest of red weeds, drifted by in a great harmless cloud on the sea breeze. Then, with a low groaning thunder which grew louder and louder, came a new

noise, a turbocharged roar, and I looked up to see a trio of triangular Typhoons flying in formation high overhead, safe black dots against infinite blue sky. Devices which had utterly failed to beat the Blight – but, in the end, it didn't matter. They hadn't been needed. I sank to my knees and, after careful consideration, quietly sobbed, for in an instant I knew it was over. All was right with the world.

Throughout the day, wherever they stood, the machines stopped and died. Some toppled over, slain mid-stride, but most froze rooted to the spot. The red weed decayed, faded, and vanished, leaving no biological trace of itself. And all around stood the extinct tripods. These things which had been so alive and so terrible were dead – and to all, this death was incomprehensible. To this day, we don't know why they died. They just did. They just all died. Some may say that God repented, that they were slain by angels, or lowly bacteria, or some indefinable syndrome, or they just ran out of fuel. We don't know – we've no evidence for anything and speculation is all we'll ever have for this ridiculous deus ex machina. They all just died. We would, in time, try to forget them and the collective nightmare they wrought. And we'd forget them quicker than you'd think. The final death is in the mind.

On my knees, I stared at the dead tripod, the falling sun striking the world into purple darkness. This mighty machine, so wonderful in its power, so unearthly in its idiosyncrasy, rose weird and vague and strange from the shadows. I looked to Penbeagle and saw the same had befallen the other on the hill. It must have been dead for hours. Across the bay and towards Godrevy, another machine was a tiny stick figure on the landscape – it, too, was motionless. The birds, I could hear through the dark, fought over the flesh deep within the tripod's metal crags. At the sound of cawing I looked back to the one I'd confronted, the huge fighting machine which would fight no more, as tattered red shreds of flesh dribbled down onto the spectator terrace. Death had overtaken it as it cried to its companions, perhaps for help or out of sorrow, and its voice had gone on perpetually until the force of its machinery was exhausted. I knew how it felt – but my voice was still there. The tripods vanished now, just harmless metal towers, as the sun departed and darkness arrived. Naked beneath clouds, the Moon came, veiling Cornwall's silent wilderness in sombre white robes.

And as I looked at this wide expanse of deserted country, of calm and happy ocean, of trees still billowing and splendid old farms and mines, all silent yet somehow breathing, as I thought of the multitudinous hopes and efforts of my life which had gone into feeling worthy of living on this human reef, and of the swift and ruthless destruction which had hung over it all, I realised that the shadow had rolled back. I might still live in these streets. By my existence alone I earned my place in the universe – and this dear vast dead land could once more be alive. The universe was not uncaring – for, as I looked out on the place which was once home and could be again, I was part of the universe, and I cared.

# IX.

And now – if you can believe such a thing – comes the strangest part of my story. I remember, clearly and coldly and vividly, all that I did that day until the time came that I sat crying at an old and trashed rugby club in the shadow of a dead war machine. And then, suddenly, I forget. The following three days have been purged. My memory is blank.

I've learned since that, when the end came, it was well observed by the rest of the world. For, as it turned out, it was an unconquered world. Only Cornwall had been subjugated. The tripods never crossed the Tamar; they never even tried. We don't know why. When I jumped from that ferry, had I only drifted in the other direction I would have made landfall in friendly territory which would have remained eternally so. Instead, swept straight back, I thought the world obliterated and walked west – the wrong way. So, as the joyful news flashed all over the world in a microsecond, drones and Army reconnaissance having watched the machines falter and die in the Tamar Valley, tanks and jeeps were already rolling back into liberated Cornwall, soldiers cockily posing for pictures at the legs of dead giants they could never have bettered, whole towns free and clean as the weeds dissolved into nothingness. As this unfolded, I sat on my knees at the rugby club thinking myself among a rare few survivors with no idea that a whole living world was just past the hills and quickly coming to me.

That world, chilled by fear for so long, wept with joy. Church bells rang out all across the nation. The flag of Saint Piran rose above foreign capitals. Crowds gathered and partied on terraces, in pubs, in every square and park. Fireworks painted the skies. The government vomited with relief and promised aid – a lot of it would actually arrive.

But when people ask me where I was when the liberation came I have no answer. Demented and broken, I'd been on the verge of a pit and finally, the emotion and the absurdity too heavy to bear, fell in. Psychotic breakdown swallowed me whole. When, at last, I became aware of myself again, it was in a service station hotel outside Truro – the military had commandeered the property as a survivor's refuge and were kind enough to permit me an en-suite. The Scottish lance corporal who found me later related, with a smug grin, that I'd been found wandering and raving through the streets of St Ives, mostly naked, singing some jingle about being "the last one left, motherfuckers! The last one left!" So things had been going well, then.

Troubled as the military were with the demands of reoccupying three and a half thousand square kilometres and rooting out every survivor, they still found time for me, sheltered me, and protected me from myself – even if their way of doing that involved handcuffing me to the metal bed frame. But I was a lonely, shattered individual, and they were kinder to me than they needed to be. For four days I stayed in that room, at one point interviewed from my bed by a German news channel, my meals brought to me each day by the corporal on a plastic tray – I'm not too proud to admit I cried at the sight of a Cumberland sausage – and I passed the time with a notebook where I tried recording a half-remembered diary of the fortnight *before* the invasion. There was in me a vague but growing craving to cling onto the little life I'd had before – it seemed in retrospect, knowing what nightmares would follow, so happy and bright. But wasn't I miserable? Was I really any happier than I was now? This diary gathered pages like a rolling snowball until it became the story you now read; with its tales of battles and slaughters and horrors and alien beasts and its prose that I've tried to make sound sophisticated but have probably failed at, but I admit it's the pages mentioning Disco that I kept flicking back to.

Eventually, after those four days elapsed, a local psychology teacher with a voice like a soft lullaby judged me ready for release back into the big wide world. I picked up my things and, without signing a single piece of paper, was out. Truro, I was startled to find, was clean of the red weed it should have been drowning in – a man in a newsagents explained how quickly it vanished from existence, as it had at my touch in St Ives, and that not a strand could be found anywhere in the county. Even the cathedral, which had been choking on the grisly vines just a few days earlier, was clean again. Services were restarting this coming Sunday.

Already, Truro was busy with returning people – the newsagent was not the only venue open; a McDonald's, a coffee outlet, a building society branch, even a designer handbag shop had reopened. At a kiosk, a soldier was handing out free phones to replace those which might have been lost – but not chargers, and the one he handed me needed one. Even the buses were back on a skeleton service and I joined a quiet queue at the depot. A pair of maintenance workers were trying to reconnect the plumbing in the neighbouring public toilets while a pensioner stood over them and loudly shouted advice. After twenty minutes, the bus still hadn't come and the electronic sign indicating its due time wasn't working. The man stood next to me, all slicked black hair and rhinestones on his jacket, lit a tightly rolled cigarette.
"Once you light a cigarette," he said to me in a gravelly Polish accent, "the bus comes." It did, a half-full single-decker to St

Ives, and I joined it – the service was free, subsidised by the government for the next four months, as the county tried to shake itself awake. The council had asked for a year.

The day was mockingly bright for my second melancholy pilgrimage to the little house in St Ives – I wasn't quite sure why I was going back but I couldn't think of anywhere to go. Again, the sense came that I was bumbling through a dream, for this wasn't the Cornwall I'd grown used to. People weren't meant to be alive! The streets weren't suppose to have traffic! Where were all the dead dogs and skeletons?! Truro was punctuated by military uniforms and high-visibility jackets as workers in cherry pickers reattached telegraph cables and food parcels were handed out from a lorry to a patient queue. Normality was unstoppable in her return. A purple-haired busker played guitar at the bus stop. Two overweight teenagers smoked and chattered besides the public toilets. An elderly woman, sat on a wooden bench, chewed a steak pasty. It seemed incredible that this place was emerging from genocide, blinking, into the sunlight. But then, as the bus pulled away with a lurch, I noticed the people sat around me – when I looked, I mean really looked, I saw their skin was pale, their hair and beards shaggy and overgrown, many in dirty clothes, yet their eyes still found a way to be so bright. Outside I saw few signs of Blight mischief, besides the odd demolished building now cut off by alternating red and white caution tape, until the bus exited Truro and passed through quiet new-build suburbia onto the A390.

Just outside Highertown, as we passed a car wash, the trees behind it disappeared and from behind them appeared a tripod, stood alone in a field. A moment of panic seized me, seized everyone, until we remembered it was over – some still averted their eyes, a couple even sobbed, unable to face the Thing which had done so much evil. At the silent behemoth's feet was a ring of military vehicles – a column of scaffolding was rising around its body like metal vines.

As the man next to me got up to leave, the bus skirting around the sealed-off wreck once known as Hayle, soldiers manning every roadblock, I realised from the example of the person sat opposite me – who with my neighbour's exit I could now see – that there existed a USB port beneath each seat. Asking as politely as I could, hoping I wouldn't somehow reveal that I was the type of person to bury an axe in a person's skull, I borrowed his charging cable and was able to breathe life into my new phone and log onto my old accounts for the first time in a long time.

Twitter was a storm of commentary, of course, but not so much about Cornwall – already, the world was moving on, now transfixed by a controversy over plus-sized models, a Netflix documentary about people who have intercourse with sow, and the upcoming *Spyro the Dragon* movie. But I did learn from the aggregated news that in a mere few days the examination of the dead machines was already producing results. Their gyroscopes and advanced circuitry were said to be of great interest – harnessing them, it was claimed by those who usually knew what they were talking about, could accelerate mechanical and electrical engineering by decades if not centuries. Autopsies of the invaders themselves might yield great discoveries in biology and genetics. Even the Death Ray, if its ridiculously complex functions could be disassembled, might revolutionise the energy sector. What they still couldn't find, however, was the one thing everyone really wanted – what killed them. The chief scientific officer had created headlines when, in a press conference, he bleakly said the words I've said myself – "they just died."

After simply posting "hey, I'm still alive" to my followers, not having particularly missed them during our time apart, I put my phone away and sat with crossed arms, looking greyly at the sunlit devastation flowing past the windows. Those words reverberated in my mind and I still couldn't believe they were true. In a way, sensing that this test had only proven bad things of me, I wished they weren't.

The bus kept going. Burned and abandoned cars had been shunted into ditches either side of the mostly empty carriageway. Junctions were sealed off with cones and emergency vehicles, officials in ghostly hazardous environment overalls everywhere, and the sight made me wonder what new and exciting cancers I'd developed from inhaling the red weed's spores. As of yet, the DNA of ourselves and the Blight being so foreign as to be entirely incompatible, I've only nursed a mild cold – and that's the fault of all these people returning to Cornwall at once.

Just outside St Erth, the bus joined a snaking queue of traffic which advanced spasmodically – the roundabout ahead, the same one where Drake and I had talked with the soldiers, had, perhaps identified by the Blight as a target of great importance given its flower arrangements, been blasted to a crater. All who came had to creep along the one lane still in existence. Either side of us were shattered and blackened ruins where houses and chestnut trees and the Victorian railway station with its expensively expanded Park and Ride system once stood. The American nuclear bomb had exploded near here and it was no surprise to be told. I stared down into the crater as our turn eventually came to shuffle by – a car lay on its side within, half-invisible in the pool of murky water which had collected after two days of thunderstorms. Soldiers with berets and young faces carefully guided the bus around the obstacle, the headphones of the bundled up man behind me buzzing with house music amid the suspense, and then we were on our way.

All down the road after St Erth the country was gaunt and unfamiliar, its wide and open fields an unbroken stretch of crisply burned blackness, and the sight was so disturbing it became painful to look at. There was no sign of the vast Blight foundry which had puffed all that green smoke in the early days – I later learned that, on the final day, it disintegrated as completely as the red weed, as if its metal and their leaves were one and the same. My gaze went with relief from the scorched blacks and greys of the foreground to the green softness of the westward hills, where only the terrible gas had rolled rather than the Death Ray's infinite heat or our own equally loathsome, but frustratingly useless, atomic firestorm. Across these spared fields I saw a great camp of tents had sprung up where buses were disembarking. There were hundreds, maybe thousands, of volunteers bussed in nationwide who distributed clothing, food, toys, anything people must have lost and must now regain. We on the bus, however, were the lucky ones; we had a place to go – or, at least, believed we did.

Treva Croft Wood, its pines healthy and unburned, felt like a fresh drink of water as we trundled through – but unmarked vans were parked outside houses, corpses still being found and removed as teams went door to door, and in one front garden I saw a line-up of black body bags each two metres in height and clearly full. When we came through the woodland's other side it was to pleasant green fields again – but there was still one place of inhuman disturbance to be found. This was the site of a capsule which had come down, unseen by me, whose pit was like a ruptured blister in farmland along the St Ives Road just before Longstone. For some reason the machine still nested in the hole, having never woken up – it must have come down on the final day, raising fresh questions nobody could answer. A number of people were standing a safe distance away, some with television cameras, kept back by soldiers in white overalls, while other troops swarmed in its midst. On one of the Land Rovers flanking the Pit flaunted the Union Flag, cheerfully flapping in the morning breeze, and a Chinook passed low overhead, a cable beneath its fuselage suspending a crate of supplies.

Again, with so many holes punched in the roads and Royal Engineers hurriedly filling them in with rapid-dry concrete, the traffic slowed to a crawl. I ditched the bus altogether after some frank words with the driver and chose to walk the rest of the way. This past however-long-it-was had left me very sore, yes, but I felt fitter than ever – my lungs no longer tried to murder me each time I ascended a flight of stairs.

I returned to St Ives through Steeple Wood, feeling some vague superstition that this route hadn't killed me when I walked it with Drake and so, obviously, any other route would. At times I realised that I walked with light steps, head stooped, sticking close to cover, and had to remind myself that things were different now. There was a brick gastropub on the wood's edge called the Lazy Fox; a laminated sheet on the door announced its sale "due to the passing of the owner." A woman unloading her car at a cottage down the road nodded at me as I passed and, moved by curiosity, I stopped to gawp as a field overgrown with buttercups opened up in front of me, decorated also with the warped and whitened bones of cows. For a while I leaned on the wooden fence, regarding these ornaments, until snapped back to attention by the hum of another helicopter circling above. I returned to the path which took me back through the woods, within sight through the trees now of the broken secondary school where a community hub was forming, and those trees became houses as I reached the southern edge of St Ives.

Crossing the decimated industrial estate, where a gang of laughing children threw rocks of tarmac through the windows of what remained of Ironside Envelopes, I ventured through Penbeagle yet again, its terraces broken up by Blight footsteps which had shredded homes and blocked the roads with uprooted trees. A squirrel, confused but undaunted, hopped along a horizontal trunk. The machine which had done this, which I had seen on the final day, was out of sight – it had been toppled over and private contractors were busy chopping it up. I could hear their roaring saws over the birdsong. At one moment I realised I stood where I had seen my first tripod, when it loomed from the thunderstorm at the rugby club, and I hurried onwards to rid myself of the reminder – without the need for anxious triple-checking over my shoulder or hiding behind trees or pinning myself to nearby walls or dodging around wreckage, which was slowly being towed away bit by bit, I was back home within a few minutes.

Quick flashes of hope had been bursting inside me with each step to the house that, maybe, it wouldn't be empty this time, but once I arrived and again took in its sullen grey exterior, I saw for certain that it was just me. It was always just me. Fetching the spare key from where I'd left it, I slowly creaked open the door and went inside. I tried the television, but the power grid was dead and probably would be for months – we've been assured that generators will be distributed and I'm still waiting for one. I sat on the sofa, looked around, and sighed.
"What the fuck do I do now?" I mumbled.

After some time sat there with my eyes closed, the distant whir of helicopters and the chopping up of the tripod drifting through the window, wondering why they were now able to cut into it so easily, I fluttered upstairs – Drake and I's muddy footsteps still led the way, the carpet ruffled and discoloured where I'd crouched, soaked to the skin, on the catastrophe's first night. The house, somehow, looked different – was it at all possible that, last time I'd been here, it hadn't been my house at all? Was *this* definitely the right one? It felt like it was. This time.

I found my bedroom window, from which I and Drake had watched the dawn and burning Godrevy, still open. I wondered about his fate and whether, if he did survive, a court martial awaited his desertion, or if he'd come looking for me, perhaps vengefully, given he knew my address. Rain had come in through the window and ruined the sheets. Black mould climbed the walls. My hardback, a silly romance about a telekinetic lesbian, still lay on the Ikea bedside table with a Hufflepuff bookmark protruding like a bone from an injury. For a minute I stood reading over its abandoned words until I dropped it without care onto the bed. It bounced twice and slipped down the gap between mattress and wall. I walked back to the stairs.

So, it was as I feared. My home was desolate. Deserted. Nobody had been here but me – nobody had escaped but me. Staying any longer, I realised then, would only torment me. The faint hope I'd spent so long cherishing was folly – I decided then and there that I'd move upcountry, where devastation wouldn't be around every corner and where I could start anew. And then I heard something behind me. A soft little mewl. Startled, amazed, afraid, I turned and on the sofa where I had sat there now sat Disco, unhurt and, in fact, fattened. I gave a faint cry. How was it possible?

"I came," I whispered. "I knew–"

He interrupted with another meow, that shrill demand for food I remembered to the note, his purr like a locomotive. I made a step forward and, sneezing from all the dust, gently picked him up in my arms.

# X.

It's a shame, I guess, that despite writing this whole account I can't actually offer much in the way of originality. There's plenty of hunger for first-hand accounts but, after a while, they all start to sound the same. "I saw the tripod. I ran away from the tripod. I hid from the tripod. I was hungry." And so on. Yet mystery remains. Unsettled questions abound about what has come to be known as the Cornwall Event, as if it were a festival or mid-sized corporate retreat, but I have nothing to offer which might resolve them – I'm in the business of droll observations not settling world-confounding queries. The reason for the Blight's sudden death remains unknown and will probably continue to be unknown forever. Here, ignorance isn't bliss – it's torture.

We don't even know what the hell the red weed really was – and here we really never will, because when it died it quite literally dissolved into immeasurable nothingness. Physics says that shouldn't be possible – and yet it happened. Even those specimens which had been retrieved and spirited to laboratories far from Cornwall vanished on the same day as the rest. No further research, therefore, is possible. To call it a puzzle is an understatement. Examination of the weeds before their death, involving everything from transmission electron microscopy to genetic mapping, points unmistakeably to the presence of exotic elements within their structure. Things that Earth-based biology has no equivalent to – the best comparison we can draw is with the throbbing electrical signals which dart through the brain. Plants have long been thought to possess something resembling neuronal networks but for the brief period we could study them the weeds looked like so much more. Like they could think. Some believe it is erroneous to regard them as plants at all and that they were just as much an animal as we or their Blight gardeners. Life, if you go solely by Earth's example, is a fairly limited thing which can be neatly categorised into families and groups and so on. The prospect that entities can exist outside of our cataloguing, so far outside it that they can never relate, is a source of unrelenting horror to some.

The Blight themselves, as biological things a little more within our grasp, are remarkable for how unremarkable they ended up being – we have come to understand almost entirely how these giant tentacled gastropods work. Only a finite number of specimens exist – reduced in quality, obviously, by the intervention of various animal pests before we could get to them. They must have been quite tasty with all that gooey protein just sitting there. Magnificent and almost complete specimens are on display at the Royal Cornwall Museum (though the best ones have, of course, been sent to London) for children to laugh at, already unaware after so little time of what monstrosities these things were and how, in their brief foray on our planet, they turned one corner of it into Hell. But while the punters fixate on the creatures it's the weeds on which the experts dwell. Some believe it was they who were the masters and the Blight their servants – or even that the two were the same and had the weeds matured it would have been into fully formed Blight beings. How English of us; aliens came to Earth and we found their herbology more fascinating.

So too, apparently, did the Blight's concentration on this county do much to promote what my MP calls "the conception of Cornwall's commonwealth." We are now a (much depopulated) nation recognised as such – through the pressure of global pity Westminster gave us a devolved assembly in Truro. Street signs are being rewritten to better reflect the near-dead language, Cornish fairy tales are being retold by the BBC, and we're even getting our own national sport teams. Recently, I visited the new Kernow Community Stadium with friends who don't know what I am to bask in this pseudo-independence, as footballers dressed in Saint Piran's sable and white were trounced 5-1 by Norwegian visitors. Shortly before they dinked in a fourth, and with the hymn of Trelawny ringing in my ears, I pondered the gains made from our tragedy and how long it would be before the memory of the carnage slipped away for me, too. Already, it felt like everybody was moving on, or had just forgotten altogether, while I sat trapped in dark recollections of the things I'd seen – and the things I'd done. While the ball zipped from one end of the pitch to the other, I spent most of the time with my eyes to the stars, taking in the universe and reflecting on my changed place in it.

Certainly, our view of the universe has been broadened to a ridiculous degree. Before the first capsule fell, there was a general feeling that though life must exist in abundance beyond our minute sphere, space's gulf was too vast for them to even know about us – let alone reach us. Now we know better. The Milky Way might be a very busy city and we the residents of a quiet country lane, not yet quite hearing the developers with their clipboards in the woods next door. In this city, with us just a piece of dust in the cosmic waterfall, perhaps the Blight are rather weak and puny little things by the standards of the universe. They might be their equivalent of Paraguay. After all, if they were fleeing their own world, as some theorise, something might be out there which made them flee – and what if it followed them?

These questions are of grave – and universal – interest. Will the Blight return? After all, not a metal foot crossed the Tamar – their conquest of Earth never touched soil which wasn't Cornish. For many people, the only answer that makes sense is that they merely intended a beachhead, a starting point, before the full swarming masses arrived. As of yet, they haven't come and Oumuamua has disappeared, thought to have died herself and drifted into the void. The world thinks itself prepared for the Blight's return, whether through the signing of a global space defence treaty or extensively researching how to penetrate the exotic metals which constitute their machines, but with each passing day old international rivalries and domestic squabbles rekindle and the threat drifts further to the back pages. I remember watching *Newsnight* one evening; an eminent Oxford scientist was explaining his view that the Blight would never return. With a scattershot approach, he said, they had aimed for every spot in the sky and hoped for a single result. Those who miraculously touched down in Cornwall were all who made it and they are all who will ever make it. Mathematics makes a second successful landing – given the inconceivable size of the universe – impossible. It is the viewpoint which I reflected at this book's beginning, if only for the comfort which cold and hard numbers can give us, like when you're on a plane shuddering through turbulence and you remind yourself, over and over, of the statistics that insist you're not going down. Or maybe that's just me.

At any rate, whatever the reasons behind the invasion, my view of my own future – and of myself, and my past, and all the forms of time which contain me – has been irrecoverably changed by these events. Never had I anticipated the evil lurking beneath my skin – I think constantly about Raymond's murder, of his round eyes, of the decadent sounds which accompanied what I did. And I did do it. This story is my confession. So, too, did I murder all those on Bodmin Moor. I could have warned them about the gas – but I didn't. Cynthia and Linda, too, are my victims – they might have lived if I tried to find them. But I fled without a word. That was the theme of this story – running away. Poor decisions. Being stupid and thinking fear an excuse. Shame must be the rock I forever roll uphill.

Each night I'm haunted by images, by questions, and by answers. It's the answers which hurt most. I know what happened. How lovely it is that the harvesting of the Blight has brought great fruits to human science – but I haven't the faintest clue what to do with those things when I can't sleep anymore. I think about that machine whose last sight before death was me and I wonder why it didn't strike me down, even when I begged it too. Did it know that I deserved death – and so wouldn't give it to me? Many would claim my butchery was perfectly justifiable – reasonable self-defence against the certain doom which Raymond was summoning. Perhaps. But my guilt festers regardless. It burns my heart. The Blight knew something of me. They came in search of me and every time they found me they did me no harm. Raymond thought we were conspiring together – maybe we were but I just didn't know. They even, if that lunatic I met is to be believed, knew my name. I wish I knew what they knew. Let them return so I can ask. What am I, I would say, that you are mindful of me?

An abiding sense of sadness lives with me now. So, too, do the images of those days. I sit in my bedroom with my laptop on my knees and, when I think I'm just rewatching *Glee*, suddenly I see again the headland of Godrevy set with writhing flames and feel the house about me empty and cold and desolate. I go out into the road and cars pass me, colourful butterflies tackle each other mid-air in the throes of mating season, a coach of German tourists trundles by, cyclists in lycra follow, children in their bright uniforms go to school, and suddenly they become vague and unreal. Suddenly, I am hurrying again, sometimes with Linda and Cynthia, through the hot, brooding silence. When night comes I see its darkness as the black gas darkening the silent streets and the contorted bodies shrouded beneath. They rise towards me tattered and dog-bitten. They gibber and grow fiercer, paler, uglier, mad distortions of humanity, and all the while look familiar – they wear the faces of those I could have saved. I wake, cold and wretched, and I know that in the end I didn't even save myself.

I go down to the harbour and see the busy multitudes on Fore Street or the Wharf and it comes across my mind that they are but the ghosts of the past, haunting streets which I have seen silent and dead, going to and fro, phantasms in a graveyard, the mockery of life in a galvanised body. And it's strange, too, to look out of my bedroom window, as I avoid doing when I can these days, to see the rebuilt lines of houses, now of a cheaper material, to glimpse people walking to and fro from the Co-Op to the Post Office and back again, to watch the sightseers about the Blight machine that still stands over the old rugby club, to hear the tumult of playing children from the rebuilt school just behind the trees, and to recall the time when I saw it all bright and clear-cut, hard and silent, dying and dead, under the dawn of that last great day.

And strangest of all is to hold Disco again and to think that I had counted him among the dead – and to wish that, after all I survived, I was among them, too.

# ABOUT THE AUTHOR

## Samuel Paxton

Samuel Paxton is an author from Bristol. He was born in Bristol in 1997 and lived in Cornwall from age 4 to (with the occasional nine-month-or-so breaks for university terms) 24, when he moved back to Bristol. His favourite film is probably Richard III (1995) and he won't stop talking about Disco Elysium.

Printed in Great Britain
by Amazon

21851507R00243